Music on the Wind

A Collection of Irish Short Stories

❖

Gardiner M Weir

Gardiner M. Weir

PublishAmerica
Baltimore

© 2006 by Gardiner M. Weir.
All rights reserved. No part of this book may be reproduced, stored in a retrieval system or transmitted in any form or by any means without the prior written permission of the publishers, except by a reviewer who may quote brief passages in a review to be printed in a newspaper, magazine or journal.

First printing

All characters appearing in this work are fictitious. Any resemblance to real persons, living or dead, is purely coincidental.

At the specific preference of the author, PublishAmerica allowed this work to remain exactly as the author intended, verbatim, without editorial input.

ISBN: 1-4241-3403-X
PUBLISHED BY PUBLISHAMERICA, LLLP
www.publishamerica.com
Baltimore

Printed in the United States of America

Dedication

These stories are dedicated to my Northern Irish family and especially those who have passed away and who were such a positive influence in my early years—my parents, my maternal grandmother Martha McDonald Kennedy, and my uncle William Kennedy, and to my many aunts and uncles and cousins who gathered at the family farmhouse on many occasions and from whom I heard many wild and wonderful stories: also to my wife Hélia and our four children who have made life so rewarding and who tolerated my hours behind a typewriter hammering away at my imagination.

Contents

	Page
Music on the Wind	7
If Only	18
As If a Stranger	29
Alive on the Page	61
Son of Thomp	69
The Phantom in the Hedgerow	80
The Dog with the Blue Eye	92
Lesser Shadows of the Day	104
Passing Through	124
At the Bottom of a Long Hill	127
All Flesh is Grass	134
Feathers	154
The Wild Skelter	170
The Terrible Sin of Martin McCabe	210
Dr. Simon's Night Out	218
The Guy from Belfast	233
Paradox	243
Devil Take the Hindmost	267
The Land of Eternal Youth	292
Say It with Flowers	301
The Quark Syndrome	325

Music on the Wind

In the spring of forty-six my uncle Danny was around forty and still not married. His mother could not understand it at all. "Ye need to be fruitful and multiply!" she would remind him.

"Aye!"

"All the hard labor Ah've put into raisin' ye a Christian. An' ye know why?"

"Aye!"

"So yer soul can dwell at ease and yer seed can inherit the earth. That's in the Psalms, so it is. So yer seed can inherit the earth. Can't ye see?"

"Aye!"

"It's this farm Ah'm talkin' about. This farm! All eighty acres of it!"

"Aye!"

Danny's mother had done her best over the years to help her son fulfill the spirit of the biblical text and, on his behalf, had sorted through the young women in the townland and many townlands beyond. "Ye don't want to marry a hussy, so ye don't!" A little lipstick and high heels was every indication of the wrong woman for her son. Those were hussies! But, from what I could gather, inheriting a few acres of land would fully compensate for any flights of fancy the candidate might have. "Don't ye realize a' the wimmen o' yer age are marriet already an' hae children? There's no a wan left." There was always an intense glare in her eyes when she confronted her son on the topic of marriage. But uncle Danny was not to be rushed. "Agh oh!" she would sigh.

Auld Mrs. McKillop had watched her son grow older, more withdrawn and now, thick set, a bit humped on the back and hardly handsome, who would look at him? Only some penniless widow like Martha, and her with a child to rear. "Go talk to Martha, Ah tell ye. Ye'll wait an' ye'll wait an' she'll marry the schoolmaster."

"Aye!"

"She has sixty-wan acres an' needs a man. Sixty-wan acres! Think o' that! Sixty-wan!"

"Aye!'

Danny had indeed thought of Martha, a kindly woman whose farm joined his. "Martha! Whyn't you an' me get marriet?" He looked at her with his tight little eyes as if that was the most logical thing in the world. Martha simply shook her head. "Why not?" he continued, an intense argumentative tone to his voice. "Ah got eighty acres, so Ah have. An' over forty ewes this year an' maybe sixty next. What ye say, hi?"

"Ah can't Danny."

"Why not? Ah'll make ye a good husban', so Ah will. Your land an' my land put together is somethin' tae think about. A hunnerd an' forty-wan acres altogether! Ye'll lack for nothin'."

But uncle Danny went away a disappointed man. "What is it wimmen want, anyway?" he said to me.

It was Easter and I was off from school. Uncle Danny and I were out one afternoon counting the newborn lambs when the dog barked and pointed his nose down the hill. A woman was cycling down the lane with a bundle tied to the handlebars.

"Now, who could thon be?" uncle Danny asked of the world at large.

She stopped the bicycle and untied the bundle. Uncle Danny watched for a bit and you could see that curiosity was getting the better of him. The woman set up what looked like a table and got busy taking stuff out of a box. It was then that our dog set off running.

"Come on!" whispered uncle Danny. "Ah got tae see what she's up to."

I was right beside him for my curiosity was getting the better of me too. "Maybe she's only having herself a picnic," I suggested.

"Nah! She's up to no good, by the looks of it!"

The damp soil of spring and the thorn bushes covered up the sounds of our getting there. We were right down by the stone hedge that borders the lane before she heard us and turned round. "Oh! You scared me." She looked at us with bright blue eyes staring out of her head. When she realized we were just a couple of harmless crayturs her mouth crinkled up at the corners in a friendly way. She had beautiful white teeth. "I hope I'm not trespassing?"

"Naw!" uncle Danny assured her. "It's a right-o'-way. Ye can do what ye want, so ye can."

"That's nice. I'm trying to paint the scene before me. Your house over there, is it?"

"Aw aye! It is that!"

Danny gave the woman a thorough going over with his eyes, sizing her up and down on the sly; her face in profile, the line of her nose and chin and her lips pouted as she concentrated on her work. She would look up and down at the scene before her and draw her brush across the paper, wash it out and try another color. In no time at all she had captured the scene of the glen as if she had taken a photo, only better, and in color; uncle Danny's thatched house with the trees around it and the figure of his mother standing out front in the yard tossing scraps to the hens. Even the auld turkey gobbler was in the picture, and the hillside behind and the glen sloping down to the sea.

"Can Ah take a wee gander?" asked uncle Danny for he was still standing off to the side looking more at her than at the painting.

"Certainly!" There was music to her voice that hinted she was not from those parts. She sounded like what we heard on the wireless. Danny wandered over but kept a wee bit off. I could tell he was wishing he were not dressed in dungarees that smelled of sheep. But what can you do when that's your life, working with animals. The woman before us was too dainty for that kind of thing. She was a town woman.

"That's gae like it." A big grin opened up on Danny's face.

The woman kept on adding more paint with dainty small hands all white and smooth like they had never seen a day's work, certainly not like the widow Martha's or Danny's Ma. Their hands were all red and rough. And she was a wee slip of a thing too, not much taller than I, a silk scarf neatly arranged around her neck and a fluffy pink beret on her head. The perfume of flowers surrounded her. My uncle Danny was beginning to move around in a nervous way, shuffling his feet and stretching his neck to see the painting. The lambs were clearly forgotten. "What they call ye, hi?"

"Margo!" She looked around at him with a flicker of amusement in her wide blue eyes. "And you?"

"Danny. Danny McKillop. That's my place over there. Ah got sheep."

"That's nice. You're a farmer then?"

"Aye! Ah got eighty acres, so Ah have."

"That's nice." She played paint across the paper, washed her brushes in water, dipped them again in paint and went about the business of constructing the scene as if Danny were not there. I could see Danny's mother looking our way.

"Where ye from?" Danny blurted out.

"Ballyaghone."

"Oh, Ah thought ye might be passin' through, like, a tourist. We get them ye know. Them an' their cameras. Ye sound like ye're from across the water, so ye do."

"I am. I'm really English. But I live here now." She did not look up from her work.

"Oh!"

"There! Finished! That didn't take long." She smiled, turning her blue eyes to Danny.

"Naw, it didn't. Ye're quick, so ye are. How do ye do that?"

"Practice. I'm an artist. Have you never seen an artist at work before?" Her blue eyes took in the rough look of Danny and brought a smile to her lips. "Well?"

"Naw! Never! The only pictures Ah've ever seen are on the calendars me mother gets at the grocer's."

"Well then, now you know." She stood back a little from the table and began to wash her brushes and place them in the box as if in a hurry.

Danny edged over to the table. "It's gae like it, so it is. Gae like it! Aye!"

She placed the watercolor inside two sheets of cardboard and began packing up the table and the box. Danny shuffled his feet. "Ye're off, then?"

"Quite! I'm finished."

Uncle Danny looked helpless. "Ye wouldn't give me that, would ye? Ah like it a lot, so Ah do. Ah can pay ye, so Ah can. It would be nice to have, so it would."

"Maybe next time." She smiled at Danny. "Now I've really got to go. I want to paint the harbor at Carnlough before the day is out."

"Ye wouldn't bide a wee, would ye?"

"What?"

"Stay for a cup o' tea. Me mother'll make ye a nice cup of tea if ye want. That's her standin' over thonder."

"Well, that's nice. Next time."

"Next time. Right ye are. Next time. Right!"

She pulled the belt of her raincoat tightly around her waist. It showed how small she was, a slip of a thing. She set one leg across the frame of the bicycle and, with a foot on the pedal, mounted up and was away.

"Next time?" uncle Danny called. "When's next time?"

"Bye!"

To uncle Danny's ears it was a single note of music on the wind. For a moment I thought he was going to run along side her bicycle as a small boy would. "So long then!" he called out. "Come back when ye want." She was already fifty yards away. "Margo!" It was a one-word poem of despair.

We walked slowly back to the house where his mother still stood watching us. "Who was thon wumman ye wor talkin' to?"

"Just some wumman from Ballyaghone. Out paintin' picters."

"Has she no name?"

"Her name's Margo."

"Margo. Ye wor gettin' gae close tae know her name."

"Agh Ma. Why ye askin' me?"

"Because ye got that look on yer face."

"Agh Ma. Ah hae nae look on me face."

"Aye! Ah hears ye. She was some hussy out o' the town. Ah know! All youse men get that same look when there's a hussy around ye. Sure Ah saw ye wi' me own eyes, standin' there thaveless. What were ye thinkin'? Are ye a goat?"

"Agh Ma. It's no like that."

"Ye've no sense. Stay clear Ah tell ye. Go an' see Martha! She's the wumman for ye! She has sixty-wan acres. An' if ye don't watch, she'll marry the schoolmaster."

Uncle Danny whistled for the dog and the three of us went back up the hillside to continue counting the lambs.

With the Easter holidays over I returned to school in Ballyaghone. I had forgotten the event until one day I was wandering around town and stopped before a gift shop on Linenhall Street. *Macushla—Souvenirs* it said above the door. I gazed idly into the window. There were linen tablecloths on display and napkins embroidered with shamrocks and fair maidens. There were Beleek porcelain dishes and piglets and Waterford glass, all artistically arranged on little tables and shelves; and several watercolors, all with that same look, a kind of faery-land in the mind's eye. One was a scene that I immediately recognized—a glen sweeping down to the sea, with stone walled fields and a cottage set amongst hawthorns and rowan trees. It was clearly the painting of uncle Danny's croft, framed, glazed and on sale. I got on my bicycle and rode the several miles out to the farm. I was breathless when I arrived. "Danny! I found her! The woman! You know!"

"What woman?"

"The one who paints. You mind the time, don't you?"

As I told him the tale of my discovery his face lit up.

"An' she's shorter than me! What are ye doin' Saturday?"

"Why?"

"Sure won't I be in at the Fair Hill sellin' lambs and can't ye show me thon wee shop!"

So it was that on the Saturday I met Danny at the Fair Hill. He was a different Danny to the one I usually saw out at the farm. For that matter he was a different Danny from the one who came to the Fair Hill each Saturday. Gone were the dungarees and the scoop cap, the white scarf around his neck and the rubber boots. The Danny I saw that day was dressed in a blue suit with a white shirt, starched collar and tie. He was shaved to perfection. His hair was combed back and there was a scent of strong soap and hair oil. His shoes shone from polishing. He spread his lips in a wide grin.

"Lookit!"

He had even brushed his teeth.

"You're looking great," I ventured, wondering how he had managed to get himself so dolled-up without his mother's objections.

"It wasn't easy!"

"I'll bet!"

"Aye!" And he ruffled my hair. He was excited. "Let's go!"

On Linenhall Street I pointed out the gift shop and the painting in the window. Danny grinned in delight and pushed open the door. There was a ringing of a cluster of bells that announced our entry.

"Yes?" said a woman, stopping her arrangement of some knick-knacks in a cabinet and turning to face him. "May I help you?" It was the woman we had seen in the lane. It was Margo.

Danny halted. There was a strange atmosphere in the shop, a diaphanous green, and it smelled of lavender and heather. The woman Margo approached and stood before him looking up at him with those strange blue eyes. There was no sign of recognition. The determination with which Danny had entered

MUSIC ON THE WIND

the shop melted.

"Ah don't know. Ah, eh, Ah'm kinda lookin'."

"Something for a present maybe? Your wife?"

"Oh no."

"Lady friend?"

"Oh no."

"Would you care to look around?"

"Well, Ah'm thinkin' Ah'm really interested maybe in the painting in the window. The one o' the glen."

"Isn't it a lovely scene? I painted that just a few weeks ago, as a matter of fact." She retrieved the painting from the window. "It's a true scene between here and the shore. In fact, you can see just a tiny bit of sea in the distance there." And she pointed with a delicate finger. There was still no sign of recognition, either of him or me. "Yes, indeed. There are so many beautiful scenes. I took the day off actually. It was such a lovely day for cycling."

"Aye!"

"Would you like to buy it? It's really one of my best."

"It wasn't what Ah came in for."

"What exactly? May I be of help?"

"Agh, it's just you see...."

"It won't stay there long in the window, you know." She held the painting out to be admired. Danny shifted his feet. She kept looking at him, looking curiously into his eyes. There was a smile on her lips and she held her head slightly to one side as if to say, "Well?" She had totally forgotten him. The few days had wiped away any memory of his face. Uncle Danny was lost. He was confused. Her blue eyes searched his face for a decision.

"Ah'll take the picter." His voice was choked.

"Very nice. A wise choice. Your wife will treasure it."

"But Ah don't have a wife, Ah said. Ah came in here tae…"

"Your lady friend then?"

She got busy wrapping the painting in brown paper and tied it with string. Uncle Danny paid, but he still stood there. It was as if he could not leave her presence. I tugged at his sleeve. "Danny! Let's go."

"Ah! Ah was thinkin'," Danny began when the door opened to the chiming of the cluster of bells. A tall young man dressed in military uniform entered. The peaked cap pulled slightly down over his nose made him stand erect with his head back. A quick glance took in his polished leather belt and the pips on his shoulder straps. He was an officer, a captain in the regiment stationed at the Castle. He carried a bunch of flowers neatly wrapped around the stems with colored tissue paper. The woman Margo turned away from us.

"Roger!" She cast a radiantly bright smile at the officer.

"Darling Margo! Sorry I'm late." His voice had the same inflections as that of the woman. He was English. He handed her the flowers.

"Oh Roger, you shouldn't have." She stood up on her tiptoes and caressed his cheek with a kiss. Roger put a strong arm around her shoulders in an affectionate hug.

"Oh Roger, please." Amidst her happiness she found a moment to remember that my uncle Danny and I were still there. She turned. "Will that be all?"

We walked back to the Fair Hill where Danny had left his horse and trap. He asked me to carry his purchase and I did, gripped tightly under one arm. "She didn't recognize you all dressed up," I tried to explain.

"Agh, what the hell! Wimmen!"

I went out to his farm taking my bicycle with me so that I could return later. His mother was waiting. "An' so? What kept youse?"

"Ah brought ye a present."

His mother unfolded the wrapping from the painting, flattening it out and folding it to preserve for another occasion. Finally, the painting was on display. "Mmmm! Did ye manage to sell the lambs?" She laid the picture aside.

"Ah did. They'll get picked up next week."

"Hmmm!" The old woman kept unusually quiet. She turned to me. "Look at him. All dolled up like a scabby knuckle. That's how ye court disaster. Ah knew it, so Ah did. Ah knew it from the moment ye left here this mornin', ye were off coortin' thon hussy. A present for me, ye say! Ah'm no daft. Ye spent yer hard earned money tae please her, so ye did!" She shook her head vigorously at the senselessness of it all. "Here, hang the blasted thing up on that nail over there. It'll do tae remind ye o' yer foolishness." She handed me the painting. Danny went into his room like a dog with its tail between its legs. I felt sorry for him.

"It's really a good picture," I said. "He thought you would like it." It was a lie, but a white lie. I hung up the painting. The old lady stood in front of it.

"Hay ho! But it's money, money that cudda been put tae better use."

MUSIC ON THE WIND

Danny came out of his room dressed in his dirty old dungarees, the old Danny. He had taken off his starched collar and replaced it with his white silk scarf. A scoop cap was on his head, pulled down on one side.

"Son," his mother said. "Ah've taught ye everythin' Ah know and still ye know nothin'! Houl' tight tae yer money. Forget the hussy. Martha's the wumman for ye. She has sixty-wan acres. Think o' it. An' the schoolmaster'll marry her. You wait an' see."

When school got out for the summer I spent a great deal of my time on uncle Danny's farm. I helped him in different ways and he would give me a ten-shilling note now and then for my effort. Never a talkative man he would open up now and then and say things like, "Thon Englishman! Thon officer fellah! She was already sweet on him, ye know." I would let him ramble on, searching for his excuses. "Thon dandy! Never did a day's work in his life. Agh oh!"

"She wasn't the kind of woman who could milk cows either," I said trying to put the matter in perspective.

"Aye. She was perty, right enough." He shook his head at the memory. "An' shorter'n me!"

"Your mother is right. Martha knows the farm life. You should look seriously at Martha."

"Aye! She's a big wumman. Hard workin' too." He looked off into the hills. "But she turned me down."

"She did?"

"Aye! Me with eighty acres and her with sixty-wan. Can ye believe it? That would make a hunnerd and forty-wan acres o' the best hill side in the country."

"Maybe you should take her a bunch of flowers like the officer took to the Margo woman."

He looked at me with an odd expression. "Ye know, ye're right. Wimmen! Their heads are filled with all that nonsense. Flowers! Bejappers! Ye're right! Flowers! Where can Ah get a bunch o' flowers?"

"But ye'll need to say the right things."

"What right things?"

"Like the officer! Darling! And maybe sweetheart. Words like that."

"Agh tae hell! Ah'm no that fool!"

A few days later, with a pound note from Uncle Danny in my pocket, I went to the nursery in Ballyaghone and bought a bunch of flowers. "They're for my uncle to give to his fiancée," I explained, exaggerating a little, "so I want the best you got."

Danny was waiting for me, dressed in his blue suit, white shirt with the starched collar, shaved and smelling of hair oil.

"Ye're out o' yer mind!" his mother cried. "She's a common sensical wumman. This is all faldelal! What would Martha do with a bunch o' flowers? Ye've been goin' to them picters in the town, so ye have. Yer heid's addled with what ye see. Them actresses! Hussies! It's the devil's work! Ah've toult ye a hunnerd times!"

But Danny had thought the matter through and had his mind made up. He would give it his best shot. He had been practicing what to say for several days. "Darlin'", and "Sweet heart". He had even tried out "Martha, me love."

"Why don't you tell her you can't live without her," I suggested. "You dream about her every night."

"Agh! Have sense! When Ah go to sleep Ah'm out cold!"

I walked over to Martha's house with Danny. On the way he stopped several times to rehearse. "So Ah give her the flowers and then what do Ah say?"

"You say, 'Martha darlin'!"

"An' then what?"

"Whatever. Tell her you love her. You can't live without her. Romantic stuff. Like in the pictures. Imagine you were Charles Boyer. Women love that."

Martha was throwing a basin of soapy suds out the front door when we arrived. The chickens flew up in the air with the suddenness of it. The auld turkey gobbler set off a racket. "Oh Danny, sorry. I didn't see ye." She looked at him, a surprised look hovering on her face. "You're all dressed up. And flowers? Has somebody died?"

I pushed Danny forward. "Naw! Ah'm here tae see you," he said gallantly.

"Well, come in."

Danny nodded his head to one side to tell me to stay away. I took a seat over by the pump, not too far off. I could hear everything. Danny stood in the threshold of the door. He was shorter than Martha who really was a big woman. He looked up at her with those wee tight eyes. Martha looked at him curiously. He thrust the flowers into her hands. "Martha, me darlin', whyn't you an' me get marriet. Ah ha'e eighty acres o' great land an' you ha'e sixty-wan and together we would have wan great place. What ye say?"

Many years have passed since that day. Danny is still unmarried and has no desire to even try again, no matter who the woman is. But he's coming up to sixty now so it hardly matters. He's an old done man getting. His mother passed away in disappointment some years ago. I go out to visit him every now and then. He takes out a bottle of single malt and we play a game of checkers and sip a glass or two. The painting still hangs on the wall gathering flyspecks. He never mentions Margo. Nor Martha. She married the schoolmaster. It appears he wrote her poetry. The woman Margo sold her shop to somebody and it's believed she went back to England, maybe even married the officer.

I learned a big lesson from it all. There's a young woman I met up in Belfast when I was at Queen's. I write her letters filled with romantic thoughts. We go out dining now and then and sometimes to the theatre. On a weekend we'll drive along the shore and, if the weather is fine, walk barefoot on the sands. We hold hands. We're getting close. I have a strong feeling that one of these days I'm going to have to really tell her how I feel. I've even written her a few poems about it, but she hasn't seen them yet. I'm keeping them for the right moment. Her name is Mary. I've thought about it a lot. Maybe I'll just surprise her and say up front, straight like, "Mary, darlin', Ah love ye, so Ah do. Whyn't you an' me get marriet."

If Only

From the moment I arrived at the airport I had a feeling of apprehension. Too much time had passed. I had been gone too long. The people seemed as foreigners, not just in their speech and dress but also in the pallor of their faces. I thought of this on the ride to my hotel in downtown Belfast. The taxi driver quizzed me in a friendly way, more to break the silence than to pry into my affairs. "Ye come in from London on that flight, did ye?"

"Yes," I said, not wanting to admit that London had only been a stage in my long journey. I looked out over the small fields with their neatly trimmed hedges, the cattle grazing, and the green-ness of the countryside that had inspired countless songs.

"The weather must be great over there, so it must," he continued. "Ye've got a great sun-tan, so ye have."

I could see his eyes in the driver's mirror looking at me in a new light; but he did not need to know from where I had come. "Yes," I said and left it at that for a moment, then added, "Don't take the Ligoniel Road if you please I'd prefer if you....."

But he was ahead of me in anticipating my request. "No way! I wouldn't go thon way through Ligoniel even if ye asked me. No siree!"

"Oh?"

"I don't want to get shot at, that's why. They're all armed, so they are. Somebody might take a pot shot at ye. A body's not safe." But I had no interest in the sectarian turmoil that had enveloped Northern Ireland for several years while I had been gone. I was here for other reasons. "I always take the Antrim Road," he continued. "It's a whole lot safer, so it is." I thanked him. That was what I had wanted in any case. I would catch a view of the massiveness of the Cave Hill on my right and gaze out to my left across the waters of the Lagan estuary. It had been a long time. The scenery was indeed beautiful and made the more so by my own nostalgia. The driver was quiet for a mile or two but his curiosity was aroused. "Ye've been gone a while, have ye?"

"Some time, yes."

"Well, it's great to get back home, so it is. I mind the time when I was in the army. Stationed in England, so I was. Couldn't wait to get home. No place like home, ye know? No place like yer own hearth."

I assured him that home always held one's respect. He fixed his attention on the traffic as we continued down the Antrim Road. Over the gray waters of the estuary I could see the gantries of the shipyard where great ships such as the Titanic had been built. I saw the spiraling chimney smoke from countless rows of houses that provided workers to the many factories that had made Belfast a cornerstone of British industry. At Carlisle Circus he caught my attention in the mirror and said, "I'm going to have to take ye the back way to yer hotel, ye know." He drove the car into Townsend Street, heading west. "With all the troubles ye can't drive up Royal Avenue any more, so ye can't."

"Oh?"

"Aye! Sure they've put up barricades and turnstiles, so they have, just about everywhere. It's all pedestrian traffic now, so it is. Didn't ye know that? Ye can't go anywhere without being searched. Guns and bombs! That's what they have to mind out for these days." He looked at me quizzically, testing my imagination. "Ye know?"

I was forced to admit that I had been gone for several years, too long perhaps, and that I was out of touch with the troubles. The driver found this admission a strong reason to fill me in on all that had occurred. He talked fast as if rhyming off a well-rehearsed text. It gave the impression of a synopsis he had given many times to other travelers in need, in his estimation, of being clued in. He took a certain relish in the absurdities of sectarian killings and bombings as if it was just an extension of the stereotype Irishman, something to add to the myth of boozing and belief in the little folk. "There's no end to it, so there's not. Sure somebody fired on a funeral there a couple of weeks ago. Right in the graveyard, so it was. Ye're not safe even when ye're dead. An' the British Army and the Constabulary are everywhere and can't stop it. No, they can't! What's a body to do? Ye could be laughing one minute and dead the next, so ye could. I'm telling ye, hi, it's not easy. Naw! " All he needed was a little fiddle music in the background and the clink of glasses. Yet the cadence of his voice brought back old memories tinged with nostalgia emphasizing strongly in my heart of hearts that I had cut myself loose from those very same tribal roots. "Aye, if only people would come to their senses!

Ye know," he went on.

Though he had a point I replied with remarkable lack of pity in my tone. "Do what I did. Get the hell out!"

"That's all very well for you to say." There was anger bordering on despair in his voice. "Where'd I go? What'd I do? A body can't! This is home for the rest of us. Ye hear? We can't all just rise and fly like some people. This is home, so it is. Ye just can't rise and go! Ye know!"

I wondered could it be possible that he got some obtuse pleasure out of the situation; or was it a means of maintaining one's sanity.

At the hotel I paid him the fare along with a handsome tip for I now saw him as a decent person trying to survive the best he could; and he had been pleasant and interesting company.

"Take care, now," he said, slipping the tip under the mat at his feet. "Don't go wandering around! Ye hear? There's a power of bad people about. An' ye look like ye would be good for a pound or two. So mind now!"

I thanked him for the sound advice and checked into my hotel. It was not too late in the afternoon and, despite the length of my journey I still felt energized. Perhaps it was the excitement of being again in the city I had once called home. So I left my small suitcase on top of the bed and decided to take a stroll and make the best of the remaining hours of the day. I would refresh my memory of the sights that had been so much a part of my life when a student at the University. I put on my raincoat for to me the air was quite cold and damp and, as I soon found out, the wind gusted along the street and penetrated my light tropical clothes. I walked fast as if late for an appointment and just another citizen going about his business, except for my suntan that seemed to single me out amongst the pallid complexions that passed me by. But no one seemed to notice or bother me. Thus, after a brisk walk of an hour or so, I had taken in those sites that had remained so strongly in my memory— the Queen's University dressed in red brick Gothic, the Academical Institution where I had attended dances so often on Saturday nights, the City Hall in Georgian white, the memorial to those crew members who died in the Titanic disaster and the many buildings of Victorian architecture, and, to cap it all, the statue of Queen Victoria, herself. In contrast to where I had been for the last few years there was a pervading British-ness around me – a cultural sea that brought back my days at grammar school, a period of my life that probably made me what I had become. There I had learned British history from Queen Boadicea through to the First World War; so much to be proud of including the contribution made by Ireland as a whole and by the province of Ulster in particular. Like so many from the Northern six counties I was Scots by descent. I had a British passport. I believed in and was British. Everything around me seemed to say so. But for the manner of speech of the citizens, Belfast could have been any city in England, except for the pockmarks in the buildings' facades where exploding bombs or gunfire had gouged out chips of sandstone or brick. There were soldiers armed with sub-machine guns on patrol around the city center and on the neighboring streets. Armored vehicles were stationed at intervals. A military helicopter could be heard somewhere overhead, hidden from my view by the tall buildings. Groups of taunting youths stood on corners watching the soldiers go by in combat fatigues, in single file, their arms at the ready and their eyes scanning in every direction.

I was saddened. Belfast, a city that had meant so much to me during my student days was now a city under siege. With trepidation I approached one of the barriers on Royal Avenue. Two guards checked me out for hidden weapons and I passed on not knowing where I would go next, just following my nose of curiosity. Somehow I had turned down a side street by a theatre and noticed a pub that had been a landmark many years before, was now refurbished in the manner of a lounge, all shining wood, chrome and glass windows etched with mythic Irish scenes.

By now I had slowed up in my step and the cold was seeping into my bones. Without a second thought I entered into the warmth of the bar and looked around for a spot to sit, relax and get warm. But, being late, the place had already filled up and so I stood there undecided.

"Park yourself here, young fellah," said a kindly voice. I looked around and found a friendly face. "Grab a seat! Here!" He pushed a chair forward with a foot. "There's room for another if ye don't mind drinking with a stranger." I sat down, thanking him. He did not realize that it was I who was the stranger.

It was a single seat beside him at a table for two. Next to it were other similar tables, all occupied, mostly by men but quite a few women. Many people were standing, elbow-to-elbow, at the bar and in the available space in between. Judging from their dress they seemed to be from the offices around. It was a Friday evening after all. There was a lot of talk and laughter giving the impression that the week's work was finally over and they were ready to enjoy the weekend. I had participated in many scenes such as this before I had gone overseas. It gave me a pleasant feeling to be amongst them. In a way I was back at home. These were my people, good people, and good citizens. There were probably similar scenes across the city and probably in every town and every city in Scotland, Wales and England too. It was part of the culture that I knew and had been part of. I turned to the barman who was at my elbow. "A small Jamison and a bottle of stout."

The friendly fellow said, "Ye chose well young lad." He raised his glass in confirmation.

He was a shortish man but of broad build and possessed a protruding belly that pushed against his side of the table. His round happy face was decorated with a beard of wispy hair that hinted at a bohemian lifestyle, as did his lack of a recent haircut. His clothes were shabby with every indication that he had either worn them daily for some time or had purchased them from a second-hand shop in Smithfield. All in all he was comfortable with himself but, though radiating that confidence, seemed to have some compelling reason to be affable and engage me in conversation.

"Ye've been here before despite yer suntan. Where ye from?"

There was pleasantness to his voice and the same cadence just like my taxi driver. I rose to the invitation to converse and had no hesitation in telling him,

"I've been overseas. Africa!"

"My! Ye've come a long way. Where in Africa?"

The barman brought me my drinks and I paid him. All the while I was wondering how much I should say to my inquisitor. He raised his glass to me. "Here's to ye! And Africa!" I responded with similar gesture and replied that I was stationed in the Cameroons. "The Cameroons? That must be a wild primitive country to be named after crawfish." He smiled knowing he had scored a point in mentioning the origin of the country's name, a name given to it by the early Portuguese explorers commemorating the quantity of crawfish in its rivers. It indicated he had a modicum of education that was not quite in evidence by his speech or appearance. I had a moment's hesitation as I wondered whether to discuss my business further with this stranger. Fortunately at that moment the man and woman at the next table got up to go and two women, one with a guitar case, emerged from amongst the standing and pushed their way into the empty seats. The friendly man gave them a welcoming smile. "Are ye going to play for us, hi?" he bantered as a way to engage their attention.

"Not if we can help it," the older one of them said, and then turned to the ever-attentive barman. "Two coffees, please."

The friendly fellow beside me was clearly in need of not just conversation but a larger audience and, pointing to me, said, "Yer man here with the suntan is all the way from Africa. What do ye think of that? An Irishman out there amongst the heathens."

The two women looked at me. The older one was in her forties and carried a face that showed wear and discontent. She turned away in indication that she had no interest in me or in the talkative fellow. The other was much younger, in her late teens or early twenties. She had a classical colleen face with dark hair and blue eyes and a couple of freckles across her nose. She cast me a disarming smile that caused a dimple to appear on either cheek and revealed beautiful white teeth. Her eyes looked into mine in a strange way and stayed there for several moments. I felt stirred by her beauty and that something one sees in the eyes of a woman. I reached my hand over. "I'm Donald." I smiled. "And I've no idea who this fellow is."

She took my hand in a brief but warm grasp. The whiskered fellow chortled and put his hand out also. "Willie. Just call me Willie."

The young woman did not give her name but it hardly mattered. We still shook hands, the three of us. The older woman took no notice as she paid the barman for the coffees. The two women raised their cups while my new friend and I sipped our drinks. I could feel the whisky warm my innards.

"Aye," began the talkative fellow again, "so there ye are out there in Africa, another Irishman taking civilization to the heathen."

"Hardly," I replied. "I simply manage a research station for oil palm and rubber."

"Research ye say? For an English company, no doubt?"

I agreed, pointing out that it really was an Anglo-Dutch concern. He pondered that for a moment, stroking his beard and frowning at me. "Research? Call it what ye want. Ye don't know yer Irish history so ye don't." There was an edge of authority to his voice. "The Irish civilized this world. Didn't ye know that?" He looked over at the two women, the younger of whom seemed as if she did not want to be drawn into any controversy.

The older looked at the talkative fellow. "What are ye, a school teacher?" she said aggressively.

"Naw! If I was a schoolteacher I'd only be able to teach history the fools in the Education Ministry would allow me. Naw! I'm a historian, so I am." He laid that point out with an element of pride and an underlining nod of his head. "Ye see," he took a deep breath, narrowing his eyes with conviction and leaning as far forward as his belly would allow. "If only the world could realize it! The Irish are great people. Great history, ye see. When Europe was in the depths of the dark ages, overrun by Vandals, and civilization as they knew it then was destroyed, Irish monks took Christianity to the farthest reaches of the continent." He looked round at me. "Ye didn't know that now, did ye, hi?" I could only reply that I did not know much about Irish history. "Naw!" He grunted. "Ye're a product of a British upbringing, so ye are. So was I! A product of the invading culture, all of us. At one time, anyway, I was myself! But you ladies knew that, didn't ye, now."

The colleen nodded yes. I had the fleeting thought that with her classic Irish beauty and knowledge of Irish history she must have been a pupil at a Catholic Convent. My own upbringing put me on the other side of the political, religious and cultural fence. But I was long, long past thinking in those terms. Travel and living in other countries had changed my outlook. There were good people everywhere. I knew and believed that, no matter the ethnic origin, no matter the religious point of view. I was opposed to tribalism no matter the basis.

Her beauty aroused my interest and there was that look she gave me. Perhaps, I imagined, she was feeling the same attraction. Maybe it was my healthy suntan, that different look, almost foreign. I sat there in hope that there was some way to get to know her better. The older woman had been listening. "That's the trouble with yer government schools, they don't teach ye anything but what serves the English purpose." She waggled a finger at me. "If only ye knew the truth! Ye know nothing about yer Irish history, so ye don't. Nor you!" she accused Willie. "Not one half of it!"

"But missus, I most certainly do." His tone was peevish. "I'm very well versed in Irish history. But I admit I had to study it up by myself. But isn't that the best way?"

"Whatever keeps ye happy." She returned to her cup of coffee.

"She's right," Willie nodded his head at me while waggling a hand at the woman. "Oh, she's right. Ye know," he studied the ceiling for a moment, "the Irish monks got as far East as Kiev in Russia. I bet ye didn't know that either. But she did!" Again he waggled his hand. "She's had an Irish education!" The older woman looked over at Willie, a pleasanter expression on her face. Maybe she felt that he wasn't such a bad fellow after all. Willie was warming to the fact that now he had a captive audience of three. "And that's not all. Did ye know that the leading church in Vienna to this day is the Irish Church? Imagine!"

The older woman nodded agreement. The younger one, who had still not volunteered her name, was looking at me furtively, glancing away when I looked at her. She appeared uncomfortable. I wondered about the cause. Had the others not been there would we have begun a conversation? Would we have looked into each other's eyes and dreamed of possibilities? I cast my glance around the lounge hoping that talkative Willie would keep quiet, perhaps even leave and give me a chance to get to know this lovely person. The whiskey was warming me and urging on my courage. "You haven't told me your name," I ventured.

"Eileen."

The older woman scrowled at her and nudged her with an elbow as if to say that was enough. I had the feeling that she had already identified me as being on the other side, correctly so, but what of it. I was not a rabid Unionist, just a prodigal who had returned home for a three-day visit, and then I would be gone.

Willie had finished his drink and ordered another with an invitation to me to join him. But I declined. One was enough. Already I was feeling the effect on an empty stomach. He invited the two women to have something stronger than coffee but they too declined saying that they had to go any minute. They had just dropped in, they explained. Willie took this as an indication to get on with his sermon. "Ye know, that's the big difference between Ireland and the other countries of Europe. The Irish, you see, weren't out to conquer other cultures and rob them of their native language and natural resources. Ye know, like the English and the Spanish and the Portuguese, even the French and the Belgians. Think of it!"

He had more to say but I was watching Eileen. She had finished her coffee and seemed anxious to go. Her older companion by comparison was listening to Willie, nodding her head in agreement, a captive audience of one. Willie was enthused. The guitar case sat between the two women and I wondered which one of them played the instrument inside. Probably Eileen I thought and hoped. I had a sudden vision of her playing for me by a pleasant fireplace with logs glowing, glasses of wine and all evening to ourselves.

The lounge was now packed with people, a possible indication of the attractiveness of its decor; something new, chic.

"Ye see," continued Willie, "we Irish took civilization with us wherever we went. Not just the re-introduction of Christianity to a pagan Europe but we founded several universities as well. Did ye know that, hi? Naw ye didn't! Ye're just ignorant! Agh, if only ye knew half the things we Irish have given this world. And you out there in them heathen parts a tool of the English!"

By now he had elevated himself to the belief that he was an equal participant in the Irish missionary works. He was waiting for my challenge. "What universities? Where, for instance?"

"Bobbio in Italy! Founded by Saint Columban, an Irishman." He smirked in triumph.

I shook my head in amazement. I had never heard of such a thing. But, I admit, I felt a certain element of pride. "And where else?"

"Luxeuil and Annegray!"

"Where's them?"

"Agh, sure ye know nothing! Ye're a heathen, so ye are. G'way back to Africa, hi. G'way serve yer English masters." He was in his element.

The older woman was amused by his display of Irish history, but the younger woman was tugging at her sleeve. "We shouldn't be here. Let's go. He'll be waiting."

I tried again to catch her attention. "Do you play the guitar?"

"No! Come," she said to her companion. "We've got to go."

"Can I invite you to dinner? I'm staying at the hotel. I invite both of you." I didn't want to give her the impression that I was on the make.

"No! I'm sorry. I can't. We've got to go. Come along Bridgit! Gimme that case! I'm taking it out of here!"

"No you're not! It's with me so it is."

There was a brief challenge for who had the guitar case.

"Well then, you bring the case. I'm off. I'm going to find Sean and put an end to this." She rose and quickly edged her way through the crowd; and I thought, if only I had had more time.

The older woman slipped over towards Willie and clasped his arm as if she had found a long lost friend. The guitar case began to slide. She caught it, holding it tightly, and then placed it between her knees where it would be safe. I had finished most of my drink but no longer felt the desire. I rose and, thanking Willie for the education, I began to pull on my coat and make for the door.

Outside the air was cool with more people on the footpath than I expected. Across the street at an angle the young woman was shaking her arms at a man standing off from her by several yards. "No! Don't Sean! Don't!" I heard her cry out. "Bridgit's still in there! For God's sake don't! Please don't!"

I was about half way towards her when the bomb exploded. The blast and bits of debris threw me to the ground. As I lay there I could see that she too had fallen. She was screaming at the man. I could make out the words "You bastard! I told you no!" She was now crying hysterically as she struggled to her feet. The man was running down the street without her. She stood up unsteadily and saw me. There was a fleeting look of recognition and then she too was running away. I got up and tried to follow but she disappeared into the throng of people, police and military rushing towards the scene of explosion; and I thought, if only she had looked back, just once.

Within the time allotted I had completed the business that had brought me back to Belfast—the closing on the sale of the modest farm in the Braid Valley that I, an only child, had inherited from my parents. A transfer of the money to my bank in London was arranged. I paid the hotel and asked for a taxi to the airport. To my surprise it was the same fellow who had brought me to town. "Ye're bravely, hi?" he inquired, putting my small suitcase into the trunk. "Ye're all in one piece too!" I assured him I was none the worse for cold weather but concealed the fact that I had come close to being killed. "Did ye hear the bomb blast, the other night?" he asked me.

"Sort of." I had no inclination to let him know I was anywhere in its neighborhood.

"Wasn't thon something, hi?" he said with a cheery chuckle as if the event had done credit to the Irish character. "Boys, can ye imagine. Nine killed and fifteen injured. And that's the second time Murphy's got his place blown up."

"Murphy?"

"Aye, the owner. Didn't ye read about it in the paper? Sure it was on the front page."

I let him know that I only glanced at the article; the photos were horrendous and I was sick to my stomach.

"Aye! Sure he didn't pay up his dues to the terrorists the first time round and they put a bomb in his place." I shook my head in disbelief. "Aye," he continued, "and with the compensation he got from the Government sure didn't he rebuild the place only much finer with all the trappings. Ye shouldda seen the place! All glitter and chrome and all. Like ye'd see in the pictures."

"And?"

"He wouldn't pay up again. So they blew the place up once more. That's what ye heard the other night, so it was. Letting him know!"

"So what will he do now?"

"Nothing. He's dead. Blown to smithereens!"

The taxi made its way back out the Antrim Road. I took my last look at the estuary and at the dark hulk of the Cave Hill, engraving them for the last time into my memory. "What caused the blast?" I asked the driver. "Do they know?"

"Oh, they know, so they do. They went through the rubble with a fine toothcomb, analyzing everything they could find. Ye know? And sure wasn't the bomb in a guitar case somebody brought in and left there, all innocent like. Just left there. No one would have noticed. And then the police think it was triggered by remote wireless. Ye know? From a distance, like."

I thought of Willie the historian and Bridget who perhaps had found in him a new friend to lighten her life. Yet she had brought that guitar case in. I had seen it! And it had contained explosives. She must have known, and Eileen too. They had to have known in order to take a circuitous rout to arrive at the pub without passing through a checkpoint. The thought entered my head that the older woman may have forgotten her mission when the possibility of romance entered her life? And Eileen? I remembered her anxiousness to leave because someone was waiting for them. She left and had I not been so enamoured with her face, her eyes and her smile, I too would have been dead, as was Willie. Poor man!

The taxi delivered me to the airport and I bid farewell to my driver, leaving him to eke out his life in a troubled land. "Tell me," he said, "where ye headed for this time? It can't be London for ye don't get a sun tan like that in a big city."

He deserved a truthful answer. "Africa. I'm going back to Africa."

"Africa! Good God! Out there among the heathen! Where abouts?"

"I work in the Cameroons."

"Ah!" He pondered a moment. "That'll be named after the Scottish Highlander Regiment. Wouldn't it?"

I stifled a smile. There was no point in embarrassing the man in his error. "Yes, you could say, more or less," I replied, nodding my head in affirmation. "Yes!"

He was so very happy at that. "Take care now!" He gave me a playful slap on the back. "And come back and see us soon. Ye hear?"

As If a Stranger

The wet cold of winter lay across the Glens as Billy walked the last few yards to the farm where he was reared. He was returning but not as a prodigal for he loathed the fields around him. Every inch of them spoke to him of poverty and labor without reward. They were barren and acid and, through their meager covering of soil, granite rocks stuck out like the bare knees of a hungry urchin child. They held the futile lives of his father and his father before him for all they had left to show for their effort were the boulders they had wrested from the soil and piled in walls to mark the boundaries of the fields. No plough could work here safely and many an acre had been dug by hand. It had put his father to an early grave but he had sworn it would not put him. So he had left. He had not returned looking for forgiveness. He was back for the only reason that would bring him back; and he was back for the hardest reason of all, to wait, for it was January and January is the month in Ulster that takes the old people.

The snow layered the naked hawthorns with its dripping whiteness. It fell subtly and silently, as once did the blight among the mist never hinting of its creeping death. He picked his way through the slush and the water-filled cart tracks of the lane, past stonewalls that framed the sodden fields, and the clumps of rushes that grew even to the edge of the road. He had been foolish to wear his city clothes though now it was too late. With every step his shoes swept the mud from each foot and smeared it on the opposite trouser leg. His suitcase was also beginning to hang heavy on his arm and it too suffered from splashes of mud. It tended to hang forward and plough into tufts of rushes and hoof-marks of mud. He regretted not having put his small typewriter in the middle of the suitcase for balance; but soon he would be there, just another hundred yards.

He could see the house ahead, a dull limestone white with the thatch sodden from the wet and the weeds in it wilted from the winter cold. A little smoke from the chimney fought its way into the sleet; and quietness, as of isolation, cupped its hands around the place. It stood remote and lost, as a dog-rose petal that had fallen in mud and slush. There was but one to share this solitude, a donkey in a paddock by the lane, standing in the pockmarks of its own feet, facing the old house, waiting, a thin layer of snow on its back.

Uneasiness shivered the young man's soul as he stepped over the ash-plant swung across the mouth of the lane and into the gutters of the yard. The melting snow trickled down over the black cobblestones and he noticed that those by the door were, as he remembered them, gray from catching the soapsuds from the tub; and the tub itself and scrubbing board still hung from the hook on the gable wall under the roof of the lean-to shed. Nothing had changed. He had once sat in his room in London seeing it in his mind's eye, not as it now was in the somberness of winter, but in early summer. In the despair of loneliness in a big city and the reality of his being there, he had tried to capture the past in his diary,

> *The pump on guard beside the door, hook nosed and iron clad,*
> *Its handle, looking kind of sad, drooped down – a cold and lonely,*
> *Rusting sentinel.*
> *By its foot the whetting stone whose smooth curved cheek was used to hone*
> *Each work-dulled blade until, the rubbing of a thumb could tell*
> *Its readiness. Beyond the fence – potatoes, cabbages and chives,*
> *An apple tree and two beehives. The privy by the lilacs, door askew,*
> *With lupines round about as floral kilt.*
> *The worn, treadless motor tire covered in a lace of netting wire,*
> *Marigolds beneath. Of simple things like these are memories built.*

For a moment he halted as he recalled that moment and then, as if a stranger, he knocked on the door and thumbed the latch.

Pleasant warmth and the odor of burning peat in an open hearth were all about him. He could not help but hesitate a moment and let his nose wallow in this long-forgotten smell. Then, nostalgia satisfied, he closed the door and stepped into the fire-lit shadows of the room. He was home, among warm familiar things, the black bog-oak rafters and the white washed walls, the hearth big enough to stand in and topped by its tapering chimney, the worn yellow tiles of the floor; and beside the hearth the settle-bed where lay the reason for his return.

"Hello, Granny!" He laid his suitcase aside and knelt to kiss the wrinkled velvet of her cheek.

"Billy, my son!" She stirred a shaking hand that reached for his. "Bless you, son, for coming back. Ah, Billy, I'm sorry to bring you back like this. But I fell and you know that's not an easy matter at my age." She sighed with a voice tired from endless waiting. "It's good to see you back. Are you here for good?"

He lied to her. "Yes, I'm back…" He hesitated for lying was not for him. But he had to. "…for good. You need someone to take care of you." He lied, for what did it matter? He was back and would never leave so long as she was alive. He removed his heavy overcoat and set it aside across a chair.

"Are you glad to be back?" she asked, her eyes searching his.

"Yes, I'm glad to be back." He lied as he thought of the poverty and the barren fields and their stone hedges built by his forefathers who toiled them. He lied as he thought of the donkey standing in the pockmarks of its own feet.

"That's good," she said turning her face away. "You were so eager to get away I was worried."

He felt his heart sink in fear that she knew, but she smiled and he turned to watch the fire lest she saw the liar in his eyes.

The fire burned, its flickering flames casting long dancing shadows on the walls. A black enameled pot of potatoes hung from the chain on the iron crane that reached its arm across the hearth. Droplets of water boiled over and fell hissing to the white powdered ash below. Peats tumbled into the fire as the heart burned away. Watching it all he saw his father's life, working the land that eventually became his grave. But was his life any better? He asked himself. He saw the streets of London again, in Camden Town and Hammersmith, the streets of smoked gray brick and his search for a place to board. He remembered the cards posted on the glass-encased message boards outside the grocery shops. *"Room for rent. No Irish or Coloureds"*. He was Irish, a stranger no one wanted except as labor on a construction site or dish washing in the kitchen of a restaurant. He had walked miles, street after street, until finally in Hammersmith, in a house owned by a Scotsman, he was accepted. His room had a bed and a gas stove, a simple room with the toilet down the hall that was shared by others. What else did he need? He remembered something he had written on a slip of paper once, away at the beginning when it was difficult to adapt to being called Paddy. It was still in his breast pocket.

The names of London streets –
Epitaph to my dying soul.

Could it not equally have been,

Boulders of the fields –
Headstones for my grave.

What was life about anyway?

"How did London treat you?" The old lady's whisper of a voice cut into his thoughts. Was she testing him to see if he really was back for good, he wondered? How could he tell her of the despair involved in being a stranger?

"It's money," he said, hitting on the main reason for being there. "I can't complain." She nodded as if the words meant nothing to her. "But you know," he continued, searching for the words, "it's a bit like one of the fellows I work with says, money, what else? He's from Kerry. Aye, what else? Money!"

"I know Billy, I know. I don't know how I'd have done without you these last few years." Her voice was just above a whisper, her eyes half closed with the effort of staying alive. "Aye, the land's not like it used to be." She shook her head at the memory of it. "You know, I mind the time your Gran'pa had nine rucks of hay in thon wee low field, and twenty ewes in the top field. We had three sows then too. Now nothing. Only the aul' donkey and he can hardly keep his ribs apart." She sighed and turned to him. "At least I have you."

She continued to shake her head as if there was no understanding of it all and looked with old gray eyes up among the rafters. He sat watching the fire in the hearth. He saw his own days labouring in the fields as a youth, season upon season until his hands and fingers grew thick. And then he left. All he had was muscle and the desire to make money; money that it wasn't possible to make either in the family fields, or in Ballyaghone or up in Belfast. He needed to make money but somewhere away from all the pain of poverty.

They had the same old donkey now as the one they had when he left and still it stood in the same spot, a stubborn old fellow that seemed to know the futility of life. Like so many he knew.

"I missed you at Christmas. Couldn't you have come over?" the old woman asked.

"I couldn't. I was up to my ears in a matter and I just couldn't. Sorry!" He avoided mentioning what it was that kept him in London. It was so important he had to stay. Finally, realizing that there would be no quick resolution he had come home. Now he was hoping for a letter that, with luck, could possibly decide his future life. He kept quiet. He carried an old fear that talking about it might make it not happen.

"Well, no matter," she said. "Johnny Thompson and his wife invited me down for Christmas and they came up for me. But I fell on the ice in their yard the day after and you know the rest. Here I am." He put his hand on her arm to assure her all would be well. But his presence seemed to have given her energy. "Why are you speaking like you're an Englishman? You sound like one of them fellows on the wireless. What's got into you?"

"Oh, I guess it sort of grew on me. I've been gone a while, you know. Since nineteen and fifty-seven. That's five years, you know." He could not tell her that it was a matter of not being called Paddy, a question of being accepted as a human being. He changed the subject. "Has anyone thought to give the donkey a bite to eat?"

"Well, no." She seemed unwilling to say. "Mrs. McGill says there's only a colour of hay left and she was kind of tholin' it till later in case the weather gets worse. Don't you know?" she added as if to justify herself.

"I know. But the donkey maun eat! I'll buy a clatter of hay later. Johnny Thompson should ha'e a wheen o' bales." He deliberately spoke in the voice of the local dialect. So easy, he thought, to undo the years of exile, the English voice he had to adopt to survive.

"Don't be long!" she whispered. "Mrs. McGill will be over soon to take those spuds off the fire and make us a bite to eat."

He put on his overcoat again and found an old pair of rubber boots in the scullery that he exchanged for his shoes. With his trousers tucked into the tops of the boots he went out and into the wet silence. The snow had tapered off. He stood a moment fighting the cold sniveling wind that sought the warmth of his body, and then he moved over to the donkey in the paddock. The donkey had no greeting and even when he slapped it on the rump only shifted feet in a token gesture and settled back as before. He had the fleeting thought that here was the image of his ancestry. Why oh why, he wondered, hadn't one of his forefathers left and gone to Canada, or Australia or wherever. Why had they stayed in this glar-bed of futility? Could not he have been born in some country of promise?

Turning he walked back to the lean-to shed where he grabbed an armful of hay. He held it out to the animal. Almost suspiciously it sniffed before taking the smallest of bites with a tugging shake of its head. Billy then turned heel and walked away holding the hay behind him. The donkey followed but without hurry. He put it in the stall in the lean-to shed and placed an ash-plant across to prevent it leaving. The donkey now had shelter with sufficient hay to last some time and water in the trough. So he left. The donkey watched him go oblivious of the food about its feet.

It was still early afternoon and Billy did not feel like returning to the house. Instead he walked the gentle slope of the hillside lane as it ran down over the boulders to the better land of the valley; past where the stone walls gave way to thorn hedges and the colour of the fields changed to a darker green. The houses down there were bigger and roofed with slate whose blackness shone like the tarred roads that wove through the clusters of trees. One of these was the old school building built on the only piece of flat land in that part of the glen. By happenstance it lay between the better land and the heather infested hillsides. There was a small play-yard behind and, on what remained of the level piece of land was the graveyard. It was separated from the school by a six-foot wall, built of stone gathered from fields and from the opening of graves over the years. It was an acre or so of sacred ground that held two centuries of ancestors from the area. The headstones formed up in rows as if a battalion of memories on a parade ground of time. Billy stopped to wonder how, in a land of so little, so much effort went into marking the graves of those whose rented lives lasted only moments in the unknown. Outside of the few inhabitants of the townland did anyone care? Many of the granite slabs told of whole families wiped out by the famine. Where had the money for the headstones come from? What sacrifice and why?

Trickling past the graveyard over mossy boulders ran the burn, a docile trickle of a stream that swelled only at the Lammas flood. Yet it was for this reason that a wall had been build where it curved past in case it swept the graveyard away. And the wall, where it reached the road, became the parapet of the hump-backed bridge. From where he leaned against the parapet he could see into the school, now abandoned with cobwebs in the corners of the windows. Some of the limestone had fallen off the walls and the stones peeped through at a world that had plastered them up some hundred years before. Though dark inside Billy could still remember the desks where he had once sat listening to an aging schoolmarm, Miss Barbour, a spinster long past the point of frivolous life. She was a dedicated person who, knowing the futility of passing on knowledge to the sons and daughters of peasants who farmed the soil, did her best to make it somehow interesting. There he had learned of English history and of the Empire. It was an accepted thing. That was the way life was. But who amongst the heather had cared what the English had done in India, or of Wellington's battles with Napoleon or why the Boer War. It was how many beans make five and how many sheep can one feed per acre of hillside, scattering manure from the pigsty to make the grass more lush, things that could only be learned at home through hard work. That was how his family had survived. Yet he believed she took joy in telling the offspring of peasants of what lay beyond the fields, of the world at large, Canada, Australia, the United States, South Africa, places where the Irish had emigrated and made good. He looked back and wondered if she could have been encouraging them all to escape.

Billy had actually liked school. And he liked Miss. Barbour. Maybe she was a substitute for his mother who had died when he was an infant. She gave special attention to him. Maybe, too, he was the son she might have had, one who liked learning. She introduced him to the great Irish writers, poets and dramatists in the English language, Swift, Goldsmith, Yeats, Wilde and Shaw and many others, lending him their works from her own library. He read them eagerly by the light of a candle before going to sleep. And yet, when he went to England where those authors were revered, he was a stranger. *No Irish or coloureds.* He was simply just a Paddy; and he wondered if they too had suffered that indignity.

Looking through the dusty windows of the past he remembered Eileen. She sat in the desk across from him. Her family had a dairy farm with cows, something his family's hillside farm could not support. Her father had a car and a tractor and, with over eighty acres it was another world, a world he saw from further up the hillside of the Glen, suitable only for sheep. Yet there were some Saturdays and Sundays when he was asked by her father to come over to help with the cleaning of his byre and pigsty. He paid well for Billy's work as a farm labourer; and that was the only reason why he was there. What he was. Nothing more. He would have the mid-day meal at their table. Eileen helped at the big iron stove in preparing the meal and serving it; and she would lay the dish of stew in front of Billy but avoiding his eyes as he told her thanks. She was fourteen then and had begun to attend the girls' school in town, a school where they wore green uniforms and learned to speak without the accents of the Glens. In his adolescent way he believed she was way beyond his hopes.

While in London he had often had nostalgic thoughts of the old school and had tried to capture his memories, perhaps a little over romanticized. But then, the burn began well up in the hillside behind his family's few acres and had often been a source of adventure.

> *Perched on the hill that heap of stones*
> *Was once a school—three windows, a chimney*
> *And a bell. Down below there ran a stream*
> *Where boys would go to sit and dream, toss pebbles*
> *And the truant spirit quell. The water spun*
> *Past trailing vines of low hung*
> *Willows catkin weighed, and waterfowl,*
> *Their nests betrayed, ran hen-toed tracks*
> *In the fine grained silt. In a shadowed pool*
> *The water slowed to sleep, a moment's pause*
> *In the clasp of straddling roots; the minnow shoals*
> *Like silver coins in the dark cool deep.*

Billy stood some time reminiscing. The fir trees along the ridge stood like naked fish bones against the sky's watery gray. Cloud crept low over Slemish Mountain until their shadows blended with the night. All became dark. There was no visible moon as he walked back up the hill. A yellow light glowed from the window. Mrs. McGill had arrived. He was now ready and looking forward to a good old Ulster fry of soda bread, fadge, eggs and bacon with a large mug of stewed black tea.

"Ah ha, Billy, maun but ye're lookin' like yersel'," she said in her characteristic voice of the Glens as he entered the house.

"How're you, Mrs. McGill? And thanks for looking after my Granny. How is she?"

"Hale and hearty. Nary a worry 'cept wonderin' where ye got till."

"Agh, sure I just took a wee strole. Was feeling a bit closed up in here."

"Well, now ye're back, draw up till the table to ye get yer supper. Yer Granny already has had hers. She hardly eats a bite. An' I've remade her bed an' given her a bit of a bath. An' she's done her necessaries. She insisted she put on her best nightgown. Can ye imagine? All them frills. Why-for in this damp weather I don't know. But she has her hot-water jar an' all, so no need to worry. She'll be warm as toast all night."

He sat down at the table while Mrs. McGill flustered about the hearth.

MUSIC ON THE WIND

Mrs. McGill was a pleasant middle-aged woman whose husband worked as dairyman and general farm laborer for Eileen's father. She had a happy disposition and that, plus doing regular weekly cleaning of eggs for the market at several farms across the valley, helped keep her well informed on gossip. It also paid her a fair income. She had been hired by his grandmother to come help with the meals and other items and Billy had sent money home for that purpose as well as general upkeep and food. Like all the people of the valley she was honest. For whatever reason she had no children so she was on call from those that needed an extra hand.

"Yer Granny says ye're home for good, Billy?" It was a clear question aimed at keeping ahead of whatever other gossip might involve him.

"Well, I'm thinking about it, Mrs. McGill. It's likely though." He continued the lie.

"Aye," Mrs. McGill nodded her head vigorously to herself. "Mind ye, my man must be wrong. He was just saying that now ye've seen a bit of the world ye'd be gone again in no time at all. Five years in the likes of London would sour ye for the likes of these here parts. Ye've got used to it over there. Aye, ye're not the only one went and never came back." She eyed Billy over the fat apples of her cheeks. "But, for my likein', yer own door step's hard to beat." Politely he agreed. What did it matter? "Sure, look at thon time," she continued, "Samuel John and I went up to Belfast of a Saturday when we were first marriet. Sure they were diggin' an' pushin' one another like the end of the world was come. An' that was away back then. Years ago, mind ye! Ye never saw the likes of it. I tell ye, it was like the Fair Hill in Ballyaghone of a Saturday save you couldn't tell the people from the herds. It was that bad we took the next train home or we'd ha' been trampled tae death. An' what they were goin' to charge us for a room ye cannae imagine! Aye, ye can take it from me, far off fields look green but divil the wan will shift me from me own habs." She waved a fat finger at him with a look of horror on her face. "I never saw the likes of it, I can tell ye."

Mrs. McGill continued extolling the wonders of home until his meal was over and she had washed the dishes. "Johnny Thompson asked me to tell ye to drop down to see him some time."

"Oh! Did he say what it was about?"

"Naw, but I'm thinkin' he'll be interested in them fields o' yours. That's if ye're goin' back to England, ye know. They're good sheep grazin'."

"Aye, I'll make a point of it, Mrs. McGill."

"Right ye be, Billy. Goodnight Missus," she called over to the settle-bed.

"Rest content now till the morrow. I'll be up just as soon's I scatter a handful of corn to the fowl. An' Billy, I made up yer bed in the room there and there's a hot-water jar at the foot. An' ye ha'e a nice warm eiderdown on top. Goodnight now. Bye." She had hardly taken three steps when she turned around and looked at him. "Did ye know Eileen Thompson is back home again?" Her eyes were bright at the mention. He shook his head as if Eileen was of little importance. Mrs. McGill shrugged and inclined her head in a statement of having tried. She went out leaving a welcome quietness behind her.

His grandmother stirred in her bed, leaning towards him. "That woman, she's a hard worker but she talks too much. Agh oh! What'd I do without her? Billy, come and sit down by the fire, son," Her voice was a tired whisper. He sat down on the low armchair that had been his grandfather's and his father's, beside the hearth. He threw on several lumps of peat and watched the sparks fly up the chimney. She looked at him intently. "Billy, you know all that I have is yours when I go?"

"Agh, Granny, don't be talking like that. Sure haven't you many a year yet. Aren't you only eighty?"

She nodded her head. "You young ones are all the same. Agh, Billy, it's an old woman I am. I'm the last too. Aul' Ferguson's gone, when you were in that factory place. And so's aul' Pat, and Sarah wasn't long after him. Aye, in January! And you know what that means around here." She fell silent and in the silence he was hesitant to speak.

"You're not going to die for a while," he finally said and realized the words sounded silly.

"I can't last for ever, now can I. We all die, even you. My father died and his father before him, and so on and so on. It has always been." She paused to think again. "You know, if you hunt in the bottom of that chest of drawers in the room you'll find a kind of book of photos. Maybe you'd like to fetch it."

In the drawer he found the album lying among folded clothes that looked as if they had once been his Grandfather's. He lifted it out and felt a moment of curiousness made all the more strange by the thought that he held in his hands the record of almost a century. An excitement of the unknown quickened his heart as he thought that in a moment he would see the faces of many who were his blood, persons he had only known of by name and deed. Almost reverently he carried it to the old lady's lap and laid it there. He handed her the steel rimmed spectacles that lay on her bible on top of the bedside table She lifted back the leather-covered board of the album. "That's your great Gran'father, aul' Peter," she said, pointing. "Your Gran'father's father."

He looked at a man held forever in a yellow print. "Yeah, the old boy himself, " he said and realized there was nothing else to say. That was aul' Peter who had been dead long before Billy was born.

"And that's my father." She turned over the linen covered mount and leaned her head back a little to see better through the lower lens. "He was a good man. And here's your mother before she was married." She let her breath out in a long sigh of life's pain. Billy understood. He had no memory of his mother, just a photograph.

For about half an hour the old lady showed him many photos of uncles and aunts and far-off relatives he had only heard about. He looked at them one by one, sometimes touching the discoloured bits of paper held in place by the four corners. These men and women were dead. Many of them he had never met. They were his blood, people who had lived and pleasured in their lives. But they were dead. And his Granny would die and then.... he realized that those people, though dead, were living a resurrection in the memory of the old woman. And she would die though now she passed the memories on to him. No, not the memory, she had known them when they were alive; to him only the names and the stories that surrounded them. When his Granny died they died also. It was as if they had never existed. It was then that he realized the role the photos had played in the lives of hard-working but poor people. There were no items of value hanging on the walls of their rooms, no paintings, no pieces of exotic porcelain on the mantelpiece, or on windowsill or brass urns by the fireplace. Yet money had been spent on photos instead and the trip to town to get them, each person dressed up in their Sunday-go-to-meeting clothes. The photos were their heirlooms with their faces on them, to be passed down to the next generation and that was he; now there was only Billy.

"Here's one with your father and Johnny Thompson. They must have been around twenty-something back then. You can see where you got your good looks. Your father was a handsome young man. Hardworking too. So was Johnny. Both good-looking fellows. There wasn't a dance in the countryside where they didn't drive the girls crazy. And look, here's Johnny's daughter Eileen sitting on his knee when she was about five or six. She has his good looks. And her mother's too." His Granny looked up at him and smiled. "She's a smart young woman. She would come up here some time to keep me company and, you know, she'd ask about you and how you were getting on."

"I didn't know that."

"Aye, she's a school teacher now. While you were away she graduated up at the Teacher's College in Belfast. I bet you didn't know that either."

"And what's she doing now?"

"Teaching. What else?"

"Where?"

"At the new school in the village. Didn't you know? Miss Barbour retired years ago and the old school is all locked up. Kinda sad. We all went there to learn our a-b-c's. Can you imagine?"

He had seen the abandoned school but of the people he had no knowledge. He was a stranger even in his own townland.

He lay in bed with his eyes open. A dull glow that seeped under the door from the fireplace was the only break in the monotony of blackness around him. Sleet tapped gently on the window and the smell of dampness, filtered through the thatch of the roof, joined up with that of the whitewashed walls and the feather-filled eiderdown of his bed. There was a kind of shivering cold everywhere that even the crock hot-water jar at the foot of his bed failed to remove. It was not that he was cold but the dampness touched to his very bones and he could not sleep. He went over in his mind the few hours he had been home and how Mrs. McGill had made deliberate mention of Eileen, a comment left as if to provoke his memory. And his grandmother had mentioned her also, a smile inviting him to agree that she was beautiful. He clearly remembered how beautiful she was that Saturday night before he left. There had been a big send-off with a dance in the main room of the old school. The partitions that divided it into separate classrooms had been pulled back and the wooden floor polished with shavings of candle wax to make it slippery for dancing. There had even been dancing out on the road. Couples sat along the parapet under the two big beeches and McGovern's ceildhe band had finally come out to play in the cool air. Miss Barbour was there along with other miscellaneous adults and parents. She came over to wish him well on his journey. "And don't forget to keep writing," she said, encouraging him with a hand on his shoulder. He thanked her and assured her he would. "You have that rare talent, you know. Keep notes. Write a diary." He assured her he would do all of that, taking observations on life around him.

He had danced with several girls that had once sat across the desks from him and with a couple of mothers but had not asked Eileen. She was the pick of several young farmers' sons and was eagerly sought after. Then, when it came to the lady's choice, Eileen raced across the floor and grabbed him. She was intent, her cheek against his while the fingers of her left hand wrote poems on the back of his neck. For an eighteen year old like Billy it was sheer heaven. Her mother watched them with the eyes of a careful parent. Eileen and he danced all of the remaining dances together until the festivities were over at which point her parents made certain she went home with them. He smiled to himself as he remembered that was how things were back then.

He had not slept that night because of thinking about her. By seven in the morning, after a bowl of beaten eggs and milk and the promise to send money home, he walked the two miles to the bus stop on the county road. He had that wonderful feeling of adventure while riding into town, getting the train and later the boat to Liverpool, then the train down to London. But he was younger then and that feeling had long since disappeared.

Sometime in the night he heard the old lady wheeze and once she coughed. He felt like going to see if she was comfortable but the silence afterwards suggested that she was asleep. Many thoughts trickled through the damp of his mind as he lay the hours of darkness in painful fatigue. It was not until well after midnight that he got asleep. He awoke to the screams of Mrs. McGill amongst which he made out the words, "Billy! Billy! Yer granny has passed away!" Mrs. McGill was crying uncontrollable and expressing her thoughts between sobs and tears. "She waited until you got home. Dear God, she held on. Poor woman. She held on, Billy. She held on so's she could see ye and talk tae ye."

Billy looked down at the face of the person who had played such a role in his early life. Her face was at peace, her glasses slightly slid down on her nose. Her hands clasped her bible where it lay open on her lap. The candle in the saucer on the table by her bedside had burned down into a hard ring of wax with the black wick bowed in a final statement. It was over. Mrs. McGill sniffed back her tears. "God bless her. She's at peace now. Poor woman."

Death has no politics. It is there for everyone, free; but it is the living who pay the price. He felt remorse that he had not returned home several days earlier, that his business in London had given him only a few hours with her. Later he realized how, in those few hours, she had given him so much, not just that he would inherit the farm but the stories of his dead relatives and their photos. He was now the keeper of the family record.

Mrs. McGill urged him to go immediately to the Thompson farm and use their phone to call the doctor. A death certificate was needed, and he had to get the undertaker organized, and there was the gravedigger of the cemetery. The need for putting things in order overcame her sobbing. She wiped her tears with the corner of her apron. "Go!" she cried.

He assured her he would go to the village and do all these things. "Can you stay here with her?" he pleaded.

"No! I can't. We'll close the door. She's safe here. Just go. I need a while away from death. Yer granny was a very close friend, so she was. I just can't stay. Later."

They both left, she to go to her own home and he to ask Johnny Thompson for the use of his phone.

The weather had cleared and the wintry sun held little promise for the days to come. Wrapped in his warm overcoat and rubber boots he made his way down the lane, avoiding the cart tracks filled with mud and melted snow. Mr. Thompson was out in the field with his farm worker McGill checking his sheep but Mrs. Thompson was at home and, on knowing the reason for his visit, cried in sympathy. He called the doctor who told him to pass by his office.

"Eileen's not here," Mrs. Thompson informed him. "She'll be so sad when she hears. She often went up to keep your Granny company, you know. She's down at the school at the moment even though school is out because of the weather. But she had things to do. I'll let her and everyone of the old friends know, Billy. I'm so sorry." He thanked her and set out for the village.

It had been a long time since he had walked through the village, so different from the streets of London. There were the usual whitewashed houses on either side of the main street, each of a single story and a window on either side of the front door. Almost every window had a potted plant, the proverbial aspidistra. The front doorsteps were all washed to a grayish shine. There was the grocer's shop, a dress shop and a pub. The doctor's office was further along, and two church spires that pled to heaven.

"Hi there, Billy!" someone called. He turned around. It was the elderly grocer who had come to the door as if to check on morning customers. "For a moment there I thought it was your father," he said. "You're so like him."

There was laughter in his voice. "Like when him an' me were young fellers. So you're back I can see." Billy assured him he was. "What can I do for you?" the grocer asked. "We've some nice apples just in from South Africa."

"Nothing for the moment, Mr. McGregor. I'm really going down to see the Doctor."

"Ye're alright, I hope?"

"Sure."

"And the Missus? Yer granny's alright too?"

There was no escape. If he didn't say it now there would be idle talk afterwards. "She has just passed away, Mr. McGregor, sometime during the night."

"Oh! I'm really sorry to hear that. She was a dear old soul. God have mercy."

"I really must go and take care of things," Billy said. Mr. McGregor nodded and Billy could see the cast of sorrow in his eyes.

The doctor was straightforward. "Yes, she fell a couple of weeks ago or so, on the day after Christmas as I remember her telling me, and I went out to see her what must have been a day or so later. There was no serious injury but I checked her out and her heart was weak. Just old age. It was a question of when. I'll be right out to give you the death certificate. You'll need to take that over to the Births and Deaths Registry in Ballyaghone." He was matter-of-fact with no show of emotion. Death was his constant companion.

Billy thanked him and went to the undertaker. He too had traveled with death for many years and, with a professional voice filled with sympathy, showed him the range of coffins from which he could choose. It was not a hard choice. He could only afford the simplest version. The undertaker accepted that with no expression on his face as something fully understood. Billy was glad he had quite a few ten-pound notes in his wallet. Billy paid him and the undertaker assured him that the coffin would be there in the afternoon; and no, the muddy lane was not a problem as he had a special vehicle for that purpose. As with the doctor, he had been through this ritual many times before. "And you'll want to talk to Jack Carson, the gravedigger, to have everything ready. He'll be at home on a day like this. You know where to find him?" That was explained and then he said, "I expect your grandmother had some thoughts on a headstone." Billy shook his head. He had no idea of what his grandmother had in mind. "Just go over to McCready the stonemason two streets down and turn up left and you can't miss it." Billy thanked him and left.

Billy soon realized that Mr. McCready also lived with death and knew in detail the life history of most everyone in the Glen. This was evidenced by the filing cabinet within which he had a file on Billy's family. "Here it is. We did the headstone for a Mr. and Mrs. William McDonald quite a few years ago. She was an Alice McDonald nee Craig. And, oh yes, we have a headstone that has a Mr. Morris McDonald already installed these many years in the graveyard out by the townland school." He read further from the document. "And yes, it has to have an addition when his wife Martha passes on. I have all the particulars here, even the biblical verse. So?" He looked at Billy for further information.

"My grandmother, Mrs. Martha McDonald, died this morning."

The stonemason was silent for a moment. "Sorry to hear that. We'll take care of everything. It's already paid for, you should know." Billy did not know but, despite a feeling of puzzlement, thanked him. The stonemason nodded. "Ye'll have to go see Jack Carson now. With this bad weather he'll need to get started. The ground will be hard. And tell him I will need the headstone of your grandfather as soon as he can get it to me so's I can add on your grandmother."

Billy had the impression that these good men worked in some kind of collaborative service to the community. There was sympathy and concern. Certainly it was a business but they were there to make death less stressful for the living.

As he walked back along the footpath there were few people out-of-doors as would be expected from the weather. Yet the bit of sunshine had encouraged those with errands to fulfill. Some with the usual "Hey there, Billy! Ye're back home I can see." Despite the reason for his being there it was a pleasure to hear his name called and to recognize old faces and see their smiles of recognition. He did not stop to talk for he needed to get to the Post Office on an urgent matter. There he explained that he was expecting a letter from London but, because of the state of the lanes due to weather and the possibility of further snow, it would be alright if they held it for him. He made no mention of his grandmother's death as something that would take up his time and mind for the next few days.

Billy started back to find the gravedigger whose house was just a short distance from the country graveyard. He understood the situation and said he would get started that same day. Billy thanked him. As he came out to the lane he could see a young woman coming his way; Eileen, an older Eileen, mature, not the young girl with whom he had danced so many years before. He waited.

"Billy! It's so nice to see you again. It's been a long while. When did you get back?" Her face was alight with welcoming smiles.

"Yesterday," he said.

"We all thought you'd be back for Christmas," she said brightly. "We had your granny over, you know, when we heard you were not coming." Her eyes were glued to his making every effort to find his feelings.

"So I heard. It was nice of you."

"What kept you if I may ask. A girlfriend? Several?" She was on the edge of giggling, yet a serious giggle.

He had to smile. Women had the knack of getting right to the point. "No. I don't have any girlfriend. It was another matter."

"And what brings you into town so soon?" She smiled with her head held coquettishly to one side. "You're visiting our Piccadilly Circus in the Glens?"

There was no way out of that so he said as quietly as possible. "My granny died during the night. I've been making arrangements."

"Oh!"

Death has a way of spoiling the intent of fun. She choked on her breath in a sob that transformed her from a happy and beautiful young woman to a torrent of tears. "Oh, Billy, I didn't know. I shouldn't have teased you. Oh God! I am so silly." He put his arm around her shoulders and let her know that he understood. He walked her home. "She was so nice to talk to," Eileen sobbed. "And the stories she could tell of the people in the valley. She was like the lady of the chimney corner. You know? Like in the book."

Eileen invited him in but he explained that he had to get home. He could not stay and, thanking her and her mother for their sympathy, he walked the rest of the way. He was just in time for the arrival of the doctor and the funeral furnisher.

The doctor handed him the death certificate stating that she had died of natural causes. "Just old age. It will happen to all of us. Such is life!" With a slap of sympathy on Billy's shoulder he said, "Remember to record the death at the Registry in town." And he left. The undertaker and his helper brought in the coffin. Billy was surprised at how elegant it was. "But I ordered the more simple coffin," he argued.

"That's no problem, Mr. McDonald. The old lady left a deposit with me every now and then and it has mounted up. Everything is paid for."

"But why didn't you tell me. I paid you also."

"I know. But Mrs. McDonald deserves the best. Your contribution plus hers did just that. This is the best. You'd want that for your granny wouldn't you?"

He let it go. The rather elegant coffin was in the house, paid for and there was no point in arguing. He certainly did not want it said that her grandson had so little respect and love for his granny that he only wanted a plain pinewood box. And he said, "That's very good of you. She certainly deserves the best." He looked down at the still body. "Do you mind," he said, "if I just leave you and your man to take care of things. I just can't be here."

The undertaker said that was how it usually went and they would take care of everything.

Billy went outside. The weather had decided to warm up a little. Most of the snow had disappeared. He took a lane that he had not walked along for many years. There was nothing but isolation on the hillside and a view down over the stone-hedged fields. Soon he passed the broken-down walls of a house that had once been the home of a boy with whom he had gone to school. Charlie and he had been close friends and often ran the hillside with their dogs hunting for rabbits and whatever they could scare out of the heather. When they could find the money they would go into Ballyaghone to see the latest offering at the Picture House; some Wild West film that transported two country boys into a world of masculine make-believe where the women were simply gorgeous. There were also those films where everyone wore dinner jackets and bow ties, women in long dresses, and scenes of sophistication that the boys would never see in their lifetime. It seemed that everyone in America drank cocktails and smoked cigars on every occasion. No one seemed to have any work to do but had vast resources of money that took care of all necessities. Then the boys would make their way home, back to a world of stone hedges and sheep, pigs and hard work. Charlie had often talked of how he would one day head off to another world and constantly talked of Canada and other parts of the English-speaking world. Even before Billy himself decided to leave Charlie had emmigrated to Australia and escaped the heritage of the hillside. Mr. Thompson bought his family acres and, with the money, Charlie's parents emigrated also to live with him. On a visit some years later Billy saw how time had taken over and he wrote in his notebook,

MUSIC ON THE WIND

Familiar things had bred disdain and held for him no sentiment.
A restless youth, he simply went, no thought to what it would become –
An orphan left to fend alone
With sightless eyes and vacant stare midst brambles growing everywhere,
The thatch sunk in, the lime washed off the walls revealed the naked stone.

He turned back and was soon on the lane to home.

A figure was coming along the main lane, stepping carefully around the puddles and patches of mud. Judging by the figure, the clothes and the headscarf, it was clearly an older woman. He waited and then recognized Miss Barbour, his old teacher. "Billy," she said, "Mrs. Thompson called over to tell me about your Grandmother. I came up to see if I could help." He was deeply touched. She still had that motherly feeling for him. He thanked her and she gave him a motherly hug.

"The undertaker is inside taking care of things," he said.

"Yes, I can see his vehicle. May I go in?"

They went in and he was pleased to see that the old lady already lay in the long narrow box with its brass accoutrements. The undertaker had left her dressed in the same nightdress in which she had gone to bed, a rather elegant piece of confection. The thought crossed his mind that she had known, sooner or later, and she had dressed for how she wanted to be laid to rest. The old discipline of a place for everything and everything in its place had followed her to her death. It was a code of behavior she had instilled in all around her, including Billy, though sometimes he forgot.

"She looks so peaceful," Miss Barbour said, reaching over to touch the old lady's cheek. "She's in heaven now. God bless her. Isn't it wonderful how she held on till you got home? She just had to see you one more time. There has to be a heaven for such as her." Miss Barbour held a small handkerchief to her tears. "And she's in her best nightdress too."

"That'll be all for the moment," the undertaker said. "I'll be back on Tuesday with the hearse. The horse-drawn one because the motor vehicle won't be able to handle the lane."

"That's fine." Billy was impressed by that offer. It fitted the elegance of the coffin.

"She was a nice old lady." The undertaker nodded his head sadly in confirmation. "So was your Grandfather, a good man. I took care of him too." He left taking his assistant by the arm.

In the quiet of the house Miss Barbour turned to Billy. "Billy, us old people know when the time has come. Your Granny knew and she did her best to make it easy for you." Billy nodded. Miss Barbour touched his cheek with a soft hand. "I'll go talk to all the old friends and let them know about Tuesday. But at what time?"

"Eleven at the graveyard by the school."

They walked outside.

"Billy, how have you been? Have you kept up your writing?"

"I've tried to."

She touched his cheek again and smiled. "Good luck. I'll be praying for you."

"Thanks."

"Did you notify the Pastor?"

He drew his breath in through is teeth in realization of his forgetfulness.

"I'll drop by," she said. "It will be something for me to do. I don't have much these days. And the weather is not so bad. At the moment anyway."

Billy was alone again in a small house that had once rang with laughter. Death has no voice. It just is. He had to re-light the hearth, hang a kettle on the chain to boil water and so make tea to accompany his buttered soda bread. That was all he wanted for his evening meal. He looked down at his granny in her final splendor, in the nightdress she had kept for the eternal sleep. He then pulled the top of the coffin all the way up and closed it so she would have her final evening of privacy. He then sat down on the armchair by the fire and fingered his way through the pages of photographs of his departed family. He got out a pencil and notebook and focused his thoughts. Soon he began to hear the words and wrote them down.

The Night is long and empty as a sleep
From which no Prince's kiss can lift the spell.
Words of Love which once caressed the lips
Are cold and silent as the chiseled stone is still.

He did not know when he fell asleep but he did and only wakened in the morning when Mrs. McGill came in. She spoke quietly in marked contrast to her usual voice as if not to waken the dead. "Billy, I'm just here to make you some breakfast. Would you like an egg and a couple of rashers of bacon?"

He assured her that was just the thing.

"And maybe a sausage?"
"Sure."
"Fried soda bread too?"

Mrs. McGill kept on talking about the delights of the breakfast she was making and he realized she was doing her best to carry on life as if death had not happened.

On Tuesday the day began with light snow. The horse-drawn hearse made its way through the dirt of the lane with its two attendants suitably dressed both for their mission and the weather. Mr. Thompson had come to the house as had Mr. McGill, both somber faced as they expressed their sorrow. Billy thanked them. Together they loaded the coffin into the hearse and set off for the cemetery, the three of them walking behind. There were no flowers. It was winter and a long way from the nearest town with a florist.

The snow by this time was heavier and it was difficult to see beyond a few yards but they kept going. There was really no choice. The grave had been dug and a mound of earth was heaped up at one side. There were several people from the village, the grocer Mr. McGregor and several others that Billy guessed were from the congregation of the church. Each one came to him, their hats off in respect to the dead, and the snow layering their heads and seeping down their collars. They offered him their sadness and sympathy. The solemn figure of the Pastor stood under a large black umbrella held by Mr. Thompson. Eileen stood on the other side across from him. The coffin was laid across two planks of wood and the service began. Billy felt no emotional participation in the ritual. It was simply of necessity in this corner of the world. His mind wandered to ask himself why he had not come home earlier; to why he had not had the sense to realize the importance of his being there, to hold her hand, to talk, to let her know she was loved and would always be remembered in his lifetime. Yet he had allowed the agent in London to delay him with promises until at last he asked him to send a letter. Whether it was good news or bad Billy could not wait any longer.

The cold of snow flakes landing on his bare forehead made him aware of the Pastor's sermon, his voice raised to follow the skyward gaze of his eyes peeping past the rim of the umbrella. He was describing heaven in a flow of wonder, a city of angels, and a paradise whose streets were paved with gold. At every scene painted with words and sightless gaze his head shook from side to side as if to emphasize the assuredness of it all. The members of the church nodded their heads in agreement of every detail. Billy got the feeling that the Pastor was appealing to him to join his flock and rejoice in all the wonders of Heavenly Love. He looked across at Eileen. She had her eyes closed and he wondered if she too had drifted into that land of eternal youth somewhere in the sky. The Pastor muttered a soft amen and she looked over at Billy. He saw in her eyes a tenderness and feeling he had never seen in the eyes of anyone before.

The sermon had ended and the planks were withdrawn so that the coffin could be lowered into the depths of the earth to lie atop the coffin of his grandfather. There they would be together through that eternity dressed in gold and song the Pastor promised for those who believed. Everyone stepped back from the open grave as the gravedigger took up his shovel to toss the dirt into the hole. Billy began to walk slowly by himself along the gravel paths between the rows of headstones, some inclined as if drooping with sorrow. He could see the names of families he knew or had heard of, families that had lived in that area of the Glens for generations. The headstones were their only proof that they had lived on this earth, if living it could be called. Now his grandmother had joined the voiceless, the soon to be forgotten, but for a headstone and an album of photos.

Mr. Thompson came over to Billy and put his arm across the young man's shoulders. "Come on down with us, Billy, and share a moment or two. We have a nice meal prepared for you and the Pastor and these good folks."

The Pastor jumped in quickly with a remark that he had another very important visit to make and, wishing Billy God's presence he left. Several of the other mourners explained that they had animals to feed and must be off to visit their barns across the Glen. Billy thanked them for coming out on such a day and for their sympathies. In the end there was only him, two older married couples, all of whom were from the village and Miss Barbour. Eileen was looking at him and her eyes urged him to join them. Miss Barbour touched his arm and closed her fingers on his arm in a gesture of support. He was amongst friends, friends who cared not just for his grandmother but also it seemed for him; and yet, in his own mind, he had come back to them as if a stranger.

"Yes," he said, "that would be very nice. Thank you."

The meal was laid out in the seldom-used formal dining room of the farmhouse. Billy knew it was the room kept for special occasions such as the Christmas dinner and events such as today, otherwise all meals were eaten in the large kitchen. He was given the place at the end of the table, the place of honor. Mr. Thompson sat at the head. Eileen sat beside her father and the other guests were spread around the table. Mrs. Thompson sat next to Billy as if taking a motherly role.

A comment was made on how nice the Pastor's sermon was. There were comments on the weather and how it seemed that a ray of sunshine had come out at the end of the service just as the coffin was being lowered. "It was a nice sign," Miss Barbour suggested. "Nice."

None of the comments were addressed to Billy as if to leave him alone in his sorrow. Billy was silent. He had not been in that dining room ever before. He was conscious of the symbols around him. It was a room that seemed to reflect a country family's visit to the pages of a magazine, the kind he saw on news-stands but never had any interest to buy, magazines that laid out the rules of décor and style. He had flipped through several on occasion when waiting in his usual barbershop in London. Yet, though not an expert in the topic, he had the feeling that the décor was somehow from an earlier period, perhaps some fifty years previous, certainly in the beginning of the century. There was an enlarged photo of Mr. Thompson's father, somewhat faded, but framed and on the wall; and of Mr. Thompson's mother, both long since dead. There were several gilt-framed scenes of peaceful country scenes in the manner of Constable. On the sideboard was a set of silver teapots sitting on an equally silver tray. There was a tall thin-structured table in the window with a brass pot and a leafy plant. Above the fireplace, on the mantelpiece, sat a clock in the center and bordered by a porcelain Pekinese dog on either side. He had seen something similar in antique shops in London. Billy took the scene in with subtle looks between each bite of food. He felt he was out of his field, not socially as not being among peers but in interest of life's values. Then, a moment of reflection and, despite the more jovial conversation around the table, he realized that he had no material values; he was just a young man still searching for a path in life. He looked down the table and saw that Eileen was observing him. She did not smile when their eyes met. There was concern. He looked down at his plate. The dog in the yard barked.

"That'll be the postman," Mrs. Thompson said. "He always gets here around this time. Can you go Eileen and see what he brought today?"

"It's tough on the mailman this time of year," someone remarked as if to fill in the break in conversation that Eileen's departure caused. There was a reply as to their hardiness and then the topic changed to the coming lambing season and how the market would go. Eileen returned with a smile and, looking over at Billy, said, "Billy, there was nothing for you. I asked the man if there was so as not to have him go all the way up the glen in this weather. If there is he could leave it here and one of us will take it up to you. How about that?"

Billy nodded thanks. "I might just go down to the post office and check it out myself. But whatever."

"Are ye expectin' a love letter young fellah?" the grocer asked.

"No," Billy said quietly. "Hardly." But his heart was beating faster. He did not expect the letter so soon. He calculated it would take more time for a decision to be made.

"Some English wumman," the grocer chuckled.

"Please, Sammy," Miss Barbour said, "it's hardly the moment for that."

"Well, a love letter brightens one's sorrows so I hope he'll get good news when it comes."

"Thanks, Sammy," Billy said. "I'll let you all know later. It's a business letter."

"Oh? Are ye goin' into business? Are ye about tae become a businessman, are ye?"

"Sammy!" Miss Barbour showed a stern schoolroom face. "Enough!"

"It's alright Miss Barbour. No, Sammy, nothing like that. Just trying to get somewhere. I'll let you all know in good time."

"Are ye thinking of going back to England then?" Mr. Thompson asked.

"Not for a while. I'm just trying to search out a few things for the moment. Still trying to get my feet under me."

"Well, what do you do then, for a livin' like?" the other villager asked.

"This and that."

"Agh, leave the young fellow alone, you men. It's not the time for all them questions," Miss Barbour insisted.

"Just trying to help. I need someone down in the store," Mr. McGregor said. "And Billy's going to stay a while." Billy thanked him and said he would remember that. The grocer chuckled. "Aye, I can see folks coming in to hear that English accent ye have on. What happened to ye? Ye sound like ye're reading the news."

The meal was finished. Billy thanked the Thompson family for their kindness and asked to be excused.

"I'll be up to see you sometime later this week," Mr. Thompson said. Billy replied that would be all right.

"And come down and see me," the grocer said.

"Thanks folks. Forgive me but I'd like to just go and take a moment to myself. You know. It's been a very unexpected event."

"Aye. True."

He saw Eileen looking at him in concern again. She came over and brought his overcoat helping him put it on. He could feel her fingers grip his arms as if to tell him something. "Thanks everyone!" he said at large. "But I must go."

Miss. Barbour came over. "Take care, Billy. Don't forget all the things we used to talk about."

He nodded his head to assure her. "I never have. I may have some news for you soon."

Miss Barbour inclined her head and smiled.

The guests expressed their understanding and he left, making his way back in the darkening afternoon, the thought of what might be in the letter foremost in his thoughts. When he arrived he found that Mrs. McGill had backed up the hearth with peats and set a pot of hot water on the hob to make tea. He had a feeling of being thought of as a member of the community, something that he had not felt during his five years in London. There he was just another person on the tube train, another manual laborer, or a set of hands on the bottling line in the brewery.

He was tired now and glad that he had not yet received the letter. He was not ready for disappointment, not on top of the sadness of the day. He lit the oil lamp and sat down. He leaned back into the cushions of the armchair, the same cushions he had seen his father relax into years before. Time had marched on. He could feel the loneliness within the old cottage, the generations that had passed through and gone on. If only the old rafters could speak. What would they say? And today? Just another death of just another! Just a moment in time! He could feel the emotions of the day calling in the distance of his mind, calling to get his notebook and pencil and write down as Miss Barbour had always encouraged him to do. It would bring peace, but what to write? He thought of his insensitivity of coming back late, of giving more importance to talks with his agent than the health of his Granny. He thought of the love the old lady had for him and the good people who came to express their sacred feelings, the Pastor's description of Heaven and the appeal for Billy to join the faithful of the church, the solemn clothes of the mourners, clothes they seldom wore and that hung amongst mothballs in a wardrobe most of the year. He searched for the words that would bring him some relief but the words did not come. He slipped off into sleep and awoke some time later. What was it of the graveyard scene he had recalled through the medium of a dream? It was love, a different kind of love, a heaven on earth. Something he had almost missed. He reached for his notebook and pencil and began to write, scratching out a word here and there and entering new ones.

The graveside rite of passage – a traditional display –
White shirt, tie and pinstripe suit, bowed heads bare
In shuffle-footed silence, straight of face to pray;
Then mournful smiles that say how much they care.

The Pastor's solemn sermon is eyeballed to the sky.
His scriptural quotes describe what Heaven holds,
Where God is Love – in wait for when I die –
What I must search for as my lonely life enfolds.

This final rite – half the church decides to come
To comfort me, assure me they are standing by
To help. And yet withal my mind goes numb
For letting go of her for them is how I must comply.

How can I explain I've been to Heaven above
Through what it was to know her, what it was to love.

It was eight in the morning when Billy was awakened by Mrs. McGill knocking on the door. "Ye're still in the armchair I see. Yer feet and legs must be frozen from the draft from the chimney. Look, the fire's dead, so it is. I'll set a match to it if you could go get some of them sticks in the wee shed. There's plenty of peat here in the basket."

In a short while the fire was blazing, the kettle steaming and the frying pan sizzling. Billy had shaved and was ready. Mrs. McGill talked on. "Mrs. Thompson tells me the service at the gravesite was very nice. I passed by this morning to lay a wee wreath of pinecones from us and the headstone is already up. My, but it's a nice one." He had not expected that so soon. "Mr. McCready is very good at that," she continued. "Most of the headstones there are his work. He does a nice job."

"Yes," was all Billy could say, but the cost of such fine workmanship to people with so little? It was something he could not understand, and the finely crafted coffin for his grandmother? It was not only in London where he was a stranger but now in the emotions of his own townland.

January soon passed into February. Billy had gone to Ballyaghone and registered the death. He stayed to see a cowboy film just as he had done as a teenager. But the thrill had passed. Long before the film had ended he got up and left and caught the bus back to the village. Then came March and soon it was the beginning of April. Billy was in despair. The letter had not come. He had visited the post office in the village many times asking but the reply was always the same. "It'll get here when it gets here. Dinnae worry yersel', young fellah. It'll get here." He thanked them and deliberately stayed away for several days. Miss Barbour would come by and ask him how he was getting on and talk about old times. She would often bring a book or two and Billy would thank her, omitting to say that he had read them. For that matter he had read and studied just about every author of the last hundred years.

"Have you talked to Eileen lately?" Miss Barbour would ask often. Billy would answer that yes, he had passed by the Thompson farmhouse several times mostly to discuss with Mr. Thompson the rental of his grandmother's fields.

"Your fields now, Billy. Your fields."

"I know. I'm not used to it all yet. But what do I do now?"

On another occasion she walked over to the kitchen table. "I see you have a nice portable typewriter."

"Yes. I got it second hand in London."

"But the page is blank."

"Oh, I was just about to start."

"Good. That's good." And, nodding her head in emphasis, said, "I'll leave you in peace then."

His stock of money was getting low and was past the point of buying a ticket either by boat to Liverpool or plane to London. Even the field rental would not be paid until the lambs were sold. He was stuck where he was and if the situation did not improve he would have to ask around for a job, either at the grocer's but most probably in Ballyaghone or even up at Belfast. The letter was his only hope. To alleviate his worry he typed pages of text and conversation. He had a new theme and tried desperately to develop it; and when the inspiration dried up he would walk the country roads noting the change that was happening as the year progressed, the heather coming into purple flower and the gorse shooting up in yellow buds. It was in such a moment while standing on a hillock looking down the Glen that he slowly became aware of the beauty of the countryside. Certainly the stone walls reflected the poverty of the land and the effort of the past but now they added a beauty to the scene, a human touch as if farmers were part of the natural habitat. There were scattered white-washed houses with thatched roof and spirals of smoke signaling that there was life within. There were sheep in some fields and the bleating of lambs, their tails shaking with the pleasure of being alive. The weak rays of the sun seemed to herald a new beginning and hope around the corner. It was inspiring. He felt as he had never felt before. What was London to this? Or any other city? Even Belfast? There was a feeling of belonging. And yet he had fled from such five years before. Maybe one had to see beyond the fence, those far off fields that rumor called so green; but here they really were so green. As if in agreement the sun seemed to expand its rays of light down into the deeper valley of the Glen. Billy turned quickly. He had the feeling he was about to take a fork in the road. But then, he had done that before. It had lead to London. He started back, taking the low road that ran past the old school and the graveyard. He would take one more look before he made that decision he knew he had to take.

It was now late afternoon. The sun had changed its mood as he entered the graveyard. He made his way to his grandmother's grave and that of his father and mother beside it. The wreaths that had been placed there with time were wilted and dead but the newly carved letters of the headstone spelling out his grandmother's name were still bright in their newness. The headstone stood all of three feet tall. There was a carved pattern of flowers around the top and ivy leaves continuing down each side. The words "In loving memory" announced to whoever would pass by the names of those who had gone before; simple people, honest, hardworking, leaving no mark in the history of the world anymore than one of the sheep on the hillside. He looked around at the other similar headstones. Beyond lay the old school. Further down the Glen was the village. Everyone knew everyone else. There was no tube train. There were no double-decker buses. No crowded streets. No Piccadilly Circus. No large neon advertising signs. No hamburger restaurants. Yet, the headstones stood out against the simplicity of the surroundings more than any city landmark did in London. He smiled to himself at the thought and, turning he made his way to the Thompson farmhouse. He had a question to ask.

Mr. Thompson was finishing up the milking of his dairy herd. Mr. McGill was carrying in hay for their evening feed. It was still too early to release the cattle to the fields as the grass had not yet begun its growth. There was an air of busyness in the byre as Billy entered.
"Looking for a job, young fellah?" Mr. Thompson greeted him.
"No. Just curious. Wanted to ask you something."
"Then stay for supper. Go on up to the house. Eileen is just back from Ballyaghone. She was in there getting me a few things."
The evening meal was that of tradition – fried eggs, fried soda bread and bacon. Billy settled down across the table from Mrs. Thompson and Eileen. They were curious in their questioning. Why had he not gone back to London? What was he doing all day, every day up at the cottage? Why did he not drop by more often? To these he was hesitant to answer other than to say he was waiting for the letter he expected from London.
"But that was three months ago," Eileen said.
"I know. There's nothing much I can do about it."
"Well, why don't you phone?"
"How? I don't have a phone."
"But we have one here."
"Oh, I'll wait another couple of days. Thanks."
"And what was the big question you had for me, like when you first came into the byre?"
Billy kept silent for a few moments while he sought the right words. "I cannot understand why the headstones in the grave yard are so grandiose. They are works of art in many ways. They each cost a lot of money. Why? I understand my grandmother put away money just to pay for the headstone. And the coffin!"
"And what is strange about that?" Mr. Thompson asked.
"These folks have lived hard lives, all work and no play and very little on their backs. Yet the money spent at their deaths seems to me to be out of all proportion."
There was an uncomfortable silence around the table.
"Do you resent that money was spent on your grandmother's funeral, her coffin and her headstone?"
"No! Not at all! I added to it with my own money. It's just…well…"

Mr. Thompson laid a hand on Billy's shoulder, a fatherly gesture. "To be remembered," he said quietly. Billy was silent. Mr. Thompson continued. "This is our little world. It doesn't matter what happens in London, or New York or Paris. Here is what matters. We will remember. No one is alone. Even in death."

Billy could feel his question had been inopportune. The eyes of the women were downcast and Eileen's were moist with tears. "I'm sorry," Billy said.

"Your grandmother was one of us, your grandfather, your father and all before them. Our family line too. Family is all we have, and our good neighbors. That graveyard is our Westminster Abbey. Our history is all there."

"I see. In a way."

"But of course there are those who went off to far-off fields, Australia, Canada and wherever, England even. We stayed. And you might ask why. I couldn't tell you. Maybe lack of ambition. Maybe we didn't know any better. Or maybe we just liked it here. Friends you see. Family. Not being alone, Billy." He hesitated a moment and, with a catch in his throat said, "Being loved."

Mrs. Thompson reached across the table to grasp her husband's hand. Billy looked down at his plate. He knew he should not have asked his question. He felt again that he was a stranger, a permanent loner not fitting in anywhere. "I apologize. I should not have asked."

"But you should have. I'm glad you did. You know, Billy, you're going to have to make a decision. Are you going to stay or are you going away again. Where do you fit in? And where do you want that eventual headstone? Whether it's large or none at all. Where? How will you be remembered? And do you want to be remembered? By whom?"

"I guess so. Yes! You're right."

"And," Mr. Thompson looked at him, "what about that letter you've been waiting for. Will it make a difference? What will it decide?"

"It all depends on what it says." He tried to smile.

Two days later, a Saturday mid-morning, Billy was brushing the coat of the donkey when he heard his name called by a voice in the lane. "Billy!" Eileen was hurrying towards him. "Billy, your letter. The postman came by but he had a puncture in the front wheel of his bicycle and he asked if I'd bring it up to you, seeing as we live so close and I was coming up anyway."

"You were coming up anyway? Why?"

"Well, you were so unsettled last time at our place that we were worried about you. Here! Here's the letter. Open it. Good news or bad, I'm here for you. We're all here for you."

Billy opened the letter, leaning across the back of the donkey as he read to himself. A smile began to break across his face.

"It's good news?" Eileen asked

"Very."

"Well? Can't you tell me?"

Billy looked at her, his eyes flashing, a large grin showing teeth. "A publisher has accepted my first novel. They are going to give me an advance and are asking if I can write a second one within a year and sign a contract with them for a series of four."

"Oh, Billy, that's just wonderful." She leaned across the donkey's back and landed a kiss on Billy's grinning lips. "You never told us you were a writer. What happened?"

"Only Miss Barbour knew. She is the one behind it all, ever since I was at school here."

"My! And you kept it all a secret. Oh what will people think of you now?"

Billy shrugged.

"So now you will be going back to London?"

"I'll think about it."

"Let's go tell Miss Barbour, Billy. She'll be thrilled."

"Let's! Good idea!"

The sun was still in the early state of Spring but it shone its mild splendor nevertheless across the Glen as they walked hand in hand along the country lane. The few bushes of hawthorn were beginning to show their buds and robins were pulling worms from the thawed out ground.

"Billy," Eileen said meditatively, "I'd never want to leave here. I was up at the Teacher's Training College in the city as you know but I wanted to come back here. I'm at peace here. Why aren't you?"

Billy walked along in silence. He had no immediate answer. He knew he had been at peace while living the last three months in the solitude of his grandmother's farm cottage. He had no interruptions while writing, only worry over the non-receipt of the letter. But now, things had changed. What would the future hold? He looked down over the stone walled fields, the heather and the gorse in bloom, the sheep, and the whitewashed houses, each nestled in a circle of protective trees. He wondered how anything so beautiful could at times be so cruel. Beyond were the Irish Sea and the harbor of Carnlough, the Antrim Coast Road and more natural beauty than an imagination could conjure in a lifetime. What was a city compared to this? Any city? Did he need a city in order to write? He realized the peacefulness of the oak-beams in what was now his own home, the open hearth, the white washed walls, and the smell of time.

"I've been working on a new novel while I've been here. It's a sort of detective story, the kind that sells, with a love interest. And I've a couple of more themes in the works."

"Oh, Billy, that's fantastic. But do you have to go back to London?"

"No, I don't. I can write just as well here."

They had arrived at the house of Miss Barbour. She was in her front garden when she saw them. She waved. "What brings you two lovebirds over here on a Saturday?" She smiled at the thought of her question.

Billy held out the letter to his mentor. "Read this!"

"And, Miss Barbour, Billy is going to stay. He's not going away again," laughed Eileen.

Miss Barbour looked up from the letter. She looked at Billy with a question in her eyes. Billy put one arm around the shoulders of Eileen while his other drew an arc across the Glen. "I believe I belong here. I'm not a stranger any more."

"Do you really believe that Billy?"

"I do."

"Why?"

Billy felt his throat tighten as his thoughts and memories rushed to find the answer. Further down the glen he saw a ray of sunshine glance off the rows of headstones. "Many things. I'll explain them sometime. But, thanks to my grandmother mainly, and you and others." He gave Eileen a tight hug with his arm. "This is where I belong. I'm not a stranger any more. No, I'm not a stranger any more."

Alive on the Page

"Agh, look at that!" Mrs. McKilt folded the newspaper across her lap, the better to control its bulk. "Do you see that, hi?" She peered intently through the lower part of her spectacles, her head tilted back as was her manner when reading. "He's dead! Agh-oh! Auld Johnny McGavin of the Academy is dead!"

The pendulum clock on the wall ticked off the seconds in a slow ponderous way that emphasized the silence in the big farm kitchen. The work of the day was over. Night had settled down. The collie dog lay stretched out before the hearth.

Mrs. McKilt had lately taken to reading the obituary column of the Ballyaghone Telegraph. It was as if she was keeping count of the number of people who stood between her and the grave.

"Is he?" Mr. McKilt glanced up from his book. "My oh my!" And as quickly dismissed the matter to hurry back amongst the daring-do's of the hero of his tale. With milking over and all the animals settled in for the night his greatest enjoyment was to read a cowboy story set in the wild west of the U. S. of A.

"Do you mind him and his goings on about Dickens, hi?" Mrs. McKilt directed the question to the others at large, her sister-in-law and her son. No one answered, nor were they really expected to. She often spoke her thoughts aloud. Mr. McKilt continued reading the book he had chosen that day from the Carnegie Lending Library on Linenhall Street. His lips moved in his enjoyment. His sister, the one who never married, sat furthest back from the fireplace, continued her knitting, lifting the yarn over the points of the needles with rapid dexterity. She was a demon knitter, turning out jumpers and cardigans by the score. Soon she would have her nephew stand before her to measure the latest item across his back. He was a favorite recipient of her labors.

"What about Dickens?" the sister asked, more to keep the conversation going than a search for knowledge.

"Mr. McGavin was a great one for getting you to read," Mrs. McKilt said. "Many's the homework I had. Charles Dickens and Jane Austin." She reflected for a few moments, looking off into some cranny of her memory that seemed to be hiding in the farthest corner of the big farm kitchen. The pendulum clock kept its slow account of time. "Pride and Prejudice! I'll never forget the first chapter. And Trollope! Barchester Towers!"

"What good did it do you?" The spinster sister-in-law never looked up from her needles.

"Oh well," was the reply. "It did no harm."

Mrs. McKilt had passed through the Academy before marrying and settling down to farm life. Yet there were moments when she still hankered after some world outside her own. There had to be something more and as if to satisfy her own longing she had tried to encourage her son. "Get an education!" she had told him often when he was a boy. "You'll never regret it. It's so very easy to carry with you." Sadly, her son had not responded to this wish. Instead he had three pig-fattening houses and a pile of money in the bank as proof of his vocation.

"Do you mind the time, Willie," she said to her husband, "when there was you and me and all of us. Jack and Alice. Do you mind, hi? And Anna!" She listed several of the folks of the town and surrounding countryside that had sat in the same English classes taught by Mr. McGavin.

"Aye! When's the funeral?" asked Willie without stopping in his reading. He was a man interested only in the essentials.

"It's been a bad summer this year," she continued, ignoring her husband's lack of feelings. "First, auld Surgenor over by the Ross. Now McGavin. It's all this rain. Pneumonia! Poor Mr. McGavin!"

"Why poor Mr. McGavin?" Her son looked up from his ledgers spread over the kitchen table.

"Agh! Just poor Mr. McGavin, a harmless creature. Pneumonia!"

"Sure didn't they only get pneumonia after they went into hospital. Wasn't it a broken hip from falling down, did it, both of them," he argued. "And auld age!"

"Agh oh! Well," his mother sighed gently.

"They both had a long innings," said her husband Willie, still able to follow the trend of the conversation while reading his book. "If we all last as

MUSIC ON THE WIND

long and go as easy we'll be alright."

The spinster aunt stopped her furious pace of knitting and was counting off rows. Satisfied that all was in order, she started up fast again. "You should stop reading the death notices and give yourself peace," she said.

"You don't know what I'm talking about, Martha. You had to have been in his class."

This was not intended as an unkind comment on the fact that Aunt Martha had not gone to the Academy. Since leaving school at fourteen she had lived in a world of chickens and milking cows by day and now, a spinster, knitting by night, producing woolens for her nieces and nephews. She was a happy woman, unencumbered by the trappings of learning, totally down-to-earth. She read only the Bible. She turned to her nephew. "You had McGavin for English at the Academy, too, didn't you?" There was the hint that she wanted her nephew on her side. The young man nodded. Indeed! He knew Mr. McGavin well or as well as any pupil who sat through two years of his English classes at the Academy would ever get to know him. Two years of it. Two years of doing his best to outsmart the teacher, as he had tried to do with all the teachers there.

"Billy! How much did it put in the bank?" his aunt asked. "Heh?" And having made the point and not expecting an answer, Aunt Martha motioned for Billy to stand up. She measured the makings of the sweater across his broad back. "You've grown!" She had a great affection for her nephew and delighted in his way with the farm animals and his calculations in the big ledger spread out before him on the table.

"Agh, Martha, that's not it, at all," Mrs. McKilt said. "There's more to it than that."

"Like what?"

As Billy listened to his mother's eulogy on Mr. McGavin he remembered his last encounter. It had not been a very pleasant one and perhaps for that reason had stuck in his memory over the years. It was the last week or so of school, just before the summer holidays, the end of his senior year. Mr. McGavin had given the class homework to do over the weekend, based on the lesson of that day.

"Now," said Mr. McGavin, "you've seen how Joyce did it in the story of the priest, now, what I want each of you to do is the following. I want you to think of a person you know well and write two pages describing them in such a way that they become alive on the page." That was a favorite expression, alive on the page.

63

Billy shuddered. His weekend would be wasted. He was helping lay cement blocks as the foundation for a new pig house, and, even if he had the time, who did he know would come alive on the page. His father farmed, a quiet man. His mother kept house, cooking and cleaning and reading women's magazines. His aunt fed the chickens and knitted cardigans. The farm laborer milked cows and carted the manure out to the fields, though sometimes he sang Bing Crosby songs. He could see no Martin Chuzzlewits in Ballyaghone; nor a Pickwick or Peggoty. "I always thought him an auld cod!" he said.

"Aye!" his aunt mused. The matter was closed as far as she was concerned.

That weekend before school ended for the year, Billy labored with his father at brick laying and by Saturday night they had a recognizable half-built building. Sunday, being the Sabbath, there was no work except the routine of milking twenty-two cows and feeding the other stock. After church Billy was too tired to even think of doing homework, and then, poking around in the orchard, too close to some beehives, he got stung.

Even as he nipped out the sting that sat throbbing its venom into his flesh he was elated. Now he had an excuse for not having done the homework. All he needed to do was tell Mr. McGavin he could not hold a pen. The teacher would see the proof for himself. The hand had already begun to swell. By tomorrow it would be a convincing sight. Billy hid the maimed hand, going to bed in pain but contented.

Mr. McGavin made the rounds of the classroom collecting homework books. Billy held up his swollen hand much as if it were a prize. "I couldn't hold a pen," he explained.

The teacher surveyed the boy over the pile of exercise books held across his extended forearms. "I can wait," he said. "I expect to see it Wednesday. Wednesday! You hear? Wednesday! No excuses!"

"Yes sir," Billy said.

Mr. McGavin looked sideways at the swollen hand. "When did you get that?"

"Saturday morning," the boy lied.

"Haven't you put any medicine on it?"

Billy shook his head. At least that was the truth.

"I think you had better go to the office and show that to the matron." Mr. McGavin said with concern. "Then get back here. Quick!"

Mr. McGavin was a small man, maybe five foot four. What he lacked in height he made up in aggressiveness. When the boy stood up to go to the office he was several inches taller than the master, built accordingly, a big farm-bred fellow, all of sixteen.

The matron was alarmed at the sight of the swollen hand. "Dear me! What is your mother thinking of?" Billy felt it best not to explain that his mother did not know. "Set yourself down while I put something on it." The matron began to fuss about looking for cotton wool and the appropriate medication. "You boys, especially you boys out on the farms, just don't take enough care of yourselves."

Billy sat quietly while the matron administered treatment to his swollen hand. His thoughts ran to the new pig house he was building, to the many pigs he would fatten and the profits he would make. He had almost enough to begin the purchase of a car.

"There!" said the matron. "How does that feel? Now you treat that hand nicely and it will be better in no time. Back to class you go."

But Billy did not go back to class. He looked at his watch and knew if he left immediately and ran the two miles to the farm he would get an early start on finishing the roof. He would have the building stocked within a week. He took off at a run, out the school gate and down the street headed for home. Mr. McGavin could go to the Dickens!

Mr. McKilt laid aside his cowboy book. "Is the kettle on? Shouldn't we have a wee spot of tea? Mother, slide that kettle there forward." The kettle was slid over the hot spot of the stove. "So auld Johnny McGavin is dead! Boys-a-dear! There was a right few lugs he pulled on the lazy. Do you see that ear?" and Mr. McKilt held his head sideways so his son could scrutinize it. "He near pulled that lug out by the root one time. Godscurse him! What a bad tempered wee man he was."

"You deserved it, so you did," his wife said. "I thought he was a great teacher. I love Dickens to this day and all the others. He never laid a hand on anybody unless they needed it."

When Wednesday came and Billy was expected to turn in his two pages to Mr. McGavin, he still had not done the homework.

"Well, boy? Your homework?"

"I wasn't able to do it,' Billy murmured.

"Why not?"

"I couldn't think of anyone. There's nobody I know I can write about. I just couldn't think of anyone, so I couldn't."

Mr. McGavin's smallness of size was compensated by an equally shortness of temper. "You're a hooligan, McKilt. One day you'll look back over your life and regret."

"Regret what, sir?"

Mr. McGavin looked at the youth before him, all of sixteen, a farm boy. There were more like him in the classroom. There had always been, over the years, farm boys and farm girls with no desire to learn what he had to teach. Why? He had wasted his life here in Ballyaghone. Why had he not stayed in Belfast? He was now too old to change that. Anger at having been cheated by life began to swell up inside him. "You know something?" His voice was on the edge of a scream. "You and the likes of you are only fit for fattening pigs. You hear that? Pigs! Pigs!" And he began to beat Billy across the head and shoulders with the rolled up notebook he carried. Billy put up his arm to defend himself and stood up. He towered over Mr. McGavin. He grabbed the teachers two wrists and held them in a paralyzing grip, a grip he had developed dragging sheep forward to the dipper.

"I know sir." He tried to talk calmly. "I have over thirty pigs, and four sows. And I'm building a new fattening house that I'll fill with pigs as soon as school is over."

"Don't get smart with me!" Mr. McGavin yelled, trying to withstand the paralyzing pain in his wrists.

"I'm not sir. It's the truth." He let the old man go.

Mr. McGavin stepped back holding his wrists under his armpits. A look of shock and disappointment came over his face. The classroom was deadly silent as it watched the humiliation of the teacher. Mr. McGavin continued to stand, speechless, his face contorted in anguish. Then, as if a realization had come to him, he turned on his heel, spun around and left the classroom. The bell rang. School was out for the year.

"I've never seen thon auld cod since," Billy said.

"I was told he retired that same summer and never went back to teach again," said his mother. "Ah well, he must have been sixty something. Tired out, I guess."

Billy rose from the table and its cargo of ledgers. "I'll go check out the beasts." The collie dog rose from the hearth to follow.

"Aye," his father said, "do that! And take a look into thon wee heifer that's going to calf. Maybe she'll calf the night."

In the cool air of the farmyard Billy inhaled deeply of the smells he loved. This was his life. There was none better. He made his rounds of the several animal houses, stopping by the heifer and pausing to rub her swollen sides with gentle hands. He knew from the extension of ribs and the dilation that she would indeed calve during the night. Mr. McGavin never understood, he thought. English literature! Dickens and all that! His mother was the same. She had grown up in the town. She just did not have the touch of his aunt, great at housekeeping but no feeling for the farm. But his aunt? There was nothing she could not do on a farm. Like his father. Like he himself. Billy walked through the byre, feeling, on that winter's night, the warmth from the animals' bodies and their breath. What was it the teacher had said to him that day? If I had to live my life over again! I'd regret! But what? The collie followed faithfully behind him back to the house.

The kettle had boiled, its last task of the day.

"Wet the tea there," his father commanded. "Have you a scone?"

His wife reached for the teapot. The collie moved to avoid being stepped on and slunk under the table. "Mr. McGavin! Oh well, he's in his heaven now. Dickens and Trollope and all. He can read to his heart's content. Don't you think so Billy?

The kitchen was silent. Her son took a noisy sip from his teacup, expressing his pleasure with a gasp of breath. It sounded as if he was trying to divert attention from the question. His mother continued to quietly shake her head.

"You needn't concern yourselves." Martha looked up. "It's all water under the bridge." She counted off several stitches. Billy sipped his tea. He reached for a scone.

"Do you see the time it is?" said his father as he did every night around ten o'clock. "Time we were all in our beds." He looked over at his son. "How was that wee heifer?"

"Rightly. She'll calf sometime during the night, like you said. I'll sit up with her."

"Good! Well, lets get a good night's sleep. There's work to do tomorrow. Don't forget to wind up the clock."

Billy sat at the table putting the ledgers and other papers in order. The collie moved back to the warmth before the hearth. The night was coming to an end just like all the nights on the farm, though this one had been a little different. An old man, of seemingly little consequence in his life, had died. Only his mother seemed to mourn. A flood of old memories rushed through Billy's head, the days in school, the scheming to do as little as possible, waiting only for the bell to ring and get back home to the farm. The ledgers showed how much money was in the bank; how many more pigs would fatten in the weeks to come, how much more money would be stacked away. Mr. McGavin never understood, the old duffer. Out of touch! He thought about him and his odd way. He thought of that last homework Mr. McGavin had asked him to do. Write two pages on some character he knew. Two pages! It didn't seem much, now. Some character that he knew! For a moment Billy toyed with the pages of the ledger under his hand and then reached for his pen. On the top of the page he wrote slowly and neatly the words *The English Teacher*, and underneath, *By William McKilt, Jr.* He paused for a few seconds to think of how he could make Mr. McGavin alive on the page and then, thoughtfully and deliberately, began to write.

SON OF THOMP

"I've been thinking hard this last while," began Thompson, leaning himself back and peering at his friends through slitted eyes. "In fact, I've been giving great thought to a thing that has me puzzled." His aging face was a specter of concentration as he searched for the words that might save him from ridicule. Long experience had taught him that lesson. Express yourself! Be succinct! Choose your words! It was so very important. He knew that his friends possessed little patience and even less inclination to fathom the depth of his rather strange and often perverse thinking. They were, he told himself in moments of reflection, simply waders in the shallows of life. Certainly he had impressed them before, many times, at great risk to his esteem, and on occasion had won their respect. It wasn't easy. But he tried hard, a kind of search for his identity as a being on earth. Was he not Thompson! Thompson of Ballyclug! Their mentor in intellectual forays, especially on Saturday nights in *The Snug*. They had, over time, gravitated to a kind of tribal group, searching out each other for mutual commiseration. It was a regular event, each Saturday night, just as soon as the football scores were read over the radio. It was a way to recover from the fact that none of them had won the eight draws that week or any week. Not ever! There was a sense of failure, fifty two times a year that lasted for about an hour. By then they were in *The Snug* where it was warm and the stout would lift their spirits. It was a place to uplift the soul and look forward to the winning that one day…..one day…..

They sat around the table from Thompson, pint tankards in hand, froth on their upper lips, all four of them—Henny the skeptic, Wee Sammy the nose, Davy Freckles and ex-Corporal Matha. They were his captive audience, his following, his multitude on a hillside waiting to be fed – not with fishes or barley loaves but with thoughts! Thoughts that never ran out! Thoughts for the mind and soul! It had to be played right. Just right! And *The Snug*, that corner of Byrne's Bar those early arrivals could claim as their own, was just the place. His friends would arrive despondent and needed that weekly lift to their spirits. Preparing himself for the onslaught was not easy and the strain showed on his pallid but still handsome face. It frequently did in that way characteristic of the true thinker. At least, Thompson's interpretation of such—lips puckered up so high under his nose that the brows forced his eyes into surrender. It was not a pleasant sight, but impressive withal.

Thompson was still shaking his head in a demonstration of profound wisdom when Wee Sammy, who had no patience for anything drawn out, shouted, "Well, out with it man. Don't keep us in suspenders!" Wee Sammy, alias The Nose because of the relative proportions of that appendage to the rest of his face, fancied himself as the comedian of the group.

"Agh! Away with you!" countered Thompson, agitated that he had lost control of the suspense.

"Are you going to tell us or are you not? Let's have it! Quick!" Wee Sammy thumped Thompson playfully on the side of the head the way one might encourage a stubborn horse. It was not respectful. Definitely not! Startled, Thompson lost the thread of his thoughts and blurted the conclusion first. "I believe I have lived in another life, so I do!" He raised a hand to the disarray of his hair and smoothed it back. That impudent puppy! Wee Sammy had spoiled the timing. It was not what Thompson had intended to do.

There were several moments of silence while everyone adjusted to his pronouncement, a declaration way beyond the scope of anything he had ever uttered before, yet, well in keeping with their expectations from this long-headed fellow. It was, they knew, just another proof of being over-endowed with an education, five years at the Academy and two years at the Tech. Davy Freckle was apt to explain it in the broad accents of County Antrim, "Poor aul' devil! He cannae help it! His heid's just a bag o' brains!" It was, they agreed. There was even a touch of envy.

"Agh, is that all!" Henny looked around the little circle of cronies in a way that Wee Sammy once described as being "like one of them plastic turtles with the wiggly heads they sell in Woolworth's and marked 'Made in Hong Kong'". Henny lived in a constant state of skepticism. He kept up this cranial exercise for the required time to have its effect. "Sure you had us all thinking that you'd found some way of making money. Like, a system to beat the pools." The head kept nodding its way around the circle looking for agreement in a way Wee Sammy once declared, "Sure the sight of him would make Hong Kong sit up and take notice and you'd see a new toy coming out."

There was a nod or two of assent because money was the thing highest up their list of wants and labor the last thing they would give to get it. Winning the football pools was the thing. Lady Luck! Like being born rich. But the rich had that one cornered. The poor had no other option but to try and win the pools. Then again, as Thompson once said in one of his more sober moments, "If you're not born with money you've got to marry it! So there! Think of that now!" They did. But to marry a rich woman you needed education and looks. None of them qualified. Certainly not Wee Sammy. His nose got in the way; nor Davy, for what rich woman could abide all them freckles? Not Matha for sure, for he had no teeth and his dentures were a bit loose. Henny was too tall and skinny and too afraid to even talk to a woman, a big softy covering up with querulousness. There was only Thompson. But look at him! Poor as bedamned! Poorer even. All his life and he was near sixty, and a bachelor. Agh, it was all theory. "Sure you don't know whether to laugh or cry," he once said on finding he had the necessary eight draws to win the pools but had forgotten to mail his entry. "But," it was a moment to be philosophical, "laugh and the world laughs with you."

"Or cry," said Wee Sammy working himself into a paroxysm of laughter, " and ye have to blow yer nose! Woooaaagghhhh! Agh! Agh!!"

"Dear bless us," thought Thompson. "What on earth am I doing here?"

As each of them thought of the chance they had just missed at Thompson not coming up with a good one, they accepted life's uneven hand, took mouthfuls from their pints of porter, wiped their lips, and fell to watching the big glass ash-tray in the center of the table as if it were the pot of gold. Money was indeed the thing!

"It sure is!" Wee Sammy reminded them for he was not the man to be silent for long. "Sure I'd ha' had at least seven draws if thon big lig o' a full back for Manchester didn't have two left feet. Did ye see thon goal, hi?"

They nodded. They had all been watching the game on television.

"Two left feet!"

"It was the center half's fault," countered Hendy. "Sure ye had to be lookin'. I saw it, so I did." There could be no argument.

Though Thompson showed no sign of interest, his ears were cocked. He sat slung over the back of his chair, resting his eyes on the finger and thumb of one hand reminiscent of the pose *Il Pensatore* he had once seen in an art magazine over at the Library on York Street. Francie, the barman, came in looking very tight in a new gray bar-jacket with *Byrne's Bar* embroidered on the breast pocket. Francie was a professional. He knew his role in life. He took pride in his work. With an expert eye he sized up the nearly empty glasses. "Well, gentlemen! Same again, now? Right?" There was no need to answer. Francie knew from long custom what his customers in *The Snug* usually took. There was some movement then as everyone, including Thompson, drained the last of his glass in readiness for the new lot coming. Francie came and went, lifting the ten-shilling note and dropping some silver on the table.

"What's that you were saying there, Thompson, about living someplace else? Let's hear it." Davy, red hair, freckles and all, was very fond of Thompson's philosophizing. Life as a janitor at the University was boring. And he was treated as an underling, a serf, a peasant, a man without an opinion, someone to clean the floors. Thompson was a friend. Thompson would ask for his opinion!

"Aye, Thompson," they said, "Let's hear it!" Except Henny who was muttering, "Just a lot of aul' cod."

Thompson reached for his glass, holding his head well back and looking all around the ceiling for the right words. "I was reading the other day about the stuff we're made of, proteins and ribonucleic acids." He let the scientific words roll slowly off his tongue. It was more impressive that way.

"Who's them?" said Henny, ready to jump on Thompson's learnedness like a terrier on a rat. "Sure for all we know you're making them words up."

"Whisht, Henny," said Davy seriously. He had seen textbooks lying around the various lecture theatres with stuff like that in them. "You know fine well that's not true. Thompson did two years at the Tech. to be a chemist. 'N'at true, Thompson?"

"It is," said Thompson with great patience.

"Well, what made you give it up for then? Huh?" Henny was ready for a fight.

They looked down, away from Henny, yet not wanting to look at Thompson for fear of embarrassing him. Everyone knew why Thompson had left the Tech. half way through the course. "It was all a farce," Thompson had explained often. "Sure if you only knew!" They had nodded assent. This was the accepted explanation. It was all a farce and had driven Thompson to a nervous breakdown and a year convalescing. Thomson would sometimes elaborate. "Who'd want to be caught counting pills anyway and putting labels on bottles? Pharmacist? Apothecary would be more like it. Selling charms. Rabbits feet on a string round their necks would do more good to half of them than their aul' aspirins. Sure if you only knew!" It was all agreed that Thompson had decided to quit the rat race. They knew. "Ye got to find yer nitch, so ye do," was how Wee Sammy summed the matter up rather adequately and to everyone's satisfaction. Except maybe Henny who felt Thompson put on airs. Henny worked in the men's clothing at the Co-op and considered himself professionally a cut well above the rest. To prove it he always wore a suit with a white shirt and tie. He was always neatly dressed.

"Well, tell us about the stuff we're made of," coaxed Matha. The ex-corporal's eyelids were getting heavy. They set their glasses down and looked at Thompson.

"It's all in the chromosomes, you see. In every cell of our body there's a group of them. It's them makes us what we are. Why you're you and I'm me. The chromosomes..."

"Chromiumspuns," shouted Wee Sammy. "Sure I had a suit made of them one time. Right hard wearing it was too. By the Holy Fly, I mind the time when Devlin's dog catched the mange...." And he was off, chortling over the top of his nose. Wee Sammy enjoyed his own stories as much, if not more, than his listeners.

Thompson waited patiently. It was all part of the game. They would get around to him again. He sat quietly, his overcoat still on, unbuttoned as usual. The air was thick with cigarette smoke. There was a hum of voices from the main bar; the tinkle of glasses and the occasional jarring crash as the helper dragged crates of bottles up from the basement. *The Snug* was just big enough to hold the small party, its atmosphere warm in a friendly way, intimate.

Thompson, eyes still closed for that was the way thinkers were, listened stoically to the laughter at Wee Sammy's antics. "Agh well!" he thought. "Blessed are the pure in heart." They were decent fellows. Humble fellows. Condemned to eat and sleep and dream of winning the pools, of money, that universal currency that the whole world understood, put value on and measured others by. There they were, clinging to their little identities. They knew who they were. There was no escape. Not even if they did win the pools. Aghaneo! He reflected to himself. Was he not Thompson! Thompson of Ballyclug!

It was coming near closing time. When the bar closed he would have to go and the thought distressed him. He would have to walk along the silence of the street of terrace houses, each with one room downstairs, one room up, the toilet out in the corner of the cobbled yard and the small black fireplace with two lumps of coal already cooled into gray ash. The light would still be burning as he had left it when he went out. He always did so as not to return to a house in darkness. Yet it was still an empty house. He saw himself lighting the gas ring and setting the kettle on to boil, buttering a slice of bread. There would still be a pork sausage left over from the morning, on a saucer by the sink, cold with a skin of hard lard on it. He didn't think he would undress tonight but just get into bed as he was, take the shoes off maybe, take his collar and studs off.

"The same again, gentlemen?" called Francie.

"No," said Matha, feeling very warmed by the laughter and ready to come out of his shell. "I'll have a wee Irish with a Monk Ale."

"Make that twice," said Davy.

"That'll be three Guinness, two wee John J's and two Monks by the neck," said Wee Sammy, chuckling to himself and watching Francie's eye. It was a standing joke of Wee Sammy who always saw great humor in ordering Monks by the neck in a pub owned by a Catholic. Sammy was a member of The Protestant Boys. Needling the religious opposition was his idea of enjoying himself. "I always get a kick out of that," he assured them. "Sure you'd never get that much fun with your clothes on! Whoooaaaghhh!"

"You were saying, Thompson," prompted Davy at last. "Let's get to the bottom of this thing before the night's wasted." His head of red hair and facial mask of freckles seemed to be on fire.

"Well, your chromosomes are different to mine and mine to his, do you see, all round."

Francie brought the drinks, saying deliberately to show he wasn't fooled, "And two Monks by the neck, there." He picked up the ten-shilling note and left a few coppers.

"But what if the same set of chromosomes were to occur twice?" Thompson looked around the group meaningfully with his lips pressed out in the manner of a duck's beak. "You'd have two people the same!"

"Sure no two people are the same," said Henny querulously.

"And what about twins?" pointed out Davy who was getting fed-up at Henny for always being down on Thompson. "And if twins marry twins?"

"Aye, there's a thing," cried out Wee Sammy, his face getting worked up with laughter. "That could lead to some capers and sure a body'd never know! Kootchie-koo to a band playin'!" His features had disappeared into glee, except for the nose. "You'd never know for sure if you were in bed with...."

"There'd be other ways." Matha was deadly serious on that score. He knocked back his wee Irish with a manner confidant that, if caught in such a situation, he'd know.

"There was an article in Reader's Digest about that very same thing some months ago," said Davy.

"And what did it say?"

"Genetics it was called. About the unborn child and all. How it comes about."

"How's that?"

"Oh, I just thumbed my way through it. I don't bother my head with such things like that. Give me a good Western anytime," said Davy, loath to have to explain something he did not understand. "But the wife, she takes a glance now and then."

"You men are very quick," said Thompson. "Very quick indeed. That about the twins was good, mind you. I must remember that." They were all pleased at the compliment and nodded. "But think of this one. Supposing by chance, and mind you, in chance anything's likely to occur."

This was good. They would fill in their football pools once again on Sunday, post them on Monday and survive the long wait to Saturday when they would sit by the wireless all afternoon waiting for the results. Yes! Chance was the thing. It could make you rich!

"Supposing a person alive today, by some miraculous happening in the matching of his parents, got exactly the same chromosomes as a man that had lived hundreds of years ago. What then?"

They wanted Thompson to tell them.

"Well, wouldn't he look alike and think alike and do everything just like the man before him?"

"With some exception," said Henny, voice querulous, head nodding. "It wouldn't be that simple."

"How?"

"He'd drive a car today instead of a donkey or he'd be on the dole instead of begging on the street."

"You're right," said Thompson. "Quite right. Man you're quick. But that's only because we've got socialism today and a labor government. But the person would be just the same. For instance, if you had the same chromosomes as Brian Boru you'd be Prime Minister of Ulster today."

"Aw, hold on there Thompson," shouted Wee Sammy. "Brian Boru was a Catholic. We couldn't have that!"

"Well, take whoever you like then."

They all thought a while and Thomson settled back with his glass. They were like chickens, scratching for grains amongst straw, a lot of effort, a lot of hope and little to show for it, them and their football pools. It was true. Chickens do not understand the equitable distribution of wealth. He decided he would keep that thought to himself. Was he not Thompson!

"You know, you set a body thinking," said Matha.

"I know who I'd like to be," said Henny.

"Who?" asked Wee Sammy.

"Martin Luther, himself!" He nodded his head up and down in the prescribed Made-in-Hong Kong manner.

"Aw now, that's sacrilegious." Wee Sammy shifted up and down in his seat with discomfort at the idea. "You can't have that!"

"Well, you can be King William and between us we'd rout all the rebels out of Ireland and into kingdom come." The turtlehead on him almost ran amuck at the pleasure that would give.

"I'm all for that," agreed Wee Sammy. "All for that." And he would have gone off on a monologue of what he would do, for the mention made him get very serious, had not Matha, stirred by the mention of King William and the warmth from the wee Irish, begun to sing, eyes closed, chin dug into his chest and not opening his mouth too wide in case his dentures slipped.

"Sixteen an' ninety bein' the date of the year,
Seven days made a week an' so was the beer,

Matha had the trick of ending each line with a nasal "aaah" and beginning the new line with a convinced nod of his head.

When a glorious white horse from near Belfast town
Won itself an' its master immortal renown.

Matha was fiercely supportive of the Crown and boasted his allegiance with a tattoo of the Union Jack on one forearm and two crossed rifles, with bayonets attached, on the other. He was fond of keeping his shirtsleeves rolled up in the Italian manner – his troop ship had once anchored off Naples on the way back from Egypt—the better to display his loyalty.

Great an' very marvelous were the things it could do.
If you fed it tobacco it could spit, smoke and chew.
But stranger things yet onto yous ones Ah'll tell,

For the horse had a quare tail an' Ah have as well."

"There'll be no singing in the house, now. No singing," shouted Francie through the door with a stern face. "You have to have a license for that I'm afraid. And we're just licensed to sell likker! This is not a house of entertainment, so it's not. Sorry lads, now! Another round? It's nearin' closing time!" Francie was always the professional.

It was Thompson's turn to pay. "Bring us all a wee Irish and what we all had the last time to chase it." It was a great gesture. He knew he had just enough to pay for it and he'd have to go easy for a couple of days, but he felt pleased. "Ye've a great voice there, Matha, so ye have," continued Thompson. "A great voice. Ye could be descended from who knows who in the operatic world. Did ye ever think of that?"

"B' Jayzuz!" said Henny. "In yer dreams. Yer head's a marley!"

Francie brought the drinks and Thompson counted out the toll, having to dip into a few of his pockets to get the total.

"Let me help you with that," offered the ex-corporal for it was not often anyone paid him a compliment.

"No! Away with you! Sure come Saturday with my eight draws in the pools I'll be a millionaire."

"Do you think," asked Davy when Francie had gone, "a body could have the same chromosomes as some great financier?"

"Like Carnegie that built all the libraries half across the globe?" suggested Matha.

Thompson watched. This was the stage he liked best, when an idea had caught on and they were chewing it over. He'd leave them for a minute. "'Scuse me, men, but Nature is a-callin'." He rose from the table and ambled off to the Gents. Thompson's frequent visits to the men's room were understood. "I'm cursed with a small bladder and a weak sphincter," he had explained more than once. "It's a consequence of getting old".

In his absence they felt free to pick apart the matter.

"How'd you ever know," asked Wee Sammy. "It takes money to make money and if you were in poverty what then? You'd have to have the luck as well. Sure look at aul' Thompson, there. He has the brains. What good did it ever do him?"

They agreed. Brains alone were not enough.

"He's sure a long-headed one, alright," said Davy. "He never gives his head a moment's peace. Did you notice he never said who he'd like to be?"

"Agh, he'll always be an aul' cod. That's all." Henny would never admit praise of anyone.

With Thompson's prolonged absence, for he tended to linger at the mirror on the wall above the urinals, the conversation came to a halt. By themselves they had nothing new to talk about. After a few seconds their minds were already drifting back to the matter of money.

"What are your picks for the eight draws next week, Henny?"

"Agh, Davy, I'm keepin' them to myself. Find yer own draws. An' if ye win sure all the money is your own. I'm keepin' mine."

"Well I'll not share it with you, then, if I win."

"Keep yer aul' money!"

"Gentlemen," said Wee Sammy. "Lookit! There's a lesson to be learned. There was this man, you see, won six million on the pools. You know. An' in a while's time he had nothin' left, not even a penny. 'Where'd it all go?' he was asked. Says he, 'Sure two million I spent on wimmen, two million I spent on booze and the rest I just pissed away!'" Wee Sammy exploded into laughter at his own wit. "Whoooaagghh! Isn't that the height of it? Bejaypers! Sure Davy, there's no point in you winnin', you'd just piss it all away!"

"Ye're a daft aul' idjit, so ye are!"

Thompson returned, not too steady on his feet. It was time to get back to more serious things.

"Well, Thompson," said Davie, "You didn't let us know who you thought you were."

Thompson spread himself in his seat, chin low on his chest. "I'll be honest with you. I'm damned if I know." That was a good answer they all agreed; and certainly a true one.

"Time gentlemen, please!" Francie came bustling in looking for empty glasses. The conversation had died out and one by one they cleared their glasses and went to ease the pressure in their bladders. Except Thompson. He stood up, looking around the bar at the motley of people. Did they too fill in the football pools with dreams of riches? Where would they go home to? And to what? Had they left the light burning? Was there a fire in the grate? A warm-bodied wife to make a cup of tea? "Agh oh!" he sighed.

Henny, Wee Sammy, Davy and Matha stood at the urinals uttering grunts of relief. They could see themselves in the long strip of mirror that stretched from wall to wall at head level. Davy looked at his red hair and mass of freckles. He knew he would have to go down to the City Library and take a look at the pictures in a history book. You never knew! Maybe he could find something in the library of the University, in the history section. Yeah! Wee Sammy surveyed his big nose with tight eyes. Who on earth or under it for that matter had a nose like that? It should be easy to trace. Henny, sighing with the relief he was experiencing, said "It's all an aul' cod! Thompson must think we're simpletons." Matha urinated quietly, thinking to himself. Could he have been an opera singer? Or maybe, as an army man, he might have been a great Roman warrior. Or a Greek! Doing battle with sword and shield. It was something to think about, right enough.

They stood on the curb outside the pub door. They all had on their scoop-caps and mufflers except Thompson who always went bareheaded in winter or summer.

"Well, goodnight Thompson," they said one after the other. But Thompson was already walking down the street. No one offered to accompany him. He was going the other way, as always. Even if he would have asked they would have been loath because, away from the safety of *The Snug*, Thompson might have said, "You know, I've been thinking lately about something," and they would have been lost. Even Wee Sammy would have been hard-pressed to utter a joke.

Suddenly Henny rose uncertainly on the tips of his toes like a cockerel about to crow. His head bobbed. "Thompson! I know who *you* are, so I do," he shouted. "You're Thompson, so you are. Thompson! Son of Thomp! And that's about bloody-well all! Son of Thomp! D'ye hear? Son of Thomp!"

But there was no laughter. Thompson walked on, slowly, rocking slightly from foot to foot, his head thrown back, eyes upwards, searching. If it had not been for the rain-laden clouds of a Belfast night he could have seen the stars.

The Phantom in the Hedgerow

It was a Sunday morning in thirty-nine. Uncle Phil was getting himself ready to take part in the usual Church parade. He handed me his khaki tunic and said, "Here young fellah. Polish me brass buttons for me an' ye'll not see what ye'll get." That was a standing joke with him. "Ye'll not see what ye'll get!" But I always did see. I always did get, like the pair of binoculars, a terrifying gift for a wee lad.

I polished those brass buttons till they shone. By mid-morning I stood at the door with the family and waved him off, me, a little fellow of five, going on six, thinking that being a soldier was the greatest thing in life a man could be. He walked the mile or so to the town, straight as a ramrod, his chest out and those brass buttons gleaming. I was not to know that The Territorials would be marched from the church to the railway station as soon as the service was over and he would not return for over six years. When he did he was still the hero he had always been, perhaps more so.

Uncle Phil was what the family termed a bit of a carry-on, always joking and laughing. He entertained us with ridiculous pantomimes of things he had seen overseas—Arabs in their robes begging for baaksheesh, Italians in states of inebriation singing O Sole Mio and Germans strutting their way through desert sand. "Them krouts all got a brush handle up their backsides," he laughed. I listened with delight and perhaps a little envious of uncle Phil and the adventures he had in foreign parts. He could say the strangest things in Arabic, Italian and even German. He described the taking of prisoners in Benghazi and whooping it up in nightclubs in Cairo where belly dancers offered more delights than Ali Baba. That he might exaggerate never entered my head. He was my uncle Phil, Corporal McCurry, of the Eighth Army. And of course the binoculars. He brought me back a pair of binoculars he'd taken off a German soldier he personally killed in a skirmish somewhere in the Western Desert. "One of Rommel's men," he said, winking heavily to let me know the magnitude of that feat. "Sure it was the shine ye put on me buttons blinded him t' death." He ruffled my hair and laughed. Not many wee lads get honored like that.

I loved those binoculars. The soldier's name was scratched on one barrel – Kurt. It was not an elegant signature, just a man's attempt to mark his property, possibly scratched there with the point of a penknife during a moment of respite from the terrors of war. Kurt! I used to wonder about him. How could he ever imagine that his binoculars would end up in Ulster, in the hands of a wee lad on a dairy farm? He was one of Rommel's men! That was something special. I took good care of those binoculars, always. I have kept them in a drawer well wrapped up. Back then I used them to go bird watching or simply scanning the fields for whatever. They're more than a valuable souvenir. They're a memory; one I intend to pass on, soon.

Uncle Phil had been a schoolteacher before the war but after his return he worked on my father's farm as a hired hand. When asked why he did not continue in the teaching profession he would reply, "Nah! No interest. There are better things." But what? He showed no inclination to pick up his life. The family worried about him. I would hear them discussing his lack of ambition. "What a waste! He can't seem to get hold of himself." or "Nah! I've seen it before. The war's to blame. It's the war that did it." And this conclusion was supported by tales of those who had returned from the Great War, thirty years before and ended up as drunkards lying in their own vomit on the street. "They were terribly gassed, so they were. Poor fellows. Their lungs all burned out!" was offered as an explanation. Aunt Florrie would consider this for a moment and then declare, "Aye, so ye say, but the Devil finds them, so he does," she assured everyone with vigorous nodding of her head. "It's all an excuse. They forsook the Lord. It's the Devil I tell ye."

There were other times when the discussion of my uncle Phil would reach a point when someone would whisper, "Shusssh!" and I knew I was not supposed to hear. My aunts would become very intent on their knitting or glance at the pendulum clock and remark, "Aye, the pubs will be closing soon." To which aunt Florrie remarked, "The Devil, sure I've told ye that before, so I have. It's the Devil! It's in him. What else can ye expect?"

I was eleven then and happy that uncle Phil stayed on our farm. Certainly the farmhouse was big enough for us all. There was my father, his two unmarried sisters who had moved in when my mother died, and me, six bedrooms in all. That left one for uncle Phil when he returned from the war and one for uncle Thompson when he came down at weekends from Belfast.

I followed uncle Phil around at every opportunity after school and on weekends. I wanted to become a soldier and travel the world. I wanted to learn languages. I wanted to hear more. And I did but it was not what I expected. It was a Saturday. I was up in the big field after completing a tour of the burn and the bog with my binoculars. Birds of all kinds had become familiar. I carried a book to help me identify the various species and I proudly knew them all. Rabbits and hares also. I had even seen a fox or two dodging along secretively. Sometimes I caught people in the lens but would turn quickly away for that was eavesdropping and did not feel right. Except one day I caught uncle Phil. He was bringing in the cows from the meadow for the evening milking when suddenly he stopped. He stepped to the side of the lane and said something as if to someone hidden in the hedgerow, except there was no one there! My binoculars gave me a close-up of his face that was distorted with apparent anger. His lips moved hurriedly, his hands cutting the air or nervously smoothing back his hair. He even stood silent for a moment, listening, then a sudden outburst, an explosion of words as if he was replying to an insult from some phantom in the hedgerow. I hurried down to the farmyard guilty that I had dallied so long. Being a Saturday I had to help with the milking. Uncle Phil greeted me as if nothing had happened and asked me to help him chain up the cows in their stands. I did and later milked my share. The binoculars sat on the window of the byre. I kept to myself the experience that I had seen.

I observed many other such conversations between uncle Phil and the phantom in the hedgerow over the ensuing months and years. Some of the words were not in English but guttural as if coughed out of his throat. I assumed it was German. The many members of the family had noticed also and it was often discussed in his absence. I remember one Sunday night after church in the winter of forty-nine. Uncle Phil was down in the byre helping a heifer calve. Uncle Thompson, down from Belfast for the weekend, was holding forth in his usual way to the assembled family in the big farm kitchen. He had taken his favorite position standing in front of the hearth, letting the heat soak into the backs of his legs. "Sure it's nothing," he said. I was seated at the long table with my nose in an exercise book getting ready for school on the Monday and pretending I wasn't listening. "Didn't the prophets of the Old Testament rant and rave and hear voices." He rubbed the seat of his trousers where the heat from the hearth had scorched the cloth and stepped away, still on his theme. "The prophets! There was Zechariah and Jeremiah all raving lunatics, if you ask me." Then, seeing the look in my aunt Florrie's eyes, he added, "Though it depends on your point of view." There was always that religious streak in the family.

"It was the war, so it was," my aunt Minnie would explain, shaking her head in sorrow. "He was never like this before."

"Nah! Bad company, more like it. Sure he's never out of Cassidy's pub."

"He has no ambition. He was a schoolteacher once. Now he's just a laborer."

"Florrie! Shame on you! He's your own brother."

"He's no brother of mine while the Devil's in him."

"He can't find himself, no-how. And the talking to himself don't help none."

The war was blamed along with the Devil. It was even said he had come under the demon's spell out in them foreign parts, in the desert like in the Bible.

"'Cast yersel' down' and all that, like it says in the Book of Matthew," argued aunt Florrie. "Egypt! Libya! Italy, where the Pope lives! And where not else? I'm convinced, so I am. Temptation everywhere! He casted himself down. The Devil has him in his grip, I tell ye."

There were more theories to explain my uncle Phil and his peculiarities than there were hares up in the whins and heather of the top field. "He should get marriet!" was another strong suggestion that at least everyone agreed upon, except aunt Florrie. "Nah! That would just cause grief to some poor unfortunate wumman." There would be silence then. "Who would have him?" aunt Florrie would add, backing up her point of view with vigorous shakes of her head. "Maybe the Widow Johnson!" suggested Thompson, an evil smirk on his lips and his eyes sparkling with the possibility.

"She needs a man, that's for certain!" confirmed aunt Minnie.

At that uncle Thompson said, "Why not Phil? Sure he can do the work of two men, maybe three." Indeed! Uncle Phil was a big muscular fellow over six feet with hands on him could choke a bull; a man made for farm work, not school teaching.

"Not if he wants to be part of this family!" Aunt Florrie moved uncomfortably in her chair, agitated by the idea. "He's too good for her!"

"But it's all a question of where your values are." Thompson had the habit of changing one argument into another.

The Widow Johnson lived over the ways a bit. Since her husband died of a heart attack, and he still a young man, she had run the farm to perfection, even better, it was said, than he had. She was tough on the farm help and they were apt to quit all of a sudden and leave. She was a real hard woman, a farmer's daughter who had attended the woman's agricultural college up by Derry for two years and got a diploma in dairy sciences and poultry keeping. She had learned how to do things right; make money, instead of just breaking your back all your life with nothing to show for it. She had land. It was all hers.

"I'd say that farm has about ninety-five acres." Uncle Thomson threw the thought out with artful carelessness. It was received with silence. Aunt Florrie looked up at him from her knitting with a look that dared him to continue. Thompson smirked and turned the page of his book. He winked at me. It was a very important point and he knew it.

Land is something you always have to take into account in our part of the country. Land! You can't be born and bred in the Braid Valley and not put high value on an acre or two of land; even better when there's a woman attached to it. You know the old saying, "If ye don't inherit it ye have to marry it." That's the way land is. Nobody had the money in them days and the banks were not lending; at least not to a fellah like my uncle Phil. Uncle Thompson's idea was not such a bad idea after all.

I knew the Widow Johnson through my binoculars. Her farm lay across the fields from ours with only a burn between. There were tall beech trees surrounding her farmyard with its dwelling, a byre, a barn and hay shed. The trees were filled with rooks' nests and the noise of the birds could be heard in spring from two fields away. I would train my binoculars on the treetops and follow their antics during the spring and summer. That was how I learned so much about her movements and the visitors she received from time to time. I knew I was eavesdropping but I convinced myself I was a soldier in training to be a spy. I had the binoculars. Kurt, Rommel's man, had surely done this kind of thing. It was a sort of game.

She employed two laborers to work the fields and milk the cows much as we did on our farm, and, like us, she had the vet visit frequently to check the animals for tuberculosis and other problems. The Pastor of the Mission Hall in Harryville also visited. Once I saw the vet put his arm around her and she pushed him away playfully. Then they went into the hay shed and were there for some time. The two laborers were at work in the lower field. On other occasions I saw the vet go into the house. The Pastor always went into the house. It seemed that the laborers were always out in the fields when the

MUSIC ON THE WIND

visitors arrived. I never said a word of what I saw to anyone.

It was that same year the Widow had the notion to put the big field, the one with the pillars on each side of the iron gate, into potatoes, all 15 acres of it; and it on a slope. It was a Saturday, a pleasant enough spring day with a watery sunshine trying to lighten things up. We were up at the Fair Hill in the town nosing around. I had waited while uncle Phil went into the pub and had a few pints. When he came out we were going to look at some machinery when the Widow appears from nowhere. "Hello there Phil," she called. "Do ye have a moment?" They had known each other since they were at school together, well before the war, before she married. Uncle Phil gave her his big toothy greeting and asked her what she had in mind. "I'd be that behooven," she said, "if ye'd plough thon Pillar Field o' mine for me and get it ready for plantin' spuds. Thon gype of a tractor-man quit on me an' the tractor's not workin'. I'm really in a bind. What do ye think?"

He gave her a look like he was asking "Why me?" for the Widow Johnson was well known to the whole town-land as a no-nonsense woman. She could easily have got the garage in town to send out a mechanic to fix the tractor, so why my uncle Phil?

He looked at her, sly like, sizing her up. She was a good-looking woman if you like them strong of face and blue eyes that see through you. She had broad shoulders could carry a bale of hay with no bother, maybe two; and broad hips would please any man bent on raising a family with a woman could do her share of the work out in the fields; to say nothing of feeding the hens and cleaning out the pigs and milking her share of the cows. That kind of woman! No nonsense! Practical! Not someone you'd be apt to whirl around the floor of the Orange Hall at a dance of a Saturday night though there were those that tried when she was a young thing, the accordion and the saxophone blaring out the Sets and Lancers. No! The Widow Johnson was solid material. On a festive night she was in charge of the food table or collecting the money at the door, content as all get-out to be doing it. At least that's what we all thought, at the time. She was getting on in years, around thirty or so, a year or two younger than my uncle Phil and he coming up to maybe thirty-five.

"What are ye payin'?" asked uncle Phil all toothy smiles.

"Ah'll pay ye well," she said glancing at him sideways in a peculiar way. "Come on over some night and we'll talk about what Ah need ye to do."

"Right, then! Ah'll be over." He watched her walk away off, taking in her stride and her legs, well made with the calves nicely turned and remarkably small feet for such a big woman. He had a smile on his face and his lips were moving. I could see a glint in his eye. "Nah!" he said, as if to someone standing beside him. There was nobody there of course. Just me. But I kept quiet. I was only a wee fellow of fourteen at the time and not supposed to know anything about those things. But I was reared on a farm too and I wasn't as green as I was cabbage-looking. I knew plenty. My binoculars had come in handy.

The next night, being a Sunday, my uncle Phil went over to see the Widow. I was ready and eager to accompany him but he had other plans. "No! You stay home, y'hear?" He ruffled my hair like he always did. "Make sure your homework is ready for tomorrow. I'll check it when I get back." He was still very much a schoolteacher where I was concerned. When he returned, rather late, it was obvious the negotiation with the Widow had gone well for he asked my father for the loan of the tractor.

"N'aye!" My father thought for a moment. "But I'll have to charge you by the acre." My father was no dope! "I hope she's paying you well."

"Agh, to hell!" exploded uncle Phil. He spun on his heel and set off into the dark. We had never seen him behave so abruptly like that before.

"The Devil's got into him. That wumman!" Aunt Florrie shook her head knowingly. "Agh, that wumman. The Devil's own."

He did not come home that night. When I came back from school on the Monday the Widow's tractor was working and uncle Phil was out in her Pillar Field ploughing. He never came back home after that except to pick up some clothes. He stayed permanently over at the Widow's. My aunt Florrie was agast. "What will people think?"

My father assured her uncle Phil had taken over the end wing of the house that had a separate entrance. "But he eats in the house," he added smiling. He thought the situation quite humorous.

"Oh dear!" It was clear to aunt Florrie that the worst was about to happen if not already. Aunt Minnie agreed.

I would watch uncle Phil from our orchard as he sat on the tractor, looking behind him now and then to make sure the furrows were straight. He was still talking to himself. I could not hear from that distance and of course the tractor made one helluva noise. It was one of those big-bellied Fordsons, all engine. I could see through my binoculars that there was a smile on his face. He was happy. Gone was the angry face like there was somebody agin him. This time he was happy talking to himself. It was quite a change. It occurred to my adolescent mind that the Widow Johnson had a hand in it.

A month or so had gone by. I was scanning the fields and there was uncle

Phil strolling up along the hedge that ran from the burn to the Widow's farmyard. He stopped every hundred yards or so and I could see him talking to the phantom in the hedgerow. Sometimes he laughed, standing back and showing his rather large teeth. Then on he would go shaking his head. For several days after that neither him nor the Widow were seen either around the farm or in town. When I got home from school one day my aunt Florrie was in a state of nerves, her face streaked with tears. Aunt Minnie was doing her best to keep her calm. My father called me out of the house and down to the byre. "Ye better stay down here till them wimmen calm down."

"What's up?"

"Agh! Yer uncle Phil and the Widow went up to Belfast and got married. All on the q-tee." Somehow I felt cheered with this news.

When we all got round the supper table there was a free for all of accusations. Aunt Florrie led the charge. "Thon conniving wumman! I'll bet she got pregnant on purpose! She trapped him! Oh dear God!"

"So what's wrong with him marrying the Widow?" asked my father.

"Have you no sense of propriety? The tales that go round? She's a loose wumman!"

"Ninety five acres!" he responded. "And twelve farrowing sows! Twenty-six cows milking and ten heifers in calf! Good gracious! I should have thought of it myself!"

"Agh, sure ye're not one bit different from Thompson. Ye've no soul in ye. None!"

"Aye! Ninety five acres!"

"What would yer poor wife say if she heard ye? An' her in her grave." Then she spied me standing there listening. "Don't you dare set foot over there. D'ye hear?"

"Why not?" I asked. I could see no harm.

"Let the wee fellah be. Phil's his uncle. He has every right to go visiting, so he has."

I did go over visiting and it was clear by the size of the Widow that she was pregnant. As they say on the farm, she was well sprung.

A son was born before nine months had lapsed from the date of the marriage.

"I knew it!" declared aunt Florrie. "That's what comes from forsakin' the road of righteousness. The sin of it! The Devil!"

The birth took place in the hospital where the Widow lay for several days. Despite the fact that she was uncle Phil's wife, Mrs. McCurry, she was still referred to as the Widow. Even now! My father took me into town on the excuse of buying some parts for the tractor and we visited her. Uncle Phil was already there. There were warm greetings and the Widow thanked us for coming. The baby was a tiny little creature cradled in her arms as it fed. It had surprisingly fair hair, almost white and when its eyes opened, even the slightest, it was clear that they were of the brightest blue. He was going to grow up into a handsome fellow.

"Have ye got a name for him yet?" I asked. The Widow was about to speak when uncle Phil burst out. "Sure we have. We'll call him Kurt." Uncle Phil looked very pleased with himself. The Widow looked at her husband, the slightest trace of surprise in her eyes. Uncle Phil looked at her and I thought I saw a message. "Yes," she said, giving a slight nod of her head. "Kurt. That's a nice name. Yes! Kurt it is." She kissed the top of the infant's head.

Some years passed. I overcame my desire to be a soldier and roam the world. There was no special reason why. I just grew up to know and realize as an adult that I would inherit my father's farm. That was the way life had been preordained for me. It was my responsibility as the only son. So I finished school and did a year at the Agricultural College up near Muckamore. Then I returned to work the farm with my father and become a man in my own right. I had no need to go out into the world and make my way. My father and his father before him had prepared the way for me. I would work the farm, make a good living and interest myself in whatever took my fancy. So I bought an old car and, with the skills I had learned in the college, put it into great working order so I could spin around the countryside after supper as I pleased. Often I would drive around by the road to visit my uncle Phil and play with my new cousin. He was growing like a young goslin, tall for his age, a skinny fellow with straight blond hair and blue eyes. He looked more like a young Viking, not at all resembling the usual wee Ulster lad with mousey hair and freckles. I could see no resemblance to my uncle Phil. On those few occasions I brought him over to visit at our place my aunts would be graceful if a little distant but always motherly around the little fellow. It was as if he filled their own spinster dreams of having children. Gradually the old bad feelings faded away. He was "My wee angel" to my aunt Florrie and "Aunty's little man" to aunt Minnie. The boy Kurt was the key to uniting the family again. He was a happy child, well mannered and set to please all around him. But, even as he became the center of attention from everyone my uncle Phil was becoming stranger in his behavior. Now he did not wait until he was alone in the fields to talk to himself. It was as if the phantom in the hedgerow followed him around. Whatever the cause uncle Phil would burst out into a rage at his phantom whether in the farm yard, or in the byre or even up at the Fair Hill on a Saturday. It came to the point that the doctor advised the Widow that it was best to commit him to the hospital up in Antrim. I drove both of them there while my aunts took care of Kurt.

When something like that happens to a family there is a search for cause and feelings of guilt. Aunt Florrie still had her theory that it was the Devil had got hold of him out in, "Those foreign parts. The loneliness of the desert, I tell youse! The Devil finds ye in yer weakness! Cast thyself down and if ye do ye're a captive in his might for ever." And with vigorous shakings of her head to emphasize the validity of that she would quote the Bible. "Read Matthew, chapter four, verse six." Uncle Thompson, not to be out-done in his knowledge of the Scriptures though more to get a rise out of her would say, "Ye know ye're right. All them prophets of the Old Testament ranting and raving out there in the desert, Ezekiel and the like, its enough to make ye think, so it is. The Devil is a desert dweller I'm convinced. Ye'll not find him in the green hills of Antrim, so ye won't. Nah!"

The doctors of course had their own medical term for uncle Phil's condition but no one in the family would admit to that. "He takes after his mother's side of the family. Sure look at aul' aunt Agnes. Wasn't she round the bend." That seemed to me clear confirmation of the medical diagnosis. He had been born that way. Yet somehow the theory of the Devil felt better. It was easier to explain.

Uncle Phil was in the asylum for quite a while. With medication and sleep he became somewhat normal again. I was visiting him one weekend and in an attempt to get a conversation going I thought to ask him about his time in the Western Desert. Maybe subconsciously I was searching for something else. "Tell me about the time you were in battle and killed the German!" I asked hoping to cheer him up. He was standing by the window, hands in pocket, looking out with a dismal expression on his face. Up to now he had not spoken to me, not even a greeting of hello. He continued in silence. I began to be concerned that I had done the wrong thing. Time passed. Without turning round to look at me he said quietly, "Thon poor fellow!" He did not speak another word during my visit. Eventually I went to him and gave him a hug around the shoulders, then left.

The months passed into years and we grew accustomed to uncle Phil and his antics. He was still the great worker on the Widow's farm even though he did talk occasionally into the hedgerows. Young Kurt grew taller and more strikingly different to any other young lad around. "Who does he take after?" was the question Thompson posed to everyone at home during one of his weekend visits. There was silence. It was a delicate matter. The seven months pregnancy was still in everyone's mind. Not even aunt Florrie dared comment. She kept on knitting as if she had not heard. Thompson continued. "Them blue eyes and thon straight blond hair. He's not like any of us. That's for sure." But young Kurt was the darling of my aunts. There was no doubt for eventually aunt Minnie spoke. "Thon wee lamb!" she said lovingly. "He'll take after his mother's side of the family, ye can be certain of that. Sure his mother has them same piercing blue eyes."

"And remember aul' uncle Hector. He was kinda blond and rakish," suggested aunt Florrie. Then she added with a smile, "My wee angel."

The matter was left there to the satisfaction of all. Young Kurt was a member of the family.

It was springtime a couple of years later and Kurt was well into school. I was working the fields with the tractor. The trees and hedgerows were in leaf and the birds were building nests. For some reason, maybe the sheer joy of release from winter, the birds singing, the sun shining, I took out the binoculars from the drawer where they had lain wrapped carefully in an old towel. They were beside me on the tractor. Across the fields in the Widow's land I could see my uncle Phil. I stopped the tractor and put the binoculars to my eyes. It was the same uncle Phil, toothy smiled, older and going gray haired. He was talking into the hedgerow. I watched for a second or two. Something seemed to move on the other side of the hawthorns. I shifted my focus and, as I watched in expectation I realized there was someone there. Uncle Phil stepped closer to the bushes pointing with out-stretched arm. I was intrigued and held my binoculars focused on the spot. In a moment or so a blond head appeared, popping up through a gap in the bushes. It was Kurt, pulling himself up to stand pointing into the bushes. The two, father and son, talking excitedly to each other, moved along the hedgerow a yard or so at a time. Kurt, again pointing into the hawthorns, climbed back in and was out of sight. It was then I realized he was following my old interest of bird watching. Being springtime he was checking out birds' nests. I also realized that now was the moment I had been waiting for these many years. Leaving the tractor I walked across the intervening field. I carried the binoculars in my hand.

They were too engrossed in their interests to see or hear my arrival until I was almost upon them. Kurt saw me first and cried, "It's a wren's nest.

Look! That's her up there creating a row." He was full of excitement just as I had been at a similar age. "She thinks I'm going to wreck her eggs."

"You can't blame her now, can ye," I said. "It's her nest."

"Show him yer book," said uncle Phil and Kurt held up a bird identity book that was clearly newly bought.

"My Dad got me that!"

I looked at uncle Phil and I could see the pride in his face. "You know Kurt," I said, "when I was about your age your father gave me something too."

"He did? What?"

I brought the pair of binoculars from behind my back. "These." I held them out. "They're yours." But he held back. As when I was a boy the present was too grand to believe. "Go on! Take it!" He was still hesitant. "Look, it has your name on it." I pointed to the name scratched on the gray metal.

Uncle Phil laid a gentle hand on his shoulder and said. "Take them son." Kurt raised his hands and carefully took the binoculars. At last they were with their rightful owner. Uncle Phil looked at the boy then shook his head slowly and turned to me. "Thanks." There was a catch to his voice and he turned away so I would not see the tears welling in his eyes.

The Dog with the Blue Eye

Herbie was not given to talking much. He was a quiet, hard working farmer who went about his own business and never bothered others. But something came over him, a feeling in the air at that time of year, perhaps. It was early morning when he stopped his horses on the roadside just as my cousin Rose was setting out the milk churns and says, "Rose!"

"'Morning, Herbie. That's a brave day," says she.

"Aye!"

There was the look in Herbie's face of a man who, while his mind is made up, wasn't altogether certain, and then,

"Aye, well!" says he. "Maybe I'll drop round the night after quettin' time for a yarn." And he drove thon fine big pair of Clydesdales of his on up the road to the wee field.

Spring had come early that year as I remember and the sycamore trees that sheltered the house from the north wind had already sprouted big fat sticky buds like fingers pointing at you. And the current bushes and the gooseberries in the back garden too were all over green and it was great, so it was, after the silent winter to hear the birds singing in the hedges. At night you'd have seen courting couples taking to the lanes or down by the bridge over the narrow gauge tracks, sitting on the hard black stones of the parapet till their backsides got numb; and myself and Sean Fluter from over the fields, sneaking down under the arch to listen to the talk of them. Many's the night I listened to my cousin Rose, her, at one time, being courted by half the country on account of the fifty acres of auld Tam, her father; big Rab and the likes of him, all eager to marry Rose. But Rose was all work and money making and the nearest a man got to her was sitting a good span away listening to her telling him the great ways there were to make a farm really hum. That was my cousin Rose all right. She was a fair looking girl but, despite the fifty acres, she was getting on and there was no sign of her getting married. Besides there wasn't that many men left, most all having already found women more given to baking and mending and maybe looking after a wheen of turkeys in the stack-yard. So there was Rose with the best chicken-runs and herd of Ayreshires about the country. All auld Tam did was the heavy work and good he was at it too, mind you. Her mother looked after the house but it was my cousin Rose ran the place. And an unheard-of thing in those days, Rose kept everything written down in big exercise books and ledgers and all, adding up and figuring out the costs and profits and things; and her getting on for thirty odd and unmarried.

That evening should have been just like any other of a Saturday, the folks coming in early from the fields to finish milking on time, you know, get the hands and face scrubbed and away off to the pictures in the town. For about an hour you'd see bikes tearing along and then the sycamores around the house would stand out dark and the wee garden would hunker down into the shadows of the wall, you know. The auld sun would be on its last legs out there sitting on the ridge of the hills away to the west lookin' at us with thon big red sleepy eye on him.

We were all in the kitchen so we were, auld Tam, her mother and Rose and I had come over from our place to help scrub eggs for going to the pictures was not permitted in our house. That was a sin. What with the minister shouting hell-fire every Sunday and my Granny that good-living. There we were, as I said, the front of the grate open and the red-hot coals pressing against the bars sending out a heat would have blistered you and the glow shining off them big willow-pattern plates on the dresser and them two china dogs on the mantelpiece. Auld Tam had begun to lean forward to the fire the better to read his paper. "There's no much light getting!" says he, sitting up and looking about and the auld half-moon glasses of him dropping to the point of his nose. "Put a light to the lamp, there!" he says to me. "And go easy with the mantle." For mantles were precious things in them days before the Board put in the wires for the electric light.

Taking the lamp off the window-sill I could see the night out was darkening down rightly and not a sign of a soul and I'm just trimming the wick when there's a put-put-a-put coming from away off, the sound of it rising as it topped a hill, don't you know, and fading away in the hollows or where the trees grew. And Tam was peeping over the half-moons. "That'll be Herbie on thon new Excelsior of his I was hearing about. Soul, he's late for the pictures the night!" And the put-put-a-put came on and on and, "Be-blowed!" says auld Tam as the bike turns in at the pillars and, "Boys-a-dear!" Auld Tam to the window and my aunt too, wiping her hands on a dishcloth. But Rose just sat there, scrubbing the muck off the eggs and never letting on. "What's he come about?" says auld Tam. "He'll be after the loan of my new disc harrow. That's what it'll be."

"But he's wearing his good Sunday blue suit," says my aunt. "Rose! Do you hear? Go and brush your hair! Tam! Away you go out to the yard and see what it is he's wanting."

Auld Tam had a couple of collie dogs powerful given to the barking and letting on there was somebody come to steal the place. "It's yourself," says auld Tam over the din.

"Aye," says Herbie.

"A brave night," says auld Tam and draws off at the dogs with a studded boot. The two dogs leap away off and then turn to sniffing at the legs of Herbie's trousers and Herbie sets the new motorbike up nicely against the wall for fear it will fall down and scratch the paint. And the big dog, the male one of them, a wild hairy beast he was too, goes over and waters the rear tire. Herbie just stands there grinning, as auld Tam told it later, "with his two legs the one length and his mouth wide shut." Auld Tam was a great turn when he got going, you know. "You'll be coming in, so you will?" says auld Tam nicely.

"Aye!" says Herbie, and he marches over, the Sunday suit choking him up under the oxters. "Aye," he says and steps in all smiles looking 'round for Rose.

"You're looking bravely," says my aunt from the scullery.

"Aye," says he and wanders in, his trousers still rolled up in bicycle clips and his toes pointing in like he was about to trip himself.

The two men got seated by the stove and my aunt and me further back scrubbing eggs.

"You're plowing hard?" says auld Tam.

"Aye," says Herbie.

"Up by the wee field there, first, where it's driest?"

"Aye."

Well that was that. Auld Tam let his chin rest. Herbie wasn't much of a one for making conversation. Then Rose came in from the hall with her hair not one bit better for all the brushing she was supposed to have done. "Hello there, Herbie," says she. "I heard your motor-bike. I just knowed it was you."

"Aye," says Herbie and Rose settles down to the egg scrubbing again.

There wasn't a sound spoke for a long time until, after I had nearly addled my brains thinking up something to say, I says, "We've got pups, Herbie, so we have. The collie gave pups a wheen of days ago."

"She did not!" says he and those were the first words he had spoke other than 'Aye' that night.

"Pups!" I says. "Six of them and one with a blue eye like the da."

Well, Herbie has on a big smile and you could see he was fair fidgeting to go see the pups.

"Come on down," says auld Tam. "Maybe you'll take one." And out we goes, the three of us, and down by the hay-shed with the bitch dancing on ahead to get in over the top of the pups afore we arrive.

Herbie had a way with dogs and the bitch licking his hand as he turns the pups this way and that and setting them in again to the tits. Auld Tam, he's over by a pile of hay reaching in. "Away up and help your aunt and Rose with them eggs," he says to me. But I can hear the clink of the bottle and glass. I go, for drinking was a thing you had to keep out of the way in our family what with my Granny having the Minister out every week to pray and him terribly set agin it. Agh well, you know, in them days....But wait to you hear.

"He's got sixty seven brave acres," my Aunt was saying, "and it lies into our Forth!"

Rose was boxing up the cleaned eggs, setting them into the pasteboard trays that kept them from getting smashed; six trays on each side of the division was thirty six dozen eggs in a crate and she could turn out several crates a week, and all marked down in an exercise book, how many, what they sold at, and how much to feed the hens. She had a great head on her had my cousin Rose. And a right bit tucked away in the bank.

"Rab has eighty three," she says without pausing in the counting.

This fellow Rab was a big fellow with a good farm of land over the fields a bit, turning some forty years old to the day and hardly ever away from a widow woman with seven weeuns up by The Water. For all that there was talk of many another woman too. But Big Rab had shown no sign of marrying any of them and he dropped in now and then to see auld Tam as it were, and keep his hand in with Rose. He'd walked her out the lanes a wheen of times and set her on the bridge for a yarn more than once.

"You can't mean that, Rose," says my aunt. "He's a terrible scrounger and he's been seen coming out of Cassidy's pub."

There was ay that thing in the family agin drink. As auld Tam was apt to say, and mind you, he liked a wee drop now and then too, "They were that feart of the Devil gettin' them!" What with my Granny agin likker and the

Minister describing the Hell just waiting for all us sinners...agh well.

"He runs the best farm in the townland for he knows how," says Rose. "And when I marry it'll be to something worth while."

"Herbie's a nice man, so he is. A decent soul and hard working."

"But I could make nothing of him!" And the dirt fair flying from them eggs till they were spotless. "But with Rab I could!" And thon eggs were cleaned to fill up another crate with them. There was no end to the hard work Rose could do or the money she would write down in them ledgers.

One thing about the house, the back door made plenty of noise to let you know a body was coming in and there was Herbie and auld Tam scraping the door over the step. Maun it was noisy.

"Isn't them the quare pups," says my aunt to Herbie.

"Aye," he says, and pleasure all over his face for there, whining in his two big hands, was a ball of fur and a wet nose peeping out.

"You have got one I see."

"Aye," says Herbie. "It's a brave while since I had a dog."

"That's the one with the blue eye. Isn't he too wee yet?"

"I'll put him on the bottle. Feed him myself so I will." And Herbie sat down with the pup sucking in around his waistcoat for a likely tit.

There was a sparkyness in Herbie's eye that wasn't there before and me, sitting fornenst him, I could smell the color of his breath like when you're passing a pub door.

"I had a dog once," he says, nodding and you could see the memories crowding up behind his eyes. The drop of John J. he'd had in the hay-shed must have done something for he burst out with the most words anyone had ever heard him put together in a lifetime. "Aye! And if it hadn't ha' been that he was black and white and as hairy as bedamned with four legs, sure you'd never ha' known he was a dog at all. Naw!"

Auld Tam says, "Is that so!" in that kind of way which means, "Tell us more."

"Aye," says Herbie. "You'll mind my uncle Davy that used to shovel coal on the train to Belfast, well, he got him from a signal-man up at Muckamore Halt for the taking away, so he did."

"You don't say."

I'm sure if it hadn't have been for auld Tam's prodding with the "You don't say!" and "Agh no!" and "Boys-a-dear!" we might not have heard about the dog at all. But auld Tam was good at that, drawing a body out, don't you see.

MUSIC ON THE WIND

"Aye," says Herbie. "And the night Davie brought him to our house telling us he was of a great ratting strain there wasn't much to him except fur and a tail that short and thick you couldn't tell which end of the beast was the business end."

Auld Tam was fair delighted and my aunt was listening too. I was listening. Faith, we were all listening for we'd never heard Herbie say that much before. But Rose was letting on to doing nothing but scrubbing eggs.

"What did you call him?" asks auld Tam, but Herbie was away.

"I was ay clipping thon tail with a pair of shears and sure, with the hair growing back faster than weeds the looks of it didn't improve none."

"Did you not have a name for him?" I asks.

"Agh," says Herbie, grinning and nodding, "thon tail, the ugly beast that it was, ugly I tell you as a religious man's sins. And the burden it musta been to him from the weight of it. But it was a god's-send when he grew up. You know, a prop to sit on in damp ground and steering him across them auld moss-holes. You know, all the stupid dogs used to catch hold of it in fights. Agh, thon auld dog."

Herbie's eyes were moist. And all the while the wee pup is getting the best fondling a pup ever got. Not even its own ma could have had it more contented lying there in the hollow of Herbie's lap, with the blue eye of it cocked.

I could see by the suspicious look in my aunt's eye that she was forming notions and doing her best to catch a whiff of Herbie's breath. Auld Tam was chortlin' and enjoyin' himself and when egged on about it later says, "Well, it was a brave size of a bottle and gae full, do you know, and there was only a color of it left by the time we were through. There were times he took two to my one. When I think of it, bejaypers, it was the first time I ever saw Herbie take a drop. Never knew him in a pub at all."

"Well, what did you call him?" I asks again.

"What ever was in my mind at the minute," says he.

"Had he no real name?"

"Aye, he had. My ma called him Bunyon on account of the burden of his tail."

"Was he any good at ratting?" I asks.

"Ratting! Hadn't he a nose on him coulda smelled a rat in an acre of honey flowers and ears could hear the grass grow in a storm-gale."

"And fighting?"

"Wasn't fighting the thing he was born to. Ratting and fighting! Wasn't he only three months old when we put him inside the wire netting 'round a cornstack at thrashing time and didn't this devil of a big rat jump out and catch him by the nose. Boys, that wee dog squealed like the train going over Kinearny and the rat let go in astoundment. I killed it, deader than a door nail, with a rake. But the dog ran 'round all day with thon rat dangling from the buckled nose. Buckled! Buckled was no name for it. With the rat bites and the fighting he got into, thon nose got like a tin can kicked out of shape. He had a hump on it like a Leicester ewe. Maun, with thon thick tail and the buckled nose thon was some dog. I'll tell you this much. You should ha' seen him after Kerr's bitch."

We were wondering what errand had brought Herbie over. There was no mention yet of borrowing the disc harrow and he was paying no bother to Rose.

"Did you know we had pups?" I asks.

"Naw!" says he. "I did not or I woulda been over sooner."

So that was that. Auld Tam must have been thinking the same thing for he ups and says,

"Thon new disc harrow I bought is a good one. Fair breaks up the sod."

"Aye, so I believe." And back Herbie goes to fondling the dog.

"Did he ever have pups?" I asks.

"Naw! He never had pups. He was 'round Kerr's bitch night and day but not a pup did he give her. Many's a time I saw him sitting outside the door trembling but it never amounted to nothing. And then thon big dog, thon big beast of a mastiff of Rab Mullin's was over after Kerr's bitch too and grabs him by the front leg and breaks it. He musta been sitting on his tail, do you see. Agh! You couldn't ha' kept splints on him he was that fierce, so the leg set all crooket. You should ha' seen him. The nose all buckled. Thon tail of his and the leg set like a barrel stave."

There was a wet look to Herbie's eye and he into fondling the wee pup like a good one.

"Maun aye," says auld Tam and leans over and spits into the ash box.

"A cup of tea?" says my aunt.

"Aye," says Herbie and goes very quiet.

My aunt goes into the scullery and brings out a kettle of water to set on the stove.

"Tell us more about the dog," says I.

Saying that was like putting a match to a haystack he brightened up that much.

Out in the night you could hear a wee Austin Seven rattling down the road and the two collies set up a powerful barking when it too turns in by the pillars.

"Now who's that?" says auld Tam.

"G'way out and see," says my aunt.

Out goes auld Tam with me at his heels. I mind it well. The moon had come up that big and round and clear. If you had got up on the hayshed roof you could have reached up and touched it. It had turned out a great night, the kind of night a man would go dolling. And there's Big Rab easing himself out of the wee Austin. What a powerful size of a man he was, with a neck on him like a Friesian bull. It was no wonder the wee car was ay down on the springs on one side.

"Hi, Tam!" says he.

"You're bravely keeping!" says Tam.

"No complaints." And you could see he was taking in the motorbike propped up agin the wall.

"You're for coming in?" says auld Tam.

"I will," he says. "I will that."

I on in ahead of him for I was afeard he'd get my stool up beside Herbie for I was set on hearing more about the dog.

"Howye, Herbie!" says Big Rab.

"Aye. Keeping rightly," says Herbie.

"What's that you got there? A dog?" says Big Rab.

"Aye!"

"We have pups, so we have," says I.

"Come on down," says auld Tam "and you can have your pick. Mind that pup of Herbie's there," he says to me, "and help Rose with them crates." And auld Tam had the pair of them out and down to the hay-shed in two shakes of a dead lamb's tail and me left with the wimmen. But I knowed rightly what he was up to. I knowed auld Tam was dying for another go at the John J. And Herbie had a smile on too. Well, they were gone a brave while.

"Them's both your suitors for ye," says my aunt and Rose says nothing. "You think a big strong man like Rab woulda been caught by some woman long ago. Herbie too for that matter." My aunt was in the scullery in among the smell of damp crockery and the bucket of water with the lid on it. You could hear her rattling the things around. "And if you wait too much longer," says she, "neither them nor any other body's going to ask you. You're too pernickety. Too pernickety, so you are." But Rose has the egg-crates ready for the egg-man coming the morrow and has the griddle out and a bowl of flower and sweet milk whipped up with eggs. "You're not making pancakes at this hour, are you?"

"I am," says Rose, and you know, when she wanted, Rose could be as tight-lipped as could be.

The kettle had boiled and the tea wet and the griddle turning out the pancakes by the half dozen when in they come, the three of them, chortling and keyhooing and Herbie's flying before the wind. Auld Tam and Big Rab weren't a hair better but it was Herbie was the boyoh. Later my aunt got on about it and auld Tam was gae repentant. "How was I to know," he says, "that big Rab had a hip bottle and Herbie a weakness. Sure how was I to know? Tell me that! How was I to know?"

Well, the kitchen was filled with the smell of baking and the men sits down, their hunger fair roused. And mugs of tea were set up and pancakes hot and melting with good yellow butter Rose had made herself. Oh, Rose knew her stuff all right. None better at it than her. And when I think about it I can see she had it all planned. That was Rose for you. She had a great head on her. But there's Herbie and Big Rab digging into the pancakes and the pup with the blue eye sneaking up to Herbie and Herbie putting it in his coat pocket. "You can talk about your dogs," says Herbie to Big Rab, "but I had a dog the like of none. He could spake just looking at you."

Big Rab wolfs into a pancake and eyes Herbie. One thing I can say about Herbie and Big Rab, there was never any ill will between the pair of them. But I'm thinking the smell of them pancakes was having them on and there was Rose working on a ledger at the table totting up pounds, shillings and pence like a good one. I'm thinking the pair of them was thinking they could fall glad to all that gae easy, like. She was a well-built girl too, was Rose, strong of it.

"You never had no dog was worth a curse!" says Big Rab.

"I had so, so I had!" says Herbie, fairly bristling. "Me and him up the burn ratting. Sure we had the country cleared of rats. I mind the time me and him got fourteen in the while of an afternoon. Fourteen of them I tell you, and me no more than ten at the time!"

"That wasn't thon auld terrier that my Keeper chewed the leg off when we were weans? Thon auld fleapit with the bowleg? Thon was no dog! Thon was a big tabby cat pretendin'!" No doubt Big Rab was having him on for he was

MUSIC ON THE WIND

like that. Herbie's eyes were getting very wee and tight with a white ring around them.

"Aye, there's some great dogs," says auld Tam by way of keeping the peace.

"Eat up now," says my aunt, getting the teakettle from the hob. "Rose!" she says. "Stir up a lot more of that batter there for more pancakes, these good men is half starved." She pours Herbie another mug-full of tea and, as she turns away from the stove, I could see her give Big Rab a look could have flayed a worse one.

"Tell us more about your dog," says I, and thankful we were that Big Rab had caught on and kept himself quiet.

"I'll tell you something about my dog so I will," says Herbie quare and big like. "I mind him and me up the burn chasing whatever moved."

For a man nearing forty Herbie's memory was like yesterday. He told us about rats as big as badgers that dog of his had caught, and rabbiting up in Kerr's whins. Agh, sure there was nothing thon dog hadn't done nor couldn't do. Herbie could ha' talked the hind leg off a donkey telling us about that dog. As auld Tam says when it was all over, "He'd been injected with a gramophone needle, so he had!".

Big Rab hadn't got a word in edgeways the whole night. Nothing but the dog, the dog, till Big Rab, sitting there with the John J. and the tea and the pancakes getting the better of him and his eyes drooping down till he's near asleep, mumbles, "You should ha' been a dog yourself!"

With that Herbie's eyes get wee and tight again and he ups and grabs Big Rab by the throat. Big Rab's half-asleep. My aunt screams. "Herbie, you'll choke him so you will! You'll choke him! Leave him go for dear sake! Leave him go!"

But devil the chance of choking Big Rab. He had a neck on him like a bull as I said. And arms, bejaypers. Big Rab was the man could handle a pair of Clydesdales and a plough with one hand. He was built like the gable of a barn, so he was. He rises and he shakes Herbie like he was one of them rats we'd been hearing about. Oh, it was a sore sight to see, so it was. And the wee pup still in Herbie's pocket and the yelps of it too were fierce.

"Get on your motorbike!" says Big Rab. "Go on! Get on your bike and away off with you!" And poor Herbie, very bedraggled, mounts up on the Excelsior.

"You shouldn't ha' done that!" says my aunt to Big Rab. "Naw! Ye shouldn't ha' done that." But by then it was too late.

One day that summer Rose marries Big Rab and a fine wedding it was; a big strong man like Rab and a strapping lass like Rose with her head well screwed on. That was her fifty acres and Rab's eighty-three put together was more than a hunnerd. There wasn't a farm like it in the country I can tell you. Rose fair made it hum and what with the war on and the price of things Rose was in her element. You never saw the like of them ledgers.

But poor Herbie wasn't the same man again after that, at all, so he wasn't. He never said much to anyone again after that but was ay like he always was, no talk at all out of him. And his farm just wouldn't go. And you'd see him and the pup, well growed up in the meantime, dandering about the lanes. And there was talk he could be seen coming out of Cassidy's pub. When I'd be in the Fair Hill of a Saturday I'd know for sure he'd been in having a glass for there'd be the dog sitting outside the pub door and the blue eye of him skinned on who was coming and going. Thon fine big Clydesdales were finally sold and the proceeds went down his throat. Agh oh! He piled the motorbike up one night against a stonewall and that was that. He got ten bob or so for the parts. That was the way of it.

You'd have thought Big Rab had kinda landed on his feet having Rose for a wife but after auld Tam died and my aunt became an invalid with the pains, things began to go sour. Rose was an overpowering woman and ran things the way she wanted. It was ay "Rab, you got to do this" and "Rab, you got to do that." No scounging the countryside for Rab after the wedding. Big Rab's life was not his own. Not a bit of it. Keeping the ledgers was the thing.

And then one day Big Rab was seen coming out of Cassidy's pub. The war was over by then, you know, and there wasn't much to do on the farm. Aye, Big Rab was seen often coming out of Cassidy's pub. That he was. I saw him myself, would you believe it, linked on Herbie the very man. Big Rab and Herbie, the pair of them, holding up Cassidy's wall, and the dog with the blue eye waiting to go home. "Herbie!" says Big Rab, and you could hear him across the square clear over to the Fair Hill gates. "You're a lucky man!" he says. "And you don't know it! You're a lucky man, so you are!" He looks down into Herbie's face and his eyes were all bleared. "And you have a fine dog there. I'm telling you, so I am. There's nothing to beat a fine dog."

We buried Herbie that winter. Aye! We did! He fell down the steps of his own barn and broke his neck. He'd a drop in, don't you know. And the howls of the auld dog brought us over to see what was the matter and we found him at the foot of the stairs with his neck all thran. Aye! The coroner called it misadventure while under the influence. We buried Herbie and Big Rab took the auld dog, all gray haired about the face and half-blind by now. For that matter Big Rab's not one whit better himself, an auld done man. The pair of them dander out now and then to sit on the bridge over the narrow gauge but the lines are gone, lifted during the war to make guns.

Rose is not as active as she used to be and she has a girl in to help. My aunt's dead long ago. I work our family farm as you know, the hunnerd some acres, and I bought Herbie's place at the aution after he died. To tell you the truth no one else wanted the place it was so rundown. But it lies into our place and it seemed the right thing to do. There's a woman over in the next townland that'll fall to forty-five of the best acres and a hayshed put up with corrugated zinc bought from the army surplus. I visit there at times.

But I'm thinking of getting me a dog. Herbie's auld dog with the blue eye is about done. What Big Rab'll do when he's gone I don't know. But I'll get a dog like I say, one for my own self. You can't beat a good dog for company, you know. Maybe I'll take a dander up the burn or away up by Kerr's whins. I'd like a good ratting dog, one that would give you a bit of sport. Aye, that's what I'll do. When I get them ledgers into shape I'll go and see if I can get myself a real good dog. I might even find one with a blue eye. I just might.

LESSER SHADOWS OF THE DAY

"He's not coming!" Mary cast a glance at the wall-clock.

"Seems like it." Thompson checked his pocket watch with the clock, its pendulum swinging lazily to and fro. "He should have been here by now so he should. But we'll give him a minute yet."

"Oh, he'll be here. Have no fear," said George, keeping watch through the window of small panes that looked out onto the lane. The beech trees that lined it were in bright green summer colors.

"Sure it's not like Samuel John to miss a chance of seeing the pair of you," said Mary. "That I'll guarantee. It's not that often you're down from the city."

There was the best part of a twenty people gathered into the big kitchen of the McKiltie farmhouse and Mary, turning scones at the griddle, was voicing what they were already beginning to feel. In one way or another, nodding heads, scuffling feet, they acknowledged agreement.

They had gathered in at Jock McKiltie's invitation; Davy McKay and Sarah, Herbie Duncan with two soup spoons sticking out of the breast pocket of his coat, Alice and Archie McGrew with the fiddle case laid across his knees, Martha Kelsoe and her brother Will who carried his fife in an inside pocket where it wouldn't be seen, the Surgenors from the bridge and the widower Hamil who was thought to be sweet on Jock's sister Mary, and the McClugs with their son Quigley who was hoping he'd be able to talk about his pigs. And of course the visitors, Thompson who was Jock's brother, and George, a long standing friend, both of them down from Belfast. The neighbors had come just as soon as the Saturday evening milking was over and they had got themselves scrubbed and dressed. There was a row of soft scoop-caps on the pegs by the hall door and a row of handbags in the recess of the window that looked out on the yard. Everyone was somewhat quiet, hands folded on laps. Conversation after the initial "Hello, how are ye?" and "Are ye bravely?" had dwindled. There had been some enquiry of Thompson and George about "What's it like there up in the city, hi?" They asked politely, not really interested but as if the visitors had to be given this attention. Most of them had gone to school with Thompson and George, to the country school, long since knocked down that used to stand on the edge of the town. They did not feel free to talk to them in the familiar way they used among themselves. It was hard to find something to say to men who had left your way of life for that of the city. Thompson was a Chemist and George an Optician. They had soft well-kept hands. And the two men from the city talked and joked in a way that was too easy, too smooth; words came readily to them, that it made their former schoolmates hesitant. They were glad in a way to see Thompson and George again but where was Samuel John? They were anxious. Samuel John should have been there by now, not just to play but also to represent them. It would not be the same without him if he didn't come.

Archie McGrew took his fiddle out of its case and was sitting with the instrument held vertical, ready to sweep it under his chin at the slightest hint. He wanted to play but, without Samuel John to set the pace, it wouldn't be the same. He picked a couple of times at the strings to make certain they were in tune. His thick, callused fingers caressed the fiddle like it was a lover's hair. He finely tuned the top string. The slow steady tick of the wag-at-the-wall stressed the quietness of the big farm kitchen.

"Give us a tune there, Archie, and get us warmed up," said Mary.

"Agh, I'll wait. He's bound to come. Give it a minute."

Beside him on a stool, Herbie took the two soupspoons out of his pocket and, holding them between the fingers of his right hand, rattled them over his left arm and knees. Herbie was not of the same generation as the others. He was younger and eager to show what he could do.

"Did you ever see two skeletons tap-dancing in an old tin bath?" George exclaimed, his eyes dancing with good humor. "Boys, Herbie, you have it! Two skeletons is nothing to you. Nor a whole dozen."

"Get away on, George." Herbie's face was wrinkled up in pleasure at the compliment, for George was from the city. George knew a thing or two, what with fitting glasses and all. The encouragement sent Herbie into an orgy of flourishes with the spoons. "Go on Archie," he shouted. "Give us a tune. Away ye go!" and he bounced a rattle of rhythmic tin off his heels. "Give us the Harvest Home, there. Away ye go now!"

Archie struck up the fiddle, filling the tune in with grace notes to give it the full flavor. The men were tapping their toes on the tiled floor, the studded soles of their boots setting a background rumble like a small army was loose in the room. It was good music. But it wasn't the same as when Samuel John was there. Thompson got up and went over to Mary by the stove. "Where's Kate?"

"Agh, sure you know her. After all these years don't you know where she'll be."

"Is there anything wrong?"

"Agh, Thompson. She wouldn't listen to fiddle music, not since that evangelist from Belfast pitched his tent up by the cross roads, which is hardly yesterday. Don't you know she's that good-living she can't abide a night's fun."

"Doesn't she know Samuel John's coming?"

"Of course she does. Isn't that why she's sitting up in the parlor on her own."

"But she should be here, Mary. Samuel John's a decent man!"

"We all know that!"

"Couldn't you persuade her?"

"Away up and persuade her yourself."

Thompson pressed the latch on the hall door, closed it and went along to the parlor. "Katy, is that you?"

"And who do you think it would be?"

"Aren't you coming up? Samuel John'll be here in a bit."

Katy firmed her lips and turned the page of her bible. "No I will not! I'll not demean myself!"

"There he is now!" cried Quigley M'Clug who had been posted in the scullery where the window looked towards the town. "He's coming up the railway, so he is!" George, Martha Kelsoe and Mary went to the window. A new feeling had come over them. "What's that on his shoulder, hi?" Quigley asked. "That's his fiddle," said Mary.

Samuel John was a tall, well-built man. Though he was no longer young he carried himself straight. On his left shoulder he supported the black violin case, holding it as if he were on rifle drill. In his right hand he flashed a yellow cane.

"He still cuts a fine figure," said Mary. "Is it any wonder half the lasses in the country fell for him? And still do!" She gave herself a knowing half nod.

Despite the passing years there was still about Samuel John the cut of a dandy. His gray Donegal tweed suit was neatly pressed. His white shirt was set off with a blue bow tie. But it was the faded red button sewn onto the left lapel of his coat that set him apart. He had worn this button for so long that people had stopped remarking on it, for it was the most ordinary button, made of horn, of about two inches across and whose outer edge was stamped with an uninspired design of wavy lines.

"He'll be here in no time at all! I'll put the kettle on!" And Mary went back to her stove.

Samuel John came striding on, his head inclining from side to side in a slow curious motion as if listening to the whispered sound of the countryside about him. He knew the railway, sleeper by sleeper. A thousand times and more he had walked along its steel lined path, the thick creosote soaked sleepers a step apart and the gray coal cinders, like bird droppings, filling the spaces between. In the summer afternoons, on Sundays, rain or shine, in the winters with the sleet falling or the bright moon-sparkled frost on the grass, he had walked its straight miles, an ear cocked for the narrow-gauge train whistling down from Larne with box-cars full of coal. He had paid court to every lass in this townland and the one next, and the one beyond that and there were a few townlands on either side where he was known as well. "Samuel John! The hay will be in next week. We're holding a bit of a dance. My father will be expecting you out. You won't forget now?" Always, "My father will be expecting you out," when it was them, with their high stepping dancing and their smell of soap and lavender, that wanted Samuel John, the man with hands for anything and the sweet music at the tips of his fingers. The sleepers passing underfoot seemed to pick off the hours, the years of his life.

"What have you there, Samuel John? Bring it up here!" Miss Brawbit, so thin and flat chested, with the big hands that would have served a farm laborer, clouted him across the back of his head. "You'll stay in after school till we knock some sense into you! And we will!" Miss Brawbit who wore a wig with a bun, and steel rimmed glasses, had beaten the towns of Ireland into him with her cane. "The principal towns of Cavan are? You Samuel John! Come up here! You lazy boy! You'll never be good for nothing till you know the towns of Ireland!" The pain of the cane across his fingers, one, two, three, four, on each hand. "You, Thompson, the towns of Wexford are?" She flexed the cane while Thompson rhymed off the towns of Wexford in a singsong voice. "Good. Now you, George, the counties in Connaught are?" Thompson and George had survived it, the brutality, the bullying by ignorant teachers and the endless lists of things to learn by heart. "The principal towns of Antrim are?" "What is Dublin noted for?" "Huddersfield produces what?" "The river Guadalquivir is in?" The voice raised on the last word, the eyebrows holding the note waiting for the cowed pupil to answer. It was a relief at fourteen years of age to rise at six o'clock in the morning and go to work in the linen mill where the noise of the machinery flooded out the towns of Cavan. It was years since he had seen Thompson and George. And fancy now! Coming down from the city and getting his brother Jock to set up a night of fiddling like in the old days. He couldn't refuse, even though it might mean meeting Katy again.

He found himself subconsciously counting the sleepers and forced the numbers out of his head. He already knew there were five thousand three hundred and twenty one from the turnoff at the town to the style into McKiltie's meadow. Five thousand three hundred and twenty-one. He had counted them that night, it was so long ago it was hardly worth remembering, the night he had to keep himself from thinking. And yet, "Agh, Katy!" He executed a yellow-headed benweed with his cane. "Little did you know, Katy, you, with your head filled with that tent mission and the hallelujahs!" His yellow cane was soiled with the green juices of the weeds that sprang from the side of the meadow path. He tucked the fiddle case under his arm to allow himself to see the faded red button. He touched it. It had torn from her coat when she turned and ran away. Its rosy color had bleached in part and there was an etching of cracks spreading out from the center.

"It's yourself, mister!" said Thompson, going to the kitchen door. "I'm pleased to see you. You're looking great, hi!"

"I feel great, Thompson. I feel great. But time is taking its toll. Time. What did the poet say? Mary, you're as lovely as ever!"

"Agh, you're always coddin', Samuel John. You don't mean a word of it. Set the fiddle down there and have a cup of tea. It's been stewing these five minutes. It'll bring you back to your senses."

"Senses, Mary? I haven't been in my senses since, oh dear, since when? George! Yourself it is!"

"How are you, Samuel John?"

"Bravely! Bravely! Archie! You're holding the instrument of the devil! Music bewitches the soul! King Samuel learned to his sorrow. Too late!" Archie smiled in embarrassed pleasure, showing a row of stained teeth in a soap-scrubbed face. He nodded back and forward. Samuel John passed on.

MUSIC ON THE WIND

"Davy and Sarah! It's good to see you. I hear great things about your boy up at the Academy."

"He's sittin' over there, Samuel John."

"A fine young man he is too. He has your looks, Sarah. A good-looking young man. Keep up the hard work, son. The ball's at your toe now. Not like your father and me. We were cast to the wolves of ignorance. Will! How are you doing? You're off the stick I see. You'll be showing us a reel later!"

"Oh, Ah'm not that spry yet," said Will, laughing and stretching the injured leg. "But Ah'm mendin', like."

"Good man. I hope you have the fife with you."

"Oh, Ah do. It's here," laughed Will and drew the slim piece of wood out of his inner pocket. "It's never far away from me han'."

"You're a hardy man, Will. Herbie Duncan! You rascal! You have your spoons with you! You'll be in the pictures yet!" He ruffled Herbie's hair and Herbie chuckled in glee, rattling the spoons off the arm of his chair for good measure.

"Quigley! The Andrew Carnegie of pigs. You'll be owning the bank soon. I must come over one day and learn all about how you do it."

There was a lifetime's intimacy in Samuel John's eyes. He had sat in the same schoolroom with most of them, men and women; pulled the lasses' pigtails, danced with them, walked them along country lanes. With the men, he had played chestnuts in the schoolyard as boys, robbed orchards of their green apples and swam in the dammed-up burn with nothing on but their notions of Man Friday. They were friendly eyes, of the blue on willow-pattern plates. A high-bridged nose any Norman would have fought over, dominated a strong boned face whose mouth kept a serious expression as he talked. His hair had been fair but had fled to silver over most of his head, receding from the forehead and leaving him with the look of a man that might smoke cigars and sip port after dinner. But he touched neither or any kind of alcohol and the lifetime's careful living had left him with a face clean in line and healthy of skin. Thompson could not help nudging George, whispering to him under his breath, "Do you see him, hi! Maun, George, he should have been in His Majesty's Diplomacy!"

"You're right, Thompson. Wouldn't he have been great in politics? Or the pulpit!"

"Aw, George, the pulpit, the pulpit, George! A man of his talent should have been in the pulpit. He'd have made another Wesley, so he would. Goodness, to think of it. Was that what my sister Kate had in mind? Eh?"

George looked at Thompson with concern. "Whisht now, Thompson. Don't mention that here."

"Agh, George, if we'd only have known. And us counting pills and fitting glasses! What were we thinking of, at all?"

Samuel John took Martha's hand. "Martha!" Martha smiled, trying to purse her lips against the pull of happy cheeks. Samuel John greeted them all, one by one, and on each he bestowed an affectionate remark or gesture. These were his people. They were strong people hardened by a hard life that did not permit weaklings. They were hard and of hidden emotion. They never said gentle things to one another but he, Samuel John, had spent his life saying it for them. By word, by gesture and by rapturous music he made on his violin, Samuel John had helped them all express themselves, all except Kate. She was not there but he had kind of been prepared. Setting the violin case on the table he said, "And how's the great metropolis of Belfast, Thompson?"

"Just about the same," said Thompson, with a sigh. "Murdering each other for brass. Life's worth about a shilling!"

Katy still sat, leafing through her bible. It had a black kid-leather cover bent down around the edges. A blue silk ribbon, running from the top, was held between the pages and projected beyond the bottom edge like a tail. It was a soft book with its own friendly feel, a caress to the fingers, and a comfortable smell not unlike that of gloves. Inserted amongst its pages were narrow cards, each illustrated in the top left-hand corner with a posy of flowers—roses, snapdragons, honeysuckle—twisting about the enlarged first letter of a gilded and strategic quotation. Below it, to the right, was the source, the name of the chapter, with its number and verse. They were the cards selected from the many that had come her way, selected because of their meaning to her and kept because they were entwined in her life. She read them often in moments of need, to reassure herself or, more often than not, just for the sheer beauty of their sacred words.

For God so loved the world that He gave His
only begotten Son, that whosoever believeth
in Him should not perish but have everlasting life.

She read the words to herself, her lips moving and then, in an audible whisper, "John, three and sixteen," as if to impress the fact in her memory like a child learning an important lesson. She selected another, turning the card and holding it off away from her eyes.

*Yea though I walk through the valley of the shadow
of death I shall fear none ill for Thou are with me,
Thy rod and Thy staff they comfort me.*

She held the card tenderly. It meant so much to her; the peace that its reading brought, a peace deep within, beyond the reach of sighs.

There was a larger card held in the fold of the flyleaf. A primrose flower, dried and lifeless, was pressed against it. She removed the flower gently, encountering a little difficulty in picking it up with her fingers. The card showed a man standing before a wooden door. It was a door reinforced against him, iron studded and barred. Creepers of thorn grew about it and weeds sprouted from between the stones of the path. One hand held a lantern; the other was raised to knock. This was the first card, the most precious of all. Looking at it brought back the whole experience anew—the ecstasy in the mission tent, the canvas lifting and falling unconcernedly in the evening breeze. She could smell the raw linseed oil of its tarpaulins and the crushed grass and the smell of bodies and breath. And the power of the words the evangelist cried out,

"Behold I stand at the door and knock and if any there are that hear, I shall come in!"

She had wept. Jesus was calling her! Her heart was barred against him! The thorns of neglect and the weeds of sin threatened to suffocate the only way! *"Softly and tenderly calling...."* The choir, brought down from Belfast, was calling the sinners forward. The ushers, sharp eyed and practiced, showed the way to the feet of the evangelist. The soft voices of the angels, *"Jesus is calling you now!"* The sweet close harmony reached into her heart as she kneeled. Through the words and the music she felt the power of the evangelist whose hands rested on her head. The tumult rising, writhing within her, ready to spill over and drown her in its ecstasy until, with a cry, she grabbed the hands that touched her head and held until the sobs that shook her had calmed and she rested, weak and spent, against the wooden edge of the platform.

"Belfast hasn't changed in a hunnerd years!" continued Thompson. "Dog eat dog! They'd steal the eye out of your head, so they would, and come back for the eyelashes. It's fierce. I'm telling you. You don't know how well off youse are."

"You don't mean to tell us, Thompson," asked Samuel John, "that you'd have stayed about your own doors. What would you have done here?"

"Aye! I suppose you're right, sir. What would I have done?"

"Well then, aren't you well off?" said Davy McKay, with bantering good humor. "What would you do if you were the likes of us, the price of eggs away off and the hay not all in yet. And here we're sittin' talkin' about Belfast and doin' nothin' when we could be out workin', a good night like this, just made for work."

"That's just it," cried Thompson. "Maun, you never said a truer word. Isn't that what they're doing in Belfast! Work! Work! Work! Isn't that why I'm here? To get away from it all! The eternal slugging match! Money! Money! Money! Do you want to be like them, hi? Glory bless us!"

In the silence that followed it seemed that they were all turning over in their minds that this person talking was Thompson, the long-headed fellow, Thompson who had stayed on at school and gone up to the city. And there he sat, stretched out in an armchair, telling them that they had found a better life. He didn't seem as big as when he stood before them in the classroom and knew it all. And now? "What shall it profit a man should he gain the whole world?" asked Thompson. "It's nice this, you know, down here. I'm sorry I ever left it. Aren't you George?"

"Oh, I don't know. There's not a man in this kitchen with bad eyesight. How would I make a living? It would be impossible. I'd be on the dole. Heh? Wouldn't that be the height of it?" There was laughter around and a few commented, "Dear knows!", "Right enough!" and "Now ye're talkin'!"

"Agh, George," said Thompson, feigning anger, "You've been won over! You're lost to the industrial city. The god Mammon!"

"The industrial city," said Samuel John pensively, "was an evil invention."

"It was!" said Thompson.

"Dickens exposed it!" said George.

"Yes," said Samuel John. "The great Dickens!"

"Sure," said George, "if Dickens were alive today he'd turn in his grave!"

"He would indeed," said Thompson. "There'd be no Great Expectations at all."

"Do you remember The Old Curiosity Shop, Thompson?" asked Samuel

MUSIC ON THE WIND

John.

"Well I do."

"And that beautiful recitation you used to do about Little Nell?"

"Aye, I mind."

"You'll give us it later I hope?"

"Vox populi, vox dei!"

"He'll give it anyway!" said George. "Hasn't he been waiting all week!"

"I'm an honest man, so I am," said Thompson, twitching a smile of self-deprecation. "I have waited. But haven't I always dreamed of going on the stage. Samuel John and me! We'd have been great!"

"But the die was cast, Thompson!" said Samuel John. "Our destiny lies not in our stars! You remember that?"

"Aye, Samuel John." Thompson, having stood up, struck a pose. "You've read the bard too. So did I! Once upon a time."

The neighbors, who had come for the fiddling, listened to this exchange. They did not quite follow what it was all about but they knew it was all part of the entertainment. They sat looking on but smiling cautiously and not knowing how to enter the conversation.

"Aren't them the pair of daft articles!" said Martha at last.

"Martha!" Thompson turned in his pose towards her, taking the center of the big kitchen floor with its earthen tiles and the furniture pulled back to the walls. "You remind me of some woman in history!" and would have said more but Samuel John had taken the fiddle out and delicately laid a handkerchief over the chin rest. He put the instrument to his shoulder.

"Heeeeeeeeee—hah!" Herbie yelled, rattling the spoons as the music of a jig set the room alive. Thompson dragged Martha into the dance, setting his feet down with exaggerated deliberation.

The night was still clear with only a tinge of red in the west from the setting sun. There was no need to light the oil lamps yet as it was summer. In the parlor, Katy tried to concentrate on her Bible. Her toes fidgeted to the rhythm of the music. She let the book rest on her lap. She heard every magic note of Samuel John's fiddle and the cries of the folk as they called for their favorite songs.

"Give us The Cuckoo Waltz, there!" a voice cried.

She could see in the setting sun a young man tucking the violin under his chin and singing as he played. The voice had changed little over the years and the music was still as sweet. She fought back the desire to dance as through

the closed door and down the long hall came the delighted squeals of several listeners.
"Cuckoo! Cuckoo! A-tit-tit-a-tat-a-tee!
Cuckoo! Cuckoo! A tit-tit-a-tat-a-tee!"

It had been a night like this then too.
"Now here's a fine box, beautifully, just beautifully wrapped and must surely belong to some lass worthy a man's most gallant attention!" said the master of ceremonies. There were some twenty boxes on the platform table, each box containing a picnic supper for two people. "Come now gentlemen! Let's make this box-tea both a romantic and a financial success! Who'll make me a bid now? Come on there! This beautiful box could belong to the girl of your dreams. Who's the lucky man who'll sit down to supper with the lovely lady whose dainty hands made these tantalizing tasties just for you?"
"A shilling!"
"A shilling I'm bid!"
None of the boxes were labeled as to their owner.
"A shilling and sixpence!"
"Two!"
"Two and six!"
"Four for the money!"
Three young men were bidding against each other and casting anxious glances at a pale girl with blond ringlets and too bright lipstick.
"Five!" said a tall fair-haired man.
"Five I'm bid! Are there any more bids?"
She could see the young man smiling eagerly at the blond girl.
"Five it is to that young man there. And the lucky lady is?"
The young man was moving towards the blond ringlets when the girl shook her head. He hesitated, looking around foolishly.
"Here I am over here!" whispered Katy.
He turned. Samuel John and Katy looked each other over and, without a word being spoken, knew that something irreversible had just happened.

"George, you're for giving us Danny Boy?" Samuel John's voice carried to her clearly. "George for his pleasure! I'll give you a wee introduction. Wait on it, now!"
George sang.

MUSIC ON THE WIND

*"Oh Danny Boyyy, the pipes, the pipes are ah-caw-aw-lin',
From Glen to ah-G-lennn, and ah-down the mountain siiide."*

His voice was a light tenor that reached with ease the high notes and wrung from the music a strange sadness that tinted the words with a hundred years of sorrows. There were handclaps and cries of "Bravo there, George!" and "That was great! Great, right enough!"

Katy sat. She was disturbed. Her photo on top of the piano showed her as a young woman. Her hair, in tight waves over her head, and the sack dress and the string beads around her neck, showed the fashion when she was twenty. Perhaps because it caused comment even in the town, there was a provocative joy in her face and a hint of laughter about the mouth. The eyes smiled. It was a photograph that caught a point in time and held it bravely against the damp stain that was already advancing around the edges.

"And now, Thompson," said Samuel John, "Lets have that recitation from Dickens. Little Nell!"

Sitting stiffly on the sofa, too distracted to read her bible, Katy felt the distress of doubt at not being with her neighbors in the kitchen. But it was too late now. There was no going up to the kitchen to have them stare at her and talk about her for weeks to come. If only her brother Thompson had stayed in the city where he belonged. "But it's for old time's sake, Katy! I knew the fellow when we were at school together! Weren't him and me as thick as thieves! And it's years since I seen the man. Have a heart!"

"Katy, it's yourself!" they'd say. "Come in to we see you!" And she'd stand in the hallway door. "And she looked thaveless, don't you know. You never saw such a change in a girl!"

They had gathered in the kitchen, but why? she asked herself. Not because of Thompson. Thompson lived in another world. They had no interest in Thompson. To hear Samuel John like they used to? The women would look at him and, once behind their own half-doors gossiping over their knitting, they'd say, "Did you see how old he's gettin'?" "An' he never married!" "Katy was the one. Wasn't she?" "It was funny that! Odd!"

"Them's lovely!" said Sarah McKay. "You'll have to write me down the recipe."

"Do you like them?"

"Them's better than anything in Bridge Street Bakery," said Martha. "Home baking's the best." Nan Surgenor and Mrs. M'Clug both agreed the scones were good. "I wouldn't mind another," said Martha. "That leppin' to the music fairly gives a body an appetite. Mind you, it's a gae wheen of years since I felt so feght." Martha, being from the Ross, was very fond of country expressions and was well know for her use of them.

The women, whether by maneuver or by accident, had come to sit together and, with cups of tea and platefuls of scones to work on, were ready to exchange comments on anything.

"Boys-a-dear, that Thompson and his brother Jock are very like one another in the face," Nan Surgenor said when Mary was up attendant on the men with a plateful of sandwiches. "But Jock's so quiet. He's hardly said a word all night."

"Thompson was doing the talkin' for him," said Martha in a joking way.

"With so much kee-hawin' goin' on it's a wonder Katy didn't show her face," said Sarah. "She'll be sittin' up in the parlor, you can be certain. You'd wonder, you know, what ever came between her and Samuel John."

"Sssshhhe now. Don't let Mary hear you say a word," admonished Martha. "It's not for us to pass judgment, so it's not."

The men had grouped themselves in the remaining chairs. Both Samuel John and Archie had laid their fiddles aside and Herbie had pocketed his two spoons. Will had returned his fife to the safety of the inner pocket. A few jackets had been laid off. There was a good deal of sweat on their shirts and the widower Hamil had his starched collar off and sat sprawled on a chair, his neck-band sprouting two brass studs. Everyone felt more relaxed. Thompson, the long-headed fellow, was still as odd as ever and George hadn't changed a bit. There was Samuel John who could still make a fiddle speak and, as Martha Kelsoe would have said, "Draw tears from a cannibal's een!" Everyone felt better for dancing a few steps, a mug of tea, a couple of sandwiches and a scone apiece was "bringing home the far fields!"

"You'd a good crop of hay in the wee meadow this year, Davy!" Will Kelsoe said.

"Aye, not bad! If I had as good a one in The Forth I wouldn't have to bother about fodder this coming winter."

"They tell me the price of ewes off the mountain is gone up something fierce, nearly doubled," commented Hamil. "I was in the Fair Hill last

Saturday and there was nary a one. They say you could walk from here to Slemish and not see hair nor hide of a ewe."

The music and dancing had brought them together. Every crop and beast and its current condition was gone into. The Kelsoe's new Ayreshire bull was discussed and Quigley's large white sow that produced sixteen piglets at a time.

"An' her with only twelve tits. Sure I'm heart scalded feedin' four of them on the bottle."

"I say," said Thompson, who was getting to feel out of it, "You lead a rich life down here, so you do."

"Aren't you the man who left it for far off fields," responded Davy McKay. Thompson said nothing. "If you hadn't got all them exams wouldn't you still be here?" There were good-natured smiles and chuckles from the men.

"Aye," said Thompson. "Sure it was idiocy anyway."

"Thompson!" called Samuel John. "What are the principal towns of Cavan?"

Thompson smiled broadly, his eyes darting with pleasure. "Do you mind thon, hi? And the principal rivers of India are?" adding to impress them, "The Ganges, Godavari, Mahandi and Kistna," pointing out their positions on an imaginary map sketched in the air. "Like that! And Captain Cook discovered Botany Bay in the year seventeen seventy! Boys, my head was dizzy with facts. And Miss, what was her name, thon aul' frustrated maiden, standing over you with a ruler. Thon gulpin. She'd no more brains than a kippered herring. To think of the lives she ruined!"

For all Thompson's bombast about the futility of learning, Samuel John often felt envy. Thompson had gone on to study and live in the world that lay beyond the countryside and its small market town. There was a world of culture out there, he knew, a world of music and theatres. It was a world that Samuel John had often dreamed about. He knew that his music could hold spellbound the people of his own countryside. He loved the way they listened to him. Once there had never been a dance or a party without him being called to play. Even now, with the young people going off on Friday and Saturday nights to the picture house there were still many occasions when he was asked.

"Do you remember simple interest," asked Davy McKay. "A penny a pound interest a month for a year is a shillin'! Where under God would the likes of us poor people ever get our hands on stocks and shares?"

"Or if a train was traveling at twenty miles an hour and a fly up ahead was going at ten, how long would it take to land on the boiler man's nose?" said Surgenor, slapping his thigh and grinning broadly as he remembered that one. But Samuel John was remembering the year of the musical festival.

His handling of the traditional music showed great instrumental dexterity combined with a deep feeling for the authentic charm of its Irish heritage. In the standard piece, taken this year from Beethoven's Violin Concerto the contestant demonstrated his range of emotional interpretation. Should seek further competition in Belfast.

He still kept the clipping from the local newspaper. It was only twenty-eight miles to Belfast and the train went there every day. Thompson had gone! George had gone! George had even gone to Dublin and taken exams there, returning with a diploma could paper a wall. Samuel John had stayed. "What do you find in this one-horse town? Sure there's nothing!" Thompson had said during a visit from the Technical College. Samuel John had no answer, none that Thompson would have understood. The farmers' daughters in a dozen townlands? Or the look in the faces of the people when he played the violin? The eyes of the people who held horses' reins in their hands all day, steadied a plough and did any and all work that coarsened the hands and sensibility? To have had a head dizzy with facts! The crazy lists of facts that opened doors!

"Where's wee Tam Slattery now?" asked George.
"Dead!" someone said.
"Agh no!" said George. "Do you mind the time he dressed McCartney's goat up in the Orange regalia and tied him to Father Kearney's Manse?" The men laughed loud at the memory of it.
Samuel John felt the cold realization of being apart from them. He could see the people with whom he had spent his life, decent people, hard people, whose hidden emotions he tapped like a vintner his barrel, and sipped, and sipped again till he was drunk with the warming spirits of their adoration.
They were laughing now at the grotesque escapade played on the long suffering McCartney and his goat. Samuel John listened. Thompson was telling a tall yarn about Belfast and, "The greed and the lust of them would put Sodom and Gomorrah to shame!" The farmers stared at him with wide eyes.
"Is that so?" said Hamil, shaking his head in wonder.

"I'm telling you!" said Thompson.

Samuel John looked at his aging schoolfellows. Every one of them had suffered the outrageous scholarship of a country schoolteacher. They had grown older as he had, worked the farms their fathers had worked before them. Some had married. Some hadn't. He wondered if any had loved, but found no names. If asked, he would have listed the events in the lives of each person present; incidents that had made them or had destroyed them. He looked for a meaning but no meaning presented itself.

Samuel John listened and found no pleasure in the animated conversation around him. It was time to go. "Well, it's near the Sabbath," he announced. "Time to go! Remember the Lord's Day!"

"Sure you'll play us a few more before you go! Now won't you?" someone asked.

Samuel John stood up. Their eyes asked him to play inner unsayable words and unleash them from the prison of themselves. "I'll play one more. That's all. Then I'll go though it pains me to leave." He spread the handkerchief over the chin rest. "I'll play a favorite of mine" The violin was tucked under his chin as he played and sang the accompanying words.

"Oh, my Kathleen, I'm going to leave you, all alone in this terrible place!"

They watched the stroke of the bow and the firm press of the fingers on the strings. Every one of them heard the beautiful words singing in the soul's rapt ear. Samuel John played and sang with his eyes closed, drawing every note with special feeling and tenderness. The music filled the old farm kitchen like a balloon swelling against the sides of a box and none heard the scratch of the front door as Katy let herself out and fled across the fields.

Katy's face had survived well the passing of the years. She had filled out in body the way farmwomen often do. There was none of the girl in the photograph. Neither the laughter in the eyes or the flirtatious cut of the clothes. Katy had settled, dressing herself in the dark, woolen, hand-knitted jumpers she worked on during the winter nights. The dress was equally somber and her stockings would have seemed dull to a nun. The feet, which had tapped so lightly with the rhythm of the lancers, were weighed with inelegant boots. The bible caressed her fingers like the soft touch of a kitten. The words of the evangelist rang in her head as they rang that same desperate evening, "Go ye into all the world and preach the Gospel! Take the word of Jesus to some loved one, Kathleen," he said. "Invite him to come to the Throne of Grace!" She remembered the pain in Samuel John's face when she told him. "But Katy!" he had pleaded. "Katy!" His way of saying her name carried an echo along endless corridors of pain. He had said it the night he had left her home from the box-tea, standing by the pump in the yard, "Katy!" Kissing her with a gentle sweep of his lips across hers, the light touch of feather-down that made her reach out and press him to her. There were a thousand Katys. There was "Katy!" called at the top of his voice across a field; "Katy!" in the midge-biting heather of the peat-moss, "Katy!" in the winter; "Katy!" in the Spring, in the Summer and in the lamp-lit Autumn evenings of the parlor before the onset of the cold winds, "Katy!" But it was the "Katy!" in his voice the day she crossed the street to avoid meeting him that she remembered now. He caught her up. "Katy! What is it? What have I done?"

Belief in herself had given her the strength to look into his eyes. "Samuel John! Our ways are different now. It's no use."

"But what have I done?"

"Nothing, Samuel John."

"Then?"

"Samuel John! I've been washed in the blood of the Lamb!" She could hear the evangelist's voice saying it. "I've accepted Jesus Christ as my own personal Savior! I'm saved!"

"But Katy! From what?"

"From sin!"

"What sin are you talking about?"

"Worldly sin!"

"You mean there's no more dancing?"

"No!"

"Or anything? All the fun we've had?"

"No!"

"What kind of a way's that?"

"I'm happy in the Lord's Saving Grace, Samuel John!"

"Katy! Oh Jesus! Katy!"

He tried to hold her. It was mid-morning of a market Saturday. There were many people in the street. He tried to hold her, putting his hand about her waist as if to encircle her, as if to touch her would break the thing that had come between them. Some of the curious had stopped. Eyes, dressed up in wicked smiles, were watching her, storing up the moment for an hour's gossip.

"Let me go! Do you hear?" And swirling out of his grasp she ran. Two streets away she saw the hanging threads where the button had been and remembered the tug at her coat when she twisted away from him.

The fiddle was holding the high note ready to descend to the last phrase when Katy slid the bolt on the front door and slipped into the falling night. She ran. The dew on the grass washed her boots. Her stockings and skirt were darkened by its wetness. The grass seeds clung to the cloth.

"Now when I passed by thee, and looked upon thee, behold, thy time was the time of love."

She had to see him.

The men, one by one, reached for the scoop-caps off the pegs. The women took up their handbags from the windowsill. One or two people were in the yard, standing idly by, waiting for others to make the first move. The widower Hamil was wrapping the bottoms of his trouser legs inside bicycle clips in readiness for the ride home. Archie started his Austin Seven, pressed the horn a couple of times.

"Anybody for home? I'll give you a lift!"

Davy McKay and Sarah said they'd walk to get a bit of the night air but their son was eager for a try in the car. The Kelsoes had come by bicycle and the Surgenors by horse and trap. The McGrews had a Ford Eight and the McClugs rode with them.

"Well, Samuel John! Just like old times!" said Will. "That was great playing. We'd like you up at the Ross sometime. There's a wheen of folk up there would like to hear you again."

"Set the night, Will. Set the night. It was a pleasure. Keep the fife dry, now. No slobbers!"

"We'll do that. You'll be hearing from us."

"Good. Give my regards to everybody," said Samuel John, knowing that Will would say to everyone he met, "Saw Samuel John the other day. He was asking about you."

Herbie, a scarf about his neck, kicked his motorcycle awake. "Samuel John! Don't forget next month out at Cross Keys!" Samuel John clapped him on the back assuring him he'd be there and Herbie went off, taking the bend in the lane in great style. The widower Hamil and the McKays said goodnight and went.

"Well, Samuel John," said Thompson. "Which way are you going to go?"

"I'll go in by the railway," he replied. "The sleepers are a good stride apart and it makes for a healthy walk."

"I'll go a bit of the way with you then. It's a fine night."

"I could do with a bit of a dander myself, as well," said George. "I'll walk a bit of the way too."

"Ye'll not mind me," said Jock, "not going a ways with you. I've a wee heifer down there in the barn needs some attention. She's for calving the night by the looks of it."

"No, Jock. You go ahead now. I'm alright."

But Jock felt he had to say what had been bothering him all the evening. "I'm hoping you'll be out again, Samuel John. I'm sorry some things are the way they are."

"Now, that's alright Jock. We'll not mention it."

"Well then, I'll be seeing you." And he walked in his deliberate farmer's way to the byre. He had felt the need to say something about Katy, make some sort of apology, and he had, in the only words that could come to him.

"Mary," said Samuel John, "you're an angel for putting up with us all. Feeding the five thousand you might say."

They looked at each other a brief moment, looking away immediately so as not to embarrass the other. Jock had apologized for Katy. Mary didn't have to mention any more about it. "You'll come by again!" was all she said.

The sun had gone down and the roosting birds were whispering in the shadowed hedgerows. Warmth from the ground mixed with the cool that tumbled down from the night air.

"You can make an instrument speak," Thompson said after a while. "You're an artist, so you are."

"You have the touch, Samuel John," said George. "I've always said it. The touch. It's a rare thing mind you, the touch."

Samuel John adjusted the fiddle case on his shoulder.

"The touch," said Thompson, "is a God given thing, so it is!"

Samuel John knew that they were, in their own way, trying to make up for Katy not being there. Yet he knew also the compliment was sincere. He searched in his mind for something he could say that would let them know he was past the point in which he took offence. "I've always believed," he said, "that God speaks to everyone in His own way."

"He does. He does indeed." Thompson thought that the shadows down by the slew bushes moved. He couldn't be certain. "I think I'll leave you here, Samuel John. My arches are killing me."

"Aye!" said George.

"You'll come up some day to the city for a run. You'll mind that!"

"I will, Thompson. I will."

"Goodnight, then."

"I'll be seeing you."

The night had darkened. The birds in the hedgerows had fallen silent and a chill was in the air. The red hues in the sky faded into gray until Samuel John, Thompson and George, going their separate ways, and Katy leaving the safety of the bushes, were as walking shadows. Slowly, imperceptibly, the great shadow of night swallowed up the lesser shadows of the day.

Passing Through

He was standing outside the door of the pharmacy, dressed in a white dispensary coat, his hands clasped across his front. He looked up and down the village street as if to check who was about at that early hour of the morning. There was just me, cycling to a stop before him. He smiled as I approached and, anticipating that I was a customer, slipped back through the door into the shadows. He was already behind the counter as I entered. Again he smiled, this time accompanied by a slight lift of his brows, a professional expression that asked how he could serve me. I showed him my swollen hand.

"Ah!" he said. "A bee sting?"

I confirmed his diagnosis and asked could he do something to take away the pain. His expression changed to one of deep thought as he scanned the shelves of bottles that lined the walls. Then, in a matter of moments, he had taken one down and was applying a wad of cotton wool soaked in cooling liquid. I could feel the benefit immediately. I was impressed and sought to tell him so. "You're a marvel!" I said happily. "You're quite a genius!"

He drew himself up, grasped the air with one hand and claimed in theatrical tones, "I," there was a pause, "am a Chemist!" He leaned forward to look straight into my eyes as if to enforce my appreciation of that fact. Apparently I was not as influenced as he had expected for he continued in a more intense manner as if compelling me to understand. "A Pharmaceutical Chemist, that is!" He was a tallish, slim man, dark complexion with heavy eyebrows and a straight nose. His hair was brushed straight back from his forehead and gave him a remarkable resemblance to actors from the forties, a Charles Boyer. It seemed he thought so too and pronounced his words in a deliberate slow fashion, each one clearly enunciated as if reading from a script. "You might say an Apothecary!" he continued, "A latter day Druid. Maybe even, you could say, a modern Merlin." There were many pauses for dramatic effect while his hands drew fantasies in the air.

By now I had accepted a chair. There I sat, in a low spectator's position, surrounded by his gallery of bottles of all sizes, shapes and colors. I could only nod my head before he was treading the boards again. "You see, I dispense magic elixirs for the sick in body and potions and aids to guarantee and improve God's original handiwork and so," there was considerable arm flourish at this point, "further the aims of the Devil!" He looked at me intently. "That's a line I quote from the Reverend. He accuses me of being in league. You'll know him, I'm sure." I shook my head and told him I was just passing through on a cycling trip. It was really my first time in this village. "Aye!" he continued as if I had never spoken. "The good Reverend lives in a world occupied by God and the Devil!" He stared at me meaningfully and with a deprecating smile admitted, "Not that I believe in either of those fabulous personages. Not me. No, not me! I... am a scientist! A scientist, you see." He gave me a knowing wink. "And that creates a conflict not easily resolved by simple faith. A question of the intellect!" He looked off into some distant part of his mind. "And yet I deal in faith. For what is medicine, the greater part of it, but faith. And faith is in the mind."

He reached forward to hold the wet compress to the back of my hand. I was a prisoner. "Yes! I dispense the accoutrements of health and beauty to the sick of body and spirit and they have faith in me. In me! Yes! You know, when I think of it, the Good Lord," he paused for several seconds, "that is to say, were He alive today, would make his mark as a pharmacist!" He looked at me to ascertain if I understood the significance of that pronouncement. "Oh, if the scriptures had only read, *They that are whole need not a pharmacist!* Wouldn't that be something! Dispensing aspirin and penicillin instead of barley-loaves and fishes. What!" He leaned towards me with a wry smile. "I once put that thesis to the Reverend, you know." I could only shake my head in astonishment. "Aye! He was left without words! Now I'm a sinner, he says! A sinner! Doomed to the Fires of Damnation!"

I nodded my head silently. I had by now accepted my role. I kept quiet! "He's either ignorant or stupid. Which do you think?" he said, looking at me with astrange glare.

"Who?"

"Thon shaman of a Reverend!"

I shrugged.

"The difference is this." He looked intently into my eyes from a distance of about a foot. "Ignorance can be changed. But stupid! There's nothing you can do with stupid." Having made that point the pharmacist posed a moment before a mirror that carried an advertisement for some effervescent fruit salts. "Pharmacy, you know, is a wonderful profession!" he said to his image, sweeping his unbuttoned white dispensary coat in a wide swath. "Once, we were called apothecaries! Did I ever tell you that? I did, didn't I?" He had strange intense gray-blue eyes that turned away to focus on some notion in the distance. "You know, I can repeat every word of the British Pharmacopoeia as if I had only qualified yesterday."

"Goodness!"

"Just wait to you hear!" And he began to recite incantations, ingredients, herbal cures and prescriptions. I rose and, interrupting, asked him how much I owed for his services.

"Nah! It's nothing. Take care." He seemed to change character as an actor who has just left the stage. There was a look of hurt and disappointment on his face. I smiled to show I was not trying to offend him, just that it was time to go. I thanked him for his treatment of the bee sting. He grabbed my arm and looked at me intently. "For in much wisdom is much grief: and he that increaseth knowledge increaseth sorrow." I could only stare at him. "That's from Ecclesiastes." He smiled deprecatingly with a downward tip to one side of his mouth. "You know, young fellow, there's a lot of wisdom in the Good Book."

At that moment there was a shadow in the light from the door and a man stepped in. He was dressed in black with a white clerical collar. The pharmacist stepped behind his counter, a smile once again on his face, his brows slightly raised to enquire how he could be of service. The Reverend laid a prescription on the counter top. I hesitated for a second wondering how best to say goodbye but he turned to me first. His face was blank of expression.

"Good day to you, sir."

It was a beautiful sunny sky as I mounted my bicycle and rode along the narrow street. I noticed the chapel with its stately spire and tall windows, its graveyard framed by stonewalls, the weathered headstones. I continued my run through the back roads and lanes of the valley until I reached the high slopes of the mountain. There I stopped once again, looking down the long incline, looking for the village in the distance that I had just passed through. It was sheathed in the foliage of trees with only the spire of the chapel to be seen.

At the Bottom of a Long Hill

The graveyard lay at the bottom of the long hill in the townland of Ballymaclug, almost an acre surrounded by a stonewall that kept the sheep and cattle at bay. It had been founded out of despair when the famine struck more than a century before. No church was attached; it simply belonged to the borough of Ballyaghone whose council paid Quincy McCairn a small stipend and allowed him the use of the thatched cottage built into one wall.

Clusters of yew trees caught the force of the wind that swept from the east in winter; and in summer the walls trapped the weak northern sun. On days without rain Quincy cut the grass with a scythe and weeded the graves of those who paid him to care. Occasionally a grave would be opened to receive its final guest, the last in the passing of a family. Rarely was a new grave dug though several unused plots still remained paid for in freehold by some far-sighted forebear, the younger generation preferring plots attached to a church or at the cemetery in town with its wide open space, its asphalt pathways and hundreds of markers and headstones. By comparison the graveyard of Ballymaclug was a very lonely place indeed to spend eternity. Quincy liked it that way. The graveyard was not just his home but also the office of his calling, the place where he took care of the dead and, as opportunity arose, interested himself in other matters.

Out by the northern wall where it trapped the sun, the soil was rich and easily prepared with a spade. Each Spring Quincy planted herbs that he tended with care, harvested when ready and hung to dry from the rafters within his cottage. When the winter settled in and the snow fell and no one in his right mind would walk the roads, he roasted barley, fermented it in drums and distilled it in a copper still set under the arch of the open hearth. The smoke from the peat fire carried the fumes up the chimney and released it into the cold night air. When spring came the herbs had long been aged with the product of the still and bottled, ready to treat the million aches and pains mankind is heir to. He was renowned throughout the townland. Even Heale the pharmacist on High Street envied his skill and had been heard to declare, "Sure, if I only had half his knowledge I'd be twice as smart as I am." Those who heard this stamp of approval nodded sagely and swore personally to the power of Quincy's elixirs, pick-me-ups and cures; for hadn't they been using them these many years.

"I wish I had your brains?" the pharmacist said to Quincy one day.

Quincy sat in the dispensary of the Chemist Shop. Shelves of colored bottles, each one labeled in Latin, surrounded him. There was one display of white porcelain jars with gold lettering and onion shaped lids. To Quincy they were the very essence of science. He was in awe. What his life might have been had he had an education: a certificate, just like that of his friend Heale, to hang on the wall—Pharmacist! It would say – Quincy McCairn, Ph.C.

"What's in them jars?" he asked.

"Nothing! They're just for show."

"Ah! Then you're just as ignorant as me."

The pharmacist looked at Quincy with a smile, inclining his head in acknowledgement. "So what can I do for you?"

"I'll take a bottle of aspirin, Mr. Heale." Quincy said.

"Aspirin? For a man in your profession with cures at your fingertips? I'm prompted to ask why."

"I've got a headache."

The pharmacist produced a bottle of aspirin. "There you are!" and continued to question Quincy with a penetrating look.

Quincy smiled. "And I'm also not stupid."

There was a friendship between Quincy and the pharmacist that had developed over the years based on mutual respect and admiration for the other's knowledge and skills; the pharmacist on the one hand representing the world of accepted medicine and Quincy the world of nature and faith. Mr. Heale loaned him textbooks from his days as a student at the Pharmacy School in Belfast while Quincy explained the folklore and skills he had acquired from sources long forgotten.

"I'll try a bottle of that stuff that gives a man zest," said Heale on his first arrival at the point of experimentation. And a week later declared, "Sure I'm feeling like a new man, so I am."

Word spread that even Heale the pharmacist took Quincy's pick-me-up elixir for wasn't that the reason he had taken a notion of Hannah McKilt the sister of Willie McKilt out at Ballymaclug; and even she sipped of the same essence for wasn't there a sparkle in her eye which was strange.

One day a new police constable by the name of McGroin arrived from Belfast, that city to the south of Ballyaghone where things are quite different and the outlook on humanity's frailty somewhat less constrained. The new constable was a man of ambition looking for some way to make a mark for himself in the one-horse town of Ballyaghone.

"I have reason to believe, sir," said Constable McGroin to the sergeant at the police barracks in Ballyaghone, "there's a man working a wee still out by Ballymaclug, so there is!"

"Is there indeed? Well, I wouldn't listen to rumors if I were you."

"But it's not a rumor, sergeant. My lady friend swears to me it's true."

"Your lady-friend! So you've got yourself a lady-friend now?"

"I do. A Miss Madge McKilt."

"Ah, Willie McKilt's daughter, a farmer out that way. And she has the notion there's a wee still in Ballymaclug?"

"Aye! She heard from another lady that takes a drop now and then."

"Another lady. I see. And from where did the other lady get the notion?"

"Oh, it's no notion. The other lady takes a wee drop now and again for her asthma and swears by it. That's how she knows."

"I see. She swears by it. Hmmm."

"And the other lady, being my lady-friend's aunt Hannah, it's a true story," continued the constable nodding his head to underline the truth of it all.

"Hmm! How long is it since you came down here from Belfast?"

"Three months, sir. I've been here in Ballyaghone three months, so I have!"

"Have you indeed. And you already have a lady-friend. My oh my."

"I do that, sir. A fine woman she is. A farmer's daughter like you said. Miss Madge McKilt."

"And she fills your head with gossip when you're out courting?"

"She wouldn't tell a lie, sir. It's the God's truth, so it is."

"The God's truth, no less. Dear me, is that all she can find to talk about when you're out courting?" The sergeant looked the fellow up and down. Three months in Ballyaghone! A lady friend! Now he wanted to upset the applecart. The sergeant sighed. What could you expect from a fellow from Belfast. "Constable, it's all just gossip. Sheer piffle. Take my word for it."

"She says even the pharmacist in the Chemist Shop up by Church Street that's courting this other lady, her aunt Hannah, takes a drop himself. Mixed with herbs and stuff, it is, like a potion."

"Ah! Then that would be medicine, it sounds like to me!"

"It's against the law, sergeant! A wee still is illegal! Illicit alcohol!"

"You don't have to tell me what's against the law." The sergeant looked out the window with a concerned expression. The problem with Constable McGroin was that he was too eager to upset a peaceful community. "Who's the suspect?"

"His name's Quincy McCairn, sir."

"The grave digger?"

"Aye! Him by the graveyard at the bottom of the long hill in Ballymaclug. He lives in thon old thatched house built into the wall."

"Ah! You've been out there snooping around, have you?"

"No sir! My lady-friend Madge and me kinda walked past when we were out together, like. And she told me."

"Well, your lady-friend Madge is ill-informed. Next time you're out give her something better to occupy her mind. Grab a hoult!"

"I'll try sir."

"Now get along with you. The Picture House will be getting out in about five minutes and it's past darkness so you'll need to check that no one is riding a bicycle without a light. G'wan! Wee still indeed! Imagination!" But the Sergeant was disturbed. He had known Quincy these good many years, a man who did a great service for the townland. His graveyard was the best kept in the county; and he, the sergeant, had even taken a few drops himself of Quincy's magic elixirs from time to time.

One evening that Spring, the matter of the still was bothering the constable greatly to where he confided his concerns to his lady-friend. Madge was alarmed for wasn't Quincy treating her mother for rheumatism with some potion and wasn't her mother improving daily. "What are you going to do? Sure he does no harm. You should try a wee drop yourself. It would make you a more pleasanter fellow to be with, so it would."

"It's against the law! It's a crime!" And the constable's tone forbad any argument.

They continued their walk along the country road but for Madge the romance was over. No matter, for Constable McGroin his mind was made up. He would do something. Immediately! Knowing he had lost his lady-friend he decided he would show her a thing or two, be firm, prove himself right if nothing else. He cycled the mile or so to the bottom of the long hill. He knocked authoritatively on Quincy's door.

"Open up in the name of the law!"

The winter was long over and, with the reputation he had achieved, all of Quincy's bottles had been sold. Not one remained, not even an empty. The evidence the constable was looking for was gone.

"What are those?" the constable asked, not so easily put off and pointing to a few remaining herbs that dangled from the beams of the roof.

"Them's herbs."

"For what?"

"For putting in my soup. That's what!"

The constable peered up into the darkness, squinting his eyes to see. There were a few cobwebs that swung across like nets hung out to dry. He took out his battery lamp and let it search the darkness under the thatch. A reflection off copper caught his eye and in a moment his frustration turned to glee. He had found the still. "Sure I told you, so I did," he said triumphantly to the sergeant.

The courthouse in Ballyaghone was filled with folks from town and country who had come to hear how the constable from Belfast had done such a despicable thing. They were in a raw mood. Even Heale the pharmacist had closed up shop to be there; the constable's ex-lady-friend Madge and her father Willie, her mother and aunt Hannah also; they all were there to offer proof of Quincy's cures. The constable gave evidence. "And that your honor, is how I found the apparatus. Hidden up under the thatch roof." He pointed to the copper kettle and spiral condenser that sat atop the evidence table.

The circuit judge, himself from Belfast, looked severely at Quincy. "How do you plead?" His voice was gruff for he had no patience with petty criminals.

"Not guilty, my lord!"

"Not guilty?" The constable and the judge exchanged looks of pity for the poor deluded fellow. "How can you plead not guilty when the apparatus of your guilt is before the court and plain for all to see? Even for one like you!" The judge smiled confidently and looked to his fellow enforcer of the law for support. The faces in the court were focused on the defendant. Poor Quincy! He would get six months at least, maybe even a year. Who would dig the graves then? And no quick fixes for ailments for all that time. "The apparatus!" screamed the judge, apoplectic at having to deal with such stupid country folk. "You had the apparatus!" He pointed with a trembling angry finger at the copper still. "Don't you understand? The apparatus!"

"Well then, your lordship," Quincy stood up. His voice was calm. "I ask for another crime to be taken into consideration."

"Ah!" exclaimed the judge. He had always known that once he broke the poor devils' spirits they would confess their sins, all of them. "Well! Let the court hear all of your miserable transgressions. Out with it! The court will try to be lenient."

"Your honor, I'd like you to take into consideration the fact that I seduced your own good wife. Raped her you might say. God bless her, it was all my fault. I take full blame. Yes sir, full blame. Rape it was."

There was a ripple of body movement in the court. Someone sniggered. Several looked across at each other for wasn't this why they had come, to hear one of their own!

The judge's face turned white at the shock of effrontery. Slowly a reddish color spread over his cheeks as his anger took control. He could see the newspaper reporter from the local newspaper with a grin on his face. What would he print? The judge rose from his seat leaning forward and yelling out of control. "There is no evidence before this court concerning the rape of my wife!" He heard his voice scream at the defendant. He stopped in the realization that this impertinent bumpkin was making him look a fool. He sat back in the chair. The courtroom was deadly silent. In a breathless but calmer voice he repeated slowly, "There is no evidence before the court." He realized the gossip would spread the incident even to the halls of Belfast.

"I know, you Lordship," said Quincy, an apologetic look on his face as if he too suffered for the judge. "I know there's no evidence before the court for my rapeing your wife, sir. But sure don't I have the apparatus for it. I have the apparatus. Look!" Quincy stood up, his fingers feeling for the buttons on his trousers.

They carried Quincy from the court on shoulders of triumph. "Case dismissed!" The reporter from the local paper hurried to write up an article that would portray the judge as a latter day Solomon with insight into human frailty. The constable would be portrayed as the goat, a person who should find better things to do, preferably back up in Belfast. He would make Quincy a cross between the Good Samaritan and St. Luke, a man who made innocent but highly recommended herbal remedies for his neighbors; and, as a last dig at authority, why didn't the medical profession investigate the wonderful cures that were possible with herbs.

"You're a celebrity!" said Heale the pharmacist.

"Aye!" But Quincy was not the same person any more.

"What wrong with you, man?" pursued the pharmacist.

"It just don't feel the same."

"Look at the money you'll make!"

"It isn't the money."

"More fool you!"

"Nah! People will expect things now. And it's no longer something hidden."

"So?"

"It will affect their faith."

"But faith in what?"

"In whatever. What does it matter?" Quincy pulled on his coat. "I'll take another bottle of aspirin with me. I get these headaches."

Summer marched on. The wall around Ballymaclug graveyard caught the weak sun and warmed the soil, but the patch of garden in the graveyard at the bottom of the long hill stayed covered in weeds.

All Flesh is Grass

"Irma," said old Guthrie Wilcox, "you're one brave, good-looking woman, so you are." He looked at her intently, nodding his head in affirmation. "You take after your mother, you know. She was a stunner in her day, I can tell you. She sure was." He had wanted to say that for some time and smiled the way an uncle smiles at a favorite niece.

Irma said nothing. There was more important business to do. She coaxed the bull a few steps forward, his step heavy, his nose stretched outward. She noticed the leer on the face of McHern, Guthrie's farm laborer.

"You should get married!" McHern said in the belief that the topic of Irma was still open for comment. There was a broad grin slashed across the stubble on his face; but there usually was when he was around women. "Huh huh!" he added with the tone of a self appointed expert in such matters. "You should, you know."

"Bring your heifer forward more," Irma scolded, ignoring this invasion of her personal affairs.

McHern held the heifer steady by the rope attached to its horns. The beast's eyes stared out of its head in anticipation of the approaching nuptials. "Sure I should offer for you myself," continued McHern, the grin turning to an ugly leer. "Aye!" He made it sound like bestowing a favor. The heifer was restless.

"It'll take a better man than you, McHern," replied Irma. "That I'll grant you. A better man than you. Can't you hold that heifer steady?"

McHern's face flushed with humiliation, then paled as anger surged within him. He was not accustomed to woman answering him back. The flesh around his eyes grew tight. He was known for his fierce temper. Guthrie, who knew McHern's temperament well, intervened with an edge of warning to his voice. "Rob! That's enough! Pay more attention to that heifer and less of that kind of talk! Do you hear? We're here to get that heifer in calf. Leave the socializing to later. Now, keep her head high. Irma, can I hold that bull for you?"

"No, you can't. No one handles him but me. He's not used to anyone else." Her voice held authority. "It's me he knows, ever since he was a calf. I'll handle him. Stand back."

Old Guthrie took a step back but kept a close watch on Irma. It was not right that a woman should do this kind of work, he thought. It was dangerous. He was ready to step in at any sign of her losing control of the enormous animal, one of the biggest Ayreshire bulls he had ever seen.

Though usually a man's work to handle a bull, this bull belonged to Irma. She had bought him as a calf from the Agricultural College and was the pride of her dairy herd. No one else handled him. He was a valuable animal of proven milk lineage, part of the plan to improve her herd. She also sold his services to the neighboring farmers. The College kept track of his performance, all of which was written down in a book.

Irma gripped the pole with the hook on the end attached to the ring in the bull's nose. A chain, its metal shining from being dragged along grass, also hung from the nose-ring. It was a ruse to slow the animal down in any encounter with his handlers, should he become unruly. Irma gave him some slack. The bull lifted his tender nose up in appreciation of the scent from the heifer, rolled his eyes back and mounted. Irma held the pole in a way not to stress the animal.

"There he goes, bedad!" A broad grin lightened up McHern's face. It pleased him that this act between animals was being performed in front of Irma. To him it was not an act of breeding animals for milk production but a peep show, made all the funnier in his mind by Irma's presence. The bull lunged hard then dropped back onto his four hooves and bellowed. Saliva dripped from his muzzle. His long slender penis retracted into its sheath. Irma jerked the pole to pull the ring in his nose upwards. The bull calmed as the tender flesh of the nasal septum felt the pull. She looked over at McHern defiantly.

"Aye, that'll do it!" called Irma's father from the brow of the farmyard where he stood hunched over and leaning on his cane. "You'll find that's a job well done, Guthrie. Worth every penny."

"Aye!" said Guthrie. "If he passes on the milking strain, sure it's worth it. What do you say Irma?"

"That'll be five shillings, Guthrie," said Irma coldly, letting him know who ran the farm. She stood straight, dressed in dungarees and rubber boots like any farmer in the townland. "You can pay for it now," she said. "I'll enter it in the book for the College."

"You've a great daughter there, Davy," said Guthrie, "How could you run this farm without her?"

"Sure, don't I know!" Her father chuckled, raising his cane in a quick wave of proof. What would he do without her? She ran the farm. The two older men were playful in their exchange. Guthrie's voice was jovial, Davy's tinged with pride. They had known each other since childhood, their respective farms just a mile or so from each other.

Turning her back on them, Irma led her bull back to the paddock where she unlatched the hook from his nose and turned him loose to graze. The bull ambled off, slowed by his great weight and the chain that dangled from his nose. He held his head sideways to avoid stepping on it. Irma laid the pole in the cradle that ran along the fence where it could be reached at a moment's notice, even in an emergency.

"Five shillings, Guthrie!"

Old Guthrie reached into his trouser pocket and drew out two half crowns. "She's all business, Davy. I like that."

"She is that!" It did not seem to concern either of the men that they discussed Irma in her presence. In a way they were paying her a compliment, one they wanted her to hear. Her father nodded his head sideways accompanying this action with an exaggerated wink of his right eye. It was a sign of deep belief and sincerity. "You're right there, so you are. I couldn't get on without her. Naw, I sure couldn't! She's a great worker!"

This was indeed true. Irma took care of the farm, doing the larger share of the work, feeding pigs and cattle. At milking time, both morning and evening, she hand-milked more than her share of the twenty cows. The chickens and the turkeys she took care of by herself. She didn't complain. This was the life to which she had been born and she didn't question it. She was an only child, twenty-five years old, in full bloom and a spinster. One day the farm would be hers. It was her duty to take care of it.

"Guthrie!" said Irma. "Next time you bring a heifer over here to be served by my bull, maybe I'll let your man, McHern there, hold him. He seems to enjoy this kind of thing. He'll get a better peek at the whole show! And maybe even he'll learn a lesson or two. What do you think?"

McHern grinned broadly, delighted to be the center of attention. But one of these days, he thought, that bitch Irma will come to heel, his heel.

"I'll do that Irma." Guthrie smiled. She had certainly grown up to be a feisty sort of a woman, tall and strong of body with a well-defined face. Could hold her own. He liked that. Her mother had been that way too. A pity she had married Davy Geddon. A pity! He was already an old, done-man. Arthritis was killing him.

"You'll take a mug of tea?" asked Davy. "The kettle's boiled! Tie the heifer up there McHern and let's go inside. It'll only take a minute."

The heifer was tied to a ring on the wall and they walked to the house. The two collie dogs that had lain stretched out in the sunshine stirred themselves and ambled along, keeping close to Irma's feet.

The clock on the wall by the fireplace measured time with long swings of its pendulum, tick, tock, tick, tock, the slow rhythm giving a feeling of peacefulness to the large farm kitchen. There was a soft glow from the hearth and the smell of hot flour from the griddle. The three men sat quietly in chairs pulled up to the long deal table waiting to be served. Mrs. Geddon set a plate of buttered scones before them along with mugs of tea.

"Has anybody had any word of the men at the front?" Guthrie broke the silence.

"Nope! Not a word," replied Irma's father. "Have you talked to Farley Goode's mother lately?"

"Saw her a couple of Saturdays ago but no word since the last letter before he got shipped off. Nobody knows where for sure but they think it's North Africa. Egypt, they say. The Eighth Army. Up against Rommel, they say!"

"Aye, he was always gae full of fight, Farley was." McHern had the ability to talk and chew his buttered scone at the same time. One cheek protruded out with the quantity of food stuffed into it. "He'll get his fill before this war is over. You can bet!" He reached for his mug of tea, drank and swallowed hard. The bulge in his cheek had gone.

"Why didn't you join up too? Serve your country for a change!" Irma's voice was sharp. She took pleasure at seeing her question bite into his pride.

"I'm needed here so I am. There's no conscription here in Ulster, so there's not. And I'm helping to produce the meat they eat. Fighting's for the glory boys, besides, amn't I in the Home Guard, so I am. Isn't that enough?"

"It's certainly safe enough, that's for sure. Do they issue you with real guns? Or just pick handles?"

McHern blanched. Guthrie saw the warning signs. "Here, Rob, we're wasting time now," he said, stepping in again as a diplomat. "Take that heifer back and let her loose in the top field. You don't need me. You can handle her by yourself. I've some business here with Davy to attend to."

The seemingly inevitable clash between Irma and McHern was put off. McHern rose from the table. He wanted to say something but could find no words. He grabbed his cloth cap and, going out through the door to the yard, screwed it purposefully onto his head. Davy Geddon followed McHern down the slope of the yard to the heifer, his cane moving in sync with his rheumatic leg. "Hang on there Rob!" he called. It was an act of kindness not to let McHern feel badly over being sent about his business. At the bottom of the yard the two men chatted for a few moments and Davy gave him a friendly slap on the back. The heifer took off at a trot pulling McHern after her. The two of them were soon out of sight up the lane. Davy wandered over to the paddock to inspect the bull. He was indeed one fine looking animal, and what horns!

"Guthrie, for goodness sake," said Mrs. Geddon, "that man McHern's an ignorant boor. How you put up with him, I don't know. And Irma, you're to blame. Seem's you only want to provoke him. One of these days he'll let go and you'll be sorry."

"Agh," said Guthrie, "he's a rare one, McHern. But sure he's all I can get in this day and age. Who'll do a day's work on a farm? The young men, what's left of them, can make more money in the Old Bleach or the Linen Mill. Why would they want to work on a farm, for goodness sake? It's hard labor, so it is. And those with less sense have gone off to fight. You can't get anybody. Nobody! And sure he's handy at things." He waved the matter off and turned to face her. "Here now, Mabel, leaving that aside, wasn't I telling Flora she's just like you were, yourself, when you were a lass." There was a touch of devilment in his face, his gray eyes laughing.

Mrs. Geddon smiled. "Prettier than me, Guthrie, so she is. You're getting old and your memory's bad."

"Neither. I'm as spry as ever, so I am. Boys, do you remember way back? Eh? The box-teas up at the Ross and the dance or two? Do you remember them times? We could skip around like two-year olds. That was a while ago, eh?. Wasn't it? Time flies!"

"You're still young," said Irma. "Sure look at you. You could be in your thirties." She poured him more tea, the personal attention carrying a rare hint of the flirt.

"Lord blessus!" said Guthrie. "I'm fifty and proud of it! I've still got thirty years in me. But, maun, if I was young again, Irma, I'm telling you, I'd never be from your doorstep. Sure, but you'd give a man great son's, so you would. Great sons! I mean that kindly, now."

Irma was pleased at this statement from Guthrie, clear and without a hint of lewdness. She saw no malice in the older man's face. He was paying her a compliment. "Maybe I'd have liked that," she said. "You're a better man than many. You put a lot of them to shame, so you do. The stories I've heard."

"No, Irma. No stories. There was only one girl for me."

A quietness settled in the big kitchen broken only by the slow tick of the pendulum clock. Mrs. Geddon fidgeted over the hearth. Irma looked enquiringly at Guthrie but he reached for another scone. The door of the kitchen scraped over the stone step. Davy entered, tapping his stick. "I declare that bull's getting bigger by the minute. Them horns on him are about a mile wide." He chuckled. "He'll soon not be able to go in the barn door."

Guthrie held a scone towards him, turning it a couple of times as if for emphasis. "These are good. Maun, Davy, I miss cooking like this. You've been a lucky man so you have."

Though commonly referred to as old Guthrie, he was indeed a well-preserved youngish man of fifty, lean and rugged of face, about six feet of sinew with iron gray hair. His appearance was marred only by an addiction to chewing tobacco that stained his teeth and often left a rim of black around his lips. Not having a wife who might have urged him, he didn't care much about his appearance except on Sundays when he made his way to church, an event for which he scrubbed himself in a tin tub in front of the hearth, dressed himself in a blue suit and foreswore tobacco for the day.

"Now that you've rented Farley Goode's place, what's the government obliging you to plant this coming year?" asked Davy.

Guthrie had rented Farley Goode's farm since the Territorials had been marched off to the train station. Farley's widowed mother was not capable of taking on this responsibility so, in his obligation to go off to war, Farley had asked Guthrie. They had signed a document in the office of Piddleslop & Piddlslop, Solicitors, Since 1845. "The same. Flax and potatoes and oats just like the government says I must. And I'll under-sow the oats with grass for the herd. I've almost thirty head now. That's enough no matter what the government says. It's all McHern and me can handle. I really need another hand, so I do. In fact the Pastor was out telling me the other day that he has a young fellow that's working in the mill there at the bottom of the town he'd like to get out of bad company. Asked me if I'd be interested in giving him a chance to straighten himself out."

"You don't say. That'll be handy for you. Well, I guess Farley will be home soon," commented Davy, "and you'll be stuck with one hand too many."

"Aye," said Guthrie. "This war will not last much longer. It's not like the Great War, so its not. There'll be no more charging into machine guns. The airplanes will do their stuff from up above there and that will be that. Hit the Gerries from a distance." It was as if he could hear the bugle call to climb out of the trenches, the rat-a-tat of the German machine guns. He shook his head at the futility of it. "Let's hope, anyway."

"Maybe another year at the most," said Davy. "The sooner the better for some people." He looked at his daughter but she showed no sign of interest. That was her way. She could hide her feelings.

"You could be right, Davy. But I remember them days in the trenches. There are some pretty stupid generals, you know; and politicians too. So who knows? Farley Goode could be away for some time. But, the Lord will take care of him."

"Let's hope. What do you say Irma?" said her father. It was another of his many attempts to get his daughter to talk about Farley. She lifted the griddle to a higher link above the hearth. "Them scones are about ready. Guthrie, would you like to take some back with you? Have them for your supper?"

"Well, thank you kindly, Irma. That's very good of you."

"You can even share them with McHern," she added.

"He'll be glad to hear that."

The scones were wrapped in paper, tied with string and handed to Guthrie. "Thanks," he said again. "I'll be off. Must make sure McHern hasn't got himself into trouble. He's a trial, that man. Good seeing you again, Mabel. And you, Irma, you make your father proud."

Her father hobbled alongside Guthrie down the farmyard to the entrance of the lane. They stopped to look across the fence into the paddock and admire the bull.

"A great looking animal, Davy. He's some beast! He sure is. Trust Irma to pick out the right one. Eh?"

Irma placed the five shillings in a tea caddy kept for the purpose of a moneybox. Frequent handling had worn the scenes of China from its sides and the tin shone through. It was older than Irma, but a practical solution to an everyday need. Nothing was thrown out that still had use. "How come Guthrie never got married?" she asked her mother.

"It's a long story."

"Well?"

"He wanted to marry a certain young woman once but, instead, he ran away off to war. Nineteen fourteen. Felt she could wait. And she, well, in the meantime she just preferred another."

"Why?"

Her mother shook her head in the manner of Who knows? "When he came back from France he was a different person. Maybe that was it, too worldly, maybe. Changed, somehow."

"And there were no other women around?"

"Not for him. She was the only girl he ever looked at, then or since."

"Where is she now?"

"Oh, about somewhere."

That was a strange answer Irma thought and felt that her mother knew more than she cared to say. "And the farm? He has no sons or daughters. Who'll inherit those eighty acres?"

"No one, probably. He has no relatives that I know of, or anybody else."

"You mean it will get sold?"

"Aye. And the money'll go to the church. He's pretty tied into the Meeting Hall down there by the railway yard in the town. I've seen the Pastor out at the farm talking to him more than once. I wouldn't be surprised if he'd like to get his hands on it for the church."

Irma was silent as she contemplated this. "That's hardly right. They'll only sell it. It makes no sense, at all."

To Irma a farm was a legacy, something to be passed onto one's children and their children. It was a sacred thing. She thought of her father's farm that would be her's one day and her obligation to have an heir to carry on. She knew she had to get married. She knew a son was expected and was determined to have one. It was the right of the land. "A pity. He must have been a very fine looking man in his youth."

"He was indeed," her mother replied, letting a slight sigh accompany the words. "A fine handsome man, he was. And still is."

"It's a pity he chews tobacco, though."

"Aye. He wasn't always like that. Not when we all went to the dances, like he said, when we were young. When all of us were young." She sighed again.

"Maybe because he never found a woman to take care of him. Men don't do well on their own. They're like bulls in that respect."

"Irma!" Guthrie called. They were at the Fair Hill. "What are you up to this Saturday? Where's your father?" Irma pointed. Her father was looking over some gilt sows and bargaining with the owner. Guthrie came to her side. McHern, his laborer, stood off at a distance. "I was wondering, Irma," old Guthrie said quietly, "if I could have a word with you."

She could see McHern standing in the background watching them. There was the usual leer on his face. "What about?" she asked.

"It's a private matter, you could say." His gray eyes looked at her in an intent way. "Private." He spoke softly as if to avoid being overheard. He looked over his shoulder briefly to make certain that McHern was not standing close. Irma noted that Guthrie was dressed, not in the rough clothes that most men wore to the Fair Hill, but in a blue suit, neatly pressed, the kind she had seen him wear on a Sunday. His shirt was white, with a starched collar and it was obvious that both had been processed at the laundry in town. He wore a tie with the emblems of his regiment during the Great War.

"Can it wait?"

"It could," he smiled, "but not much. I want to show you something." She saw that his face was scrubbed and clean-shaven. He seemed to have paid a visit to the dentist for his teeth were sparkling white and better than she expected from a man of his age. His hair was cut neatly and carried a glint of hair-oil. She smiled back at him as she realized he had made an effort to look his best. Why? In another setting he might have been a schoolteacher, a lawyer, a doctor.

"Can't you show me here?"

"No!" He smiled. "It's out at the farm." He really had good teeth. She remembered her veterinary class at the Dairy College. A sign of health. "It's out at home," he said. "I'd like you to see something I've been working on. I'd really like your opinion. You've been to dairying school and all." Still the earnest gaze.

She realized how much of an effect he must have had on the young women in his youth. Who had that woman in his life been? "What if I come by tomorrow, Sunday, after church? Or early afternoon, before milking?"

"That would be very kind of you. The afternoon's best. But come alone! Leave your father at home. It's your opinion I want. Not his!"

"Sure! Who else would come with me but the dogs? I'll take the dogs with me for a walk. We'll all drop by. How's thon old collie of yours doing?"

"Like me. Getting younger every day." He smiled broadly. Irma had the impression that something was afoot. He did look younger. Perhaps it was a certain happiness that shone from his face. She glanced at McHern. He too was curious.

"I can see," she said and was surprised at herself. She had not talked to a man in this easy way for over a year. Not since well before Farley Goode went away. Perhaps it was just old Guthrie, a friendly sort of uncle figure, no threat, no leers, no hidden motives.

"Well, looks like my Da has bought them gilt sows. So long!"

Guthrie stood watching her walk away. McHern joined him. "She'd make a great hoult, so she would. Broad on the beam. A good breeding woman, thon."

"Hold your tongue, man!" Guthrie said sharply. "Have you no respect?"

McHern backed off. "Hey! Just putting my feelings into words."

"Well don't."

Irma sat in the family pew in church. The Reverend was reading the lesson, a passage from Isaiah from which he was trying to abstract some obscure message. He was a mild man given to searching for meaning within the scriptures and applying it to the routine lives of his congregation, farmers and shop-keepers for the most part; some were employees of the linen mill or other commerce and a couple were school teachers.

"The voice said, Cry. And he said, What shall I cry? All flesh is grass, and all the goodliness thereof is as the flower of the field."

The Reverend, installed behind a tall pulpit, was doing his best to reach his flock with homilies that his sheep could understand. Irma heard the words in the distance of her thoughts. She heard the singsong of his Belfast accent and knew he had never in his life set foot in the lush grass of a pasture. *"All flesh is grass!"* It was meaningless. She saw his robes with the scarlet hood that denoted his University degrees—a man of learning. What if he were to see her prize bull grazing that grass and the herd of cows that produced their milk from it? The choir behind him looked down from their balcony, their faces composed in Sunday reverence. In front of her she saw a miscellany of backs-of-heads, tanned necks and ladies hats. There was a faint odor of peat smoke and mothballs. They sat immobile. This was their Sunday ritual, rain, hail or shine. *"And on the seventh day thou shalt rest!"* These were her people. It was what they did without question. *"It is written!"* Just like they farmed. It was what they were born to do, strong of muscle and belief.

"The grass withereth, the flower fadeth: but the word of our God will stand forever."

The Reverend was getting to the point of his sermon. But Irma thought only of her father's farm, of Farley Goode's farm that lay next to it, Guthrie's farm farther on. *"All flesh is grass!"* She decided to take a look at the lower fields and check if they would graze several bullocks during the coming summer. Yes, she decided, she'd talk that over with her father after church. And she'd ask around the neighboring farms as to what male calves were available. There'd be a bit of money in it. Grass meant beef. Beef meant money. Money meant land. Land meant grass. Grass meant beef. *"All flesh is grass!"* Maybe that was the point the Reverend was searching for. He wasn't such a bad fellow after all. She perked up her attention to get a better grasp of the meaning of the sermon but the Reverend was calling for the last hymn. Oh well!

Irma drove the old car slowly through town, headed back home. She was amongst the few who had a petrol ration because of the farm. She used it sparingly, reserving as much as possible for the Sunday trip to church. "I'll drop by Guthrie's place this afternoon, I think, and see if he has any bull calves he'd like to sell," she said to her father.
"Oh?"
"For the meadow. We could graze about six head for a wheen of weeks and then leave it for hay."
"And then?"
"Run them with the cows. We've enough grass for six more head."
"You're always thinking, Irma, so you are," said her mother. "Money! Even on a Sunday. Won't you take time to have weeuns? That's what a woman's for. Don't I get to have grandchildren, for God's sake?"
"You will. You will. As soon as I find the right man."
"There's Farley Goode, so there is. Isn't he the right man for you?"
"What good does it do to answer that if he's off somewhere in this war and I'm here and he never even writes?"
"It's war time. They don't allow them to write much. It's all censored. For

all you know he has written already only they censored it. Thon Peacock fellah, Farley's china, wrote one a few weeks ago and it was all cut about with scissors. You could hardly make out what he was trying to say. Only that he was in good health and all the lads from the town were together in the same Battery. Don't worry, he said, tell everyone I'm doing fine. That includes you Irma, so it does. Farley was maybe sending you a message too."

"He should have stayed home," said Irma simply. "He had a farm to take care of. He'd no business joining up."

"He was called up. He was in the Territorials. He had no choice."

The young men had been whisked off one Sunday morning after the church parade; the Territorials, young men dressed in khaki enjoying the lark of parading around in uniform carrying a rifle, the girls watching. Now all of them were overseas, that was all anyone knew. Farley might even then be dead. But then, if he were, there would be a telegram. At least that was the bright side.

"So what, Ma. He's not reliable. Even before the war. Always gallivanting instead of looking after his land. Besides he never had time for me. It was that Elsie Peacock he was courting, not me. He was never away from her place."

"Agh, sure it was only because he was great with Elsie's brother. That's all. Buddies. Willie Peacock was his china. Sure they're in the Battery together. They both were in the Territorials. Men have their best pals, like your Da and Guthrie. Elsie Peacock just happened to be there. Coincidence, nothing more. Willie's sister. That's all. Farley Goode's a fine young man, so he is. None finer. He'd make a right husband for you."

Farley Goode was the kind of son Mrs. Geddon would have liked to have had, strong of body and spirit, a staunch Orangeman and member of the congregation at First Presbyterian. One day Farley would inherit eighty acres, fine land that lay into the Geddon's own farm. Eighty and sixty would make one hundred and forty of the best acres in the Braid Valley. It would make a nice match. Her grandson would do well, maybe several grandsons. As the mother of an only daughter Mrs. Geddon was convinced her daughter would produce sons. If only the right man! Farley Goode was that man. There were moments of despair when Mrs. Geddon thought of how this fine young man might become a casualty of the war. It did not bear thinking about. He was meant for Irma, even though Irma did not know it yet.

"Ma, listen to me. I'll make my own mind up. So stop worrying. And forget Farley Goode. He's at war. And I'm here. And there are more important things to worry about."

During the mid-day meal they listened to the wireless, hoping for better news of the war. There was the report that the German army had advanced across North Africa and held both Tripoli and Benghazi. The wireless, dependant on a wet battery and a wire aerial strung between two trees, whined and whistled. Her father rose and switched it off. "Damnit! Well, it looks like the Gerries have the upper hand for now. Agh oh! We'll not see Farley for some time. His mother will be in despair. Thank God Guthrie's taking care of the farm. Ah well!" He sat down, tired. Life was not working out as he would have wished.

There was little talk amongst them from then on and that only of who had been seen at church. Mrs. Geddon had not attended and she was eager to know. The meal over, Irma put on a pair of walking shoes and placed a straw hat on her head. She still wore her Sunday dress with the flowered pattern. It was one of only two dresses she possessed. Around her neck she wore a string of pearls that had come handed-down to her.

"It's too early to bring in the cows," said her mother. "Where you off to?"

"Taking a walk, me and the dogs. It's a nice afternoon, so it is."

"Oh?"

"So you're passing by Guthrie's?" said her father. "Now, don't be offering too much for them calves, if he has any. Deal for them. You'll get more respect."

"It's a Sunday, Irma!" said Mrs. Geddon. "Can't you wait until tomorrow?"

Irma nodded her head and was out the door. The two dogs ran beside her, happy at the prospect of a walk.

Guthrie set a kettle of water to boil on the new iron range he had installed in the kitchen. Beads of moisture rolled down the sides of the kettle to hiss and spit as they touched the red hot metal top of the stove. An orange enameled teapot stood to one side, the lid off, two spoonfuls of tealeaves already in the bottom awaiting the boiling water. Two cups, set in saucers, sat on the scrubbed pine table along with spoons, a jug of milk, a bowl of sugar and six cupcakes he had bought the previous day in town. The cupcakes were arranged in a neat circle on a plate. Black raisins poked their heads through the icing. A sticky roll of flypaper hung from the ceiling by the door to intercept any flies that might enter.

Guthrie had spent the evening of the Saturday and had not gone to church on Sunday morning so as to have the house looking clean and tidy. The flagstones of the floor looked scrubbed. The brass toasting fork with the scene of Cardiff Castle at the tip of the handle—a present to his late mother from an old aunt who had visited Wales—was polished and hung on the chimney wall above the stove. The two pictures depicting the "Travels of John Bunyon" in one and the "Broad and Narrow Way" in the other had been dusted and the backs checked for cobwebs. But there was a square of lighter colored wall where the photograph of the woman he had once loved had hung. He had removed it and placed it in the cupboard. It would not be right, he felt, even though bygones were bygones, to have it hanging there. Women had a different feeling about those things.

He stood in the center of the kitchen and looked around him. All was in order. His mother, had she lived, could not have done it better. The willow pattern plates that she had so much loved were washed, dried and set up in a neat row on the dresser shelf. A fresh bucket of water with the lid on tight sat below, ready for any thirst. And, as a last thought, Guthrie had put a new toilet roll in the outside privy just in case, instead of the usual dated newspapers. He had dressed in his go-to-church clothes once again though this time he wore an argyle pullover instead of a coat, and shoes instead of boots. It made him look younger he thought, sort of sporty like the young men in the advertisements. His heart was beating fast in expectation of his visitor. He positioned himself by the window to watch. She would probably come up the back lane. That was the short cut. Maybe there was still time to take another look at the byre where he had spent so many hours of labor these last months. It too was clean and spotless, shining even. He had made certain of that after the morning milking. McHern had not been too pleased claiming he had a church parade but Guthrie had insisted that he wash down the floors and stands a second time. Guthrie was pleased. He felt like a young man. There was a sense of excitement running through him. He could hardly wait.

Irma did take the short cut. The dogs ran ahead of her poking their noses into every bush and clump of grass. One never knew where a rabbit might be hiding. They were in great fettle, working the roadsides in tandem. Who would get one first? The trees were in full leaf, birds working on their nests. There were sheep clustered on the hills, lambs with tails turning like whirligigs. To the east, the mount of Slemish rose like a hump on the horizon colored purple from the heather in bloom. A row of trees stood along a skyline. It was great to be alive. Irma breathed in the aroma of late May, the bright yellow flowers of the gorse, the white of the hawthorn and the purple heather. This was the life. This was the land she loved, the Braid Valley.

One dog barked. Irma came out of her thoughts. Both dogs began to bark, then run forward, their tails wagging. They knew this person standing in the road. They knew the cottage off by the side. They had been here before. They smelled his trouser legs, twisting their bodies in gleeful recognition of McHern.

"Irma! It's yourself?" He stood in the middle of the narrow road, legs apart, arms folded. He was dressed in the khaki battledress of the Home Guard. A pick handle protruded from where it was held under his left armpit. There was a playful grin on his face. "What brings you here on a Sunday afternoon?"

Even from several paces Irma could see that he was drunk. "I'm taking a walk," she said. "Giving the dogs some exercise."

"I see. But why up my bit of the road? Never knew you to come by here."

"Just out walking. Come boys," she called the dogs that had wandered off to some bushes. "Skkkkgg, skkkggg!" Her tongue clicked an order for them to follow. She noted McHern had washed and shaved and, taking into consideration the Home Guard uniform, had probably been to a Church parade at First Ballyaghone, the Church of Ireland in the town.

"Not so fast, Irma. I need to talk to you. Step in. Want to tell you a couple of things." Now she could smell his breath. His eyelids were none too steady. "Come on! It'll only be a minute." Without thinking, Irma accompanied him into the cottage. The dogs followed her, rushing into every corner to smell it out. He threw the pick handle into a corner. "You're a great looking woman, Irma. And a great worker too," he said, "just like your father says. He must be proud. I'd be proud too. I would. Yes I would." Some gas from the stout he had drunk pushed up his gullet. "Sorry! Didn't expect you to be coming round these parts today. Wouldn't have had that last bottle. Won't you sit down? It's not every day a man like me has the pleasure of a lady in his abode. I'm just an ordinary farm laborer. Not even a gentleman like some, nor a handsome fellah like aul' Guthrie. Would you like a bottle of stout?"

Irma realized that the stout had mellowed McHern to a point where he would soon become maudlin. Irma stood where she was. "Why don't you sit down yourself? I have to be off. Go on. Sit down."

"Don't want to sit down." McHern looked at her with drunken eyes.

"Anyway, I want to tell you something." His eyes tried to focus on Irma, looking into her eyes, while his mind searched for the words. "I want you to marry me. I'd make a great husband, so I would. I'm a great worker too, just like you." He tried valiantly to put the words together without a slur. "Will you marry me? Will you?"

Irma had never expected McHern to make a statement of his affections. Compared to the arrogant person with the leer on his face, the person before her was a pathetic creature. She would have preferred his arrogance. That she could have dealt with. "You're drunk," she said. "You don't know what you're saying. I have to be off. Guthrie is waiting for me."

"So it's that auld fart you prefer. Is it? B'Jazus!" His eyes sunk into the flesh of their sockets and his face lost its color. "Leading me on to make a fool of myself. Is that it? You and your snooty ways! Well!" He grabbed her round the waist and pulled her hard towards him. She could smell the sick stench of his sour stomach as his breathing snorted through his throat and nose. She struggled against him as he tried to press his lips to hers.

"Let me go or I'll scream!" she cried.

"Scream then!"

He tripped her to the ground and all semblance of his drunkenness vanished. He was a raging bull in his fight to get a-top her body. He had one arm pinned behind her back, the other caught under his armpit. Irma tightened her muscles for one great effort to throw him off. "Bite him!" she screamed as she arched her body upwards. The dogs seemed to sense at last that the struggle was no parlor game. Irma screamed again and the dogs responded. Suddenly they were snarling and biting whatever part of McHern they could grab. He turned his attention to defending himself. One ear was badly bitten and blood spouted down his face. He was dragged back by one leg as the greater of the two collies pulled him by an ankle. "Let go, you bastard! For Christ's sake! Let go! Call them off! Hey! Agh Jesus!" McHern twisted round to address the fury of the dogs, leaving Irma free. She got to her feet, opened the door and sprinted out into the fresh air. She whistled and the two dogs came running. They were jumping against her as if in thanks for the great sport they had just enjoyed. Their tails wagged. Their bodies twisted back and forth in delight. "Let's do that again, sometime!" they seemed to say.

"Godscurse you, you bitch. You'll regret the day." McHern stumbled to the door, holding a hand on his chewed and torn ear. "Damn you!" he yelled. "I'll not forget, you stuck-up bitch! Go to your aul' Guthrie, the aul' fart. You can have him. He's all you're worth, damnit. An aul' run-down man, so he is.

One foot in the grave! Aye! He's about your match, so he is. Go on! I never meant a word of what I said. Not a word of it. Who'd want you, anyway? You've no blood in you. None! None at all! Half dead like aul' Guthrie, so you are. Sure! You'd be some cold squeeze for any man foolish enough to take you to bed. Agh, you're a waste of my breath. To Hell with you!"

Irma, running with the dogs bounding along beside her, was soon out of earshot. She stopped to get her breath. Her heart was pounding. She doubled over to relieve the stitch in her side. It was then she noted the condition of her dress, torn across the bodice, one sleeve fallen down. There was a hole in the knees of her stockings. For the first time in many years Irma began to cry with relief of tension. She sat down on the bank of the lane, amongst the yellow gorse and let the tears run. The two dogs crept up close and nudged their wet nose against her arms and legs. They were happy with themselves and wanted her to be happy too. Why wait around here? There was more adventure probably around the next bend. Let's go, they seemed to say and bounded off. Irma sat for some time, her head buried in her lap, forearms around her head.

"Irma, what's wrong?" The firm hand of Guthrie touched her shoulder. "What's wrong with you?"

Irma looked up and instinctively placed both forearms across her breasts. One hand explored her neck. "My pearls! My string of pearls! They're gone!"

They sat at the table in Guthrie's farmhouse. He poured two cups of tea, added milk and sugar and slid one carefully across to Irma making certain it did not slop onto the saucer. "This will help," he said softly. "Drink up."

Irma rocked slowly back and forth in her chair. Her face was tight with determination. "One day I'll kill him," she said. She fiddled with the safety pins that held the cloth across her breasts. Guthrie placed a calming hand over Irma's.

"Take your tea, Irma, please. Don't fret so. I'll deal with him. Just stay calm."

Guthrie looked steadily at Irma. He had so many plans for this afternoon. All the work of the last three months and the anxiety he had suffered. All gone! He could not go forward with it now. If only he had gone to fetch her with his pony and trap by now he would have had some indication of what she felt. Instead, McHern had spoiled it all with his lack of breeding. "What can you expect from a pig but a grunt!" he said.

Irma stopped rocking. There were the beginnings of a smile. "That's a good one. Where'd you get that?"

"One of my father's sayings. He was a rustic philosopher."

"I must remember that." She sipped some of her tea. "Do you always make it so strong?"

"Aye, I do." He watched, hoping.

"I see you've put in a new range. I wish my Da would get us one. My Ma would appreciate it."

"Well it's hardly likely now with the war on. All iron and scrap is being taken to make guns. They've even lifted the railway lines running up to Larne. I just got that stove in time or I'm sure they'd have had that too. Did you see they took the railings down from around the Model School? And up at the Academy too? If I'd have known your mother wanted a range she could have had it. I've no real need anyway. There's only me here. Just me. I don't need a big range like this to cook for only myself. It was just a notion I had. I kinda got to dreaming a bit. You know how it is."

Irma had risen and was inspecting the range. She noted the number of rings on the surface where four pots could be cooking at one time. She saw the water boiler and the oven with two separate shelves. The handles and knobs shone silver, the rest a shiny black. "It's very nice." She looked around her. "You know, I haven't been in this house for years. The last time was when my father brought me here about ten years ago. He was buying a horse from you or something."

"Aye, auld Hector, a half Clydesdale. I remember well. You were looking very bonny indeed."

"You remember?"

"You looked just like your mother did at that age. How could I forget?"

She noted that the walls were still the same color of ripened oats, darkened over time from the smoke of the open hearth that had existed before the range had been installed. "I'm going to give them a coat of distemper," he said.

"You're missing a picture there," she said pointing to the lighter colored rectangle on the wall. She turned to him with a smile. "What happened? Who was it?"

He hesitated for a moment unsure of how to answer. And then, "What do you think of white?" He kept his eyes intently on hers. "To brighten up the place. What would you say?" She could divine that he had avoided answering and now he was looking for her approval. But why? "I'm planning an indoor toilet and bath. With running water and a tank for hot water connected to the boiler in the range. There's a place to connect it up. Look! Do you see there?" He pointed to the range. "That's where I'll connect up."

"Is this what you wanted to show me?"

"Partly. Do you want to see the rest?"

She had relaxed from the stress of the encounter with McHern and was now curious as to why she was invited by Guthrie, why all the renovations?

"Come!" He took her arm and led her out of doors. "Do you remember the old byre I had, the one with hardly any light and you couldn't whip a cat in it?" She nodded and he smiled. "Come! Look!" Before her was a new building built as an extension to the old; its new corrugated zinc roof shone in the sunlight. It had five windows along its front and three doors, all painted red in strong contrast to the whitewashed walls. "This is why?" He pointed. "Aye. Come inside. Look!" With great pride he showed her the new stands and drinking fountains for the cows, the pressure lanterns that hung from the ceiling, the easy cleaning system that drained the manure out to a midden. "How does that compare with your Dairy College? Eh?"

At that moment Irma knew he was asking for her approval. She had the training, the education, and the skills. Apart from her father no man had ever asked her for an opinion on matters of running a farm. Yet here was Guthrie, a man of great ability, a man who was respected throughout the townland, asking. "What do you think?" he said again.

Irma took her time. Her thoughts scrambled over each other as she sought to come to a clear understanding of what the moment could mean. She thought of Farley Goode and his carefree outlook on life, the farm he had inherited and abandoned to run off to war. She thought of the lout McHern and what he represented. There were many like him. She thought of the gentleness of Guthrie and who, even as a man of fifty years was still building for the future. But why? At the same age her father was prematurely aged and crippled with arthritis. Guthrie was alive and full of enthusiasm. But why? He was certainly not planning to die and give his farm to the church. Guthrie had plans for the future. Was he asking her approval as a test to find if what he had to offer would please some woman, the woman he had not found over twenty years before? The photograph that had been removed from the wall in the kitchen? Who had it been? The thought brought a smile to her lips. She had become his confident, as old friend, a sort of temporary substitute for the friend her father had been for years, except this was a matter for an expert to judge. Guthrie clearly valued her as an expert. That was why he had asked her to be there. But who was the woman? Irma thought carefully about her reply. She would draw him out. "I truly think it's a great pity," she spoke slowly and calmly, with great concern for the meaning of each word, "you do not have a son to inherit all this." She looked at him. "I really mean that. He would be proud of you."

Guthrie could feel his heart pounding. He took a deep breath to hide his emotion. "Aye." He swallowed hard. He could feel his eyes becoming moist and turned away for fear she would see his weakness. He cursed within that McHern had ruined his plan. It was not the day to say what he wanted to say. She had already had too much pain. Another day perhaps. He walked down the still bright cement to a lantern and removed it from its hook. "You see. These are the latest things from Sweden. They're the best. I got six of them. They were the last in stock, what with the war and all." He was talking fast to fill in between them. "They run on paraffin oil and you pump them up to get the pressure and put a little methylated spirits in here and a match and let it warm..."

Irma listened to his talk knowing he was avoiding a reply to her comment. What did it matter anyway who the woman was in the photograph? He had taken it down. It was over. She had probably married someone else a long time ago. "Guthrie!" she said. "You need a son. Why build all this if you don't have a son. You can't give this to the church. They'd only sell it for money and spend it on who knows what. It's your life all this, and your father's before you. You've got to have a son. Find a wife. You're still a strong man."

He turned towards her and there was agony in his face. "No Irma, that day's gone."

And then she knew. "It's not Guthrie. Guthrie, listen to me," she said. "You once said I was a woman that could give a man great sons."

"Agh, it was just a notion."

"No, Guthrie, listen. I'd be proud to give you that son. I'd be proud to be the wife of Guthrie Wilcox. I'll give you that son, Guthrie. I too need a son. Just ask me. Ask me, Guthrie!"

He reached forward his hands and held hers. There was no embrace, just the moment of looking inwardly on each other, unspoken thoughts passing between them.

"Will you marry me, Irma, and give us both a son?"

"I will Guthrie. Several, if it pleases God."

FEATHERS

Farley Goode's last day on earth was the Twelfth of July the year after the war ended; the Second World War that is. There was no warning such a thing would happen, there seldom is. He was a strapping, big-hearted fellow with eighty of the best acres coming to him some day—a great catch for some lass. And there were plenty of them chasing him, like Irma, auld man Geddon's daughter, herself falling into sixty-five acres that lay alongside Farley's upper fields.

That Twelfth morning started off well, like it's apt to do, with the Lambeg drums warming up Lodge by Lodge, away in the distance over the fields. Whap, whap, whappety, whap, like they were talking to each other, a noise that seemed to rumble over the hayfields and burns and rattle the dishes on the kitchen dressers of the scattered farms.

With the milking done and the churns set out at the end of the lane, Farley scrubbed off the smell of sweat and cows in the zinc tub in the scullery, hip deep in sudsy water, knees up under his chin. Three years in the Western Desert had left its mark. He was very tanned of face and neck but the rest of him was pale. Later it was something folks made a point of saying when the story was told and told again. No one could understand why it had happened, even those who had served with him in the Artillery.

Farley Goode had returned from the war as a man starting life anew. At least he thought. He had seen battle. He had seen death. He had traveled foreign places, seen other cultures and races, languages and religions, Cairo, Alexandria, Tobruk, Naples and Rome. He had discovered he had a talent for languages and picked up a passable smattering of Arabic and Italian. He had sampled their food, their music and their women and yet, ever since the bombing of Alexandria, when the noise and mayhem of the German bombardment had died down enough to allow him to think, he yearned for only one place and that was County Antrim. Home was where he wanted to

MUSIC ON THE WIND

be, in the Braid Valley, within sight of Slemish.

"What's the first thing you want to do most?" Willie Peacock of the Battery asked him one sweltering night while sipping beer, about a week before the bombardment.

"I want to walk on the Twelfth of July with Ballyclug Orange Lodge, so I do," he said slowly and with great certainty.

"You do? I thought there'd be some lass you'd want to grab a hold of."

"Nah! I'm going to be right up front there, with the banner and the swordsmen, beating a Lambeg drum. Did you know that? I can beat a Lambeg like no other man."

"Sure I know. Weren't we in the Lodge together? Well, here's to you," said Willie and they swallowed down a couple of gulps of beer. "Goddam that auld tattoo. It's still smarting." Willie pulled his arm round the better for Farley to see. "Whatja think? Isn't that a good one, hi? A peacock! Just like my name. Got that a couple of days ago." The two men fell silent. Two women of the house, their bellies round and soft, dangled silk veils invitingly over their table. Willie waved them away. "Impshie! G'wan! Beat it!" He turned to Farley. "You know what I want to do, first thing? Me, I'm going to take my bike and ride down to the shore at Carnlough and take a stroll on the pebbles. Get my feet wet in the Irish Sea. Then I'm simply going into Ballyaghone on a Saturday night for a fish-supper at Caulfield's and watch a good Western at the Picture House. Then home! Home! Can you imagine that?"

Farley could. Home! Even in the desert he could remember the smells of his mother's farm, all eighty acres of it, and the pig-fattening unit he had built himself; and the cow-byre where fifteen shorthorns were milked daily. But that was before the war. "You know, Willie, it's a wheen of years."

"Sure I know. Didn't we all think you crazy to up and go like you did. I had one hell of a job looking after them pigs when you went away. But me too, when the war broke out, I up and left too. It's luck we both ended up in the same battery. The Eighth Army, by heavens! Who would have thought?"

When Farley had towelled and dressed in his blue suit, white shirt and red tie he was still every inch a soldier that not even the civvies could disguise. Even the haircut, which he'd got at Storey's Barber Shop on Queen's Street the day before—close cropped on the sides until the skin shone through and the top plastered down with two drops of Brilliantine.

"Perfetto!"

"Ye look fine, so ye do!" said his mother.

"Shukran!

She was used by now to the strange words he used since his return home. She liked it in a way. It was proof he had seen the world, all those foreign places she could only read about, and then mostly in her Bible—Egypt, Palestine, Jordan and Rome. "Here's yer sash. Yer father wore it afore ye." With great care she stood on tiptoe and lifted it over his bent down head. "There now." She was proud of her big son. He had come back alive and a hero. Now he'd wear his father's sash with the golden fringe and the silver, mystic emblems of the Orange Order. Later, that too was seen as something strange.

"Che bella."

"An' yer bowler hat."

He placed it on his head and gave it his characteristic couple of turns, as if screwing it into place. It sat low over the eyes so that he held his head back. He was once again a soldier on parade. "My gloves, Ma, per favore. Grazie!" He did a music hall parody of an Italian, a little soaked in wine, putting on his gloves. "Multo bene. Shukran." It didn't bother him to mix two languages together. "Agh, sure that's the way we codded each other in the Battery," he explained with a long-toothed laugh. "Eyetie or Arabic, what the hell!"

That was how he was seen that morning, a happy man. But Mr. Peece and Johnny McGee thought him a bit standoffish at the Fair Hill the previous Saturday though they themselves had welcomed the man with open arms. "We need you on the Town Council, Farley, so we do," said Mr Peece. "We need a man like you who has traveled and seen foreign lands. A man like you can get things done. Hey Johnny! Johnny McGee, there!" he called to a man ambling across the Fair Hill. "Meet Farley Goode, here. Used to be a pupil of mine when I taught Latin at the Academy. Became a tycoon in fattening pigs before the war. Took my advice, so he did. Didn't you now, Farley, my man?"

"Hello there!" said Johnny McGee with a wide smile. "Mr. Peece has told me a lot about you."

"All good I hope!"

"Och aye. Great stuff. Maun, how I envy you. I never made it into the services. Bad feet. But I was in the Home Guard. Best I could do. You were a corporal in the artillery, I understand. Boys that's great. Eighth Army! Great! And an Orangeman too."

"Sure. Ballyclug. I joined way back before the war."

"Well that's great. Right enough!"

"Johnny," said Mr Peece, "wouldn't he be the very man to run for Town

MUSIC ON THE WIND

Council? What do you think Farley? We need red-blooded men that can speak up and get things done. Like you setting up your pig fattening years ago. You're known for that. With a military record like yours you would be great for the Council. You could even be Mayor one day. What do you think?"

"You're moving kinda fast, there, Mr Peece. I've only just got demobbed and I'll tell you the truth, the first thing I'm goin' to do is walk on the Twelfth. I've been longing for that these good several years."

"Boys, that's great!" said Johnny McGee.

"Isn't it though," said Mr. Peece. "I tell you what. I'm on the platform at the Field this year and it'll be a real privilege to have you up there with us. Wouldn't it Johnny? Be good for you when you run for the Town Council. All the folks need to know who you are. You might even say a few words so you might. What do you say?"

"Och, sure you're away ahead of me."

"Don't worry, now. I'll set it up. There's a power of people need to shake your hand."

"A war hero!" said Johnny. "Great! Did you get to kill any Gerries, hi, when you were out there?" Johnny's face was aglow with pleasure. Just standing beside a real hero of the war, a man who had been through the battle of Alamein, was a thrill. "Did you kill any, hi? How many?"

Farley looked at the poor miserable soul of Johnny McGee. Johnny would never understand. "Lots," Farley said quietly and walked away. Mr Peece was upset. The former schoolmaster resented being left like that. "Where you going," called Mr Peece. Farley paused in his step and turned calmly. "I've decided I need to do something, something for a fellow who can't be here. I'll maybe cycle down to the shore at Carnlough and walk barefoot on the pebbles. Maybe step into the water." They looked at him in puzzlement. "And then I'm going to eat a fish supper at Caulfield's, and maybe go to the pictures." They shook their head in puzzlement. Later it would be remembered. Farley walked away.

"Jesus!" said Johnny after a few moments. "Did you hear what he said? He's killed lots of Gerries, he said."

"Didn't I tell you," said Mr Peece. "He's the man we want."

As the Ballyclug Lodge began its walk to the Field, auld man Geddon's daughter Irma had wheeled the milk churns down to the end of his lane in the barrow. It was noted by those attending the procession, that she was not in her usual dungarees but dressed, as they said, in her Sunday best, "lookin' very unlike hersel', she was that dolled-up! Looking very pretty an' as if she had some place to go."

Her father sprawled across the four-barred gate and studied the procession before him. He was known for his commentaries on everything and anybody that caught his gaze. And there were those that remembered what he said that morning and brought it up later. "Thon young Farley Goode, thonder," he offered by way of an opener, "is as red-blooded a fellah as I ever did see." The noise from the lambeg drums and the piercing of the fifes was intense at such short distance away. "Blood tae the claws!"

"How's that Da?" shouted Irma. She kept her eyes on Farley, one of four sturdy fellows stripped to shirtsleeves, each harnessed to an enormous Lambeg drum that hung before them. They blattered in unison. Whap-whap-whappety-whap.

"Farley Goode, from over the way! Ye went to school together, don't ye mind? Ye hain't seen him since he come back from the war. That's him thonder. Maun, can he blatter a drum! Blood tae the claws!"

Irma had seen him! Had spoken to him in town at the Fair Hill one Saturday and felt her heart leap like it used to before the war began, and Farley a wild thing and neither of them had a care in the world. He had somehow changed. "Hope ye're keepin' bravely," was all he seemed able to say. The smiles that spread over his long white teeth were no longer there. "Good to see ye again, Irma. I heard ye got married," he said

"Yes, I did. But he passed away suddenly. A heart attack."

"I'm so sorry." He looked at her for a moment and then, "I must get going." He shook her hand as if with a stranger. He had never done that before. Shaking hands was something he must have picked up abroad, so strange, so distant, so foreign. "Chiao!" he walked away as if wanting to escape.

"Chiao?" she had said to her father. "What in the name of the Almighty? Has he come back crazy?"

Later she saw him talking to a young woman she knew vaguely, an Elsie Peacock, and she felt an agony in her stomach at the sight of them together. He was smiling. She knew he was. She could see his long white teeth. Why hadn't she waited for him? It was only a few years. He would have come back to her.

"I declare," said her father, "he's made o' great stuff, like his aul' Da when me an' him were in the Boer War t'gither. I'm tellin ye, hi!" he nodded his head and winked at the same time. "I hear Mr. Peece has great plans for him."

He looked at his daughter, his only child, who would one day inherit his farm. They were close companions, she working the farm almost on her own, ever since his rheumatism began to limit his movement, since she was fourteen. Now she was a widow. He looked at Farley Goode and he hoped, for her sake. "I was sayin' he's made o' good stuff. Blood tae the claws! Don't ye know! Make sure ye invite him here tonight for the fun. Mr. Peece'll be here an' Johnny McGee."

"I know. I know. Haven't I been baking all week!"

Davy Geddon looked at his daughter. She was still young. A widow. And there was the farm.

The procession of Loyal Orange Lodges made its way along the Antrim Line towards town and the Field that was the designated gathering place out the Galgorm Road. Ahead of the drums walked the sword carriers, solemn-faced men as befitted this responsibility, each one sashed and bowler hated, dazzling white gloves on their hands and a firm grip on the majesty of the claymore laid at sixty degrees across the shoulder. To these men, newly returned from the war, it was like holding a rifle. Their backs were ramrod straight and bowler hats a little too pulled-down over their eyes as if military issue and they were on parade. They were chosen men, returned from the war as heroes, men who deserved to be honored in this fashion. Some of them took turns beating a drum and passed their sword in the meantime to the man they relieved, just as Farley had done. Now he was back as a sword carrier. Somewhere behind him on the footpath, Irma walked along. She could see him and kept him in sight all the way.

The parade made its way past the Memorial Park with its nicely kept bushes and grass and the monument to The Fallen in the War of 1914. There were those amongst the men who turned their heads to the right as in a military salute to the dead. Then past the Railway Station and out the road to the Field where each Lodge found a spot for its men to cluster.

Most of the people gathered in the Field were men because Walking was something men did. The day was a day to see men at their best, clean-shaven, well dressed and well behaved. Dark blue suits with white shirts made up the standard garb. There were also women, young men, young ladies and miscellaneous youths. The ladies were able to take liberties with print dresses and now and then a wide brimmed straw hat with flowers stuck around it. The wee lads ran about everywhere getting grass stains on knees and elbows.

People drifted about to visit the tea stands, sip lemonade, chat with the ladies, slap old buddies on the back and laugh at long remembered escapades. "Hello, there!" and "Sure I haven't seen ye in donkey's years. Are ye bravely?" and "Maun but ye're lookin' like yersel', hi!" There was a general feeling of joy that the war was over and life had returned to what it should be. But Farley, people remembered, seemed odd. Irma looked for him. She needed to extend the invitation. She found him just as one of his army buddies walked up.

Farley felt a hand on his shoulder.

"Gunner Goode!"

"Crikey! It's you, Alan! Alan McMullin! Kaif halak?"

"Multo bene. Ham'dalialah!" said Alan, also not one bit perturbed at mixing two languages. They had both served in the Eighth Army in North Africa and Italy and picked up a smattering, first of Arabic and then of Italian. It was used now to cement the bond between men who had faced the enemy together, first in anti-aircraft gun sites around the harbor of Alexandria and later as lorry drivers hauling surrendered Italian soldiers to internment camps. Later they had been part of the forces fighting their way up the boot of Italy.

"It's great to see you, Alan. La mama? Cuomo e la moglie?"

Alan laughed. "Ye could always handle the lingo, Farley. Ye should ha' been a schoolteacher, so ye should! The moglie's great. Ye're not marriet yersel' yet, are ye? No bint in yer life?"

"Naw! No girl in my life. But, I got to get my feet under me with a bit of money, first. Living out at the farm for the moment. It's badly run down."

Irma listened from a little distance, hesitant to walk up and say hello. The men talked as those who are catching up after a long absence, raucous laughter, backslapping and a few good-natured punches on the arm. The feeling of comradeship was strong. They were joined by another comrade and another. Soon they were a group of six, Farley, Alan, Billy Tresdale, Matt Henry, Harry Duff and Wee Mickey Gilroy.

"If we find any more of you lads," said Farley, "we'll have the whole Battery, so we will." It was the trademark word for those who served as gunners. The Battery! They wandered aimlessly down the Field talking excitedly together, pushing each other a little to emphasize some point or stopping to gesticulate in some grotesque parody of an Arab or Italian caught in some devilish foreign intrigue around the military camp. The celebration of the Twelfth was completely forgotten and they were reliving the greatest moments of their lives. Irma followed in the hope there would be another opportunity.

"Farley!" Johnny McGee came forward. "Hey there, Farley. We've been looking for you, you know."

"Who?"

"Mr. Peece and me. You're wanted up on the platform."

"Nah! Not me."

"Aw come on. Mr. Peece wants you."

"Were ye in the Forces, hi?" someone asked Johnny.

"Unfortunately not. My feet. Too flat. I was in the Home Guard though." All eyes scrutinized him. There was a quiet moment.

"We had no choice, had we boys," said Matt. "Do ye remember? Us thinkin' it was just another church parade."

"It was a full kit parade, for God's sake! Ye might have guessed."

"Well ye didn't an' neither did any of us. None of us!"

They fell quiet as they remembered, the realization slowly growing that day as they neared the railway station. This was it. Left, right, left, right. Eyes to the front! If there was family on the footpath they couldn't see them. The engine whistled a couple of long piercing blasts. They were off.

"Harry tells me Canada is the place to go now that the war's over," said Billy. "Great place to get a start. Didn't ye say that, Harry?"

"If that's what you want. There's lots of opportunities in Canada, so there is."

"Nah!" Alan said. "I like it here. Everywhere's the same. Only here ye can drink the water. I remember the time in Cairo when I had the skitters for a week." It was the comment they all were waiting for. Another jumped in, "It was the same in Naples, for God's sake. Aqua or moya, in any language it's a cupful of germs. No place like home, so there's not."

"Irma!" At last Farley had seen her. "Come meet some of the men from the Battery."

"Hello!" she said. They nodded to her in turn. Two of them mentioned not having seen her in a long while. She made a polite reply. They stood in silence as if her presence had interrupted their enjoyment. They had heard she had married an older man in the first year of the war after the men had shipped out. There had been negative comments on why she had not waited for someone of her own age. And now she was widowed. They were uncomfortable. "My father," she said, "would like if you all would come over tonight to our place and share supper with us. And he'll have some refreshments, so he will." They gave polite smiles, nodding their heads. "That's great, Irma," said Alan.

His father's farm bordered on the other side of her farm. "Great Irma. We'll be there. Won't we fellahs?" Several nodded agreement. It was the polite thing to do. Irma thanked them.

The men watched her go for a moment then carried on boisterously with stories of hardships in the army in different places, Tobruk, Benghazi, and Tripoli. They relived moments they would never live again; and all around them was the blatter of drum and the whistle of fife. It was indeed great to be home. Johnny McGee followed along. It was great to be beside fellows like these.

A crowd of some dozens of people was beginning to gather around the platform where the day's speakers would make an address. The platform was a Bedford lorry with the sides down and a couple of Sunday School pews aboard for the Men of Importance. A microphone, atop a spindly support, was set up to the fore and connected to an amplifier that in turn was connected to the battery of the lorry. An electrician fluttered with the mike as it emitted a whine in protest. A man, somewhat bloated around the girth, got up and said, "Reverend Doswell will lead us in prayer."

The Reverend, a very tall man, strode forward, raised his hands for silence. "Oh merciful God, to whom all things we owe, we thank Thee for returning our young men to us safe and sound from the hand of the enemy. And on this day, a day of commemoration of your bountiful goodness in times past, when the hand of Satan sought to destroy all the things we hold dear, we thank Thee for the renewed fellowship of our brothers in the Order that commemorates your Servant of Glorious Pious and Immortal Memory on that day near three hundred years ago. We beseech Thee to protect us in years to come from the hand of Satan and to help us glorify Thee in Thy Way, as commanded by the Holy Scriptures."

Reverend Doswell had a voice that rose from deep in his chest. It was a voice he had practiced, a voice designed for the pulpit, one that would fill all the corners of a church. Aboard the lorry and augmented by the amplifiers his voice roared out over the Field and beyond the hedgerows. There were those who later said they heard him two miles away. He loved his voice. It took the best part of twenty minutes for him to repeat all he had to say at least three times, from as many different ways of saying it, until he was certain they all had the message. And that was simple. On occasions like this there only was one message. "If God be for us, who can be against us!" Reverend Doswell was certain God was for Ulster, and he wanted everyone to be certain of that fact.

MUSIC ON THE WIND

There were two other speakers who said nothing that stood up to the Reverend's message. They had everyday voices, the voices of farmers and shopkeepers, and they said the same thing, a big thanks to everyone for coming out to Walk on this Glorious Day and it was nice to see all the young men back safe. They were humble, sincere men who lived everyday lives and were happy.

"And now," said the fat man, "there's a soldier here amongst us that we'd all like to come up here and say a few words, a man who represents the many sons of this town, a man who fought for King and Country. Folks, Farley Goode." There was a burst of handclapping from Johnny McGee and Mr. Peece stood up on the platform clapping strongly. Others joined in. "Come on up Farley," he called. "Come on!"

Farley climbed the few steps. He crossed to the microphone. As he grasped the stem it gave off an electric whine. Some people giggled. Farley stood silent, his face very serious. "I'd just like to say that there are a few who didn't make it back." He stopped and swallowed. The crowd had got bigger. It was very quiet. Even the Lambeg drums seemed to have lapsed into silence. "There was one fellow," he looked out above the heads of the crowd, "one fellow that should have been here but isn't. I'd like a moment's silence in his memory. Willie Peacock."

He could feel his eyes become wet. The crowd felt the moment and bowed their heads. The minute ticked past. Mr. Peece slipped over to the band that had stood at the ready and whispered into the ear of the bandmaster. As the minute closed the band struck up the Anthem led by a soloist who, in speaking had one of the worst stutters anyone could remember, but in song had the voice of an angel. The soloist stood before the microphone and sang his heart out. "God save our gracious King!"

It was then the fight broke out. "Stand to attention ye Fenian bastard! They're singin' the Anthem, ye Papish get!" There was the hard thud of a fist hitting flesh followed by the grunt of a man falling. Someone cried out, "Don't! Ye'll kill him!" and a voice said, "That's Phelim Ryan ye hit, for Christ's sake. Have ye no sense! What harm was he doin'?"

Farley and his comrades ran over but by then several people were involved in the melee, pulling on the arms of the two men to separate them. The injured man was in his mid twenties, his face white with anger, blood trickling from his nose, the other, a big teenager, flushed of face and scowling.

"What's goin' on here?" the authoritative voice of the Police sergeant demanded. "What's this all about, now? Who struck the first blow? Speak up or I'll have you both in to the Station!"

The big teenager, almost six feet tall and heavy of arm and chest, a farmer's son fed on potatoes and meat, said, "I did."

"And why?"

"They were playing the Anthem, an' he just went on stackin' those crates and not standin' to attention. An', well.."

"Where's your father? Is he here?"

The big teenager nodded towards a part of the field.

"Go find him and go home. I don't want to see you around here or I'll have you up for disorderly conduct. Get going. Now, everyone disperse. Go back to your Lodge or go home." The sergeant went over to the injured man, "You O.K. Phelim? Sorry for the ruckus. These young lads get carried away. Ah, Farley and Jack there. Be good fellows and give a hand here. You know Phelim."

"Heh there, Phelim. Can we give you a hand?"

Johnny McGee and Mr. Peece came running over. "What's going on?"

"Agh, just some codology. An ignorant lout laid into Phelim here." Farley pointed out Phelim. "This is Phelim, another one from the Battery. You fellows all know each other. Come on! Tutti per uno, uno per tutti." And Farley laughed. "Mind the time in Naples, Phelim, when you an' me met them two sisters. Che bambine! Che gambe! Bejapers I didn't like the one you got. Too much mustache! But, che potrine, and those hips." And again, as he often did when he spoke foreign words, he performed a burlesque. "An' don't let that big lump get to ye. He's as ignorant as turd, so he is." They all laughed. Mr. Peece grabbed Farley by the arm. "Maun, that was a great wee speech you made back there on the platform, Farley. Just great. Just the right touch. You'll win easy in the election. Maun, I can see it!"

"I'm not up for election, Mr. Peece."

"You must! You're a shoo-in! You're what we need! Soldier! Orangeman! Businessman! You can make a speech! Why not?" Farley shrugged. Mr Peece said, "You're all coming over to Geddon's place, all you fellahs, tonight. Auld Geddon's putting on a bit of a party for you. Irma did the cooking. I can tell you you'll like that. She's a champeen."

"We know. Phelim is coming too," said Farley.

Mr. Peece looked uncertain. Phelim Ryan was a Catholic, but it could help the vote. It was a good idea. "Why not! Auld Geddon is a generous man. See you later."

Johnny McGee walked beside Mr Peece. "Are you certain, Mr. Peece?

Phelim Ryan? We don't want none of the wrong kind, you know. We'll be talking about the Town Council."

"Nah! Farley's our man! He knows what he's doin'."

The banners were being raised and the drums and fifes lining up in formation. The men got behind them and slowly, in a not too organized fashion, the lodges began the walk home. The day was almost over. They proceeded through town and toward the various streets and roads exiting to the countryside. Some of the men dropped out of the ranks and entered the pubs. It was time to relax, talk of times past and catch up on the present.

Farley and his fellows helped Phelim load his small lorry with the tent and the crates of empty bottles and the trays that held what was left of the sandwiches. They leaped on board, sitting on the crates and the folded canvas of the tent. One of them remembered he was wearing his sash and hurriedly took it off and folded it neatly before putting it in his pocket. He made a face to his companions and they too did likewise. It might not appear dignified to be seen in regalia riding on the lorry of a Roman Catholic on the Twelfth of July, even if he was a fellow gunner from the Battery. As they passed through the gate Irma waved. "See you all later!" They waved back in assurance they would be there.

It was mid-evening. They had assembled in the big kitchen of the Geddon farm—the men from the Battery, Mr. Peece and Johnny McGee. A banquet of sandwiches and cake was laid out on the table.

"All Irma's work!" auld man Geddon assured everyone. "She's a great worker." He passed around a bottle of whiskey and glasses and encouraged everyone to help himself. There was the clinking of glass and cries of "Your health!" The melee at the Field was forgotten and Phelim was hearty with everyone else. They had come through a lot together. They drank and ate and told tales.

An accordion appeared from a case hidden under the staircase and the call went up for Farley to give them a tune. "Remember them five Egyptian women playing the squeeze-box in Alexandria," said Phelim. "Where was that? The Elite Corner, wasn't it?" Someone agreed that was it and could he remember the night they all went to the nightclub with the belly dancers and that was a night the Gerries let some bombs drop. Sure, they all remembered. And they swallowed more porter. "Do ye remember buyin' thon accordion of yours from the Italian soldier, Farley? Do ye? Poor bugger. He'd ha' sold his soul so he would." "How about a verse of Lily Marlene?" someone called. Phelim began to sing as Farley opened the bellows of the accordion. Each one accompanied to the best of their voice,

"Underneath the lamplight, by the barracks gate,
Darling I remember the way you used to wait.
T'was there that you whispered tenderly that you loved me, you'd always be,
my Lily of the lamplight, my own Lily Marlene."

There was silence. Irma's eyes were moist as she thought of what Farley must have suffered so far from home. She kept her eyes fixed on him. Farley said, "Let's do that again. She deserves another shot!" and they sang in full voice this time with Phelim doing a descant in his fine Irish tenor.

"Ye'd wonder how a kraut could write a song like that. Wouldn't ye?" said Harry.

"Soldiers is soldiers, no matter what," said Phelim.

"What are ye doin' these days Phelim?" Farley asked.

"Tryin' to get by. Just tryin' to get by. Have applied to the Canadian consulate for immigration papers to Canada an' I'm waitin'. Looks like I can get a job there, in Toronto. There's also a chance for workers in the Ford factory in Windsor. So I'm goin' to give it a try. How about you?"

Farley rested his head on the top of the accordion. "Don't rightly know. The farm's run down so I suppose I'll just have to build it up again. How about you fellows?"

"Truth is," said Harry, "I'm lookin' at Australia. I've cousins there. I wrote them an' asked if there's a chance."

In a sober frame of mind they talked on about the future and the chances they had or didn't have. Irma sat quiet, hoping. She had heard Farley say that his farm was run down. Had he changed in responsibility?

"You know," said Alan, "I got this farm next to here. My father died, as you know, just after we got back so I've got this farm." He didn't need to say more. He had a farm.

"Agh, one place's much like the next," Harry said. "When it all boils down there's not a pin of difference between any place an' the next."

"You fellahs have had the great experience," said Mr. Peece, anxious to get into the conversation.

"I wish I had your experience," Johnny McGee said quickly. "But my feet!"

"An aul' excuse!" someone cried.
"Naw! Serious, fellahs. My feet!"
"Aye, sure!"
"You should support Farley here for the Town Council, all of you, so you should," continued Mr. Peece fearful his theme would get lost in the ridicule of McGee. "What about it Farley?"

"Sure I've told you, Mr. Peece. No!" Farley closed his eyes as if to shut out the thought. Irma looked at him with concern. He was still not the old friend she had known but she hoped he would not accept the offer. There was the farm. There was a responsibility.

Mr. Peece sat back. He sensed something wrong. As he told it afterwards, "It was a good thing too. You never know how these fellahs are after a war. You never know." He tried a new slant. "Would anyone of you go back an' live in Egypt, or Sicily or Naples or even England? Now would ye?" he asked. "Isn't this the best place of all? Isn't that so?" There were a few grunts and nods. The whisky and the porter had mellowed them. "So isn't it a civic duty to take part in the local government. Wouldn't you say so?" But they were not ready for that topic.

"Do ye mind the night in Alexandria," said Alan, "when the Gerries got a direct hit on one of the gun sites?" They held silent for some moments. It was still vivid. "Poor Willie Peacock. Never knew what hit him. None of them fellahs did."

"You know," said Farley, "one of the things he wanted most was to go down to the shore at Carnlough and walk over the pebbles and just dip his feet in the sea. He told me that one night, in a bar, about a week before it happened."

"Agh oh!"

"Ye didn't see any of the family on the Field today did ye, anyone? His sister, even?" Farley asked.

None had seen anyone of the Peacock family.

"There's no men left in that family, is there?" asked Alan.

"None."

Irma listened knowing now why she had seen Farley talk to Elsie Peacock at the Fair Hill. Her eyes were on Farley with a tender look.

"What was it the aul' sergeant said, the next day. Do you mind, hi?" Farley had come out of his moroseness and was chuckling at the memory, his face beginning to light up as he prepared for the punch line, "Sure ye remember, hi? Eh? Says the aul' sergeant, says he, 'Ye couldn't see the gunsite for feathers!'" Farley laughed. "Willie Peacock! Him and thon aul' tattoo on his arm. Ye should have seen it. A peacock as big as all get-out. 'Just like my name.' he says to me. Feathers!" Farley laughed, tears in his eyes, choking in laughter at the ridiculousness of the pun and then he was crying. He sobbed in great choking spasms and buried his head in his hands.

Johnny McGee looked over at Mr. Peece. Mr. Peece raised his eyebrows in a question. This would never do for a council member. No! Never! Johnny McGee felt very uncomfortable. Men did not cry. And this was the man who had killed his share of Gerries! Johnny shook his head in agreement with Mr. Peece. They both rose quietly. "We'll be going now," Mr. Peece whispered to auld man Geddon. "Aye!"

Irma moved over beside Farley and put her arm around his shoulder. "Are you alright?"

"We'll walk you home," came the offer from the men.

"I'll walk him," said Irma. "He lives right close by."

Farley blew his nose and stood up. "Sorry fellahs! It's just.."

"We know. We know." A few of them slapped him kind-heartedly on the back. "Willie Peacock was his buddy," they explained to Irma. "His china!"

"I'll walk back with you, Farley. You're going to be alright."

"I know," he said, "but I'll go home alone. Don't worry about me. Don't!"

It was a clear July night and though the sun had set there was still enough light, great streaks of red and yellow across the whole western horizon. Somewhere off in the distance a lone drummer took a few last whacks. Then he quit. In the silence could be heard the corncrakes calling to each other in the meadows.

Farley pulled his bicycle out of the shed and threw a leg over the saddle. He adjusted his bowler hat and patted the wrinkles out of his sash. He mounted and rode off, following the road towards the shore. The headlamp picked out a splash of yellow on the tarmacadam. Shadows began to settle on either side of him, darkened all the more by the hawthorn hedges that lined the road. He knew his way; out past Broughshane at a steady pace, past the hulk of Slemish on his right until he came to the long freewheel ride down to the shore. Finally he was there, in the eerie luminescence of the breaking waves. All the houses that lined the bay were in darkness. He was totally alone.

Farley rested his bicycle against the rail of the promenade and took the steps down to the pebbled beech. His feet slid and scrunched on the small round stones and he could smell the seaweed that lay in wreaths from the last high tide. He took off his shoes, his sash, his coat and shirt. There was a pleasant coolness to the air. He slid out of his trousers and underwear and stood naked except for the bowler hat that still rested on his close-cropped head. He breathed the salty air for a few moments, throwing his shoulders back and flexing his arms. It felt good. His face, neck and forearms were brown from the sun of the Western Desert. The skin around his knees formed a band of tan against the white of his legs. Farley stooped and folded his clothes neatly, shoes first with the socks pushed inside, then his trousers, coat, underwear, shirt, tie and the sash. Lastly he took his bowler hat off and laid it atop the sash to make a neat little pile worthy of any soldier. Feeling the pebbles with his feet he made his way to the edge of the water. The spread of an expired wave splashed over his toes. He waded in. The water was up to his knees with the waves lapping up around his pale buttocks. A few yards on and he began to swim, a barely visible dot that soon was lost amongst the pewter-colored swell of the sea.

"It must ha' happened around two o'clock in the morning," the coroner said. "But why?"

The sergeant of the village shook his head. "Do we know who he is?"

"Nope! He didn't carry a wallet on him, just that sash. But it has the number of his Lodge, so it won't be too hard to find out."

"Maun, do you see how sun-tanned he is on the face and neck, and his hands too, even his knees. The rest of him is all pale."

"Aye! Looks like one of the men who came back. Maybe he was out in them foreign parts. One of the Territorials."

"You could be right."

"Poor soul. With the war over and everything to live for, what would drive a man to do a thing like this?" The policeman looked the body over. He had no answer.

The Wild Skelter

When Albert went up to University in September of fifty-two, his mother had given him advise, very sound advice in her estimation. "Now, keep your nose in them books, son," Mrs. Burns said, "an' don't pay no heed to them hussies in Belfast. They'll only distract ye, so they will."

So far his life was unsullied though not from fealty to his mother's wisdom. He had a feeling that what she preached was true. Rather, Albert loved women and respected them. He would watch from afar, hear their laughter, follow their movements with hidden glances, a glimpse of a knee, the swell of a breast, and even try to smell their fragrance by sitting near them in the lecture theatre. But it didn't help. Albert was shy with girls. And he blushed easily.

This abstinence meant that he did well in his first exams. He studied all the time never going to a picture house or a dance at the Student's Union or any place for that matter where temptation might have lurked. Hussies were kept out of sight at least in practice but, as Albert well knew within his soul, they were very much in mind.

In the interest of saving the little money his scholarship afforded, Albert stayed in the city most weekends, both Saturday and Sunday, not wanting to spend the couple of shillings on the bus back to Ballyaghone to visit his proud mother. "He's up at Queen's takin' physics," she would tell anyone within earshot. "An' he's comin' back to teach at the Academy, so he is. Just as soon as he graduates!"

Preserving Albert for that great moment was the compelling reason for her advice. Teaching at the Academy would be the culmination of all her labors. Then they could sell the small farm that had put her husband in his grave. But not Albert. He would have a job. Wear a shirt and tie. On those few occasions when Albert did go back he was honestly able to tell his mother that he was behaving himself and the only place his nose had been was stuck in a book.

"I'm getting good marks in the exams, so I am. Sure I've no time for skiving away off," he would assure her.

"There'll be plenty of time for that later, son, so there will," she said, hammering home the edict once again. "Get yer education first. This is yer big chance, so it is. Yer father would be proud of ye, so he would."

But, oh man, was it boring! Even for a shy person like Albert whose idea of doing something different was to take bits of stale bread to feed the swans on the river Lagan down by the Ormeau Park, on a Sunday. But he persevered. Not even his landlady's daughter Sally had been able to break his shyness and get beyond the polite good-morning or good evening and the thank-you he always said when she laid his breakfast or dinner in front of him.

"He has manners, that wee lad," said Mrs. McIlhagga, his landlady. "A good up-bringing always shows, ye know. Ye can be sure his mother saw to that! Aye!" Which was indeed the truth. But behind the outward appearance of shyness and good table manners, Albert longed to burst out of his shell. He was eighteen, away from home for the first time in his life, alone, no one to chastise him, and the opportunity this freedom offered was waiting. But how? Albert knew not! Nor should he have worried for, beyond his control, like the innards of a dormant volcano, life was rumbling around him ready to erupt and carry him along with it.

The wintry sky over Belfast was darkening down in preparation for a rain shower. Albert sat at a small table in his bedroom, his nose poised over the book in the manner expected. But the words on the page had long since begun to blur and his mind to wander to the tirade going on below in the family quarters of his landlady.

"Mammy, I don't care if cousin Duggie is coming to live here. I'm going to do what I please. What I please, not what pleases Duggie M'Gookin! So there!"

Sally's angry voice could be heard through two closed doors and up three flights of stairs. This argument about Sally's use of facial make-up had been going on for several days now and would, without doubt, go on for several more. But, on this particular evening Albert heard the introduction of a new component in the matter—cousin Duggie. He opened his bedroom door and paid particular attention. He suspected that cousin Duggie, whoever he should be, was going to rent the front attic, recently vacated by a tenant even more frustrated by the constant family squabbling than Albert.

Mrs. McIlhagga re-adjusted her fat body on the armchair and reached two fistfuls of knuckles, gnarled with rheumatism, into the warmth of the fireplace. She could feel the adrenaline seep into her blood stream in readiness for the coming argument. Mrs. McIlhagga loved arguments that she generally won through sheer volume of voice. In consequence no one in her family bothered to speak to her in a normal tone but yelled as if to win the day before the arguing began.

"I'm seventeen, so I am," shouted Sally. "I'm not a child! And it's my face, not yours and certainly not his though God save us he could do with something to cover up thon dial he has on him."

But Mrs. McIlhagga was beyond listening to youthful reason. "Seventeen is it? At your age I had to ask please before I spoke. But naw! Youse girls nowadays! Full of opinions! An' no sense about propriety! None!" She tossed her head. "Yer eyes painted. An' yer lips. False eyelashes! Like Jezebel! An' the way youse dress the day. High heels an' your legs showin'. There's no mystery to that! None! None at all! When I was your age it was different so it was. We had a bit of mystery about us." She thrust the arthritic fingers back into the heat from the fire, rubbed them while her brain perused visions of unspeakable sin. "An' gettin' familiar with men! D'je hear? That's what yer make-up will do for ye. An' don't I know! Half exposed in them dresses and yer face painted. Walkin' around in clothes ye could see through. Aye! Well I'm not havin' it so I'm not. Ye can mark that! There's no daughter of mine goin' to bring shame to the McIlhaggas. An' not with yer cousin Duggie coming here to stay."

Mrs. McIlhagga's views on the sins of the flesh were really not much different from those of Albert's mother. Motherhood seems to spawn wisdom in that realm, probably based on experience.

"Is that right?" Sally yelled back. "If it's shame you're worried about, what about Molly and that...?"

"Hold yer tongue!"

It was a sore point with Mrs. McIlhagga that her two other daughters had seen fit to disobey her warnings. Molly had claimed she was pregnant to an ex-sailor, a condition that wore off, as by a miracle, shortly after the marriage.

"And Margie!" Sally called with lightly applied innuendo.

Margie was aptly described by the former tenant of the front attic as "frequently married but never churched." Others referred to her in less euphemistic tones as "a hot piece," and "good for a spin, hi!"

"Hold yer tongue, I say! Soul, I'll rise this minit an' take me han' to ye. Ye should be ashamed of yerself. You, you....you young hussy! If yer poor father were alive to hear ye! That's what's wrong! Ye miss a rulin' hand!" Mrs. McIlgagga became full of self-pity. "God rest him but he left me with a handful. Och, if it wasn't for me pains!"

In none of the few weekend visits home had Albert ever mentioned the constant turmoil in the McIlhagga household nor the fact that his landlady had three daughters, of which two would have decidedly fallen into the category of hussies. Though some might say it had been an act of fate, others could argue convincingly that it was a lack of money that placed him on the brink of the pit, that pit which the Pastor of the Meeting House in Ballyaghone assured him was filled with sin. The McIlhagga rear attic was the cheapest digs he could find.

"An there's something else you should know," Sally said. "I'm not cleaning up after cousin Duggie M'Gookin, no siree, any more than I'll clean up after Margie and Molly and that, that useless..."

"That's enough! Hold yer tongue! Not a bad word about Molly's man. D'je hear?"

Mrs. McIlhagga detested her son-in-law, the ex-sailor, for marrying Molly but that was beside the point. In a confrontation she took the side that afforded the most opposition to her opponent. "I'll not tolerate it! So mind that, now!"

Sally let her mother feel she had won a point. "Only Albert keeps his room tidy," she said, quietly.

Because Mrs. McIlhagga had rheumatic pains and aches and had become grossly overweight to the point where movement was difficult, Sally did most of the housework associated with the lodgers. So she knew from practical experience that Albert, in the back attic, was very proper in his habits. His jacket was always on a coat hanger, his shirts neatly folded, his socks rolled. And he did his own laundry in the scullery, even his ironing. Albert never caused her any bother. Albert was a gentleman. And he was studying up at Queen's to be something. When she tidied his bedroom she would lift the bedspread, which he had so neatly stretched over the pillows, and feel for his pajamas. She liked the feel of the rough flannel. Once she had pressed them to her face and could smell his male odor. It made her heart race.

Sally was a young woman of strong build, fair in an Irish way and a face that burst into laughter as easy as it turned to anger. She had the habit of singing when she climbed the stairs or was in her room and when she sang her voice was crystal clear. There was one song in particular of which Albert had even memorized the words and hummed a few bars now and then.

"They tried to tell us we're too young.
Too young to really be in love."

The words tugged at Albert's heart. Was it any wonder the song was at the top of the hit parade?

Sally was the kind of wholesome girl any young man would be happy to squire to a dance at the Orange Hall back home and sense with pride the envious looks of his pals. She might even get up on the platform and sing that song. Albert could see that in his mind's eye. "Albert," they'd say. "That's a great wee girl ye got there." But it was only fantasy. Albert could not bring himself to ask Sally out for a date. Not even to feed the swans on the Lagan. He was afraid. Girls scared him. Even Sally. And, moreover, his mother was dead set against wimmen with make-up. It would never do. "Why can't they be like the good Lord made them?" she was apt to say. "Nowadays they're all painted up, the colors of the rainbow, like ye'd see on a baboon's backside."

On a Sunday School outing to the zoo on the Antrim Road many years before, the baboons had left an indelible impression on Mrs. Burns. Her husband, then alive, had been amused by the spectacle. "Would ye look at thon, hi!" he exclaimed to the world at large. "Look at the goes of them!" The poor Pastor had been shaken to the core and had hustled the little children away ere their tender minds got sullied. Mrs. Burns never forgot. "Albert! Watch out for them kind. They're the worst, so they are! All painted up! Hussies!"

Sally was her own woman and with a final burst of justification, shouted at her mother, "Agh sure ye don't know! All the girls today use make-up. It's part of looking your best, so it is!"

"I do know," called Mrs. McIlhagga, the adrenaline in full flow. "Ha-hye, I know ye me girl." And, closing one heavy eyelid for emphasis, "It's just an excuse to get up to a lot of fal-de-la like ye're seein' in them pictures. Just to attract men! That's the height of it! Och, if yer father wor alive! Och, if he wor only alive!"

To Albert the boarding house had become a nightmare. There were evenings when not even the cheap rent of his attic could compensate for the distraction of the constant noise. Study on this particular night was impossible. Albert laid the book aside. Poor Sally, if only he could help. He had often thought of asking her to go for a walk in the park when he fed the swans but he had been too shy. Feeding swans was so silly really, the kind of thing for fellows without a clue. Others had cars and trips planned to Bangor, or down the Ards Peninsula, even to Island McGee; then home by dark to park the car in a quiet spot for a kerfuffle in the back seat, out of eyesight. He had imagined himself doing that. But...

Mrs. McIlhagga was warming to her theme of how her daughter would dishonor the name of their father and shame her in front of their cousin Duggie, soon to rent a room in the top front attic. "Molly marrying that...." It was a thought that stimulated her aggressiveness. "I say! Where's she an' that Englishman got to the night?"

"Dancing!" Sally called. "They'll be in any minute."

Mrs. McIlhagga should have known that. The sailor, and an Englishman to boot, her son-in-law and her daughter Molly spent most of their time dancing or in bed. And they were not in bed at that moment. Hence an easy conclusion but, there was that certain joy that confrontation gave her. "An' Margie?"

"What?" Sally called from the scullery.

"What? Who told ye to say what? Come here!" It gave her great joy to be querulous. Sally appeared in the doorway. Mrs. McIlhagga looked at her sternly. "Where's that Margie got to?"

"She's out with a man! Isn't she always!"

"Well ye can tell yer scoungin' sister that there'll be no more milarky in this family. Do ye hear? That mister milarky yer sister married is enough for a whole bloody city!"

"Tell her yourself. There's the front door scraping."

Albert too heard the front door scrape over the threshold. A cold blast of air surged up the stair well and past his door. The voice of Mrs. McIlhagga yelled. "Close that door ye idjit. Were ye born in a field? Close it this instant!" It was the kind of incident that gave Mrs. McIlhagga pleasure. She could yell at the top of her voice while finding justifiable fault with some idjit.

The front door closed with a bang. Steps stamped down the hall to the living room and a hand rattled the brass knob of the door. Some of the tribe had returned from the fray. Albert decided to slip down the stairs and go out for a walk. It was past ten o'clock. A brisk walk in the cool air and he'd get to sleep quicker. He grabbed his raincoat and trod lightly as he descended. Looking down through the well of the stairs he could see the oiled head of Basil, Mrs. McIlhagga's son-in-law, the Englishman, ex-sailor off the Bonaventure. He had met Molly at a dance in the Floral Hall during shore leave.

Basil squeezed open the door an inch or two the way a child would play with a puppy. "Helloew mothah deah!" he yodeled, and burst into song. "My wylde Eye-ah-rish rowse. The sweet-est flou-ah thayit grr-oows!"

"Shut yer bake if ye can't be sober!"

The little man, neatly dressed in blazer and flannels, grinned drunkenly. "Mothah, we're bay-ack!"

Molly pushed him from behind. "G'on in, hi! My feet are killin' me. I got to sit down for Christ's sake. God, thon was some dancin'. I'm near killed, so I am. What a night!"

Mrs. McIlhagga surveyed her loved-ones with ill-disguised horror. "Ye've been drinkin', so youse have!" observing with practiced eye. "Ye're a disgrace!"

"Yup!" said Basil who, when not dancing or in bed, was addicted to cowboy movies. He settled on his knees to open the door of a sideboard.

"Where's Margie?" shouted Mrs. McIlhagga. "Have ye seen Margie?"

"She's out with a fellah!" Molly sprawled out on the sofa. "Aw God, it's great to sit down. I'm frazzled!"

"What kind of a fellah?"

"A fellah with a googly eye and a corduroi staff in his hand." Clutching a box of darts Basil climbed drunkenly to his feet. He closed a lazy eye for the benefit of Sally in the kitchen and poised a dart.

"Ye're so funny." Mrs. McIlhagga lay back in exasperation in her chair. "God pity me. I'm at the mercy of idjits! An' yer cousin Duggie about to arrive. What'll I do? God help us!"

"Cousin Duggie?" said Molly. "Him! Dear God! Why?"

"He's asked to rent the front attic."

"Couldn't you have rented the room to Dracula instead. It would have been a lot safer!"

The footpath was already wet with drizzle as Albert set off towards the dark silhouette of the University. He crossed the quadrangle and directed his steps past the Museum. He was totally alone but for the last city buses returning to their depot, empty. The city was closing down. Each street-lamp carried a halo as if on best behavior for the remainder of the night. Albert felt a longing to be back home in Ballyaghone, away from the discord of the McIlhaggas, some place where there was no strife among friends, where everyone knew him since a child, where he had identity. Life in the McIlhagga boarding house was a turmoil of accusations and name-calling. The noise was constant, so bad that the other lodger in the front attic had moved out a week previous.

"I've had enough. I don't care how cheap it is I can't stand it any longer. I'm going batty. I'll stay in the Salvation Army hostel so I will before I endure another night. For God's sake! It's a mad-house, so it is!"

Albert had often felt that way too. But he had not been able to find cheaper digs in the long search before term started. His scholarship was meager and his mother had limited funds, and moreover, Albert was not a person to take on a challenge. He put up with things. Whether the McIlhagga household was roaring with mirth over some nonsense or fighting over some clash of opinion, he accepted it. It was the genteel thing to do. His mother had told him to be polite. Albert was polite. "And watch yer manners son. Manners maketh the man. That's an' aul sayin', so it is. An' its true," she told him often.

As he made his way back along the footpath by the river and the narrow streets, all was quiet but for the sound of a car sloshing through the rain. No lighted windows broke the red-bricked Victorian front of the rows of houses. It was long past bedtime for working people, especially on a Wednesday night. There was work on the morrow.

The front door scraped again as Albert entered. Mrs. McIlhagga raucous voice cried out, "Margie! Come on in here you out there an' none of your lettin' on!"

"It's only me!" said Albert, peeping into the family sanctuary.

"Well, either come in or stay out. There's a draft from that door would clean corn. Sally! Bring this wee lad some supper. A cup of tea, son?"

Mrs. McIlhagga was fond of Albert. He was the example of decorum she held up to her wayward flock. If Molly's husband could only be like Albert! "Look at Albert!" she would say. "Why can't ye be like Albert?" But it was like sowing oats on stony ground.

"Thank-you. Please," said Albert quietly.

"Is it a cold night out, young fellah?"

"Yes, missus. And wet, too!"

From her throne at the side of the fireplace Mrs. McIlhagga controlled her empire. What did arthritis and swollen ankles matter when you had a voice! And she owned the house, all three stories and the back yard. The insurance from her husband's death in a shipyard accident had paid it off. Now she had a little income from renting out bedrooms to her two daughters and the two attics to students. Sally got hers free for doing the housework. It was a good set-up Mrs. McIlhagga thought. "Thank the Lord for a nice warm fire an' yer own hob. Ye know, we're not half-thankful, so we're not. Here, have a sandwich." She handed over to Albert a plate of white bread sandwiches composed of slices of raw onion liberally peppered and salted. "Aye! There's some not half-thankful. Tuck into that, son!"

Despite the hour the McIlhagga family was very much alive and not ready to go to bed. Conversation was still being carried on at full yell.

"Will you throw an 'and, lad?" asked Molly's husband offering Albert three darts.

"No thanks, Basil. I'll be going to bed in a minute. I'm not feeling good."

The atmosphere in the room was stifling, a mixture of damp overcoats, coal fumes from the fireplace and onions. The old lady screwed up her face, the eyes sucked back into the veined network of her face. "There's the flu goin' around they say. Take a Beecham's powder in pill form," she ordered at full voice. "That'll do the trick. Sally! Reach into the drawer there for that box with the one or two pills still in it from my last bout." She twisted her face and winked at Albert. "You'll feel better in the mornin', so ye will."

"Thank-you. I'll be alright."

"Well?" insisted Basil. "'Ow about an 'and?"

"Come on!" cried Molly. "You an' Sally agin me an' Basil. Are ye on?"

Sally bounced in from the scullery. "Be a sport. Go on. Be a sport!" Sally smiled at Albert using the moment to give him a squeeze on the arm. She could feel the hard sinew of a young man and let go as a thrill sped up her fingers. She looked at him afraid that he noticed. But Albert was withdrawn. He looked tired. He was such a sensitive looking young man she wanted to put her arms around him and just hold him. If she only could.

"Right, cock!" said Basil as Albert got off his chair. Basil threw three well-placed shots. Albert pulled them from the board and walked back to the imaginary line on the floor. He threw a dart. It struck the wall above the board and clattered to the floor, laying there a bright green in the gray dust of wall plaster that spilled down from the hundreds of ragged pockmarks in the wallpaper.

"Are ye blind?" shouted Mrs. McIlhagga. "Look what ye're doin' to my good wall! Look at that mess! Will ye look?"

"He didn't do them all," said Sally. "Anyway the wall's rotten. Like the whole house is."

Further argument was halted by the sound of the front door opening and closing. Timidly Margie peeped in before drawing her head into her shoulders coyly and stepping into the room. Her face was red from her chin to her nose.

"Come here girl. Where have ye been to this time of night?"

"Agh, Ma!"

"Answer me this minit!"

"Agh, Ma!"

"Where were ye?"

"I was courtin' in the doorway, so I was."

"An' lettin the neighbors see ye! Was that it?"

"It was the back-door in the ally."

"Well ye'd no business bein' at the back door in the alley. Had ye anything to hide?"

"Agh, Ma!"

"Well, we'll have no more of it. Look at yer face. Ye're all sucked over! When yer cousin Duggie comes next week we'll have none of that! Ye'll behave yerself. Do ye hear?"

"Cousin Duggie?" Margie's pale face lit up.

"An' I don't want yer aunt Minnie's folk to think I reared ye a young hussy. Naw, I don't!"

"Oh, Ma! Cousin Duggie! What's he comin' here for? To stay?"

"He is!"

"Honest, Ma? Cousin Duggie?"

"Aye! Don't ye have ears? Yer cousin Duggie's takin' the front attic startin' next week."

Margie gave a little jump of delight. "What's he like Ma? G'on, tell us!"

"'Ere," asked Basil. "'Aven't you ever seen your own cousin?"

"Not since the evacuation during the blitz," said Molly disgustedly, "an' he was like nothin' then. And he's only a second cousin, so he is. Hardly a blood relative at all."

"G'on, Ma!" insisted Margie. "You saw him at Aunt Minnie's funeral. What's he like?"

"He's a fine lookin' young man. Not unlike his father. An' I can tell ye his father was a right good lookin' young fellah in his youth, so he was." She smiled at the memory of a young man in a high starched collar. There was a time when they had stepped out together to a dance or two. There had been a thing between them. But they were cousins.

"Is he good lookin'?" cried Margie whose face was filled with expectation as if a film star were about to enter her life. She had heard plenty about Duggie, a wild young man by all accounts. Margie had visions of adventure.

"Why do you ask that for," said Molly, "when you mind fine well his face was covered with skitter japs and thon hair on him like something he stole off a dead sheep. For goodness sake! The fellah was a fright even then when he was fourteen. What must he be like now? Ten years would only aggravate things. Stands to reason, for God's sake."

"Molly! That's a way to speak of your cousin Duggie. Have you no family feelin'?" Mrs. McIlhagga scolded.

"Agh well, its true. The wee lad couldn't help his looks. As it says in the Bible what's bred in the bone runs long in the flesh. Look at Aunt Minnie!" Molly laughed.

"Molly! Yer aunt Minnie's in her grave!"

Basil poised a dart. "That's what she said. Look at Aunt Minnie!" The dart struck the center of the board and Basil chuckled. Though he had long ago ceased to let the old woman's tyranny bother him yet he was afraid to meet the old woman's eyes.

Mrs. McIlhagga eyes went tight and vicious. "When yer cousin Duggie comes next week we'll have none of that back talk! Ye'll behave yersel's. Do ye hear?"

"Cousin Duggie!" Margie's pale face was aglow.

"An' Margie, I don't want yer aunt Minnie's folk to think I reared ye a young hussy. Naw, I don't!"

"Really Ma, what's he like?" persisted Margie hopefully.

"Wait an' see. An' it's high time ye were all in bed. Lookit! It's goin' on past eleven. Sally! Have ye me jar ready?"

"Your jar's ready," announced Sally. "I'll slip it in under the sheets, so I will. Your bed will be snug when ye get there."

In the momentary lull in the fighting Albert saw his opportunity. "Good night!" he said, eager to get away. Sally followed him up the stairs a little wistfully, the hot water bottle hugged in her arms. "Albert! Goodnight!" she called up the stairwell. "Goodnight!" he said, looking down. Sally looked so nice, her face tilted up towards him. There was a smile on her lips. Her eyes begged him to notice her. From above he looked down into the cleft of her breasts. He closed his bedroom door and wondered how much longer he could stand it. In her bedroom below Sally began to sing softly,

"They tried to tell us we're too young...."

When Albert returned from classes he noticed the large car parked outside the boarding house. In the family room Mrs. McIlhagga was actually standing up, a rare sight, and holding the hands of a thickset man a few years older than himself. Mrs. McIlhagga's face was wrinkled in smiles. "This is Duggie!" she said. "Duggie M'Gookin. An' this here's Albert Burns, our lodger. He has the back attic, ye know. You have the front one. Yours looks out nicely onto the street!"

"Howye!" said Duggie in a voice that could have called in a herd of pigs from a mile away, and gripped Albert's hand in a freckled vice. Albert noticed that Duggie was totally covered in similar markings, from his hairline and down over his face and neck. To Albert, Molly's description of her second cousin seemed very apt. From the opening of Duggie's shirt a handful of dull ginger hair burst out while, on his head, hair of similar hew was tiered up in waves in the manner of advertisements for a popular brand of permanent wave. The overall effect was, as Molly later described him, "like some creature has been dragged through a pot of mustard with some fungus growing on it."

"Have you seen Duggie's car?" The occasion was so exciting for Margie she was jumping from one foot to the other. "It's smashin'!"

"C'mon!" Duggie ruffled her hair, "An' Ah'll take you a spin!"

Margie's squeal of delight was cut short as Mrs. McIlhagga scolded from her throne. "At this time of night an' him just come? Have ye no sense? Sit down there, Duggie. Sally's just goin' to make supper. Ha ha, you've done well for yourself, Duggie. You know," she turned importantly to Albert, "Duggie's a sales representative now. Aren't ye, Duggie?"

Duggie acknowledged his accomplishment with a smile and nod of his head, looking at everyone in turn as if expecting a challenge to the truth of achievement in that statement.

"You should see his car," cried Margie, clapping her hands like a child. "It's as big as a barn, so it is." For Margie the size of Duggie's car was clear evidence of success. And it would have a big back seat. A lot of Margie's free time was spent in car back seats.

Duggie was now the center of family admiration, at least for Mrs. McIlhagga and Margie; an example for all to follow even better than Albert with his fine manners. It was intoxicating and was going to Duggie's head. Already he had learned that communication was carried on at the yell. He leaned towards Margie and ran a hand up her leg. "Wheeee! All the better for dollin' in!" His eyes were dancing from his head. It was a surprise attack and Margie stepped back into Basil, who, unimpressed by Duggie's car—for hadn't Basil served in the Royal Navy during the war—was still concentrating on his game of darts. "Whoooooaaagh!" laughed Duggie as Basil went tumbling.

"I say there!" said Basil, somewhat peeved.

"My God! A dart board!" Duggie sprang upon the darts, snatching them from Basil. "I haven't played darts since the time I speared McGoslin's prize turkey through the eye. Deal us a hand there!" Duggie toed the imaginary line on the floor, poising a dart. "Get a load of this!" he said. With one eye focused on the dartboard he threw with a force would have taken the dart a hundred feet. The unfortunate little green missile struck a wire and ricocheted upwards, glancing off the ceiling to plunge downwards towards the floor. "Whooooaaagh!" roared Duggie.

"I say!" said an alarmed Basil. "Easy on!"

"Look what you've done you big hallion!" Molly pointed to the green shaft that protruded from between her toes and nailed her sandal to the floor.

Duggie was doubled up in mirth. "How can I help it!" he roared. "There's a wild bit of you along the ground! Whooooaaagh! Eh, Auntie May?" He turned for support to the old woman who, humored to the point of tears, sat clutching her wobbling body. "I never see'd the like, I declare!" she said through tears of merriment.

Basil was white with anger. "I say! That's my wife you're talking to!"

"Agh, don't let that worry you."

"My wife's foot!"

Duggie leaned over him menacingly. "It could have been yours."

"I must say....This is....not the thing!"

"Oh my! I've never laughed so many! Never!" said Mrs. McIlhagga doing her best to recover from her fit of laughter. "Ho, ho, ho!"

"Think no more of it," said Duggie to Basil. "I'll forgive you where thousands wouldn't."

"Well..."

"It takes a good laugh at times," said Mrs. McIlhagga drying her face with the corner of her apron.

"Your tea's getting cold!" called Sally.

Duggie sat down at the table as Sally went forward with the teapot. "You wet a quare cup of tea," declared Duggie in the manner of a connoisseur. "You should be marriet!"

"Stop it, Duggie! Stop it!" Some tea poured onto the table. "You cheeky big thing!" Sally stepped back out of reach of the exploring hand.

"Duggie!" Mrs. McIlhagga was shocked.

"She takes after you, auntie May. She turns a man's head."

"You're as wild as your father ever was," said Mrs. McIlhagga, clearly flattered. "That's the truth. God rest him. In spite of all his faults he never harmed no-one."

"You're a wild bugger, Duggie M'Gookin, so you are!" cried Margie, smiling happily. She had a quick vision of what it might be like curled up with him in the back of his big car. Why not? They were only second cousins!

"A flipping Don Huan, if you ask me," commented Basil.

"You're a wild man, so you are, Duggie M'Gookin," Margie interposed, drawing Duggie's attention back to her. He had pouty lips that were kissy but the spattering of freckles was a scare. Maybe in the back seat of the car at night she wouldn't notice.

"Whoooaaagh!" snarled Duggie reaching across the table to grab at her.

"Ooooooh!" squeeled Margie, thrills running up her spine.

"Ha ha!" Suddenly Duggie sat down, all humor gone, and stared at the solemn Albert. "If youse'd all quieten down we'd get to hear what Albert here has to say for himself. Are you courtin' fellah? Eh?" Albert was flustered and his face shot up a red glow. "Haven't you ever had a hoult?" Duggie insisted.

"Duggie!" cried Mrs. McIlhagga. "There's Sally here. Don't talk that way."

"Agh, auntie May, Sally's a big girl. Eh? Seventeen? Eighteen?" Sally nodded, delighted with Duggie's chiding of her mother. "There you are, you see!" said Duggie, nodding over at Albert. "What you need is a good wumman. You'll have to join us all for a good skelter. There's a great dance on the night, I'm told. Are you on?"

Margie squealed in delight. "Where we goin', hi?"

"Ligonail! Up by the Crimean Arms. Next door in fact. We can get a couple of jars before we start. What do you think of that Albert?" He leaned over and slapped Albert on the knee.

"Why the night?" Mrs. McIlhagga felt robbed. "Sure, Duggie, ye've just arrived!" She wanted more of his company. It brought back so many memories of his father and the wild times when they both were young.

"Why not?" yelled Duggie. "There's no time like the present. You only live once! Eh? What do you say Albert. You might get a hoult!" Albert shook his head meekly. Duggie laughed, "Hoy-yee! You don't want to stay a virgin all your life. Good God, man! You'll end up with hair on your hands!"

"Duggie! What kind of talk is that in front of Sally?" Mrs. McIlhagga yelled from her corner, feeling she was losing control of her kingdom. "There's to be no more of that talk in this house!"

"Agh, auntie May. Isn't the word in the Bible." There was no chastising Duggie. He was impervious to the old woman. The arrival of sandwiches distracted his attention. "My God! Onions!"

"Aye, them's very good for you," said Mrs. McIlhagga, glad for the turn in events, and to demonstrate, she seized one and bit into it with every sign of enjoyment. Proof!

"Ligonail!" chimed in Basil, seeing a chance to make good in his new relative's eyes. "I say, that is a proper idea."

"What?" asked Molly missing the point.

"The Ligonail idea. Dancing. We haven't tripped the light fantastic since last Saturday!"

"Oh!"

"Jolly good idea, eh? What do you say?" Basil leaned over and squeezed his wife's knee in a weak imitation of Duggie.

"Oh, here!" responded Molly, coyly fluttering her eyelashes. "Can we all go, Duggie? Can we?"

"Why not! The car's big enough!"

Margie screamed with delight, "Ooooh, smashin'!"

"And Albert?" asked Duggie again. Albert shook his head. "Are you yellah?" said Duggie.

Basil rose from the table, dragging his wife by the hand. He swung her round in a ballroom tackle and leaned towards Duggie, speaking salaciously out of the side of his mouth. "Separate the men from the boys, eh?" He nudged Duggie with a wink and, stepping fairy-footed across the linoleum, bent his wife's back into a tango hold in what he imagined was a display of passionate abandon. "Dahling!" he said in ecstatic tones, his eyes gazing off into the distance, his eyebrows tragically arched.

"Oh, here!" sighed Molly.

"I've things to do," Albert said meekly. He moved hurriedly through the door and up the stairs. Gales of laughter could be heard from below.

"You're a beast, Duggie M'Gookin! You're a beast." Albert heard Sally shout. "You've no right teasing the wee fellow like that." It was hard to bear that a girl stood up for him.

Albert lay in his bed propped up on a pillow trying to read a textbook but it was a useless task against the noise of the excited foursome preparing to go out. There were Margie's squeals. Molly shouting to anyone within earshot, asking them if they had taken her shoes or her stockings or whatever part of her clothing and make-up she could not lay her hands on at that instant. There was Duggie suffering from impatience standing at the bottom of the stairs shouting, "Are you not ready yet?" and "Hurry up, hi! Youse'd try the patience of Job!" and even the threat of, "I'm away on by myself, so I am, an' youse'll have to walk! Are ye coming?"

But the two women and even Basil had their preparations to get ready. A dance on any day of the week was a social occasion and required preparation to meet the expectations of the event. For Molly and Margie there was the attention to eyebrows and lashes, the lipstick and the seam down the stockings. For Basil there was the knot in his tie and the cuff links. It was important for Basil to look groomed while gliding over the floor of the dance hall. He put on his blue blazer with the Royal Navy crest on the breast pocket, and the matching Royal Navy tie. He brushed his hair down smooth. It was something he had picked up from seeing George Raft in the pictures. Basil thought he looked very much like George Raft. And George danced too.

Duggie was still standing at the foot of the stairs but had ceased to get any pleasure out of cajoling his cousins. Then he remembered Albert. "Aaaaalllbert!" he called in a long whooping cry. "Aren't you coming with us for a wild skelter? Aaaalbert!" He waited a few moments while inspiration stirred somewhere below the mass of wavy hair. "Albert! Shake a leg an' come for a hoult at a wumman! Aaaaalbert!" He was beginning to enjoy this new pass-time.

"Let him alone, do you hear!" Albert could hear Sally defending him. "Do you have to? Sure he's done you no harm! Let him alone. He has to study."

"Aalbert!" Duggie called. "Aaaalbert Buuurns!"

"Stop that!" cried Sally.

"Agh! Sure he's dead if he had the wit to stiffen. Aaalbert! Ye know something, Aaaalbert? What you've never had you'll never know the want of. This is your last chance! You hear, Aaaalbert?"

"Stop that!"

Duggie was silent for a moment as a new thought occurred to him. "Why do they call him Albert Burns? Heh? For Christ sake, his fire isn't even lit yet! Whooooagh ha ha!" Duggie felt really pleased with himself now. "Whooogh ha ha!" and burst into song. "Cigareets and whusky aaaan' wiiild wild wummin! They'll driiiive youse crazy they'll drive youse insane. Are ye comin'! Aaaalbert! Baaasil"

"Coming!" called Basil.

"We're here!" chimed in Molly and Margie.

All three descended the stairs. There was a strong smell of perfume and aftershave. Basil showed two inches of white cuffs neatly held by gold cuff links. The Royal Navy emblem shone. "Ready!"

Mrs. McIlhagga had hobbled to the hallway to watch their departure. "Ye're always on the batter," she said to one and all, shaking her head at the foolishness. But there was a smile on her face. Duggie was a power of energy. Just like his father was. He would keep some life in the boarding house.

"We're off, auntie May!" pronounced Duggie and with the scraping of the door over the step and a blast of cold air up the stairs, Albert knew they had gone. There was a moment's silence. "I do declare!" said Mrs. McIlhagga and let the declarations rest there. She returned to her seat by the fire shaking her head. These young ones! She sighed and leaned back into her chair. Her arthritis was giving her pains.

"That fellah's not right in the head,' commented Sally. She found her second cousin repulsive, an ignorant lout in her estimation. Albert was refined. A gentleman.

"Can ye get me some aspirin?" Mrs. McIlhagga said to her.

"They're upstairs in the bathroom."

"Well, get them. I'm in a bad way. I am."

Sally mounted the stairs to fetch the aspirin but her mind was on Albert. Treading lightly she continued up to the next landing. The light was showing under Albert's door. "Albert!" she whispered. There was no answer. "Albert!" she tapped lightly on the door.

"Yes?"

"Are you alright?"

"Yes!"

"Are you studying?"

MUSIC ON THE WIND

"Yes!"

He was studying. That was important. Sally could not think of what might come next. Her heart was racing. What if he scorned her? Albert was so very timid. Her courage left her. Oh God, she felt foolish at having come this far. She retraced her steps to the bathroom on the floor below and got the bottle of aspirin.

Sally switched on the radio to the Luxembourg station that carried the popular songs. Soon she was singing.

"Too long, too long, I've waited too long,
To tell the world just where you belong..."

Albert laid his textbook aside and switched out the light. He pulled the cold sheets up around his ears. It was drizzling outside again and he could hear the swishing sound of cars passing by. He kept his eyes closed, willing himself to sleep but it was useless. The car noises became fewer. Sally had long since stopped singing. He heard her going to her room. There was no sound from Mrs. McIlhagga. She was probably going to sit up waiting for the party to return. They would regale her with the events of the evening and she would get her thrills second hand. "His fire's not even lit, yet!" kept running through Albert's head. He felt a failure. Eventually fatigue took over and he slept.

Mrs. McIlhagga eased her fat backside into the chair. "Thank the Lord for Sunday. Ha hye," she sighed knowingly, addressing Albert. "Six days shalt thou labor!"

"Huh! Well the good Lord must ha' starved on a Sunday, so he must ha'!" commented Sally.

"Shush girl! What kind of blasphemy is that?"

"It's the God's truth. That's what it is. I'm the one who knows. Work! Work! Work!"

"Shush, do you hear! Ye're showin' the worst of ye in front of Albert, so ye are. Albert, did ye ever hear the likes?"

Albert kept quiet knowing he was not meant to give an answer.

"Shush nothing! Why isn't that shower up this time of day? Huh? I suppose they danced all night." Sally stamped to the hall door and shouted. "Baaasil! Molliii! Duggiiiiee! Margie! Your food's on the table. If you don't come and get it now it's not my fault if it gets cold. Do you hear? Baaasil!"

"'Ere! Don't shout so! You would think I was back in the navy. Do dododo dooo do do!" Basil stood to attention at the top step and bugled through his fist. "Oooooaaaah! Gives me the creeps to think abaht it." He clicked his heels as if in farewell to the thought and stood a moment to recollect himself. With a jerk of his neck he straightened his tie and stoically descended the stairs. "Motah!"

With a little flutter he skipped into the living room and placed a hand comfortingly on the old woman's shoulder. He bent enquiringly over her. "How are you this Lord's day?"

"Up and out of my bed this three hours. Not like some I could mention. An' Albert here too. He's an early riser, aren't ye, son?"

"Ah ha! Six days shalt thou labor!" laughed Basil.

"Ye can quote the Bible when it suits you. But ye're not so quick at goin' to church. Get stuck into your plate there before it gets cold. The rest of us has started. Where's yer mate? An' Margie?"

Basil pretended to be offended. "My wife is attending to her twalette. She will be here.."

"I'm here. Say no more!" Molly drew her quilted dressing gown tighter around her shoulders and came to the table. Margie crept in behind her wrapped in a bedspread.

"Dugiiiiiee!" screamed Sally up the stairs.

A noise like a barrel rolling down stairs descended from the top story to the first landing. A rude stroning noise came from the lavatory interrupted by a gusty breaking of wind.

"I declare to my goodness," said Mrs. McIlhagga, "that Duggie's a case."

"Ha hah!" Duggie appeared in a gray woolen sweater pulled over his pajama top and feet stuck into woolen socks. Ginger stubble sprouted from his chin. His eyes were baggy from too much to drink the night before and lack of sleep. "Ha hah!" he said again, rubbing his hands at the prospect of eating. Then, spying Albert, "Heavens-to-nelly the virgin's up before me. Move over there to I sees the table. Are youse all rightly? Eh? Auntie May?"

The old woman nodded that she was still bearing up.

"I say," said Basil, "you fairly gave us the slip last night, I should say. What happened?"

"Ah hah!" said Duggie, giving a cunning nod and wink at the same time.

Mrs. McIlhagga turned from the fireplace and said, "Ye're always on the blatter, so ye are. One day ye'll find yerself with consumption."

"Ah hah, auntie May, sure I have it already. One bottle of John J. a day and a crate of porter every hunnerd miles. Wooooaaagh ha ha!"

"But I say, seriously, where did you get to last night, old boy?" Basil enquired intimately.

"Now if I told you that you'd be as wise as me."

"Go on Duggie," urged Molly impatiently.

But Duggie was giving nothing away, yet. "Well, if you want to know, I was putting an eye in a goat."

"Sure we know that. Whose goat?"

"Now that would be telling. Pass the salt, there." And he elbowed Albert to emphasize the need.

"Well, I mean," said Basil, "if it's all so secret, perhaps...I mean...well.." He prolonged his protest as long as possible hoping that Duggie would butt in. "It's a long story," hinted Duggie.

"Just give us the details," drooled Margie.

"My auntie May would put me out on the street. Wouldn't you auntie May?"

"I'll see. Where were you?"

"Well," he exhaled a long dramatic pause. "Do you mind thon wee bit of fluff in yellah sittin near the band?" He turned to Albert before anyone could speak and slapped him on the knee. "Agh, Albert, you shoulda seen her. A wee beaut! A real smasher." He gave a pally squeeze on Albert's knee as if to say that Fate had not meant such favors for him. Duggie turned to Basil. "Do you mind me pointing her out and then asking her for a dance?"

"Quite!"

"Well I took her over to McNoggin's for a drink and doesn't it turn out she's going with thon big, long drink of water that was playing the saxophone."

"G'on!" trilled Margie as if that was the last thing she would have expected.

"Well, he comes out at the interval and wasn't he going to give me a lacin'. So he says."

"I say!" Basil leaned anxiously over the table. "Did...?"

"Didn't ye hear the row?" asked Duggie. "Bejazus didn't I leave him like a butcher's hag-block on a busy Saturday at four in the afternoon."

Some of Margie's jealousy left her. "And blood and all?"

"Sure when they dragged me off him didn't I lay out eleven of the crowd!"

"Now, here!" said Basil. "I say. We can believe some things, but look here."

"It's as true as God's in his heaven."
"Well, who was the girl? Do I know her?" asked Molly.
"A wee thing from Lisburn. Naw, you wouldn't know her."
"I hope," said Basil gallantly, "you left her an honest maiden."
"Honest? There was a glitter in her eyes like chromium, so there was. Maiden, be God? Made in Sheffield! Whoooaaagh ha ha!"
"Duggie M'Gooken! I'll have ye watch yer language. Don't ye know there's a young girl in the room?"
"Honest to God, mammy, you'd think I was a child," responded Sally.
"Sally! Ye shouldn't be listening. But go on Duggie. Tell us what happened."
"Agh no, I can't. Youse've spoiled it all. I'm shy now," Duggie pretended, wobbling his head in mock self-consciousness.
"G'on, Duggie," urged Margie.
"No I'm shy. I'll tell you another time. Albert here'll tell you a story. Won't you Albert? Eh? Tell us about the time you twisted the wee girl's arm. Whoooaagh agh ha ha!" Albert rose from the table. "Here! Where you going? Have you no manners leaving the table before us? Huh?" woofed Duggie through his bite of bread.
"I'm going out!"
"Whoooaagh ha! Do youse all hear. The virgin's got a girl! Is she a good girl, hi?"
Albert went up the stairs to get his raincoat. There was a lump in his throat from frustration.
"Duggie M'Gookin, you don't know how to behave." He could hear Sally yelling. "You're a thick, ignorant clod!"
"Sally!" yelled Mrs. McIlhagga. "How dare ye speak to yer cousin like that? Apologize this minit!"
"I will not! I could kill him." Sally fled up the stairs.

When Albert descended the social activity was still in high decibel in the living room.
"Hi! Wait for me!" Sally whispered. "Where you going?"
"I'll take a walk along the embankment. It's peaceful there."
"Do you mind if I come along?" He shook his head. "I'm coming with you then. Alright?" She slipped her arm into his. "Albert, I'm at my wit's end, so I am. Aren't you?" Albert was afraid to speak.
They walked along the bank of the river in silence. They stopped and

looked at the swans gliding on the water. Sally eventually broke silence. "They look so lovely and peaceful." Albert nodded. He could feel her grip on his arm. What should he do? He was afraid. No girl had ever taken possession of him like this before. They walked further on and across the park then back through the University grounds. There was no conversation. Each was content in their own thoughts, too afraid to mention them to the other. As they approached the street of the boarding house Sally turned him gently around, looking up into his eyes. "We should go out again some time. Wouldn't you like that? I would."

"Yes. Me too. But I need to think about it? I've my studies."

"Hmmm!" She let the matter go. It would take time.

Albert had come to a decision. He would not put up with the emptiness and humiliation any further. He would act. All week long he had gone over the various components of his plan and he had it down pat. He dressed carefully in his white shirt, school tie and blue blazer with the badge of Ballyaghone Academy on the breast pocket. He had got a haircut earlier in the day. His shoes were polished. His nails neatly scrubbed and trim. He was ready. He threw his raincoat over his arm and descended.

"God save us, would you look at thon, hi!" yelled Duggie. "All dressed up like a scabby knuckle! Where you going the night?"

Albert allowed himself a smile.

"Let's see you!" called Molly.

"You're cuttin' a dash the night, hi!" commented Margie.

"Who's the lucky girl?" asked Molly.

"Agh, sure it's some wee thing he sits with during chemistry class making stink bombs. Whoooaagh ha ha! Isn't that it! Would she go for a loaf, hi?"

"Duggie! Shut up!" Sally had appeared from the kitchen.

"What's goin' on over there?" called Mrs. McIlhagga.

"It's Albert. He's all dolled up and no place to go," called Duggie. "You need to see this, so you do."

"Let's see you son!" the old woman called. Albert was not troubled this time with the harassment but instead was deriving satisfaction from the scrutiny. The whole tribe of them needed to know that he, Albert, was a dark horse, that he, Albert, was deep water. "Soul son, ye're a fine lookin' young fellah so ye are. Yer mother should be proud."

"And a haircut into the bargain," giggled Duggie running a hand up the stubble of Albert's neck. "Yeachh! Brilliantine!"

"Leave him alone, Duggie M'Gookin!" called Sally.

Albert kept his pleasant smile.

"Where you off to, hi?" asked Duggie. "Can we come too? I could hold her tail for you!"

"Duggie! Don't be so ignorant. Go, Albert. Get away on out of this before they scunner you. G'way on!" urged Sally.

As Albert walked away he could hear Duggie calling in a high falsetto, "Albert's go a gir-il! Albert's got a gir-il!"

"Stop it!" Sally cried.

"Do you know where he's going?"

"Yes I do and you're not to know."

"Agh, come on. Tell us!"

Out of earshot on the Botanic Avenue, Albert boarded the bus and took a seat. He leaned back satisfied with himself that he had pulled the moment off with aplomb and breathed a large sigh of relief. His heart was beating eighteen to the dozen. He felt into the inner pocket to make certain he had his wallet and, for the umpteenth time since he had visited the Chemist's on Shaftesbury Square, he fingered the circular embossings on the leather made by the packet inside. Albert's stomach tightened with the first tremors of fear since he started to think it all out.

Albert entered the Mecca Dance Hall, bought a ticket and checked his raincoat. In the Men's Room he relieved a taught bladder, straightened his tie and combed his hair. He noticed how his wallet weighed down one side of his blazer. Two young men entered to change their shoes to dancing pomps and he watched them surreptitiously through the angle of the mirror. A note of music came through the still swinging door and Albert followed it down to the dance floor.

Albert had never seen anything like it before—a full-scale orchestra of saxophones, clarinets and trumpets with a singer crooning at a microphone. Band and crooner were dressed in fuschia colored dinner jackets with dark velvet collars and lapels, and shirtfronts resembling those worn by Mississippi gamblers in Technicolor pictures. Their heads were brushed to look smooth. The look and the music established an aura of sophistication. Romance was provided by the subdued rose-colored lighting. A revolving globe of multi-faceted mirrors suspended from the ceiling reflected a beam of light. There was an effect of snow falling that bedazzled the mind into believing this was fairyland, a place where anything could happen if you believed it would.

This dance hall was different. This was not a Saturday night dance at the Orange Hall where he knew everyone and the men clustered on one side with the women on the other, talking and feeling secure. This was a battle field where elegant men chose partners to demonstrate their prowess with intricate steps across a polished floor; men in gabardine suits, women in taffeta dresses that swung out and revealed their thighs on the spins, the long gliding steps, the momentary rest before the next glide, the up-on-the-toes and whirl, one, two, three. Albert felt boyish in his blazer and flannels, a wee fellow up from the country. But, he was determined.

One of the men from the group beside him began to walk nonchalantly to ask a girl sitting opposite to dance. As if by cue the others followed and in a moment each had a partner and was gliding across the pond of ecstasy. Albert was alone. He looked around and saw a group of girls to his right. He had to make a start. He just had to dance. That was the only way to find a woman. A dozen pairs of eyes watched him advance, each curious as to whom he would ask. He was in front of them now. Wasn't that a school blazer?

"May I have this dance?" he asked a red-haired girl.

"Nah! A'm sittin' this one out. Can't you see Ah've jist lit a cigarette!"

He began to blush. Should he ask the girl next to her? No, she was smoking too. They were all smoking, each one gazing away from him in deliberate effort to avoid eye contact. A wee fellah! He wanted to run and hide from them. He made a sick smile. The girl at the end of the row put out her cigarette.

"May I have this dance?"

The girl got up and dismay flooded to his legs. She was taller than he. For a moment he did not know what to do. The girl was waiting. She laid a bony arm along his shoulder and thin fingers grabbed his hand. "Aren't you dancin'?" she said.

Watched by the row of girls Albert steered her onto the floor. He felt awkward, his feet would not move properly and they kept slapping down flat-footed. Slow, slow, two wee quick steps to the side, slow, slow, quick, quick, slow. Time was endless.

"It's a great band," he said.

Jesus, had he really said that?

"Yes!"

What now? The girl's face stared over his head and the down around her chin was level with his eyes. Slow, slow, quick, quick, slow. Around him nimble footed versions of Fred Astaire and Ginger Rogers glided by.

"Is this the only step you can do?" the bent down head of the girl asked. For the first time he saw her eyes. Marbles.

"Well, I'm not much of a dancer."

"Nah, ye're nat!" She took the bony arm from around his neck. "Ah'm goin' to sit down. Ah've made a big enough sight of myself already."

She left him in mid-floor. The blood was rising to his ears in mortification. What could he do? He looked around. The low balcony was just visible through the pink murk and swirling snowstorm of light. He rushed to it and saw the bar. "Whisky!"

"Sorry! Only lemonade, orangeade and milk shakes. You can have coffee?"

Albert sat at a table with his coffee. It had been a mistake to come. He should have used his bit of money to take the bus back home. There would have been something on at the Orange Hall where he could have made up for his distress. He watched the dancers gliding by below. This was what Basil and Molly did on every possible occasion. Fred and Ginger! He could not ask another girl to dance out of fear. Neither could he leave. He sipped slowly at his coffee. It had cost more than it was worth. Make it last.

"Hello!"

He looked up. Sally smiled. "Sitting this one out?" she said softly. "What brings you here?"

"If you only knew."

"Aren't you dancing?"

"Naw! There's not a girl here I'd walk round a herring barrel." He liked the sound of that; something Duggie might have said. It made him feel brave. "Except you!"

She reached for his hand. Albert felt confident as he took her hand and led her to the floor.

"I'm not a very good dancer, Albert," she said.

"Don't worry about a wee thing like that. I'll take you easy." His heart was running wild as he swallowed the lie.

"Albert, you're wonderful."

She laid her cheek against his and together they edged slowly around the floor. Albert felt strong and cursed the tall bony piece. He could feel the firm flesh of Sally's waist and her soft breasts against him. She was warm to hold. The tune being played was one heard frequently on the radio. Sally sang softly to his ear,

"You must remember this,
A kiss is just a kiss,
A sigh is just a sigh...."

"Tell me," he whispered, "how were you able to slip away from the house?"

"What would you say if I told you I sneaked out?"

"You did?"

"Uh huh!"

"You did not?"

"Honest. Honest to God."

"Jeepers! Your mother'll yell her head off at you when you go home. You shouldn't have."

She stopped. "I don't care and what's more, Albert Burns, I'm seventeen years old last October and I'm old enough to please myself. And if you think..." She was leaving him.

"Sally! Sally, wait a minute." He caught her arm. "I'm sorry. Come on, let me buy you a drink."

"A drink?"

"A lemonade or a milkshake."

"Who wants a milkshake? I'm not a child."

"But the pubs are closed! Otherwise.."

"Would you Albert? Honest? Would you?"

"Yes, I would. But the pubs are closed."

She studied his face for a moment. "That doesn't matter. Come on. I know a place."

"Listen Sally. You're mother will know."

She was getting coquettish and ran a finger round under his chin. "What my Mammy doesn't know won't do her no harm."

They walked through several streets where Albert had not ventured before. "Take this," she said, "and show it to the man at the door."

"What?"

"It's a membership card."

"It says Douglas M'Gooken on it!"

"Sure I know that."

"But I can't use that."

"Sure you can. Nobody knows you're not him."

"Where'd you get this?"

"I took it out of his wallet along with five pound notes."

"You did not? Jeepers!"

"He deserves it. Look at the way he has been teasing you."

"But he'll know!"

"Nope. He had a pile of them in his pocket tied up in a rubber band. He'll not know for a while."

"But the membership card, he'll miss it!"

"So what? It'll turn up some day in his socks drawer. Don't worry. Who cares about him? I don't. Why should you?"

Albert had a rush of excitement such as he had never had before. "Sure!" he laughed. "Show me this place."

"We're there. That door over there."

They negotiated the entry to the club without mishap. It was a social club. There was a friendly atmosphere made up of people sitting round tables for four or more and a pianist playing requests from the jovial crowd. There were framed photographs around the walls of football players from the Belfast teams, a couple of jockeys and several prizefighters. Barmen carried laden trays of beers and goblets and glasses. Orders were taken and delivered and there was an overall atmosphere of friendly enjoyment.

"A Bushmills and a bloody Mary, please." Albert heard Sally order.

"Sally!"

"Relax, Albert. It's just you and me, tonight. No Duggie M'Gooken, no Molly and none of that Basil. Just you and me." She smiled at Albert.

"But your mother will find out!"

"Eventually. So what?"

He looked at her in amazement. "You know what? I'm beginning to enjoy myself. Aren't you?"

The piano struck up the music of a request from a table near them. Sally began to sing the words softly. "*A kiss is just a kiss, a sigh is just a sigh.* You know what? I wish I could be a singer in a band. I'd have liked that, instead of cleaning up after people. Oh, God, let's forget that. Drink up, Albert." They sipped their drinks. "What are you thinking, Albert?"

He shook his head afraid to share his feelings. He was so very conscious of the difference between this atmosphere and that of the library where he sometimes went to study, or his boarding house, the lab where he spent three afternoons a week or any of the other places he spent his time. There was conviviality here, friendliness. It was difficult to imagine how Duggie fit in here as a member. Maybe he calmed down as he came through the door, just another in search of friends. "I'm wondering how Duggie behaves when he comes here."

"Oh, he's just all mouth. I bet if he opens his yap in here someone would close it for him. He's just all talk. Let's forget him. I need to order again. How about you?"

"I'm O.K.," he said. He did not have enough in his pocket to buy a beer let alone a whisky and a bloody Mary.

"The same again!" he heard her say and she folded a pound note into his hand.

"Take it. It's Duggie's treat."

Albert was now feeling good about things around him. The pianist had started another request.

"They tried to tell us we're too young,
Too young to really be in love,"

Sally sang. The several people at the next table turned to listen. Albert heard one of them say, "She should get up there and sing, so she should." There was applause for Sally when the song ended. A woman said. "That was lovely, hi. Why don't you get up and sing the next one. Do you know 'Too long, too long, I've waited too long'? Do you?" Sally nodded. "Hey Matt!" the woman called. "Let this wee girl sing for you. She's great so she is."

There were cheers of encouragement as Sally went to the side of the piano and sang. Albert basked in the looks he received from the people around and the heads nodding in their approval of Sally's voice. The whisky had been sipped dry by the end of the song. "The compliments of the house," said a voice and two more drinks were on the table before him. Sally sang again.

"A blossom fell, from off the tree,
And touched those lips you turned to me..."

When the song was over the pianist rose and with lifted arms helped the audience show their appreciation. "Bravo!" a voice called. "That was great!" There was much hand clapping as Sally returned to the table. She was aglow and happy. Her eyes shone. She took Albert's hand. "I've got to thank you for bringing me here. I've never been so happy." They held hands and sipped their drinks. "You didn't tell me how you slipped out," Albert said. She moved her chair close to his side. "You don't want to know." She laid her head on his shoulder. "I said I was going round to Maisie Mullins to baby sit. Who cares?" She looked up at him. "Albert, I think I'm getting drunk."

Albert too felt the effect of his whisky. There was a feeling of elation and all's right with the world. He had never experienced this before. The rules of math and physics seemed very far away. He had not a care in the world, lovely music, a beautiful soft girl resting on his shoulder, her hand in his. All around him were happy people. Not one of them had said a contrary word against him. One man, old enough to be his father, had even leaned over to him when Sally was singing and said, "That a lovely young woman you have there, fellah. Lovely voice too." Albert felt like he never had before in his life. He put his arm around her. "Shall we order another?"

"Sure. Let me get another of Duggie's pound notes."

It was closing time. He put his arm around her shoulder and steered her towards the street. They buttoned up their coats as the cold air hit, then wrapped their arms around each other for the walk back home. She would look up at him every now and then and reach to kiss his lips. She sang a few words of a song from the club.

"I tried so hard to show that you're my everything..."

Her voice was pure joy to Albert. He steered her into a shop doorway and kissed her. She held onto him. "Isn't it a pity we have to go home?"

"Where else can we go?"

She shrugged.

"No place."

"It's a pity I don't have my own place."

"Or me either."

"Well, let's go."

"What time is it?"

"Well after midnight."

"They're all still out until three in the morning because it's Saturday night. My mammy will be asleep by the fire. Why don't we just slip in and never let on?"

"What?"

"Sure. Don't you see? I'll sneak in while you go in like always, making a noise with the door and mammy'll think it's only you and I'll sneak up the stairs with my shoes off."

Albert giggled. "Why not?"

"Look! You see. Duggie's car's not even there and there's no light on up stairs. All's quiet!"

Albert made more than the usual noises as he opened the door and coughed a good deal as he hung up his coat on the hallstand. He stamped his feet a few times before looking in on Mrs. McIlhagga.

"Albert Burns, ye're like a Clydesdale horse with six feet, so ye are. Ye're fit tae waken the dead. What do ye mean by rousin' the house at this time of night? It's one o'clock in the mornin' Everybody's abed since twelve except Duggie an' he's still out scoungin'"

"Sorry! I didn't know everybody's home. What happened?"

"That Basil took sick. It's the flu. Molly too. I had to give them hot whiskeys an' aspirins they were feelin' so bad. The flu. Margie never went out at all she was feelin' so dreary. They're all up stairs sleepin'. So go easy. Have ye seen Sally?"

"No!"

"That wee lass went out to baby sit these hours ago an' there's no sign of her. She'll hear me when she gets home. Just wait till I lay me hands on her."

"Well goodnight, Missus."

Albert climbed the stairs to the first landing where Sally was making faces at him. She held her face forward to be kissed.

"Sssshhhh!" he whispered.

"I heard," she said and pointed upwards. She began to climb the stairs. He followed. The sounds of sleep came from the bedrooms.

At Sally's door they kissed and under its disguise she guided him into her room. Its feminine smells filled his nostrils. The end of the bed came against his legs and he steered her around it. Together they fell lengthwise on its softness. Albert felt the bulge of his wallet against his side. In the darkness his lips sought hers but his hands were nervous. Fear pounded his heart but her parted lips invited his caress.

Duggie M'Gookin had been on a wild skelter. At least he had planned it as such. But without Basil and Molly and Margie there as his audience the evening had foundered. He had met a young woman and danced with her but there was no fire. He had invited her to go with him to his after-hours social club and she had accepted. It was only when he got there that he found he had mislaid his membership card and the doorman was adamant.

"Sorry sir. Members only. I can't let you in without a membership card."

The doorman was a big fellow and Duggie did not insist. From inside he could hear a woman's voice singing. "Who's thon?" he asked.

"It's a private club sir. You're not to ask unless you're a member."

"I heard thon voice before, so I have."

"You probably have, sir. All young ladies sound alike to me."

Duggie was not satisfied. "Can't you just let us in? I know the place well. I'm a member I tell you."

"Sorry sir. No card, no get in."

At which point the doorman folded his arms in signal that he was not kidding.

A man and a woman came by and on proving membership were allowed to enter. While the door was ajar Duggie stood on tiptoes and peered over the doorman. Through the smoke he saw somebody suspiciously like Albert stand up while a girl equally suspiciously like Sally walked towards him to sit at his table. But with the haze of cigarette smoke and the coming and going of waiters he could not tell. It could hardly be possible. Albert was a wet dishcloth. And Sally was too young. It was simply an illusion. "Come on," said Duggie to the woman. "Let's go."

"It's alright, Duggie. Just take me home."

"I can't for the life of me understand how I lost my membership card. And there's five pounds in one pound notes missing too."

"They probably fell out of your pocket."

"Nah! Nah!"

By the time he had driven to the far side of the city and deposited the girl on her doorstep Duggie had explored his suspicions. He had never trusted Basil. And he suspected Margie had been in his room searching his things. He'd have to get a key for the door. Then there was Albert. But no way would Albert have the courage to steal from his room. Or Sally? She was going baby-sitting. But Albert had got all dressed up. Nah! He probably went off to some church meeting to sing in the choir. Sally could sing. Just like the girl at the club. Remarkable. Nah!

When he got to the boarding house Duggie had almost forgotten his disappointment. He was feeling very much alone and miserable. What he needed was a good story to tell to entertain the troops, as it were. Get a laugh! Thrill them with a grand yarn about his goings-on and how he had come out on top. Maybe everyone was still up and waiting. He'd surprise them. He lifted the front door up on its worn hinges so it would not scrape over the doorstep. He closed it. Stepping lightly he went to the living room from where the light seeped out under the door. He turned the handle gently and stepped in silently. There was only the old woman still asleep by the fire. The others had already gone to bed. Duggie stepped back into the hall and took off his shoes. He'd slip up to bed and leave the story until the morning. It would be better then. On the first landing he could hear Basil snoring. Margie's door was open and he peeped in. The moonlight shone on her pale face and open mouth. She was asleep. He began to climb the stairs again. At the turn he noticed Sally's door was closed. She must be asleep too. He continued. He might as well go to sleep now also. Albert's door too was closed and there was not a sound. Then he heard a creaking noise and poised to listen. Someone was turning over in bed he thought. Then voices. Old Basil was giving his wife some favors. With a grin on his face he retraced his steps and paused outside their door. Duggie had no hesitation at eves dropping. It would make a good yarn to tell next day, but no sound. Then it happened again but this time a man's voice whispered something he could not make out. He held his ear to the door. Nothing. Then again. But that was strange. The sound seemed to be coming from Sally's bedroom. Good God! Old Basil had a howlt on Sally. Good God! He sprang at the door and switched on the light in one movement. Sally was pulling up her underwear. He caught a glimpse of her breasts. Albert was standing before her, naked.

"Whoooaaagh ha ha! Albert! What's this? What's this?" For once Duggie could not find words. Albert reached for his pants and shirt and began to dress but Duggie had recovered. "Hi everyone! Albert's got a hoult of our Sally. You Judas you! Sneak in here and ruin a girl's virtue, would you!" He began to rain blows on Albert who fell to the floor stiking his face on the cupboard.

"Stop it, Duggie. Get out of here! It's none of your business!"

"What's going on up there?" Mrs. McIlhagga yelled up the stair well. There was the sound of scurrying feet.

"Whoaaagh! The virgin's trying to mount our Sally! Whooaagh! Look at his bare arse! He has his trousers down. Whoooaagh!"

Albert, still naked, grabbed his clothes and rushed for the door. Duggie clipped him over the head as he passed. "You're a bad ouzel. G'wan out of here." Duggie cried, now more amused than angry. It was the perfect finish to a dismal night. One he could recount many times in the future. Sally was pushing her breasts into the cups of her brassiere. "You're a jackass idiot!" she yelled. "What business do you have bursting in here?"

"What's all this then?" shouted Basil from the landing. "What's going on?" He saw Albert pulling on his trousers half way down the steps. "What's the matter Albert?" Albert pulled on his shirt. He picked up his socks and shoes from the step and went quickly down.

"What is it?" called Molly from her room.

"Bejazus," yelled Duggie, "thon Albert's a dark horse! Did you see him trying to mount our Sally?"

"Sally?"

"He was not!" yelled Sally. "I was trying to mount him. For God's sake! Go to bed the lot of you, you make me sick."

"Nice tits!" said Duggie.

Sally calmly reached for a china dog on the mantle piece and smashed it over Duggie's head. Duggie dropped in a lump.

Albert stood coatless in the damp silence of the street. He could feel the cold through his shirt. The lamplight gave off a morbid glow as though tired from it all. What was new? Just another night in Belfast! Albert felt the pain rising to his cheek. He felt it for broken skin but there was none. The swelling had begun. He did not feel well. The rush of adrenaline was tapering off and his stomach was beginning to retch. He bent over Duggie's car as the vomit rushed up his throat. Tears flooded to his eyes with the effort. The car was a mess. He beat the fender in his frustration, feeling the cold metal under his fist. Then, now aware of where he was, he stood back and kicked the door. The panel caved in. Albert began to run. He ran for a few hundred yards but slowed to a walk as he realized a policeman might see him and question his appearance at that time of night plus the fact of the bruise on his face. He found himself in the University quad, cold and in need of warm shelter. He stood in an archway and shuddered.

"Hi there, fellah! What ye doin' standin' there? Ye look frozen to death."

He recognized the watchman from his blue uniform and cap. "I had an accident."

"Let me look at you. You're a student here, aren't you?" Albert nodded. "Ye'll have to come on over an' get warmed up," the man said kindly. "Come on. Ye're shivering'." The yellow light from the porter's hide-away swelled out through the door and enveloped him in its staleness. "G'on in, young fellah," urged the porter. "Sammy," he said to the other porter sitting at a table, "this young fellah's got himself hurt. An' he's starvin' to death with the cold. Seat yourself up there, fellah. That's it. You'll warm up in no time."

Albert approached the fire holding one hand to shade the eye from the yellow light. He tried to prevent the pain showing on his face.

"You're looking slightly worse for the weather, hi!" said the first watchman. His inquisitive eyes were probing and his half-open mouth had the indecision of not knowing whether to ask for an explanation or wait until one was given. But the second man had less subtlety. "That's a right shiner you have there." It was half a statement of fact, half a question. "Ye look like ye got kicked b' a mule, hi." His laughter cackled like a hoarse hen, his stained teeth bared by the stretched upper lip. "What's the other fellah like?"

Albert thought about that. What excuse could he make? Duggie would have made something up, told a story of outlandish daring-do. "I was coming over Shaftesbury Square when these two guys jumped me," he began. But the lie didn't feel right. He waited wondering what to say next.

"Just shows you,' said the first watchman. "There's never a policeman around when you need one. And then?"

"Well one of them pulls my coat down over my elbows while the other hits me in the face."

"Goodness me! You're lucky you're alive. There's some terrible bad people about. Then what?"

"They tore my coat off and my wallet and money and keys are gone."

"But can't you knock the door of your digs to let you in?"

"I didn't want to bother them, so I didn't. It'll soon be morning. Can I stay here?"

"That's very considerate of you. Sure you can stay here. Just lie back and rest."

One of the watchmen began to tell a story of similar theme about his wife's cousin's husband who was on the night shift and one night... The story was listened with quiet respect and responded to with "Huh huh!" and "Boys a dear, you don't say!" But Albert had withdrawn from them. He saw the fire glowing, warming to a tingle the front of his ankles. Gradually the voices of the men faded into the distance as he relived the evening, her perfume, her warmth, the cold of the bedcover as they lay back in each other's arms. He had felt no embarrassment taking off his clothes, just the wonder as Sally placed his hands on her body, taking his face between her breasts. The nightmare of Duggie's discovery screamed through his mind, the blows about his body that injured beyond the skin.

The McIlhagga household had been in a state of turmoil since Albert's hurried exit. Everyone had something to say about the event and each and everyone wanted to say it at the exact same moment that the others were trying to give their opinion on the matter.

"Oh, how could I've been so mistaken in the character of thon wee lad?" Mrs. McIlhagga declared from the depths of her armchair by the fireside. She sighed heavily to underlie the torment this realization gave her. "To look at him ye'd think butter wouldn't melt in his mouth. Just like the good book says. A wolf in sheep's clothing." She felt justified by that and pleased she had remembered so pertinent a quotation. It deserved repeating for those who didn't listen. "Aye, a wolf in sheep's clothing. That's the height of it." She continued to shake her head in torment. "Agh oh! An' the way I treated him, like he was me own son." The iniquity of it was so appalling she had to raise her voice to a pitch that would do it justice. "Goddamn the wee bugger! Couldn't any of ye have seen it? Are these things always left to me?" The effort made her weak and breathless.

"Agh Ma, give over. Nothing was left to you. I'm to blame. Ye'd think it was the end of the world." Sally handed her a cup of tea. "Here, this'll calm your nerves and maybe quieten you down a bit."

"Me own daughter, me youngest, the one I had the most hopes for, not one bit different from her sisters. Agh oh!"

"Give over, Ma."

"It's always the quiet ones ye have to look out for."

"He was the only person who ever treated me decent."

"Decent? Is that the word for it? Seducing you? Taking away the thing most precious to a woman?"

"He didn't seduce me! I tried to seduce him! For god's sake what's the big worry? That idiot Duggie stuck his big nose into the room before anything happened."

"Thank God. Duggie, ye're the only one who has a care for how I feel."

Duggie had made himself a sandwich in the kitchen. It was a Duggie special in which two slices of large white loaf were held apart with whatever appealed to the hunger in his eyes. There were slices of onion, tomato, a cabbage leaf and two pork sausages, cold and congealed with fat that had been left over from some previous repast. In consequence the sandwich was far thicker than the average mouth could negotiate without severe elasticity of the cheeks and the considerable grimaces that this involved. It did however have the advantage of keeping Duggie out of the shouting match between Mrs. McIlhagga and Sally for the space of several minutes. Now, with a direct reference to his heroic participation in preventing what was clearly evolving into a case of near-rape, Duggie jumped into the fray. "Sure I saw his bare arse!" he said, not for the first time that night, as clear evidence that a sin had indeed been about to be committed. Eyes staring with conviction, Duggie struggled with the quantity of food in his mouth. He had taken a very generous bite, as always, and it had not yet succumbed to the chewing to which he had attacked it. But there were important things to be said that could not wait. Amid crumbs and bits of cabbage leaf that seemed to protest his lack of commitment to the meal, he shouted, "He's just one of them Queen's students. What else can ye expect? No balls and less brains! Did ye see the way he took off, hi? I scared the bejazus out of him. Wooaaugghhh!" And having summed up the matter Duggie studied the reminder of his sandwich to determine from what angle he should take the next bite. A coil of onion rings peeped out from below a slice of tomato to invite his serious consideration and, having studied their proposal, clinched the matter by thrusting the succulent lot into the cavern of his mouth. He turned once again to Mrs. McIlhagga. "The best thing ye can do is put all his stuff in his suitcase an' I'll take it up and dump it at the caretaker's office. He can get it there whenever he sees fit. What do ye think?"

"Serve him right," agreed Molly, looking round for approval.

"He'd be drummed out of the navy, in my day," reassured her husband.

"The poor wee fellah." Margie was partial to the romance of the affair and somewhat regretful that her bout of flu had kept her away from what might have occurred in her own life that night. She gave vent to a fit of coughing.

"I'll pack his things then," said Sally sadly and went upstairs. It might be her last chance. She entered Albert's room and took the suitcase from under the bed. In each drawer his shirts and underwear were neatly laid. She lifted them and pressed them to her face.

"What's keepin' ye?" Duggie's voice carried up the stairs.

"Tell her to hurry!" Her mother's hoarse voice could be heard urging him on.

Sally put Albert's clothes into the case along with some books from atop the chest of drawers. On a piece of paper she wrote "Love, Sally", placed it inside and snapped the lock.

Duggie was waiting for her at the bottom of the stairs his eyes straying up her skirt as she descended. She had the feeling that sooner or later she would have to teach him a lesson. "Gimme," he said exuding a waft of onion breath. "I take over from here." He grabbed the suitcase and went to lean his head inside the doorway of the living room. "Get yourself some sleep, auntie May. Ye've heard the last of the wee bugger."

"There's his blazer and raincoat, on the peg there. Take them too. He'll need them this cold night."

"Aye, woman. Ye're over anxious. But I'll settle his hash." He winked over a large grin and went out singing. "Cigareets an' whusky an' wild, wild wummen. They'll drive youse crazy they'll drive youse insane. Cigareets an' whusky..."

A hand was shaking Albert. "Come on there lad. Wake up! There's a fellah here looking for you. Are you Albert?"

He tried to open his eyes and pain rushed to his face. His back was stiff from the chair and his neck seemed kinked to one position. Sunshine sparkled in through the diamond pane windows.

"Whoooagh, Albert, ha, ha!" said Duggie. "Ye look like ye tripped over a straw an' a hen kicked ye. How'd ye do that to yersel'? Ye're a dangerous man, so ye are. Here! Ha. ha!" There was a strip of plaster on one side of Duggie's forehead where the china dog had found its mark. Duggie held out a suitcase and, as Albert reached for it, dropped it on the floor. "An' here's yer raincoat an' blazer. Ha, ha!" He threw them onto a chair beyond Albert's reach. "Mrs. McIlhagga was worried about ye. Had me come all this way this early in the morning lookin' for ye. Real concerned she is. An' all the thanks she gets is you up to your oxters in her daughter's knickers. Whoooaghh! Ha, ha! Ye're some pup, ha ha!" He looked Albert over. "Ha, ha! Ha, ha!"

The two watchmen looked on in wonderment as each new fact was revealed about Albert. This was the fellah who had been in a fight the night before, like he said, and now, a wummen chaser. Boys-a-dear! They saw him with new respect. Such a quiet looking fellah, too. But they were usually the ones. Students! Good God! The life some of them led. Bloody Errol Flynns the lot of them. Full of buck like a tomcat.

Duggie leaned over with great ceremony to view Albert's eye, holding his expression the way a connoisseur would view an objet d'art. "Whoooaagh!" He broke into a giggle. His shoulders shook with glee. "Boys, that's a right shiner ye got there! Let's take a look! Whooooaagh! What have ye been doin' to yersel'?"

Albert sighed. It was hardly possible that this galoot of a fellow, this ignoramus, could get so much enjoyment out of another's misery. He swallowed his mounting anger. "How is Sally?" he asked instead, keeping his voice calm.

"She's not crying after ye if that's what ye mean. Runnin' out on her like ye did. Whooaagh ha ha! Ye're some boyoo! Takin' advantage of her like that. Ye had her drunk, so ye had. Ye know that? Ye deliberately had her drunk so ye could take advantage. Of a wee girl! D'je hear? Mrs. McIlhagga's mad, so she is. Ha, ha! What she's goin' to do to ye when she lays hands on ye, I wouldn't be in your shoes. Naw! Ha, ha!" Duggie saw the makings of a great story in how he had humiliated Albert the morning after the deed. He could see himself saying, "Maun, I scared the bejazus out of the wee lad. He went in his trousers, so he did. Whoooaagh! Ha, ha!"

"Is Sally alright?" Albert asked again. He could feel the rush of adrenaline up his body, waiting for the starter's pistol, like on the annual sport's day at school. But this time it was a fearful feeling, one he had never felt before. Albert had never been one to fight, not even in the schoolyard. His mother had been proud of that, so well behaved.

"Sure, she's alright. Amn't I there to take care of her? She's a great wee bundle, Eh? Whooooaghh! Ha ha! Don't you worry about her none, I'll take care of her. Ha, ha!" A dirty leer spread over Duggie's face. "Hegh, hegh!" He gurgled sexily, as a hint of things to come that he would do with Sally. Albert struck, no warning that the anger in him would so suddenly turn to violence. It just happened, an involuntary act. His fist shot out and landed alongside Duggie's nose. There was a spattering of blood and then a gush that flowed down over Duggie's shirt. Albert threw his other fist hitting Duggie on the cheek. Duggie fell back against the wall, bumping his head. There was a telltale thud, shock, surprise and fear in his eyes. This had never happened to him before. He tried to stand up and put his fists before him, fight, do something to show he was a man, but Albert connected again on his nose. Duggie put his hands up over his face in anguish. He could not breathe. Something was wrong with his nose. He saw the blood on his hands.

"Don't!" he screamed. "For Christ's sake what's wrong with you? What'd I do? Jesus! I'm bleedin' like a stuck pig!"

The two watchmen had not moved, the attack had happened so suddenly. Albert stood poised, his fists at the ready. His face was deadly white as if all the blood had rushed to the muscles that propelled his fists. Slowly he let his arms drop, his body losing the readiness to spring. He turned and reached for his blazer and felt himself begin to shake. Duggie lay against the wall whimpering. "Oh, fuck it! My nose! My fuckin' nose! Ye broke my fuckin' nose! Christ oh!" He rose shakily to his feet and, hiding his face in his hands stumbled out the door.

Albert slipped on his blazer and gathered up his raincoat. His suitcase was before him. He picked it up. The door to the quad was open.

"Hey!" one of the watchmen called. Albert stopped and turned, slowly. "Is that fellah a friend of yours?" the watchman asked. A weight was beginning to settle on Albert as if his clothes had suddenly become too heavy. He wanted to answer. The watchmen had been kind to him, but he was too tired. All the adrenaline had gone. What did it matter anyway? Not now. "Ye need to sit down a wee moment, so ye do." The watchman said. "Ye've had a night of it. Just sit a while an' ye'll feel better."

Albert slumped down into the chair. "Thanks. Just give me a moment." He closed his eyes and laid his head back.

The other watchman looked down at Albert and shook his head. "Godsaveus. He's gone to sleep. Can ye imagine? He's all tuckered out! What's he been up to? These students. Ye niver know."

The clock on the wall could be heard ticking time away. About a half hour passed when the watchmen heard a voice.

"Is there an Albert Burns here? I'm looking for him."

The watchmen pointed in unison to the sleeping figure. One of them reached over and shook him by the shoulder.

"Come on there, lad. Wake up! There's a young lady here looking for you. Are you Albert?"

Albert tried to open his eyes and pain rushed to his face. His back was stiff from the chair and his neck was kinked to one position. Sunshine sparkled in through the diamond pane windows.

"Albert!" Sally cried. "I was worried stiff. Are you alright? I thought I'd find you here. I've looked everywhere for you. Are you alright? Really?"

The two men were setting their chairs back to the wall and making things look active. Albert stood up and, muttering, "Is it morning?" went to Sally.

"Are you alright?" she asked again. Her eyes held his. "Duggie's a complete mess."

He looked at her, seeing the strength within her. Albert felt a confidence like he never had before. "I'm O.K"

She touched the bruise on his cheek and pursed her lips in a kiss. "I love you Albert Burns," she said.

Albert smiled. He had never had anyone say that to him before, not even his mother. "I love you too." It was the first time he himself had ever said that to anyone. It felt good. He turned and called to the men, "Thanks!"

"Keep winning fellah!" they said. The remark had warmth and friendliness.

"Let's go, Albert," Sally picked up his suitcase. Albert noticed again that the sun was shining through the windows with diamond-like sparkle. He took Sally's outstretched hand and together they walked into a bright new day.

The Terrible Sin of Martin McCabe

"McCARTNEY!" The name was blurted into a sudden lull in the noise of the hall. Heads turned inquiringly. The piano stopped. McCartney and the girl looked at him, a quizzical expression on their faces. Martin hesitated.

"Well?" said McCartney. Martin knew he had lost. He felt his tongue too large and his teeth would not part. The girl giggled. "Have a seat man," said McCartney genially pulling up a chair, "and take the weight off your legs." Gratefully Martin sat down. "Now, what can I do you for?" McCartney continued boisterously.

"I..." Martin saw the girl looking at him, a trace of laughter in her dark eyes. He stammered. "I just wanted to say hello."

"Well, hello!" McCartney laughed. "Here, meet Dottie our new technician."

"Hello." His hand reached forward, cold, to drain the warmth that flowed from her long, smooth fingers.

"Oh, it's you I see in the Atomic Physics lab. opposite," she said gaily.

A moment's fear that she knew of his secret lust shook him. "Yes," he said simply and colored under the look from her intimate eyes. She knew. A voice within cried out damnation. "He who lusts after women has committed sin in his own heart." But, oh, she was beautiful. He had never thought she was so beautiful. At the sight of her Martin's courage returned. "Really, I...I really wanted to ask if you'd..." hesitantly he asked, "...like to come to the Bible Union prayer meeting at half past."

Dottie, her chin resting on her hand, inclined her head towards McCartney, silently curious. McCartney thought a moment. "Well, Martin, it's like this. They that are whole need not a physician." He raised his finger to waggle it at Martin. "Now you, for example, you spend all your time working out bigger and better atomic bombs and that I consider to be a far bigger sin than any I am ever likely to commit." The girl swiveled here eyes to Martin. "You see, Martin," continued McCartney, "if I were you, I'd never leave the prayer meeting at all I'd be so repentant."

Goaded, Martin's voice rose hysterically. "You...you..." He searched hard for the right words. "You fornicator you!"

"Bravo!" McCartney clapped his hands in mock applause as a grin laid open his face. "Three cheers for aul' Martin. And he clapped him heartily on the shoulder. "And since when, Martin lad, has fornication become a greater sin than thinking up atom bombs? Eh?"

Martin winced. "It is written thou shalt not commit adultery!"

"Is it now. And it's also written thou shalt not kill. What do you say to that?"

Martin knew that there was a text somewhere that would answer him. But he could not remember under McCartney's mocking eyes. "For every word that proceedeth out of the..." he cried weakly.

"Och, give over, Martin. You're suffering from a terrible frustration, so you are. What you need is the love of a good woman."

Martin stood up. He felt the call to save this girl. He must act. All his loathing was forced into his voice. "You're despicable!" He spat the words then turned to the girl, his voice softer. "Come with me to the prayer meeting. Please." He was surprised when she did not refuse.

"Give me five minutes to finish my tea. You go along. I'll follow."

Martin wanted to cry out his happiness. He had won. "Thank you," he said softly and sped among the tables to the meeting room.

McCartney was incredulous at what had happened. "Here, what possessed you to go and do that for?"

"He's sweet," she said simply.

"But he thinks up atom bombs. Think of all the radioactivity about! Think of Hiroshima! Cretins!"

She stood up to go and, looking beyond him with eyes full of knowledge, said with finality, "He needs the love of a good woman."

The days that followed were filled with happiness for Martin. Dottie went each evening with him to the prayer meeting and afterwards he would take her downtown for coffee before leaving her at the door of her flat. During the day she was often by the window and they would wave to one another. On one occasion McCartney had approached her to circle her waist but she had pushed him away, and Martin, watching from the window opposite, had rapped the glass and grinned, unable to conceal his triumph.

Martin's work progressed though once he stepped into a beam of radioactivity and had to destroy his clothes. Even the Professor noticed the change in Martin and was more complimentary than usual with the result that Martin, waving a page of hieroglyphics, said excitedly to Dottie before the prayer meeting that evening, "The Professor said it was a major step forward to the Ultimate Weapon. We could destroy all the Soviet Union in one go. Imagine!" Martin stepped restlessly across the room at the thought of it, "We could destroy the AntiChrist!"

Dottie, though taken aback by the enormity of such destruction, felt a glow within her. This, she said to herself, was the moment she had been waiting for. "Martin," excitement seemed to infect her, "let's go up to my flat after the prayer meeting for supper. To celebrate!"

Martin was jubilant. "Let's!"

When prayer was over they went together to the shops and bought food. Martin held his arms out as Dottie piled the parcels—meat, vegetables, fruit, cheese and bread. Martin felt happy as they walked to her flat. He had overcome the timidity that had previously prevented him from going in. But today...he reflected happily on his success and smiled at Dottie. Dottie was saved! He would talk to her about it, later perhaps, he thought as he tied on an old apron to wash some dishes while Dottie prepared to cook.

"Smells nice," he said.

"You like it? I always cook my special dishes in wine."

"Wine?"

"Yes, wine."

"But it's alcohol!" he protested.

"Oh, don't be silly. Remember," she stopped to press a floured finger on the point of his nose, "a little wine for the stomach's sake."

Martin felt confused. He wished people would not keep quoting the Bible for their own purpose.

"I..." he began, turning and noticing Dottie placing a bottle in a cabinet. "Let me see."

"Oh, don't bother me, Martin. And don't go into that cabinet. It's very private."

"Oh."

Resignedly Martin continued to dry dishes and lay the table.

"Dinner is served!"

Martin felt a rich thrill at the sound of her voice. How nice it would be if always he could come home tired from the laboratory, to Dottie, and this

MUSIC ON THE WIND

smell of cooking.

"Orange juice or lemon?" she asked.

"Orange if you please."

"Good. Sit down while I go and fetch it," she said.

"But let me do it."

"No." She kissed him lightly on the cheek. "I'm the woman of the house." And hurried to the kitchen.

Martin sat down. He had never been so happy. A sudden urge to kiss Dottie made him want to jump up and run to the kitchen. Then she appeared carrying a tray and a jug of orange.

"Up full?" she asked, clinking the glass of the jug against his tumbler.

"Full," he smiled.

"Cheers," she said, taking a sip from hers.

"Cheers, Dottie."

"To maybe a new equation."

"Thanks, Dottie. To you."

"And to us."

Martin's heart beat wildly and he took a long draught to cover up. "Hmmm, I was thirsty," he said.

"More orange, Martin?"

"Please. It has a wonderful tang to it. Hasn't it?"

Dottie smiled at him with her strangely intimate eyes. "It's my own blend."

"You're wonderful Dottie. I wish I could have you always cook for me."

For the first time Dottie felt a twinge of guilt. Yet, seeing the happiness in his face made her overcome it. She had made that happiness, she told herself, and she would make him happier still before the night was out. "I'll make the coffee now," she said, rising from the table.

"Can't I do anything to help?"

"No, Martin. Would you like my special blend of coffee too?"

"If it's as good as the orange."

Again the twinge of guilt. "Yes, Martin. Better!"

The percolator bubbled over for the last time and Dottie partly filled two cups. She glanced towards the door before going to the cabinet. She opened it. Inside was a large collection of liqueur bottles. Dottie pushed aside the vodka to reach for the brandy. She filled the half-filled cups to the brim.

"Coffee up!"

They sat down by the fire and Martin sipped from his cup. "Ooooh! It's hot but it seems to cool the throat."

Dottie smiled at him.

"What is it?" he asked.

"A Brazilian flavor. You like it?"

Martin licked his upper lip and made complimentary noises. These were better than words. Noises, pleasant sounding noises.

The room was becoming very warm and shadowed. Dottie was over there among the bronzy glow from the fire.

"Dottie!"

She laid aside her cup and leaned towards him to rest her arms on his knees. "Yes Martin?"

"Oh, I feel so different. I...I could sing...I could dance. Here, feel my skin. It's all tingly like I'd had a warm bath."

She touched him on the forehead, running her fingers down over his ear to rest on his neck.

"Dottie...I've never felt this way before."

"How do you feel, Martin?"

"Oh, wonderful." He paused. "Let me kiss you Dottie."

She saw in his eyes the moment she had been waiting for and, thrusting aside her guilt, she kissed him.

"Dottie...I...I...I'll have to go. The way I feel...it's..." He began to stand up but reeled towards her. "I must be ill."

"No Martin. It's all right. Rest a while."

He wanted to protest against the soft warmth of her arms and the hand that soothed his temple but he could not. The darkness of oncoming night seemed to creep over his brain. "Dottie!"

"Ssshh, Martin. It's all right. I'll take care of you."

Night fell.

A sparrow chirping at dawn made Martin awake. He could hear it through the gray fuzziness of awakening, a clear, fresh morning sound. Martin opened his eyes. Shafts of bright sunlight stabbed at his pupils making the world revolve in a myriad of flashes. Martin squeezed his eyes tight. Something was wrong. He lay in the deep warmth of the bed and forced himself to think. There was something different this morning. There was a strange perfume to the bed, and...he could feel the warm texture of the sheets against his skin. Martin sent a groping hand towards his loins. It passed over his scrawny body in spidery runs of exploration. Martin jumped with shock. He was without his pajamas. He lay stiff and still forcing himself to remember. The perfume was strong in his nostrils. He turned his tightly closed eyes into the pillow as he remembered. Dottie's perfume! His turning head bumped against something firm. Martin opened his eyes to stare into the eyes of Dottie. "Oh!" Martin reached the floor in one bound, the bedclothes held in front of him. "Oh!" He looked down on the girl's body left naked by this act. "I...I...I..." Frantically Martin searched for words but found none. In desperation he tossed the bedclothes back onto the bed and crouched down by an armchair. His trousers hung over it and he grabbed them, falling over in his panic to pull them on. The girl lay huddled among the bedclothes, her eyes darkly curious over the whiteness of the sheet. Martin raced for the door, hopping on one shoe as he pulled on the other. Into the street he ran, to the weak rays of the early sun and the morning chorus of the sparrows.

Martin was still running when he reached the University. Tears streamed on his face as he thought of what he had done. He had sinned a terrible sin. The voice within sobbed out the accusation. He had sinned. Yet, through the blur of his agony he saw the girl and question upon question lay heaped before him. Why had she done this to him? Why? Why? He remembered the tumblers of orange, the tang of it and the coffee that seemed to cool the throat. She had tricked him! But he had sinned. He cursed her. Delilah!

Martin went into his laboratory and sat down at his desk. A momentary feeling of comfort came to him until he looked at the window of the laboratory opposite. Her window! Martin buried his head in his hands. He could never face her again. A dull throbbing pounded in his head as the shame swept over him. Martin began to pray.

"Here! Are you all right sir?" The cleaner nudged his shoulder.

"Oh, I...." Hastily he searched for a lie. "I was working a bit late....I just dozed off here instead of going home...a long experiment...you know?"

The cleaner nodded knowingly. "You're overdoing it though. Aren't you? I mean...all night and all..."

Martin smiled through the thudding of his headache. "It happens now and then...long experiment...You know...Eh..." He glanced at his watch. It was seven fifteen. "I've some readings to take now. Do you mind if I continue?"

The cleaner made for the door, shaking her head in unbelief at one working so hard. Martin closed his eyes and muttered "Amen." When he opened up again Dottie was at her window, her hand raised as if to call his attention.

"No!" Martin stepped back and crashed into the cyclotron. The switch caught on his clothes and there was a whirring sound. He stood off, transfixed

with the thought of escaping rays, and then fled out into the quad.
"Martin!" The girl was calling him. "Martin! Please Martin!"
He ran towards the bus stop. "Get thee behind me Satan!"
"Please Martin! Let me explain!"
Into the roadway he ran his one idea to escape. A red flash of color loomed above, its black honeycomb of radiator crashed against him, a searing flash of pain and the smell of oil before the crushing weight of the wheels.

A strange peace was everywhere and there was sweetness in the air. The bustling sound of traffic seemed as if filtered through layers and layers of gauze. And the people and the buses and the cars seemed small, almost toy-like in their distance from him. Yet it was all proof that he was going upwards. Martin was going to heaven after all. He took one last look at the world below him, the bus, the driver leaning over his dead body, the man in the telephone booth, and the girl standing weeping by the footpath. "Dottie!" His soul voice whispered her name before the scene slipped into the distance. Cloud seemed to close over the earth and he was alone, floating upwards and upwards.

In a little while Martin had become accustomed to the upward movement. He began to take stock of himself. He was just as he had been on earth – legs, body, arms, head – though now he seemed strangely gaseous, like vapor. He tried moving his limbs and found that, though he could stand or sit down or even run if he wanted, he always kept moving upwards. Martin was overjoyed. He was certainly going to Heaven.

He took a few little skips in the air and kicked a passing cloud. He began to sing and run then, he halted in awe. Beyond him the sky opened into a blue, sparkling vista. A little winding road seemed to run from where he stood, away into the distance towards a golden corona. In the middle of this was a city. Heaven! He knew it had to be! Martin began to run. He could see others ahead of him going upwards, singing. He ran faster. Then, as he turned a corner, someone was passed him, going downwards. Martin hesitated and turned to watch the retreating figure with its bowed, sorrowing head. Martin felt a pulse of anxiety. What had happened? Had the other sinned? For some reason Martin found he could no longer run. Yet he was continually going upwards though he dallied by the wayside. Then another passed him on the downward path and Martin felt the first touch of panic. He called out, "Friend! Please tell me..." But the other was quickly out of sight. What had happened? Surely, surely the other had sinned. Fear shook Martin. He had also sinned.

The path ahead of him was now empty; and an old man stood by a gate beckoning him. Martin went forward. The old man said, "You took your time, didn't you?" Martin opened his mouth to apologize but the old man continued, "Heh! You're just in about time too. We were about to close. Well..." he gave a tired sigh as he looked at Martin. "I don't suppose you've ever done anything that would keep you out. Eh?"

"I...I..." began Martin.

"You're lucky you're last today. I haven't the time to go through the list of sins so you'd better just tell me what you've done. And we'll get it over with quick, like." He looked at Martin with impatient gravity.

Martin stuttered. "I've done nothing...nothing...except..."

"Except? Except what?"

"I...have...fornicated." Martin's eyes were bulging with fear. "Once...Once only...I slept ...with a woman."

The old man began to laugh a deep hoary laugh that belched from his chest. "Whoooooaaaach! That's no sin, boy! Whooooaaaagh! That's no sin! I've done it myself! Lots of times!" He wiped the tears of laughter from his eyes. "Ho-aye. What's your name?"

"Martin McCabe, sir," said Martin, a trace of hope sliding back to him.

"Well, don't be afraid, boy. Have you ever done any...any..." He forced great emphasis into the words, "terrible sin?"

"No, sir," said Martin.

"Well then, what have you to worry about? Come on and we'll fill in these forms. Now..." In a friendly fashion he put his arm around Martin's soul. "...write your name here...yes, like that...and here....occupation."

Martin wrote, "ATOMIC PHYSICIST."

The old man puckered his face as he glared at the words. "Ooooohh! That puts a different face on things. Atomic Physicist, is it? Hmmmm!" He shook his head gravely and removed the friendly arm. "I think we'll have to examine you properly. Tch! Tch!"

Martin watched in terror as the old man removed a cover from a machine with countless dials. Little lights whirled around and wires ran to a probe. A Geiger counter! The old man held forward the probe. The dial lights whirled in frenzy as it touched Martin's soul. The old man shook his head as he backed away. "Too bad, boy. Your soul is radio active!" The gate slammed in Martin's face.

Dr. Simon's Night Out

Though Dr. Aubrey Simon was not a religious man he was fascinated by the concept of the soul. Was there really such a thing? As a medical physicist he believed that he would find the answer. Of that he was certain for it was a topic that obsessed him day and night; at least, when he was not thinking about the woman across the way. The problem was that he knew as little about the soul as he did about women. It never occurred to him that perhaps the two were related in some way. He had not yet figured that out for he was, after all, just a scientist.

On that September evening in nineteen and fifty-two, Dr. Simon's mind was more taken by how he might measure up as a woman's ideal male companion and sought to enlarge on the matter in the unlit secrecy of his bedroom. He removed his shirt and looked at his torso in the mirror. The evening light through the window gave the flabbiness of his skin a grayish unhealthy color and added shadow to the hollows between the rolls of fat making them look like muscle. Aubrey liked the illusion as he flexed himself. He smiled with inner satisfaction and dropped to his hands and knees on the floor. Straightening his back and legs to a wobbling stiffness he lowered his chest to the carpet. He took a deep breath and then, with shaky deliberation he raised himself up, once, he lowered himself, up, twice, down, up, three times, down, he lay gasping on the floor.

In a few moments he had recovered. He stood up straight and held his arms in front like a diver on a ten meter board and slowly, as a priest before an idol, he bent himself all of a piece towards his toes. The fingers stopped short just below the knees. He grunted as he pressed himself down till the sinews pained to snapping point. Up down, up down. The fingers reached no further.

Evening had crept into autumn darkness when he finished his exercises and, tired but with his skin glowing warmly from the exertion, he took a talcum box from his dressing table and faced the wall by the door. He was calmer now and half-expectant. He put the base of the box flat against the wall above him and slid it down to touch the crown of his head. Gingerly he stepped back and marked the lower rim of the box on the wall. It made a mark above the other marks and caused Aubrey to smile. Yes! Science was at work. He had grown another two millimeters.

Dr. Simon was happy as he slipped into his pajamas and lifted back one corner of the bedclothes; but he did not enter to begin the sleep that would prepare him for the grueling day that he knew was ahead. Instead he removed the high-backed chair from the window to the darker shadows by the wardrobe and straddled it back to front. He folded his arms on the back as a rest for his chin and sat silent and still, looking out the window to where the night had filled all the corners of the space between the buildings to an even blackness. There were no sounds except the drone of the city 'buses in the distance. In Aubrey's room there was just the ticking of the clock and the almost imperceptible sound of his breathing. He was like a cat before a mousehole.

Suddenly, to twitch him back to life and shatter the blackness of the night, a light was switched on in a room across the way and a young woman stood there. She was tall and proportioned as would fit a painting by Renoir and Aubrey's heart leapt as he watched her move around the room. Then, as was her habit, she went to the window and pulled the blind down one third. Aubrey stared as one transfixed at the scene beyond; a body fully clothed was visible beneath the blind and above, the silhouetted gesticulations as the woman removed her sweater and brassiere. For several moments the spidering arms fought with the garments and then, the bust held in profile for the briefest second and she was gone, the window yellow and empty.

Dr. Simon came down to breakfast with pleasant anticipation warming the sallow of his face. It was 8:15 a.m. and if his landlady would hurry with his breakfast he would have, he thought, it all timed perfectly. Mrs. Todd at that moment entered with his cornflakes. "'Morning, Dr. Simon!" Dr. Simon was too busy scooping up cornflakes to notice, his mind already on the challenge ahead of him. "Morning!" almost yelled Mrs. Todd. "Will you want plain bread and butter or toast?"

"Huh?"

"Plain bread and butter or toast?"

"Oh, whatever's quickest!" He glanced nervously at his watch. "Whatever's quickest!"

Mrs. Todd went to her kitchen making faces to herself. She did not quite understand her lodger. He was too up-in-the-clouds, thinking all the time, and those smiles on his face. She often wondered what went through his head. Once to find out, when she was cleaning his room, she had opened one of the big books on the mantelpiece and glanced at a few of the pictures. They had frightened and puzzled her and she had regarded him with awe for days afterwards. It was difficult to believe, she thought, that a person like him could be cutting up bodies though, mind you, something did show on his face. It was the way he smiled to himself maybe, or the way the eyes never focused on anything, not even when he was speaking to you. And then she remembered a film about a doctor that she had gone twice to see. He had been a handsome, tall, strong, and...yes, silent type. Maybe that was where Dr. Simon, despite all, shared a point with other doctors. He was silent. And now, she thought as she carried in his poached egg on toast, he was going out to cut up something that day. Yet she was sure as she set the plate before him that he was not all there. He was smiling to himself again and, she noticed in horror, he rubbed his hands vigorously before seizing the knife and fork to burst open the egg.

Aubrey swallowed his breakfast without taking the time to chew and hurried out into the morning air. He walked quickly to the corner and there slowed his steps as a young woman came out of the next street ahead of him. She was tall and well proportioned. Her hair was a mass of golden curls that swept back in strange feminine contrast to the man's sweater she wore, long, hanging in folds about her waist above the hem that molded with her hips. Her black skirt was tight and styled to a level with her knees so forcing her to walk slowly with tiny steps. Aubrey followed some yards behind, a smile writhing on his lips.

Fifty yards more and Dr. Simon quickened his steps to pass her. Drawing level, he noticed with sickening intensity that he was still three inches short. He walked faster to escape from this unfairness and reached the 'bus stop before her. She joined the queue two places behind him so that Aubrey, on looking round, could gaze with hidden rapture at her face. She was so lovely.

A 78 'bus came and halted at the stop. Several people boarded including the young woman and Aubrey, from the pavement, watched her go. As it moved away the other 'bus on the route, a 75, pulled up and in a moment the remainder of the passengers had gone. Aubrey stood alone, a little way back from the kerb, then slowly he turned and walked up to the University but two hundred yards away, his head bowed. Life was indeed unfair. He forced his mind to focus on the more comfortable scientific challenges of the day.

Dr. Simon was, as he always was, the first to arrive in the laboratory in the morning. Immediately, in the habit of routine, he set to arranging a few bits of apparatus and let his mind drift over the day's projects. First, to annotate the points he would make in the interview with the professor scheduled for later that morning. It was essential, he felt, to let the professor see that he was at the forefront of his work, in advance really. That might be difficult to put over; the professor was a stagy old type and a bit behind the times. Should have been retired long ago to make room for younger, more progressive types, he thought, like himself. And a little smile rose to the surface of his face. Aubrey knew he was the cleverest post-doctorate in the department and the hardest working. Take that last paper for instance, *The electron cloud and the cerebral ganglion*, way above everyone's head except that Russian, Gregorkov, who wrote him a personal letter of congratulation. But the professor? Hadn't a clue what he was talking about. And today once more he would have to explain time and time again when not even McCartney, who had graduated with him and was much more up to date, could grasp all the points. Though, mind you, McCartney was a bit dull at times; no real flamboyance in his ideas, more of a solid routine man than one who pushed the frontiers of his science. Still, not everyone could be a genius.

Dr. Simon found solace in this thought. One day he knew he would be hailed as a kind of prophet. It had its sacrifices he knew, like working fourteen hours a day but it was pleasant punishment. Better than throwing the productive years away like McCartney on wine, woman and song. That thought halted him in thinking-stride and for a moment he had a glimpse of a mass of golden hair swept back by the morning air. Down inside him somewhere a little heavy weight rolled around with burred edges, gnawing and gnawing. Aubrey's heart swelled up to crush his breathing at the thought of her. Hot tears seeped over his eyelashes and blurred his vision and he was glad he was alone as he removed his glasses to wipe the mist from the lens. No one would arrive before 9:30; he had fifteen minutes. Slowly he stood poised and bent towards his toes. The fingers only reached to just below the knees.

"Hello old fellow, old rhubarb, old cock! What are you trying to do? Split the seat of your pants?"

McCartney had arrived early.

"I've got a kink in my back. Thought this would ease it a bit." And Dr. Simon continued to reach for his toes for three more times just to show that he was not being caught unawares at some mysterious ritual.

"It's rushing in here in the mornings does it. You work too hard. They'll make you professor one day if you don't watch out." Aubrey smiled and said nothing. "And there's nothing worse," continued McCartney, "than a professor with a kink. And talking of kinks, when do you see wee Willie?"

"When he arrives, I suppose."

Professor William Small arrived at 10:59 just one minute before morning teatime. He had already changed into his slippers when a technician carried in his cup. "Ah, O'Neill!"

"Yes, sir?"

"Send me in Simon and, ah, bring a second cup."

Professor Small leaned back in his leather armchair. It wouldn't be such a bad day if he could get this business of Simon's work straightened out. A remarkable chap really, Simon, but his ideas needed controlling, wild stuff, sometimes a little far-fetched, but a good thing in a way. He had been like that himself once, way back in the thirties, keen, youngest professor in the University. Now he felt a little sadly that some of the younger men were whispering behind his back. There was a knock on the door. "Come in! Come in! Ah, Simon, draw up a chair. Have you had tea?"

"O'Neill said he would bring it in, professor."

"Good! Well, it's a fine morning."

"Yes sir."

O'Neill arrived with the cup of tea and left.

"Well now, Simon, what's this I hear you're wanting to work on? I know you're interested in nerve impulses and the cerebral ganglion but where, man, where is it getting us? You see, when I was your age....."

Dr. Simon listened to the little man opposite reminiscing of his active youth. He wondered was it possible that he was responsible for the many pioneer papers on the physiology of the central nervous system. Few would think that this little man wrapped in several cardigans, his feet in carpet slippers and sitting in an armchair with sawn-off legs, belonged anywhere but in a pawnbroker's. Professor William Small. Professor Aubrey Simon! He liked that and smiled.

"Ah, you can well smile young man but when you think that all the equipment we had in those days was a piece of string, a watch-glass and a razor blade, you'll see that you had to design an experiment that was simple and efficient." He paused to let that sink in. "Now, what's this line of work you have in mind?"

Dr. Simon cleared his throat. "It's really a continuation of my last paper, professor. If you remember, in discussing the conclusion of my results, I outlined a hypothesis based on the fact that a nerve impulse can be measured in a manner similar to that of a small electric current, as it were, a passage of electrons. Now, you know that when any of the modes of perception receive a message, it is transmitted to the brain for interpretation." The professor nodded. Good stuff so far, he thought; and well outlined. Simon had the makings. "Now," Dr. Simon continued, "we can liken this system, I feel, to one of electric wires distributed throughout the body but all connected to this thing called the brain. And it's this center that I'm interested in. You see, the brain, as the chief ganglion, is a reservoir for the electrons carrying messages from the centers of perception, like a kind of storage battery with a built-in analyzer. And therein lies my thesis." Aubrey paused to extend his left hand, palm upwards. With the forefinger of his right poised above it he continued, bringing the finger down gently to emphasize each point he made. "In a battery system the electrons are stored within material walls and a liquid or dry medium. So I feel is the brain. We have the material stuff of the brain but it is, as it were, just the container of this concentration of electrons, or what I prefer to call an electron cloud." Professor Small had his eyes closed. A soporific feeling was beginning to fill the space between his ears. "Now," said Dr. Simon, "to come to the point. I have said that the brain and the body composed of the appendages are merely a kind of container for this electron cloud. Now..." He paused to search the professor's face for the moment in which to reveal the concluding points. Was the old bugger asleep? "Professor?" The professor opened his eyes. "Hmmm?" "As I was saying, professor, to have movement of electrons freely through the body we have the medium of tissue, but what, professor, if we wanted the movement of electrons from one body, or person, to another?"

Professor Small shuffled uncomfortably in his chair. "Good God!" he thought. The world of science was beginning to move far too fast. Where were the good old days?

"Can't you see, professor," continued Dr. Simon, "we could solve the problem of telepathy, thought transference, the transmigration of spirits. We might even be able to read each other's minds. All we need to do is find if it is possible to get part or all of the electron cloud contained within the tissue of the brain, outside, and the possible incorporation into the brain of another person. Can't you see, sir, it's a problem basically concerned with when a person dies. The so-called soul! Is it the electron cloud I'm talking about?" Aubrey stopped and his face wore an expression of appeal to the professor's understanding.

Professor Small continued to look at him amazed. And they sat like that for some time. "You'll have to let me think about it, Simon. You've taken me by surprise, man. I must admit, by surprise." He got up and padded to the window. Aubrey waited for him to speak and utter some kind of appreciation. The professor continued to gaze out over the University gardens. Two gardeners were working with a shrub. "How untroubled their little lives are," he thought. It reminded him of his childhood on a Scottish croft, laboring among the boulders to get enough money for his education. The early days! A piece of string, a watch glass and a razor blade. Oh God, if he had only known, he would have stayed a farmer. "Simon!" he said without turning around, weariness in his voice.

"Yes, sir?"

"Leave me now and come back in to see me in a few days and tell me how exactly you propose to do this. And I won't spend a penny on fancy American apparatus, do you hear?"

"Sir!"

"And Simon!"

"Yes, sir?"

"Have something to convince me." But silently he thought, "Or forget the whole thing."

McCartney and two technicians were laughing when Aubrey returned to the laboratory. McCartney was telling one of his lewd tales. "But boy-oh, man alive, you should have seen the one I met last week. A beaut, a real beaut! Got her all lined up for the Floral Hall dance tonight.

"Was this the one who pinched your sweater, you were telling us about?" asked one.

"Aye! That's her all right. Struggles! Great!" And he winked lecherously but stopped talking as Dr. Simon approached. The two technicians went back to their work.

Aubrey disliked McCartney's familiarity with the technicians and the way he talked of women. Yet, in a way he envied him. McCartney was tall and blond with a well-chiseled face, a kind of Nordic god. He had a sports car and a continual stream of women and always could be seen somewhere or other accompanied with one of them, sometimes two, their faces happy. Aubrey wished he too could be like McCartney, not that he wished for a lot of women, he had no experience of that, but it was the only thing at which his brains could not bring success. Aubrey felt the lack of physical beauty that McCartney so greatly possessed.

"Did you find out why is Willie Small?" asked McCartney with a wink at the technicians. It was a standing joke amongst them. Aubrey smiled his weak smile. He said nothing. Why talk to this nincompoop. "Aw, cheer up Aubrey. He's fifty years behind the times. Here, have a look at this graph. What do you think of that? Eh? Might even stretch to a publication." Aubrey looked at the graph. McCartney did good work. He had to begrudge him that despite his way of life and lewd talk. "Come on! It's twelve. Time for lunch," urged McCartney, and they walked over together to the Dining Hall.

"Did he come off with the old bleat about the string, the watch glass and the razor blade and no seat to his pants?" Aubrey nodded. "Ah, don't worry. It'll all work out. Relax a bit," McCartney went on prattling. "Take time off. Enjoy yourself. Here," an idea occurred to him as they entered the Dining Hall door. "You want to go to the dance at the Floral Hall tonight? There's a big do on. How about it? You and me and my new bird!" He nudged Aubrey significantly with his elbow. "She might even have a mate. Eh? How about it? Refresh your memory of anatomy!"

McCartney had not really meant to invite Aubrey; it was just part of his constant teasing. Nor had Aubrey really meant to accept. But he had and both were loath to go back on their word. It was late afternoon when Dr. Simon fully realized to what he had agreed. It stopped him in the assembly of a galvanometer system. He closed his eyes in the unbelief of what he was doing. He was going to be unfaithful! That she would never know made the crime more grievous. Her silhouette flickered over the backs of his eyelids and he shuddered. The little weight began to roll around and around his stomach until he felt the tears of anguish rise and he had to go to the bathroom. He stood gripping the wash-hand basin and stared at himself in the mirror. The pallid reflection stared back.

"Go on Aubrey, don't be a fool," it said. "She'll never know! Be back for eleven and you'll have plenty of time to spare." He wanted to answer that he was betraying his tryst but the fear of ridicule stopped him. "Go on Aubrey. Go on. You can get one up on McCartney any day. Take that last paper. And the time you gave the seminar. That means more to a clever woman than a sports car!"

Aubrey leaned closer to the mirror and turned his head a little to catch his profile, one that showed a few teeth, and felt pleased. "Go on Aubrey!" He leaned closer still and saw a little yellow-headed pimple on his nose. He swore. "No, Aubrey! Don't touch! Use some spirits or you'll leave a red mark."

Footsteps sounded outside. He straightened up and turned the water tap to wash his hands. McCartney entered. "Ah, you're here, Aubrey. I'm just going. I'll pick you up at your place at seven. It'll speed us up a bit and we can call in at The Eg. for a few half ones before we go."

Aubrey could do little else but agree. "Right oh! I'll give my bench a clean up."

Aubrey tidied the bits of apparatus in readiness for the following morning and put on his coat. He was going out when he remembered the pimple and returned to fill a little bottle with alcohol. The fumes of the spirit stung his nostrils as he poured. He corked the bottle and shook his hands to dry off the cool splashes. For some reason he felt better and was quite looking forward to the evening. And the idea of a few half ones in The Eglantine Bar was a comforting thought.

Aubrey changed his tie and gave his shoes a rub with the blackening brush. He oiled his hair and combed it in the three-sided mirror so that he could get many views of his profile. A tune whistled out from his lips as he jerked his head sideways to see himself better. And then he swore. The yellow postule still rose up on his nose. Aubrey grabbed the hand mirror and stepped into the light from the window to get a better look. The pimple was definitely bigger. He swore impatiently as he remembered the bottle of spirits in his pocket.

The ethyl alcohol stung the meat of his nose and brought tears to his eyes. But he squeezed again and dabbed with the corner of his handkerchief. Again he surveyed it in the mirror. A weald covered the end of his nose. He fingered it lightly and stood facing the light to see it better. He saw her over the ebony rim of the mirror standing at the window looking across at him. She smiled as she placed a scarf over her golden hair, a goddess in the red light of the setting sun. Aubrey could not move for that moment of ecstasy that surged over him. He smiled and feeling braver smiled again. Then she was gone but still he stood, not realizing the mirror had concealed all his face but the eyes.

It was a happier Aubrey that skipped down the stairs. Mrs. Todd saw him go and wondered what girl was leading herself into a parcel of trouble. But that was the girl's business, she thought, after all she herself had been a fool once, too. Still! Aubrey stepped into the sitting room and stood before the window, hands in pockets and restless, waiting for the purr of McCartney's car. He had not long to wait. McCartney arrived looking smooth and well groomed and Aubrey regretted not changing his shirt. McCartney regretted again at having invited Aubrey yet he was surprised at his cheerfulness as he climbed in. Surely, thought McCartney, Aubrey isn't a dark horse, after all. The car roared off. "Got to pick up my bit of gear," yelled McCartney in Aubrey's ear. "Squeeze yourself over a bit when she gets in."

The car roared into the adjacent street and halted beside a tall young woman standing on the corner. McCartney sprang out and enveloped her in a bear hug. The young woman squealed with delight and held a hand to the scarf covering her golden hair. "Get in, woman dear, get in!" He pushed her unceremoniously in beside Aubrey. "Have you room? Move over Aubrey, lad, and give the woman room." He climbed into his own seat. "Aaah! Good. Know everybody? Angela, this is my buddy mate, Aubrey. And ah, Aubrey, ah, my body mate, Angela." He guffawed loudly and let in the clutch fast. Their backs pressed against the seats as the car accelerated. Angela giggled and Aubrey grabbed for the dashboard grip. He felt sick.

The lounge of The Eglantine was warmly shadowed and lit by subdued lights. A log fire in a rustic hearth spread coziness around the deep armchairs and blacktop tables. Harshness was unseen and the tinted mirrors behind the bar concealed the lines of care on the clients' faces. Aubrey could see himself as he waited for the order, a little hazily without his glasses though and he squinted to get a better focus. Behind him McCartney was whispering to the girl and her laughter tinkled through the raucous noise of the pub. Aubrey blinked back the rising pain of distress and paid for the drinks. McCartney was holding her hand between both of his and shaking his head in a tilted back position as some endearment trickled from his lips. She responded with a brush of her hair against his shoulders. Aubrey set the three drinks down. McCartney still had not drank his last drink and the girl had two glasses yet untouched. Aubrey said, "Are you not taking your drink?" The girl turned towards him, her face contriving to express herself without hurting his feelings. "I think I have had enough, really."

"Well," said Aubrey. "I'll have a use for them."

Angela rested her eyes on his until her smile faded. Then she blinked and in that instant her head turned so that, as she opened her eyes again, she was ready to receive McCartney's attention. McCartney sat as before, unconscious of Aubrey's question. Aubrey swallowed the remainder of his whisky and the one he had brought for McCartney. He rose to his feet. "I've just remembered," he said, his tongue somewhat too thick for his mouth, "I have some business to attend to." He left the table and moved towards the door.

"Oh that poor fellow," said Angela, "What happened to his nose?"

"Keeps sticking it in things."

"He doesn't talk much."

"He's odd!" said McCartney. "Real odd!"

Their words were part of the blend of voices shut off by the closing door as Dr. Simon stepped into the silence of the street. The cold air chilled the rising glow of whisky and a heavy weight rolled its burred edges around his stomach. He put on his glasses to hide the tears that began to trickle down the sides of his nose. Dr. Simon walked away knowing that he would never again be in The Eglantine.

Aubrey turned into the University grounds and followed the path around the quadrangle. A peace came upon him awakened by the familiar sight of the cloisters and his own department to the left. He still had a key and let himself into his laboratory. He switched on the mercury vapor lamps and as they flickered to life a new feeling touched him. He felt safe from the cruelties of others and above their little world. He felt his own greatness and used the feeling to recover from injustice. He had a brain and that, he assured himself as he touched a piece of apparatus, was supreme.

Aubrey set the apparatus aside from his writing pad and, seating himself, took a ballpoint pen to write. He would capture once and for all the concept that others found so difficult to understand.

1. The kinetic part of the brain can be likened to an electronic cloud. It is in continuous contact with the organs of perception via connecting electron chain systems.

2. The body envelops this electron system.

   a. the brain tissue contains the electron cloud.
   b. the body and the legs and arms contain the electron chain system.
   c. according to our present thinking the body relies entirely on the brain (ie. the electron cloud) for its actions.

This poses a question. Can the electron cloud exist outside the body? This question is pertinent in view of such phenomena as:

 i. Telepathy
 ii. Spiritualism.
 iii. The soul living after death of the physical body.

He stopped writing to consider how each of these topics could be investigated. There was, he knew, the possibility of measuring a kind of potential difference between the brains of two people engaged in telepathy but that, he felt, did not lead to exposure of the electron cloud outside the brain. He let his mind flex around the problem but could find no answer. If only he were capable of experiencing some of these phenomena. If only he could telepathise or commune with spirits, but the thought had never occurred before. He threw down the pen and dropped his head to the paper. The professor was right; he was theorizing. It was better to forget the problem and be prepared to accept a mediocre one. He felt tired.

Dr. Simon walked back to his boarding house, his shoulders hunched, eyes searching the ground for inspiration. Mrs. Todd, from beneath the blankets of her bed, heard him enter and wondered why he made so little noise with the front door and climbing the stairs. But if she was aware of him he was not aware of her or anything. Mechanically he entered his room and removed his coat and shirt. He looked at his torso in the mirror and flexed himself before dropping to the floor on his knees. His chest touched the cold bristles of the hair mat and, as if the contact had been an electric shock, he jumped up suddenly and looked out the window. The window across the way was still black. She was still out with McCartney. He slumped on the chair by the window and brooded on the thought.

Time passed before his vacant staring eyes as he waited for her return. Image upon image of her silhouetted body danced before him. She beckoned to him across the alley and he went to her, floating....his head thumped against the back of his chair and he stared wide awake. The window across the way was still darkened. "Yet..." he told himself, "I have thought myself there, but... have I really been there? If in my dream I am there, where in reality am I? My body is here but my mind? Has it bridged the gap between my body and hers?"

He began to remember dreams of lust, played with her night after night since first he had seen her at the window. "Could it be," he thought, "that my mind in the form of an electron cloud has left me and crossed to her room?" Then, reflecting, he saw the possibility of this, that if the whole electron cloud left the body, the body would die! Part of it would have to remain to carry on the body functions. "Yes, my mind would not be all there. Yet, allowing for this it may be possible."

He got up as the possibility developed and, going down the flight of stairs to the bathroom, he opened the window. Returning to his bedroom he left the door slightly ajar and pulled the chair back further into the shadows and closed his eyes. Concentrate, he told himself, concentrate, and began to recite softly to himself, directions. "Out of the bedroom door....down the stairs....bathroom....out the window....down to the shed roof....now I'm on the wall, easy now, easy.... drop gently to the ground....step across to the other wall and climb....grab hold of the door lentil....easy now....on to the shed roof....gently to the window....ease it up." His mind grunted with the effort. "Into her bedroom now....there's the bed, the wardrobe, the chair where she throws her clothes....back now..."

Dr. Simon slowly opened his eyes and a smile spread over his face. He had done it! He had been there! He wanted to shout his triumph and gloated inwardly of revenge on McCartney. He heard possibility upon possibility suggest themselves and he sifted them for the most cunning. He wanted her to look at him as she had at McCartney, to be under his control and obey his wishes. "Surely," he thought, "if the electron cloud can leave my brain it can enter another, her's....and...." His excitement made him whisper his thoughts aloud. "Compel her to do my bidding for my mind is stronger!"

He wanted to cry his happiness at the possibility. He set his chair round to face the window and when seated he closed his eyes and began again. "Out the window....down to the shed roof....now the wall....climb up....up....to the window." A little squeal of delight escaped him as he succeeded, but then, just as he turned towards her bed, the noise of a sports car roared into the street and stopped. He heard the door slam and, a little panicky, he escaped back the way he came.

With wild-eyed eagerness Aubrey waited until the woman entered her room. He stood up and removed his clothes. He opened the door slightly more and seated himself in the chair. Angela stepped to her window and raised it but did not pull the blind. She stepped back from view and began to undress. Aubrey narrowed his eyelids and began to concentrate. "Out!....Out the bedroom door....down the stairs to the bathroom .... easy....up on the window sill....out and down to the shed roof....drop down....up the wall....gently to the window..."

His body twitched excitedly as his wandering mind glimpsed her shadow thrown on her bedroom wall. Now he was in her room and stayed a moment in mute worship of her face and body. "To her mind!" he prompted. "To her mind!" His mind crossed the space that separated them to one of her delicate ears.

Mrs. Todd lay unable to sleep. It was cold and there was something strange in the night. She began to think about it and with thinking sleep became more distant still. Lots of things were strange she thought, like the way the furniture creaked in the dark, yet in the day it was silent. And then, there was the way Dr. Simon had closed the outside door, not in his usual way that near wakened the dead but silently, almost stealthily. And then, hadn't there been someone in the bathroom later? That was really strange, not like him to wash at night. And hadn't he opened a window? That, she felt certain, was why she felt so cold. The idiot had left a window open.

She got up, wrapped the bed-cover over her shoulders and stepped into her slippers. She would close it and, into the bargain, give his lordship a dressing-down for having no consideration for his elders. She climbed the stairs noiselessly and entered the bathroom. Yes, the window was open! She closed it and locked it, shrugging her shoulders at the new warmth as the draught was cut off. She turned and at the door stopped. Voices? There were voices in Dr. Simon's room! Who? No! Her lower jaw dropped in disbelief. Dr. Simon had a woman in his room. That was it! He had brought a woman into the house! Mrs. Todd stood unable to move at the monstrousness of the action. Yet, something would have to be done! There would be no tomfoolery in her boarding house, giving it a bad name! She would catch them at it!

Still moving as silently as before she climbed the turn of the stairs to his door. It was open slightly. The brazenness of it! From inside came voices, definitely! Mrs. Todd took firm hold of the handle and pushed the door open. Looking in she saw a body, naked in it's fatness, sitting on a chair by the window. It was writhing in convulsions as if the brain had been cut off from reality.

Mrs. Todd stepped out. She had not been seen. Panic ran through her. She was in the house with a madman. She almost ran as she went down the stairs in her soft slippers and locked herself in her room. She held to the door to regain her breath and dared not switch on the light. She saw the phone. There was only one way. She picked it up and dialed. "Operator! Operator! Are you there? Hello! Yes, listen! Take my address. Call the police! I'm in the house with a madman. Tell them to hurry! Quick! It's Dr. Simon!" Her hand made circular motions around her temple. "He's not all there!"

The Guy from Belfast

Pastor Billy Doswell was a Man of God and his white dog collar attested to that fact. He had come down from Belfast to be pastor at the Mission Hall in the lower end of Ballyaghone, or, as the locals were apt to say, "Down there at the bottom of the town! Ye g'on over the river and across the bridge! An' when ye see the spinnin' mill ye're there! Ye know!"

In that part of Ballyaghone so easily located, the houses huddled up to the linen mill in parallel rows of narrow streets. They were redbrick houses except where yellow brick was used to trim the doors and windows. It added what one proud mother called, "a nice wee touch." Each house had a door opening onto the street, a parlor window downstairs and a bedroom window up, a tiny kitchen with a door leading outside to a W.C. at the back of an equally small yard. From there another door led to the back alley where the garbage was put out once a week for the bin-men to collect.

They were good, snug little houses built way back when the industrial revolution came to that part of Ulster. Here was the Braid River as a source of water and farms to grow the flax, and serious-minded, uncomplicated, disciplined people to do the work. They kept their houses neat. The brass of the doorknobs and knockers shone with weekly polishing and, as further evidence of pride, the cement of the footpath in front of each doorstep had been scrubbed to a shining half-moon of glittering cleanliness.

The people here were of what could be called, a fierce temperament, volunteers-to-a-man in time of war. The memorial on Galgorm Street carried the name of many a one who'd fallen in the Great War. Sundays, their survivors went to church or chapel, the head of the house walking along in his blue Sunday-go-to-meeting suit and white shirt and his wife resplendent with a hat like a flower-garden, as someone once described them. Good-living people, was the word, though apt to take a bottle or two on a Saturday night, Presbyterians most but a fair sprinkling of Wee-Free or Brethren or the like, and some Holy Rollers.

It was not the most elegant part of town but wherein lived the solid citizens whose labor kept the linen mill spinning; and as such it was the perfect setting for the Pastor's humble Mission Hall and a fertile ground for a man dedicated to the saving of souls from the grip of the devil.

"He's here!" he declared to his wife, a certain note of ecstasy in his voice at the thought of the battle ahead. "The devil is here! Oh, I can feel him! For we wrestle not against flesh and blood but against spiritual wickedness! Ephesians six and twelve!" The Pastor had a fine head for memorizing passages from the scriptures. "A pub on every corner! Full every night! Ooooh! Drink and likker are an abomination!" he cried, and his eyes were indeed moist at the iniquity of it all.

"Billy has a thing against drink, you know," his wife would explain but leave the matter there; to go beyond that was too much. The truth was that Billy had stood by as a young man and watched his own father drink himself to death and die an unbeliever in God's grace. It was a recurring memory that, now a Pastor, spurred him on to rescue more of these ungodly as if their quantity would be his atonement.

"Pouring money down their throats! Oh Lord, what a waste!" This was a sore point because he had not yet enough members in his congregation to pay him a decent stipend.

"It's enough to make a body cry!" his wife confirmed, for she too suffered from the sinfulness of this world and the poverty it inflicted on those laboring in the vineyard of the Lord.

But Pastor Doswell was made of stern stuff and took as his inspiration, "Go out into the highways and hedges and compel them to come in that my house may be filled!"

"That's the gospel according to Saint Luke, chapter fourteen verse twenty three," his wife would explain to those who she thought needed the proper authority for her husband's behavior. Thus, in pursuit of converting the damned, clearing the pubs and building a congregation that could afford him a better living, he preached on street corners, often with only one or two supporters, but loud and energetic for all that, his strong Belfast accent crying out exhortations to forego the devil drink, sin no more and follow the Lord.

He soon was to become a familiar figure, not always referred to in generous terms but respected nevertheless as "Thon guy from Belfast. The pastor fellah! Ye know, hi! Him that's for iver standin' on the street corners an' preachin'! D'je iver see the like of it?" Modest praise indeed but dear to the good man's heart for wasn't that his mission in Ballyaghone.

The Pastor's humble Mission Hall was over by the old Railway Yard, a single-story, slate-roofed barn with pointy windows of diamond shaped panes, some red, some blue, some clear—a dissenters' interpretation of Gothic. There was a pointy door, dark stained and heavily hinged in wrought iron and an equally pointy notice board beside it with the legend, Mission Hall of the Open Bible, lettered in gold gothic. Underneath that it read—*Pastor Wm. Doswell*. There too on the pointy notice board, below his, was the name of the organist, *Eliz. Doswell*, his wife and, down at the bottom, in smaller letters, the word *Soloist*. But here there was no name, nothing but a blank strip that seemed to proclaim the poverty of the humble Mission Hall.

"Oh, we got to get a soloist!" his wife implored. "No Mission Hall can be without one. Someone to lead the voices in praise!"

The Pastor did not grieve too much. He had faith! "It's only a matter of time. Wait'll you see! God works in mysterious ways."

And He did! Because one day there happened Brendan Gunn, the personification of that chance occurrence which changes the world around us, and certainly the life of Pastor Billy Doswell, the fellah from Belfast.

Brendan Gunn, a scion of this part of town, was described by his adoring mother as very willing. It was an apt description for this unfortunate young man had been born with a speech impediment of such proportions that most people avoided him so as not to be present when he opened his mouth. His life was a misery. At school, that hell-upon-earth for the unfortunate, the other boys shunned him or used him as the butt of pranks. Teachers were no better, either leaving him out of their scan of attention or selecting him out of good intention to read or comment beyond his speech capability. During those moments the classroom was either icy quiet under the teacher's stern eye or a shambles of titters and giggles as the boys took obtuse pleasure in the knowledge that someone was worse off than themselves. His stutter got worse as he grew older and became more insecure. What might have been improved by kindness became a wild sight to see. Any simple attempt to speak provoked his head to flop about at odd angles while his eyes rolled up white. He'd hold his mouth wide open to receive the words held somewhere in the depths of his chest and then, a trick he learned by accident, he'd stamp his foot on the ground and a few words would come tumbling out.

Brendan was unemployable until, out of kindness, he was taken into the Linen Mill by a well-meaning supervisor and given a job amongst the din and bedlam of machinery where speaking was unrequired. And he was indeed what his mother described him, very willing, a conscientious worker. But deep inside Brendan was another person straining to be heard. The noise of the machinery stifled the cries of despair until one day Brendan discovered that, while he couldn't speak one whit, he could indeed sing. No one seemed to notice or care. The noise of machinery was in the high decibels and others had their own worries to contend with. So, there was Brendan discovering he could hum to himself and even sing a few words, in a low voice so no one but he would know; and then whole verses and songs were possible, all hidden in the belly of the linen mill's noise.

The day came when Brendan was singing confidently and, despite the noise, his co-workers did hear and the word spread amongst them. Brendan had a great singing voice, a beautiful voice. "Ah tell ye. Ah heard him an' Ah could har'ly believe me ears." Others confirmed the fact. "Ye shud hear him, hi! Thon's great singin'! Like John McCormick on the wireless, so he is." And "Ye shud hear him sing Danny Boy, so ye shud!" So it was that a group of the men invited Brendan to join them for a pint or two at The Eupyrion Bar, on payday, for the fun of it.

The Eupyrion Bar was a working man's haven, a place where the boyos would meet to down a pint of porter and regale each other with lurid and exaggerated versions of otherwise normal happenings of the day. Topics ranged from their recollections and critiquing of the latest Wild West film at one or other of the two Picture Houses, to the antics of various well-known and otherwise respected personages around the town. On the one hand they relived the larger-than-life adventures of their screen idols and on the other gained self-esteem by ridiculing the antics of civic leaders and miscellaneous supervisors and managers of the linen mill. The introduction to character destruction usually began, "D'je hear the wan about aul' Tammy, hi?" or whoever. Everyone chosen to be the butt of ridicule was always "aul",—aul' Tammy, aul' Joe, no matter their age. And after a few colorful comments on how the person had looked silly in the given situation and laughter had duly reinforced the matter and rewarded the story teller, deep draughts of porter were swallowed and everyone felt less threatened by those who had set themselves up as superior. This brought about a great atmosphere of comradeship, reeking with tobacco smoke and the smell of stout. The air was thick. The ceiling, once an ornate rococo of entwined garlands of leaves and flowers, had a patina of condensed tobacco smoke which, with the humidity from beery breaths, had coalesced into hanging drops of amber resin like miniature stalagmites. And to here, the new Caruso of the Linen Mill was taken with all the enthusiasm as if it were the Opera House in Belfast.

Brendan went willing enough. It was great to have friends. The group of them ambled up Bridge Street where, on any evening, the smell of porter and tobacco smoke emanating from The Eupyrion Bar could be smelled from a distance of fifty yards. To some it was the smell of Heaven.

"Set them up there Sammy," Pat McCuddy commanded. "Pints apiece here!"

And Jacky McGulpin recited his usual party piece, his one and only poem he had managed to remember.

"Here's to a temperance supper,
Water in glasses tall.
Coffee an' tea to end with,
An' me not there at all!"

He then looked around with a smirk, "Ah heard that on the wireless wunst," he said to those who might not have heard it before. They all had, but no matter. It was the usual toast of the boyos and they all gave grins of agreement. "Drink up lads." And they drank as men are supposed to do, three big long swallows, then the pint set to rest on the bar while they licked the tan froth off their upper lip.

Brendan swallowed the black creamy liquid. It was his first taste of the forbidden stuff. A hand slapped him on the back and he felt great. "How did that hit ye, hi?" he was asked.

"N...N...N...Not...b...b...bad!" and the boyos cheered.

"Let's have a song! Brendan Gunn for his pleasure!"

"Aye. A song there!"

"Gi'e us a song, fellah. C'mon, hi!"

"Gi'e us Danny Boy!"

It was the first of many pay-nights for Brendan Gunn.

At The Eupyrion Bar, the cutting edge of his newfound friends' humor was sharpened by tankards of stout such that, from the rapidity of his stutter and the uniqueness of his name, they came to call him Brengun. He accepted this with the greatest of good nature, considering it a compliment to be named after the army's weapon. It had its profitable side too because the jesters plied him with free drinks. He was appreciative and responded to whatever tomfoolery they conjured up. It was like being popular. He took part in all their revelry. There was no trace of any stutter when he sang. It was like being a bird on the branch of a tree way, way up high where no one could reach him. He sang and he sang. And gradually the louts changed their opinions about this scarecrow of a man they had sought to make fun of. There were comments like, "Boys, that's great. D'je iver hear a voice the likes o' that? Didje now?" or, "Brendan," the Brengun was forgotten at times like this, "sing us Galway Bay, there!" or, "How about wan o' them John McCormack songs, d'je know any, hi?"

Pastor Doswell had spent the evening with a few of his faithful congregation standing on a corner preaching his message of kingdom-come, where, by the Pastor's own guarantee, the streets were paved with gold and its air filled with love; nothing to do all day but worship and sing songs of praise. He did not get any new conscripts to this vision because the reality of life had taught the good people of this section of town that that was as foolish a thing to do as any they could imagine. Standing around singing all day was just nonsense! Boring! Throw in a bit of eating, kicking a soccer ball, a few bottles of porter and some sex and then you had something. But songs of praise! All day? Never!

So the Pastor, like certain disciples before him, had toiled all day and caught nothing. He called it a night by orating a particularly long and loud prayer that called for blessings on the Queen and the Duke, guidance for the government at Stormont and exhortations to the Town council of Ballyaghone to close down the pubs as proof of their Christian faith. He ended with a sincere Amen. When he opened his eyes he could see that the street was empty except for the faithful few from his Meeting Hall.

The Pastor was undismayed. Student of the scriptures that he was, a chance notion to cast his net on the other side of the ship, as it were, led him to walk up Bridge Street where, within the envelope of smell which surrounded The Eupyrion Bar, old memories of his father's favorite Corner House came back. He saw again the emaciated face and heard his cough, the voice heavy with unspilled tears as he talked of the trenches in the First World War and the gas that burned out his lungs, the men who died screaming for God's help, the help that never came. "Where was God then?" his father asked him. "Where was God then?"

Pastor Doswell stood for some moments within the aura of the public house, just as he had done often enough years before without the courage to enter. He blamed himself for his father's death. He blamed his own lack of courage. But he was different now. He saw his father as the instrument of his own atonement and the salvation of the many he had brought to know God. Then, through his thoughts he heard a voice in song,

> "*Oh Dan-eee Bhoyyy, the pipes, the pipes are ah caw-all-in'.*
> *From G-len to g-lennn an' ah downn the moun-tain side...*"

The Pastor stopped in his tracks. He couldn't believe his ears. What a voice! Oh, what a voice! In a thrice he knew what he was going to do. The past was the past. In his pockets he always carried his stock in trade, his Bible with the zipper and bundles of little cards printed with selected texts. He pulled them out at the ready and, with face set in do-good determination, charged into The Eupyrion Bar.

As the Pastor held open the door of the Pub he already had his smile prepared. He took a deep breath to begin his assault on the ungodly when the stench hit him. He stood still to recover.

> "*...in sunshine or in shaa-ah-doow.*
> *Oh Dannee Bhoy, ooh Dannee Bhoy I ah looove yooouu-uu soooo!*"

Brendan glissandoed to a high note that would have put an operatic star to shame. There were cries of "Boys that was great, hi" and "Brendan, ye aul' bren-gun fellah ye, ye've wan great voice, so ye have." Several of the regulars sitting back in the booths clapped and one of them called, "Give us 'Oh my Kathleen Ah'm goin' tae leave ye!'" "Aye," shouted another. "How about Galway Bay. 'If Ah iver go across the seas t' Irelan'. If only at the closin' of me days.'? C'mon! Give us that wan, hi."

"Naw! Give us the wan Bing Crosby sang in that picter was here a while ago. Wat'je call it, hi? The wan wi' him as the priest!" "Naaah! Why not let Brengun here decide for himself. Go ahead Brendan. Sing us what ye like best. Be yer own man."

Pastor Bill had recovered from the partial asphyxiation by smoke and the smell of stout and body odor. "Gentlemen!" he bellowed from the doorway. "Gentlemen, please!" They turned to face him, this commanding voice that had thrust its way into their fun. He radiated everyone with his smile. "Gentlemen!" The sight of the white dog collar around his neck and black bib shocked them into silence. He wasn't a priest, for sure. They saw that at once because he wasn't dressed in black but in a light sports coat. Nor did he have a priest's black paddy-hat on his head. He was bareheaded. He was some kind of Protestant Reverend, maybe even a Pastor. "I'm Pastor William Doswell. Bill Doswell. Call me Billy. From the Reorganized Faith Church of the Open Bible, right fornenst the old railway yard." He let that announcement sink in for a few moments while he smiled and beamed benevolence over everyone. "I couldn't help but hear the most beautiful voice I've heard in many a year. I just had to meet a man so gifted by God. You, sir!" And Pastor Bill went into action with his hands, gripping Brendan by the shoulders, shaking his arms, patting him on the back. "What's your name?" Brendan was stunned. To be at such a pinnacle of attention was more than he could handle.

"Go easy there, Pastor," McCuddy admonished. "The wee fellah's a wee-thin' shy, so he is. His name's Brendan Gunn. Give him room now. Give him room."

Pastor Bill knew and understood these kind of men for hadn't he worked with men like them up in the ironworks, in Belfast. He stood to his full six foot five inches. "I'm Billy," he said and grabbed the hand of an astonished fellow in a scoop-cap and dungarees. "I'm Billy," he said to another, then another. In no time he had shaken hands and embraced a dozen men with bonhomie. "What a gift from God! You have, you know! A great gift." He stood back and surveyed Brendan at arms length with serious half lidded eyes. "Galway Bay," he said. "Isn't that what you fellows want. Galway Bay? What do you say? Galway Bay it is, eh? It's a beautiful song. God must have inspired it," he said, looking knowingly around the group of astonished men. "Take my word. Now," he said to Brendan very intently, "you sing the melody. I'll accompany you. And these good men," he swept his arm in a circle, embracing them all with flashing teeth, "they'll join in too. Eh? How's that! Now!"

Brendan felt the power of the man. Never in his life had anyone given him this much attention. Brendan stared. "Now!" said Pastor Billy, raising his hand like he was going to conduct the Philharmonic. "Now!" Brendan stamped the floor to release the brake on his vocal chords and he sang. Never had The Eupyrion Bar heard the like of it before or since, the lyric tenor of Brendan Gunn and the deep baritone of Pastor William Doswell.

"If I ev-ver go a-cross the seas t' Irelan',
If on-ely aat the closin' of me days,
For to see again the moonliiight over Cladagh,
And to watch the sun go down on Gal-a-way bay."

They sang the song through and repeated the chorus twice. There were loud cheers and yells of applause. Pastor Bill held Brendan at arm's length and stared intently into his eyes. The noise of the pub died to silence as the patrons watched. Phelie the barman tried to break the tension with, "What'll ye have gentlemen. Pastor, a wee sherry? On the house!" No one took his offer.

Pastor Bill eyed Brendan and slowly he said, "Now Brendan, here's a tune you must know. You must have heard it many a time." He hummed a bar or two. It was a hymn, a hymn often used in tent meetings. "Let's you and me sing it," he said confidentially. "You and me!" Brendan nodded. "Well, let's sing." And Pastor Billy led off,

"Lead kindly light..."

When the hymn was over there was silence, no applause, no comment, just silence. Phelie the barman stood back in the far corner behind the bar, ashen faced. He knew the business was over for the night, early though it was, and it was a payday too, and maybe for many nights to come. The boyos and cronies stood shamefaced and sullen at this invasion of their domain. It wasn't right, so it wasn't. The night had taken an unexpected turn. The stout had gone sour.

The Pastor hauled stuff out of his pockets, little cards printed with posies and texts. He began handing them around with great energy, thrusting them into hesitant hands, grabbing and squeezing their reluctant arms, hugging desolate shoulders. The memory of how he might have done this years before in the Corner House on his street in Belfast spurred him on. He would redeem! "Brendan," he said with great enthusiasm, "God is calling you." He laid great emphasis on that *you*. "For God," he said, "to have given you a voice like that he must have had a purpose. Respond!" he cried. "Respond to the call, Brendan." He shook the startled Brengun a little, beaming down from his great height. "Brendan, God wants you to sing in my church, this Sunday. Now, Brendan, what do you say?"

Brendan had never had a kind word said to him in his whole life. Yet here was this man, a big, big man, with a big voice, a man of God, asking him to sing in a church, and it was only half an hour ago. The tears welled in Brendan's eyes.

"A...a...a...a..."

Until now Pastor Doswell knew nothing of Brendan's affliction. He heard the stammer, he saw the eyes roll up, he saw the head gyrate around the shoulders as Brendan dug deep into his inner being to make the words come out. The boyos stood silent. This was worse than anything they had ever seen before. They were embarrassed. Yet they couldn't look away. Pastor Bill saw only a young man going through a deeply moving experience. He reached forward and wrapped the frail body of Brendan in his big arms. "And Moses said unto the Lord, O my Lord, I am not eloquent but I am slow of speech, and of a slow tongue." He shook Brendan in a hug that trapped the smaller man under his armpit. "You see Brendan, Moses too had a stutter, just like you. And, you'll remember, God called him for great things. Now what do you think of that?" One turn on his heel and he was across the floor to the doorway with Brendan still held like a rag doll under his arm. A few stragglers stopped to watch from a safe distance. Pastor Bill smiled generously at them and went out into the falling night. He was certain he had found his soloist.

"Bejazus," said McCuddy, "D'je see thon, hi? What the hell? He's made off wi' Brengun, so he has." And he looked around for some kind of support. "Thon wee fellah's feet har'ly touched the groun'." A bunch of them nodded. They were serious faced. The pints of porter were forgotten. "D'je hear thon big fellah, hi?" continued McCuddy. "He's from Belfast, by the sound of him! Godsavuz! He just walked in like he owned the place."

"Aye!" confirmed Phelie. "He's from Belfast alright."

Paradox

There's a pub in a certain city in this great country that I suppose you could call an Irish Pub. Of sorts! It has an Irish sound about it for sure, Bridget McGee's. I'll not say what city it is in or what country because there's those are partial to London or Glasgow or Liverpool and there's those far away off in Boston, Massachusetts as they say, or San Francisco, California, and so on, even Dallas, Texas. It doesn't matter what city or country at all. Best you all think it's your own city or town as the case may be. And it well might. Because, you see, there's Irishmen everywhere and we're all drawn, given time, to find someone of our own beginnings, our own way of looking at things. The right word I'm told is *culture* and if that's what I'm talking about then you're on. Men of our own culture, don't you see?

Bridget McGee's pub is right fornenst a theatre, a very famous theatre in fact. I had passed by it that night and was surprised to see that this woman I used to know, sort of, Loveen they called her, was playing a lead role. Her photo and name were plastered all over the billboards outside. That's what caught my attention. Hadn't seen her since when I was a young fellow down one night from the Teacher's Training College in Belfast spending the weekend at home. I wasn't so interested in seeing the play itself, though it was Shakespeare. If the photos were anything to go by she was still a beauty, a lovely woman. Loveen was her name. Anyhow, the show had started and I left it for another time. So I hoofs it over to Bridget McGee's for a draft I was that thirsty after a long day. Bridget McGee's was a regular place of mine when I was in that part of the city.

So there I was, drinking a bottle of Guinness—you can get a bottle anywhere in the world, you know—when the barman says to this big fellow, a giant of a man he was, "You sound like an Irishman!" says he, and it was put more as a comment than a question.

"You might say that, so you might," says the big fellow. And the minute I heard him I knew he'd been born and bred not a stone's throw from me in County Antrim, Ulster. Of course you'll not see that marked on the map. It's Northern Ireland these days. That's about the same thing, so it is, only Ulster is the name of the auld province and Northern Ireland is the political entity, as the politicians say. But so what? County Antrim is the place I want to tell you about and to hell with politics.

The big man looked sort of familiar but I couldn't place him, as hard as I tried. I had known a few like him, the fellows who played rugby when I was at school, farmers sons almost all, reared on oatmeal and potatoes with rashers of bacon and eggs thrown in for flavor, to say nothing of soda bread and fadge. A man the size of this one could, as I heard a body say once, eat a hearse and all the trimmings. What a giant of a man he was. Six foot four in his stocking soles and shoulders and chest on him like a bull. Maun, he was big. I'm only a wee fellow myself, you see, and it hurts at times to know you were squeezed behind the door when the good Lord was doling out the inches.

"Don't I know you?" I said edging near him with my glass full so he wouldn't think I was trying to cadge a free one.

He looked down at me the way big men do, like they'd found something had crawled out from under a stone. Maybe they don't know they're doing it but us wee fellahs sure notice. "Not unless you're from Ballyaghone," he says, turning his head more towards me. And the minute he did that I looked at thon big ears on him and knew instantly who he was. It was M'Clug. M'Clug, the man with the greatest pig fattening business in the county up until he up and ran away off and left it, pigs, buildings and all thon money in the bank. It created a stir I can tell you. And here he was! Quigley M'Clug. The pig farmer fellow himself! We'd even been to school together, at the Academy up on Thomas Street, though he was a year older than me. For that matter his father's farm was a stone's-throw from my uncle's place where I was reared. We even traveled out and in to school on the bus together and walked the mile or so of country lane back and forth from the bus stop. But I hadn't seen the man in over twenty years. Boys-a-dear he had changed, even allowing for the three days growth on his chin. I hardly recognized him, except for the ears; they were a landmark. Despite his size he was an auld worn-out man, the mark of despair on his face where old age had snuck up on him unbeknownst, like, and him not more than forty something.

"You're Quigley M'Clug," I said, feeling right smug about it.

"And who are you?" His tone was almost belligerent as if to ask what right had I to recognize him. Of course, not once did I stop to think that I too had changed a lot over the years. "I'm Billy Duff," said I. "Don't you remember me? Going out and in to school together? On the bus? Walking the mile and a half up the road together?"

"Billy Duff? Agh, its you!" His ugly face split into a wide grin like somebody had taken a hedge knife to a turnip. "It's yourself, so it is! Every bit of you! Maun, you've growed, so you have!" That was an unkind remark if ever there was one. I had always been a banty rooster of a lad right up until I was sixteen when there was a burst of growth for about a week or two and that was it. "You're looking like yourself," he said. "Sure I'd know you anywhere. Aye! What'll you have, now? Come on there! What'll you have?"

He pulled out his wallet and I could see there were only a couple of singles and pretty little else. Not even receipts from a grocery. You know how it is, pushing the slip of paper into your wallet when you buy something to take back to the digs to eat. Not even that! Quigley was broke, so he was! But the three-day growth and his clothes had already told me that. Oh-hye!

"I'll not have a thing, Quigley," I said. "Thanks all the same. I've still got a glass here and this is enough for me for one night."

He put his wallet away, gratefully almost. But the gesture had been made and decorum preserved, don't you see. "What are you doing in these parts?" he asked. "It's kinda far from home for a fellah like you."

I let that one go by me. A fellah like me? Did he think I was some gowp that never traveled? "I'm here for a while, so I am," I said with some authority, deliberately laying it on thick. "Was in South Africa for a while and Australia. Had a shot at the Solomons and, agh, I don't know where else, so I don't. All over the place, you could say."

"You were? So was I. And Canada too, Toronto. Where else were you?" And a friendliness came over his lined face, different like.

"Oh, I was in Canada, so I was," I said. "Couldn't stick the winters. And you? Where else you been?"

It turned out that Quigley M'Clug had travelled the world much like myself. Strange as it seemed we had never ran into each other despite having visited the same parts around the same times. But there was a difference! There was I, cattle-herding in the Northern Territory, sheep-shearing in Queensland, deck hand and so on. But he seemed to only visit the cities, and the big ones at that.

"Why that?" I asked. I wondered, him being a farmer. He might have wanted to get out and see how the other side did things.

"That's where the theatres are," he said simply.

"Oh?"

"Aye."

"Have you seen the one across the road?"

"Aye!"

"Do you know who's playing in it?"

"Oh sure!" and took a long swallow from his glass as if to tell me to let the matter drop.

And I did. We were both a couple of wild geese following who knows what. I knew what drove me on—a need for adventure, a rebellion against the smallness and the dullness of life in a small country town in Ulster where the only excitement was a cowboy film on a Saturday night at the picture house. There were two of them and they were always full, so I wasn't the only one was bored to tears. But I did something about it. There was always something gnawing inside me that I tried not to give into. I fought it through my years at the Teacher Training College thinking that once I started to earn money everything would be all right. Money in my pocket! You know? A girlfriend! Maybe marriage and weeuns! A house! It was after my first year teaching in a wee school in Belfast that I realized something. You know how it is; a thought suddenly jumps into your head from nowhere. One thing leads to another and before you know you've got a bee in your bonnet. For me I saw how, in those few months teaching, I had just experienced the rest of my life. That was it! This wasn't the life for me. I was simply not a teacher. No more! School out, I pulled my little bit of money out of the bank, said goodbye to my uncle and aunt and set sail.

Quigley was different. He had a farm to inherit. He had money by the bucketful. At least that was what was said and that was how I saw it. Yet one day he up and left it all and disappeared. Just like that!

"Where are you staying?" I asked. He shrugged. "I've got digs over the city a bit" I said. There's a sofa, if you want. A bit short for a fellow your size, you know. But I'll be glad of the company. How about it? A night or two. Come and go as you please."

"Any chance of work around here?" he asked instead.

"Sure!" I lied.
"Yeah!" He looked at me with a skeptical twist to his mouth as if to say he had been there before.
I said, "C'mon!" giving him a punch on the arm for encouragement.

He stayed at my digs for a couple of nights and as luck would have it he did get a job on a building site near by. I mean, what foreman was going to turn away a man looked like he could lift and lay as much as two normal human beings and still have finished before noon. Then a room became vacant in the boarding house and I talked to the landlady and it was Quigley's for the asking. I think she fancied him a bit for she kept looking up at him with the oddest glint in her eye and her well past the age of young love. But Quigley took no notice. He was a man with troubles in his heart. Eventually, with a few bottles and a lot of careful coaxing and listening, he led us both back through our childhood and those difficult adolescent years. It took a time to get the whole story for he would often say, "Agh to hell, what does it matter anyway. Vanity, vanity, all is vanity." There was that thing about Quigley, his whole family too. They took their wisdom from the scriptures. He remembered his Sunday school like it was yesterday.

I pieced Quigley's story together bit by bit from the meanderings of his mind under the influence of several wee glasses of the good stuff and my gentle coaxing. "Do you mind the time, hi?" I would ask, referring to some incident or escapade, some character, some landmark of the countryside. Or, "Do you mind aul' Peece, the master?" sort of knowing full well the response. But it was the richness of his memory that intrigued me. He would sit a while digesting the matter and then launch into what was almost total recall of events long past. And not just the event itself but the persons involved and how they looked and dressed and their tone of voice. He remembered it all with the bitterness of an exile, a man who believed he could not return, his voice and facial expressions showing his distaste of whatever wrong he believed was done him. Yet, beneath the venom of his hatred there was a longing. I understood perfectly. I too had suffered from the same for a long while. Not all the travels of this world can erase that inner self, that feeling that haunts the Irish emigrant to his dying day and, should he be fortunate enough to sire children, persists as race memory for three generations to come.

One day I came back from work to discover that Quigley was gone. The landlady just said he paid up his rent, put what he had in a bag and went. There was a note pinned to my door that said. "Thanks. So long. Q." That night I went over to Bridget McGee's in the hope he might be there. But no! The barman said he hadn't come in for several nights. "But you might try over there at the theatre," he suggested.

"What?"

"Aye," says he. "Thon big fellah had something to do with what ever was going on over there."

I rushed over, a feeling of great stupidity at not seeing it before. The play was closed. I asked a cleaning lady what had happened.

"It's all over," she said. "Their run was over. They've moved on."

"Do you know where?"

"No. They don't tell me those things."

When I had time to myself I wrote Quigley's story down. It is as close as I can go without a recording machine. Mind you, I've filled in here and there with my own recollections but don't let that bother you as you read on. Aghoh! Some day I want a certain lady to read it. It would be only fitting. So here goes.

It was a Sunday evening in early summer. Quigley M'Clug, pig farmer, draped himself over the five-barred gate and despaired at life.

"Cheer up, son. Ye're rich, so ye are." His mother, a small woman with fiercely concerned gray eyes, looked up at him pleadingly. "Ye're lord of all ye survey here. Ye know that, don't ye?"

"Aye, Ma. I know. But, there's got to be more, so there has."

"Ye're still young, son. Ye're twenty-five only. Unmarriet. A pile o' money in the bank. All yer life afore ye. What more do ye want? Just look out there. Don't ye see?" Before him on the brow of the hill, five pig fattening units gave off the ammonium smell of success. "Now that's all yours. Ye won it by hard work. An' there's this farm of yer father's will be yours wan day. An' that's great land, son, to say nothin' o' the house. An' all them barns an' the stable, an' the byre there. There's not a byre within ten townlands its equal."

"Aye, Ma. It's great, right enough."

"Most men would be satisfied they'd been so lucky," she continued.

"What is it ye want, son? Fancy cars? Fine clothes? Fast wimmen, son? Is that it? Fast wimmen?"

"Naw, Ma. It has nothin' to do with them things."

At least that was that, she thought. He wasn't going to turn out like her uncle Duncan. He was the man for the wimmen, alright; but Quigley, her son, was going to be different. She hoped. "Ye've always been careful, so ye have. Ye've niver been given to flights of fancy, so ye haven't. Ye're steady. We've always known where ye stan', Quigley son, ye know. Ye're perpendicular, so ye are, straight up an' down. Just like yer Da and his Da before him."

"Aye, Ma. Ye're worryin' too much."

"Ye're a good son, Quigley. Ah know that. Ah do know that, so Ah do. Ye've been everythin' a mother could want. But son, ye've everybody worried out of their minds. Why this flight of fancy, now, all o' a sudden?" she asked. "It's not like ye, at all."

"Agh! I'm human, amn't I?"

"Ye know what yer problem is, don't ye?" said his mother looking up at him with fiercely concerned gray eyes. "Ye won't listen tae yer father an' me."

"Ah do so listen."

"An' that's why Ah've asked yer uncle Thompson down to talk some sense intae ye."

"There was no need to bring Thompson intae this. Ah'm just tired fattening pigs, so Ah am, an' Ah'm not going to do it the rest o' me life. Ah want to be something, do something. Something," he said yearningly, "that a woman could admire a man for."

Quigley breathed in a deep breath of the ammonium-laden air and sighed. What did his uncle Thompson know about anything. Anythin', damn it! Of being in love, the despair, the longing, the fears, or the agony of humiliation. Not the humiliation of rejection. No, not that, the humiliation of being nothing more than just oneself, and not being able to do much about it. But, by God, he would try. He would get away from here and be something. The memory hurt.

"Quigley M'Clug," Loveen had said, looking up at him with those violet eyes. "You know, you're really nothing but a pig farmer."

In the big farm kitchen the wall clock swung its pendulum to and fro in slow sweeps, ticking the moments of silence. It was the thing I noticed most when I visited over at the McClugs. I sat in a chair well back from the others, sucked my tea with an audible gasp of relish, set the cup down and stirred it again. The spoon rattled off the china with a clinking sound that jarred the already taught nerves of Quigley's mother.

"Stop that!" she cried at me.

The family had gathered. They saw things different.

"Ye're the heir," said his uncle Davy, "just like Willie here is mine. Ye're needed to keep the farm goin', so ye are."

Quigley knew that if he had brothers the mantle of responsibility could have fallen on one of them. But he was an only son. Nor did he have any sisters.

"We've always believed ye'd be takin' over from us," said his father. "An' ye've already started with those five fine pig houses ye have. We just can't understan' it. This land's been in the family this hunnerd years or more."

His aunt Katy sat silently at the table reading her bible, as usual. I hardly ever saw her any other way, reading or leafing through it. That day was a Sunday and, as she said, "Six days shalt thou labor and do all thy work, but the seventh..." She turned the pages with gentle fingers taking care not to lose the dried petals of primrose and pansy that nestled there. Quigley's Uncle Thompson seemed lost in thought, teacup poised in the air, forgotten. Then his father, eyes moist with despair, decided to poke the hearth, tumbling peats that set off a shower of sparks flying up the chimney. His mother sat with her arms folded across her breast, ready to do battle and growing impatient at Thompson, just sitting there doing nothing, saying nothing.

"Thompson!" she burst out. "Wake up there an' drink yer tea. We're waitin' for ye to speak."

"Aye, Mary. Have patience. All in good time, now, all in good time. As the bible says, you bring forth fruit with patience. Isn't that right Katy?"

"It is, Thompson. Ye always could quote the scriptures, perverse though yer motives often are."

Thompson smiled. "You're our own Katy, so you are. Did you recognize that as Luke's gospel?"

"Don't jest. Ye know ye're just makin' fun o' me."

"Thompson! Pay attention," said Quigley's mother. "Ah asked ye here for a reason, so Ah did."

"Aye, Mary, aye. We want to get things in perspective so we do. Lookit! Here we have a young man who's been highly successful. But he's young. And he's restless. With a sense of unfullfillment. And he's about to go off and do something that's beyond your ken and sensibilities."

"Just tell him he's making a big mistake."

"Agh, Mary, patience! You have to go at this thing slow. Get the perspective like I've told you. First, we need to know what drove him to the pinnacle he's at and then, once we know that, we'll know why it has turned to ashes. Now wait!" Thompson's eyes narrowed to search among the beams of the ceiling for inspiration. It was a habit of his. "He feedeth on ashes. A deceived heart hath turned him aside that he cannot deliver his soul, nor say, is there not a lie in my right hand." He turned to Katy. "That's Isaiah. You'll want to look that one up."

"The devil in ye quotes the scriptures for his own purpose, so he does."

"Will ye wheesht, the both o' ye," cried Quigley's mother. "Thompson, stop wastin' time an' tell Quigley he's makin' a fool o' himself." In her anxiety she couldn't wait for Thompson, her long-headed brother she had called down from Belfast. "Quigley, son. That young wumman has yer head turned, so she has, her an' her seductive ways. Isn't it enough what her breed has done to ye already over the years without ye fallin' under her spell? Remember her aul' Da an' what he did tae ye. An' the aul' wumman. Are ye forgettin' what she is, an' what she did?"

"Ma, them things don't matter anymore."

"Of course they matter. Considerin' what they did tae ye, they matter. Isn't that why ye are what ye are? But only because ye have character. Character!" She turned to the family to explain. "That's what made him overcome all the badness an' villainy they did to him. Even when he wor a wean." There were nods of agreement. "Son, all yer life ye've had character. That's what sets ye apart. An' that's what ye're losin' now wi' this scatterbrained notion of traipsin' off."

"But it's simple. Ah'm just goin' away for a while. There was no need for ye to bring everyone an' Thompson intae this. It's my life, so it is. My decision."

"No it's not just yer decision. There's yer responsibility an' Thompson's yer uncle. An' he's the one with the education an' the experience. If ye won't listen tae yer father an' me an' Davy an' Sarah, at least listen tae him."

"Oh, for God's sake, Ma!"

"It's for yer own good, so it is. So discuss everything with Thompson, Quigley son. Ye'll see he can put it all in perspective, like he says. An' ye'll be all the wiser. An' we're here to listen too."

"If ye ask me," said Katy, "it's all there in the Commandments. Honor thy father an' thy mother all the days of thy life which the Lord thy God giveth thee."

Silence took over the kitchen as they pondered the force of Katy's statement. Surely Quigley would understand. The pendulum swung to and fro. I sucked my tea, sorry I had come over. I didn't like it one bit this looking in on someone else's bother. Thompson was in deep thought.

"I believe what we have here is this. Now listen to the Scriptures." Thompson had a way of spreading both hands expressively before him, then looking at everyone from slit eyes. "Happy is the man that findeth wisdom, and the man that getteth understanding. For the merchandise of it is better than the merchandise of silver, and the gain thereof than fine gold."

"Praise the Lord," said Katy.

"Hallelujah," said Davy and Sarah together.

"Understanding. You see! And wisdom!"

"Ye're a longheaded fellah, right enough," said Davy.

"It's all there in the Bible," said Katy smiling confidently.

"Now, Quigley," continued Thompson, "tell us the truth. How did you ever put so much money away in the bank? What do you have that I, and all these good folks, don't? What gave you the Midas touch?"

"What's that got to do with it, Thompson?" shouted Quigley's mother.

"Understanding, Mary, like it says in the book of Proverbs. And perspective. You've got to know where you're coming from to know where you're going. It's the way you do these things."

"Ye're sure?"

"Agh!" Thompson searched the ceiling and all its corners for understanding before turning with a grieved expression to Mary. "Didn't I just quote you the scriptures as proof. That's our foundation. Just leave this to me."

Mrs. McClug looked with pain at her brother's face. He was the brains of the family, the one who knew all the answers when they were young, the one who went on to study and hang a diploma on the wall. "Alright then," she said. "So, Quigley, tell him the wan about ye findin' the penny and what ye did next! Let Thompson see what a smart young fellah ye wor, before ye got yer head turned around by thon hussy an' her lipstick. Thompson! Now listen to this, you wi' all yer education an' thon big diploma. Listen tae this! Go on Quigley, lad."

MUSIC ON THE WIND

Quigley could see the bright eager faces of his family, shining in anticipation of hearing how his success had come about. They had heard it all before, except Thompson. He was up in Belfast. But they wanted to hear it again. It was as if his father and mother, Davy and Sarah, and his aunt Katy lived their lives through him. They got pride and enjoyment from what he had earned, the money in the bank, the car and the prestige in the townland. They were part of it through blood linkage. He was their hero. They looked up to him and he could see they were afraid of losing him. These were his family and had been there all his life, in a million small ways to help him over the ruts and ditches when he needed them. He had repaid them through his success. He leaned back, took a deep breath and said, "You mean the day Ah found the penny over by Peece's?"

"Aye. That's the wan. An' listen youse all. That's aul' Missus Peece the young wumman's granny he's tellin' youse about. That's important." She underlined this with a wink and nod of her head. "An' ye know who she is. Go ahead Quigley. There's some here never heard this wan."

"Mary! Let the man talk!" said Thompson.

"Wheesht there, all youse. Quiet. Quigley's goin' tae tell the wan about the penny. Right!" Mrs. McClug folded her arms as a sign for everyone to pay attention.

"Well!" began Quigley. He would make it good for their sake. "I was on me way home from school, ye see, with Billy over there." As he spoke, I could recall the small boys we both were, seventeen years before that final Sunday, the two of us staring at a penny lying in the dust at the side of the road. Quigley had been kicking stones along the dirt by the kerb, watching how they skidded and cannoned into other stones along the way, when he saw it, a well-worn penny with Queen Victoria's head looking up at him, stern and double-chinned. It just seemed to shine out of the dust. He bent and gathered it up with finger and thumb like it were gold, he was so wide eyed and breathless by the suddenness of good fortune, rubbing it on the sleeve of his coat to make sure. It was, indeed, a perfectly good penny despite being three monarchs old. "That must a' been nineteen forty-three," Quigley said to Thompson. "Ah must a' been eight year aul'."

"Ye wor, son," said his mother "an' things wor tough. We were milkin' less than a dozen cows then. Scrapin' pennies against each other tae pretend. An' only a wheen o' pigs."

"Mary! Let him talk!" said her husband.

"Maun," said Quigley, taking up the theme again, "thon penny was burnin' a hole in me hand. Do ye mind, Billy, hi?" he said to me.

"Sure," I said. "it's like yesterday."

"Aye, sure! You were with me right enough. An' ye'll all mind thon big, red, cast-iron slot machine outside of Peece's shop over by the Bridge. That was all Ah had in me head, thon big red thing. Have any of ye ever actually seen anyone put a penny in and take something out? Naw, nor me. Not even today! But there it was, big and red an' Ah could har'ly wait."

Now I have to explain. Times were not easy back then. There were scarcities of everything—food, clothes, shoes and things we really only knew about from advertisements in old newspapers that had accumulated in the big, slatted crate in the out-house. When a body sat hunkered over the cold hole in the plank of wood, you could read what they had to say about the flavor of chewing gum, and chocolate bars and sweets of every description from years previous, before the war started. Neither Quigley nor me could remember ever having had any of those delightful things to eat or suck-on or chew. And, even though there was a big, red, cast-iron vending machine outside of Peece's shop over by the Bridge, we'd never actually seen anyone put a penny in and take something out. But there it was, big and red and inviting. Every day we passed it on our way to and from school with no opportunity to learn what it held inside, until today. Now Quigley had a penny. All we had to do was stop kicking stones and get over there, maybe run part of the way and not cause questions at home by arriving late.

"So Ah stood there," continued Quigley, "in front of thon big, red slot machine towerin' way above me and me stretchin' from tip-toes to put the penny in the slot. Ye could hear it fall. An' thon handles tae tell ye which wan to pull if ye wanted a bar o' chocolate or a packet o' fruit drops. Ah selected fruit drops. Ah pulled an' Ah waited. Nothin' happened. Nothin'! Ah pulled again an' still nothin' happened. 'Hi! Ah shouted. Hi there, Missus Peece! Hi!'" He turned to me with a big grin on his face. "D'je mine thon time, Billy?"

I stood back because Mrs. Peece was a woman gae quick with her hands. I had taken a clout once before for not getting out of the way quick enough.

"Missus Peece!" called Quigley again.

A little girl of about our own age appeared and gazed at him from the doorway. She was fair with big violet eyes. Even after all these years, Quigley's reenactment of the event brought it back to me. She stood there in her pretty frock, little ankle socks and the ribbon in her hair. She was a lovely child. Quigley gaped.

Mrs. Peece, who owned the shop, I remember as a tall woman who still wore Mother-Hubbard dresses and laced-up boots that were the fashion in the country at the turn of the century. She was a scrawny looking individual, brought on, as people said, from eating three meals a day of nothing but thin porridge. She appeared to be all wrinkles and wisps of ash-gray hair escaping from the bun and combs behind her head. Forever blowing strands away from her face and smoothing them backwards with knarled hands, she seemed to be in constant nervous movement. Not a bad woman, mind you, just carnaptious where wee lads were concerned. And a gossip! She liked to prattle with her customers about the events of their daily lives, their troubles and their hopes. Most of all she liked to tell her customers about her grandson Warren, all at full yell because she had to shout over the aching of the water wheel round back that powered the two big stones that ground the oatmeal. Through the half door we could hear she had a customer, Mrs. Twaddle from over the ways a bit.

"Ah'll ha'e a couple pounsa yer oatmeal, if ye made it today, like," said Mrs. Twaddle in her high whiney voice.

"Ah did, indeed!" Mrs. Peece yelled back.

"An' how's yer gran'son Warren keepin'?" Mrs. Twaddle asked.

"Teachin' at the Academy!" yelled Mrs. Peece. "An' ye know.."

The cry from outside the door came again.

"Hi, Missus Peece. This machine dinnae work! Hi, there! Missus Peece!"

Mrs. Peece tossed her head and blew hair. "That sculpin's goin' tae deefen me. Just haul' on there missus tae Ah see what the wee bugger wants." She was getting angry. To be interrupted when she was just about to tell the latest news about her son Warren, now that he was Latin Master at the Academy. "Thon wee bugger o' a M'Clug!" she yelled. And she banged open the shop door that, in anger at being disturbed, clanged a battery of bells. "Wha' ye want, ye wee ouzel ye? Ye're makin' too much noise for a' the size o' ye. Wha' ye want the noo? Spake up!" Mrs. Peece had lived all her life in the Braid Valley and spoke a rich form of the vernacular that was still thick with its Scottish origins.

"Ah put a penny in thon machine an' nothin' happened," said Quigley. He was sure God was on his side. "Ah'm supposed t' get a packet o' fruit drops, so Ah am." The little girl looked up at the old woman and back again to Quigley. Quigley, sensing a challenge to behave like a man in front of her, stuck his chest out even further and said again, "Ah put a penny in there," pointing to the slot, "an nothin' happened."

Mrs. Peece pursed her lips in mock disbelief and lowered her head, her face very tight to Quigley's; so close he could see the black-heads in the skin around her temples and on her nose, see the grime etched into her wrinkles and the fuzz of dust on her face from measuring out scoopfulls of oatmeal. She smelled of peat-smoke from an open hearth. He held her gaze with a defiance born by anger and disappointment at losing his newfound penny. "Ah lost me penny so Ah did!"

Mrs. Peece put her face even closer, squeezing great concern into her expression. "Isn't that a pity now," she said in a mock whine. "Maun, but that's a pity, now." And before Quigley could plumb the meaning and intent of this pantomime, she had turned and opened the shop door. "Come, Loveen, child. No need starin' at a wee ouzel wi' no manners!"

The door jangled and hung there, slowly drawing strength to swing itself closed again. The little girl edged towards it as if reluctant to follow. She stared at Quigley with wide eyes. He stared back. Mrs. Peece returned to Mrs. Twaddle. The door was hesitatingly still open.

"You mean she stole your penny?" said Thompson.

"Aye, she did. Sort of."

"Sure that happens in Belfast every day of the week. They'd steal the eye out of your head."

"Wheesht there, Thompson. The lad hasn't finished the story. Giv'im a chance to tell the whole thing, can't ye," cried Mary.

But Quigley hesitated. He had never told the whole thing and had carried the humiliation hidden within him ever since. But I remember. The door still hung hesitatingly open. Mrs. Peece could be heard talking to the customer. "Maun, what a bad-lookin' wee fellah that is," she exclaimed. "Did ye see the size o' his ears. God save us but he's no blessed wi' guid looks. Ye'd wunder what the Guid Lord had in mind sometimes lettin' folks play wi' his image like that."

Quigley heard it all. So did the little girl who sidled through the door and disappeared from sight. Though only eight, he not only instinctively knew that nobody gave a damn about his penny, he was mortified to hear she thought him ugly. The anger and humiliation was hard to bear. He kicked out with one nail-studded boot and laid some scratches across the red paint. It didn't make him feel any better. "Ye aul' witch, ye!" he shouted. We had heard people say that about Mrs. Peece. None of us were quite sure what it meant but it felt good to yell. "Ye're nothin' but an aul' witch!" It had effect. Mrs. Peece tore open the door to bells clanging and shouted, "Off wi' ye! Or Ah'll eat ye alive! Ye're about a good-sized mouthful. Ye hear?"

The hair tingling on our heads, bravery of the moment slipped away and we sped along the road as fast as our feet could carry us. When we stopped to look back, just to make sure we were safe, we saw the little girl standing by the door. She was looking our way. Quigley waved.

"She was aye a bad tempered aul' wumman, thon," said his mother. "Isn't that so Jock?"

"Oh, aye. An aul' witch to be sure. Keep goin' son."

Quigley cleared his throat. "Ye could say Ah made up me mind there an' then Ah was never goin' to waste a penny again. No more slot machines. No siree! Ah was determined. An' as for the aul' witch, Ah'd gallop past the shop from then on. So did Billy there. Just in case, don't ye know?" He laughed, I laughed, and the family laughed too.

"Isn't that a good wan?" I said. "What do you think?"

"Katy, what do you think?" said Thompson. "A feast is made for laughter and wine maketh merry, but money answereth all things. Ecclesiastes!"

"Don't mock, Thompson. Don't mock."

I remember that day when we were weeuns. We both sped away knowing in our eight-year-old hearts that, whatever it took, we were never going to waste a penny again. I followed him down the lane to his farmhouse.

"That you, Quigley?" his mother called from the scullery.

"Aye!"

"Yer late! Wha' kept ye?"

"Nothin' ma."

His mother came out, drying her hands on a towel. "Ye're lookin' down in the mouth. Wha' ails ye?"

"Ma, how do ye get tae keep somethin' without some aul' witch stealin' it from ye?"

His mother, a wise, practical farm-bred woman, forego further questions and answered directly. "Ye put it in the Bank, so ye do. In a Savin's Book."

"Can Ah have one o' them? If Ah had any money, like?"

"Aye, Quigley, son. If ye'd like? Ah'll take ye intae town wan o' these days before the banks close, an' we'll open wan for ye. How about that?"

"Ah've no money yet. Don't Ah have tae get money first?"

"Aye, ye do, Quigley. But Ah'll start ye off wi' sixpence." And she ruffled the tousled head of her son, bringing the hands over the ears as if to stick them to his head. It was a pity his ears stuck out so—a trait he inherited from his father. Agh Well.

"Hello Billy!" she said to me. "Whyn't ye start a savings book too? Ask yer auntie tae start ye wan." But I never did. Maybe that was the difference between Quigley and me, considering the way things worked out.

"So, Thompson, what do ye think o' that? There he was, all of eight years aul' an' he knew already how many beans make five. So ye see," his mother said proudly, "that's how it all began."

"Very interesting. And then?"

It was as if Quigley could still feel his mother's hand ruffling his hair, feel the pride that seemed to exude from her fingertips. From that day forward every penny, every thruppence, every sixpence, every coin he found or earned went into his Savings Book.

"When Ah was fourteen Ah had seven pounds, sixteen shillings and nine pence. Never once did Ah take a penny out."

"Dear bless us!" said Thompson. "You have the Midas touch, so you have. And there's me laboring all this time in Belfast and don't have two brass farthings to scrape together. And you the Andrew Carnegie of pigs."

"Wheeest there, Thompson. You an' yer own problems. Isn't aul' Missus Peece the granny of the young wumman is tryin' tae steal the lad away. Lurin' the lad tae who knows what, wi' fingernails colored scarlet an' lipstick!"

"Like the sirens of Ulysses!" said Thompson. "I know their ilk!"

"The hussy, more like it. Her and her wild notions! An' her face painted like Jezebel. Gallivantin' off wi' the lad, tae who knows where."

"Calm, Mary. The lad's a financial wizard."

"Who'll have more tea?" asked his father.

"Tell them the rest o' it, Quigley," I called. "Tell them about her Da, aul' Peece the Latin master when you an' me was at the Academy. Tell them about the day he beat ye wi' his fists and you just walked out. Go on, hi."

"Dear blessus!" said Thompson. "Is that brutality still goin' on? True, young fellah?"

"Aye, sort of. It was nothin'."

"An' he niver tol' me at the time," said his mother. "If Ah'd ha' knowed Ah'd a gone in to straighten thon Latin master out. He'd no business beatin' the lad." Her face reflected concern as if it had happened the day before. She was ready to do battle.

"It's alright, Ma. He was just bein' ignorant. That's all."

"What did he beat you for?" asked Thompson. "Was there a reason?"

"Agh, who knows? He was aye ignorant, so he was."

Warren Peece, the Latin Master, saw Quigley as he saw most of the boys, just another of the big lumps on whom an education was wasted. Quigley would have whole-heartedly agreed with the Latin Master if he had but known these sentiments. He had been saying that himself for three years now. But the Ministry of Education had set the age of school leaving at fourteen. Quigley was just fourteen. As soon as school closed for the summer he'd be free. He could hardly wait.

"Goin' tae the Academy was a waste o' time," said Quigley. "What can ye do wi' stuff like geometry an' trigonometry an' who the hell are ye goin' tae speak French to on a farm by the hip o' Slemish?"

"You know," said Thompson with a philosophical air, "for some reason the mount where St. Patrick hatched his missionary vision is never accorded the respect it deserves. The hip o' Slemish, you say?"

"Wheesht, Thompson," said Quigley's mother, "an' listen."

"Ah'm askin' ye, hi! It's sheer codology!" said Quigley, smiling derrogatively and nodding his head at the same time. "An' as for thon aul' Latin, bejapers, not even the pigs speak it anymore."

I remembered how that was a standing joke in the class and always got supportive oinks from the others who knew full well they were also headed back to the farms.

"If Ah'd gone to the Tech at least Ah'd a learned how to do book-keepin'," he continued, nodding his head in affirmation.

"It's an education, Quigley," counseled his mother at the time. "All them things is an education. Book-keepin's no an education. Ye'll find them things out when ye're older. Look at Warren Peece. Born with no family but thon aul' wumman and look at him now, a graduate o' the Queen's University and teachin' Latin. He has education. Lives in thon nice house with the bay window, an' all; an' a Mason intae the bargain, Ah'm told. Now he's somebody. An' Quigley, Ah do want ye tae be somebody."

"Aye," murmured Quigley with a sigh, and leafed through his Savings

Book. He had heard it all before.

"Well, go on, then. Tell us about the Latin master," urged Thompson.

"He was known for his bouts o' bad temper. Anythin' that displeased him set it off like marking badly done homework."

I can still remember Mr. Peece entering the classroom with the exercise books piled high on his arms and thunder pounding on his brow. "M'Clug!" he yelled. Quigley's Latin exercise book came sailing across the classroom, pages fluttering like broken wings on a badly wounded bird. It landed amongst the desks and, as he retrieved it, he could see the red X's scattered across his homework. A couple of them had been done with such intensity of feeling that the page was torn. "M'Clug!" yelled the Latin Master. "You're a jackass! A great, thick, ignorant clod of a jackass! Do you hear me?" His face was getting red and more contorted up with fury as he realized for the umpteenth time that he was wasting his time and education on this and all the other dunderheads. And, as was his wont when angry, he slid from the carefully pronounced English of the Latin Master into the pure broad dialect of his youth. "Ye're fit for nothin' but fattenin' pigs! D'ye hear me! Fattenin' pigs!" he screamed. Peece's anger got the better of him. He came marching threateningly down the aisle of the class, shouting, "Git up out o' that seat an' take yersel' away off, ye great galoot ye. Ye're past fourteen year aul'. Don't ye know that? Ye don't have tae come here anymore an' waste me precious time." He was trembling in his anger that teaching louts was all that life now held out for him. No chance of teaching at an Academical Institution or a school known by a single prestigious name, like Pretora or Campbell. "Tell yer aul' Da ye're fit an' ready tae work on the farm. Fatten pigs or somethin' useful. Work, d'ye hear? Work!" He grabbed Quigley by one ear and then said something that formed Quigley's life thereafter. *"Per ardua ad astra!"* The classroom began to titter. Aul' Peece was in form, right enough. He was starting to splutter. *"Per ardua ad astra!* D'ye unnerstan' that, ye great dolt? Or am Ah castin' pearls before swine? Am Ah? D'ye ha'e any idea whatever? Ye ignoramous! So listen! Through hard work ye can reach the stars! That's what it means. D'ye hear that? D'ye hear that? Ye can, ye know, ye can! Ye can reach the stars."

Quigley had stood up. He was taller than the Latin Master who, letting go the ear, took a swing at him with the flat of his hand. As if in slow motion Quigley ducked sideways. He felt very calm. He walked slowly towards the door. Peece pummeled him with clenched but ineffective fists. *"Per ardua ad astra*!" screamed the Latin Master and there were tears of despair running down his face.

"*Per Ardua Ad Astra*? Sure that's what you have up over the pig houses. D'ye mean to tell me it was inspired by the Latin master?" asked Thompson.
"Aye. It was."
"Wheesht, Thompson. Keep goin', son."

Quigley was still waiting at the bus depot when school got out and the several boys who also lived out the Antrim Line, wandered down to take the bus home. I came up to him. "Boys, but aul' Peece laid intae ye today, hi"
"Thon aul' bugger. What the hell does he know about anything? Him an' his aul' Latin."
"Ye're no vexed, then?"
"Naw. The day'll come when Ah'll buy an' sell the aul' cod, so Ah will. Wait tae ye see! Thon aul' cod!"
Quigley was very quiet seated in the bus as it whined through the gearshifts all the three miles to our bus stop at the end of the country road. When we got out and began walking towards our adjacent farms, I asked, "What're ye goin' tae do, Quigley? Heh?"
"Just what the aul' bugger says. Ah'm goin' tae fatten pigs." Quigley jerked his head and winked an eye. "Aye! Ah'll fatten pigs, so Ah will."
"Ye will?"
"Aye! Am'm goin' tae fatten pigs." As he kicked a couple of stones we remembered the day he found the penny lying in the dust. "You know," he smiled, "Ye remember aul' Mrs. Peece. She'll never know how much good she's done me, naw!" He continued to smile. "I think Ah've just found another penny, but this time, an' oh b' the holy jeepers, Ah'm not goin' tae waste it in no aul' scrap-iron slot machine. No sirree! Ah ha'e seven pounds, sixteen shillings and ninepence in my Bank Savings Book. There's thon empty barn over at Geddon's Ah can rent to say nothin' about usin' the stack yard at home for farrowing sows." Sure enough, a plan had formed in Quigley's head. "Damn Latin. Damn the Academy an' all them aul' buggers teachin' rubbish." He punched me on the arm in glee. "Ah'm goin' tae fatten pigs, so Ah am." And in high energy he sped down the lane to the farmhouse to do a bit of bookwork. I had a hard time keeping up with him.

"Ma! Where's thon aul' exercise book ye bought for keepin' the egg-count in?" he called.

"On the window, there. Wha' for ye want it now? Don't ye have yer own exercise books for yer homework?"

"Naw, Ma. This is for somethin' else." Quigley took the exercise book and laid it purposefully in front of him on the table.

"Quigley! Are ye all right, son?"

"Never been better, Ma, Ah can tell ye." And with a strong hand wrote on the outside cover, *Perdua adastra*. He smiled, unconscious of his spelling error. I kept silent.

"What's that mean, son?"

"It's Latin, Ma, an' it means Ah'm goin' tae fatten pigs."

"Latin!" she thought. "Ye see, Quigley. Ye're startin' tae show an education. It was worth it after all, son, now wasn't it, goin' tae the Academy."

"You mean to say you saw your destiny in a quotation from Virgil?" said Thompson. "My, it's like Greek tragedy, so it is. Dear blessus! And you a lad of fourteen?"

"Sure!"

"Pigs?"

"Sure!"

"Isn't it the parable of the talents. 'And a man had three sons and to each he gave.' Remarkable! You should be proud of this son of yours, Mary." He turned to Quigley. "First the old wumman Peece cheating you out of a penny and you saving up a fortune, and then her son, thon Latin Master, beating the daylights out of you and telling you to go fatten pigs."

"Aye. Ye might say."

"If ye ask me," suggested his aunt Katy, "it's all in the scriptures. Isn't that so, Thompson? In the book of Job. 'Then he showeth them their work and their transgressions that they have exceeded. He openeth also their ear to discipline and commandeth that they return from iniquity.' Ye see, Quigley, ye hadn't done yer homework." Katy sat back feeling very good about getting her quotation in before Thompson could rally.

"Dear blessus Katy, that's good, so it is. But you're off on the wrong line of thought. It's not the scriptures at all. It's pure Shakespeare, so it is. As the Bard says, 'There's a time in the tides of man when, taken at the flood, leads on to greatness.' That's the explanation. The lad's a tycoon, so he is. If Carnegie were alive he'd be cheering in his grave."

"Agh, give over Thompson," said Quigley's father. "Didn't ye go up to

Belfast an' haven't ye been livin' high iver since? Isn't that right? Ye don't often smell of pig manure now, do ye? Ye see there's a price to pay for workin' hard. Dirt an' calluses on yer hands an' an achin' back an' on the go from five in the mornin' till ye go to bed at mid-night."

"You're right, you know. 'The night cometh when no man can work!' You hear that Katy? That's somewhere in the gospel of Saint John."

"Thompson! Ye're tryin' me patience, so ye are," said Quigley's mother. "Ah asked ye here tae put wisdom in the lad's head an' here ye are sparrin' wi' Katy over which o' ye can remember the most verses o' the Bible. Ye're daft so ye are. An' Ah always considered ye the long-headed wan o' the family."

"Patience, Mary. This is a very special young man we have here. We have to draw on the wisdom of the ages and Katy is keeping me on my toes, so she is. Aren't you Katy?"

"Just don't mock."

"I'm not mocking. It's with reverence. The three great works of reference are Shakespeare, Milton and the Bible. All our wisdom is in there. You just have to find it. Now, where were we? Quigley! What I can't understand is why you're giving up everything to go away off, as your mother puts it, gallivanting?"

"Traipsin', Ah said."

"Traipsing. What is it you want? What's this young lady like and what's her intent? These are the questions you must ask yourself. Or, why'nt you just get married to the lass? And have her settle down on this great farm?"

"Marriet?" interjected his mother in alarm, while scolding her brother with a frown. "Selectin' the right wumman is somethin' tae take yer time o'er. As a wumman mesel' Ah can tell ye, son, they're a' the same, 'cept when it comes tae work. Ye dinnae want a wife that's so fond o' the work she cud lie down beside it. Look at the length o' her nails. An' painted, intae the bargain!"

"But Quigley must speak for himself, Mary. Does he crave adventure, love, or.."

"Agh, Thompson. Ye're daft too. Don't tell me he inherits these wild notions from you an' our side o' the family?"

"Well, look at aul' uncle Bob," said Thompson. "Went off to Australia an' didn't he end up a prince of the opal mines."

"Aye, an' he marriet a fortune hunter an' that was that. None of it ever came back to his own family. That's what Ah'm afeart of. She has her eye on yer fortune, son."

"Naw, Ma. It's not her. It's me. Ah want tae do somethin' else."

"Like what, Quigley?" Thompson asked.

"She's an actress and she's been tellin' me about it an' she's goin' tae be in a picture."

"Gettin' intae pictures, she says," said Katy. "Pictures! It's the devil's own work, so it is, Quigley!"

"Dear blessus, Katy, what makes you say that?"

"Ah just have that feelin'! The way them actors an' actresses carry on."

"There's no future in it," said Quigley's mother. "An' he already has himself well set up fattenin' pigs. He's secure. What more does he want?"

"Agh, Mary, you're his mother, so you are, and you've every right to be sore. But where's your sense of adventure? The lad's young."

"Thompson! Ah'm beginnin' to regret ye came. Ye're supposed to be a help not a hindrance."

"Mary, the pictures are here to stay and there's people making millions at it every minute of the day. Look at Myrna Loy! And Ronald Coleman! Millionaires! Sure I was once on the stage myself if you remember and had ambitions, so I had."

"We're not talkin' about you. What's to become of Quigley?"

Thompson looked long at his sister Mary. He saw her despair at the thought of losing her only son to a woman she considered a hussy and to a profession she believed was full of sin. He saw the despair of a proud father who feared losing the son that should inherit the farm and carry on when he was gone. In Quigley he saw the opportunity he himself had missed. God help us, he thought. He leaned over and said gently, "Quigley, you've been very patient with us all. Tell us about this woman."

"She's just a woman from the town, daughter of the Latin master like ye heard. Loveen they call her. Loveen Peece!"

"How did she become an actress?"

"She went to the girls' school on the Ballymoney road and from there to study in London."

"The Royal Academy of Dramatic Art."

"Aye. How'd ye know?"

"I know. Sure didn't I do a bit of repertory once, in Portstewart, during the summer."

"An' she's been actin' on the stage for a couple of years an' now she has a chance to be in the pictures."

"So?"

"Well. It sounded great to me. Ah've seen just about everything that has come to the picture houses in town an' doin' that as a livin' sure would beat fattenin' pigs. Ah can ride horses an' jump off things."

"What did she say?"

"She says Ah could start as an extra as they call it, in crowd scenes."

"He's lettin' me take over his pigs, so he is. Aren't ye Quigley?" said his uncle Davy.

"Be quiet, Davy!" said Mrs. M'Clug. "Ah do believe you an' Thompson want the lad to go away. Ye'd both be happy then for yer own perverse reasons."

"The way Ah see it," said her husband, "is that Quigley has got to get this thing out o' his system, an' then come back an' he'll be happy."

"Bravo!" said Thompson.

"You too?" said Quigley's mother.

"You're quoting Shakespeare, Mary. It's just like I said. But you left out the Brutay bit."

"Agh, ye're all gone mad, so youse are. Talk sense, Thompson."

"The thing is, Mary, it's like his father says. He has to get these things out of his system. The lad has been working like a slave since he was fourteen. He's now in the prime of his life. It's not the money. There's the artist in him yelling to be heard," said Thompson. Then, gesturing with upraised hand he stood up, the better to emphasize the point that had just occurred to him. "Maun, I can see it now," he said. "It's a paradox, so it is. On the one hand is the Lord telling us to go make cash after the manner of the parable of the talents, and on the other hand he's saying it's bad for the soul. 'For what can it profit a man if he gain the whole world yet lose his own soul.'" He looked around. "Isn't that the long an' short of it? A paradox. Ye wouldn't know what to make of it. What's a body to do? Boys, if I'd a been smart enough in me youth." Thompson clenched his fists and beat himself a couple of times on the chest. "That's it. There's yer perspective for ye. 'For what shall it profit a man if he gain the whole world and lose his own soul.'" He turned again to Mary. "Let the young fellow go. The artist in him is crying for release! Isn't that so, young fellow?"

"Aye!"

"Artist? For God's sake! Quigley, where on earth did ye iver hear the word artist or artistic fuldiddle until that wumman came along?" cried his mother.

"Ah've been tae the pictures, so Ah have, ma. When ye see James Cagney an' Bing Crosby an' John Gilbert an' Douglas Fairbanks Junior an'.."

"You know them all, so you do," said Thompson in amazement.

"Ah do. Ah haven't been thinkin' about much else for a long while and then when Loveen came along and tol' me about the chances Ah had, well, Ah'm ready, so Ah am."

"You are indeed. Did you see Boris Karloff in *The Black Room*? Wasn't thon something, hi? What did you think of Paul Muni in *The Good Earth*?"

"Thompson!"

"Yes, Mary."

"What are ye doin'?"

"Two artists talking, Mary. You know, you're right, so you are. I believe he does take after our side of the family."

Long before I had finished the Teacher's College the five pig fattening sheds lay empty and a couple of the doors banged in the wind. A corner of the roof had been lifted off at some time past in a storm. His uncle Davy just didn't have the knack. M'Clug and his wife spoke often of their son Quigley and of his supposed where-abouts. It had been over two years since he left, a suitcase in his hand and a ticket to London. The sign over the gate—*"Per Ardua Ad Astra" Q. M'Clug, Prop.*—had blown down and his father didn't have the conviction or the strength to weld it back up. It lay against the bottom of one of the feed silos. The film *The Irishman's Fancy* came to the Towers Cinema and stayed a week it was in such great demand. It was about the political upheaval in Ireland during the last century. Loveen Peece was cast in a minor role as a tart that lures a despicable English officer into a trap where the brave local lads beat him to death with barrel staves ripped from a handy keg of porter. There were those who swore that a giant of a man in the crowd scene where the tart is dragged through the streets, had ears that made him damn like Quigley M'Clug.

Devil Take the Hindmost

Sergeant Kilroy held the manuscript between finger and thumb with tired disdain. Were it not that it might be evidence he would have cast it aside as waste, fit only to liven the ashes in the near-dead coals of the fire place. It was indeed a collection of sorry-looking pages, dog-eared with dried stains suggesting a cup of tea had been spilled in its vicinity. Tobacco ash had been brushed from its surface leaving a characteristic dark smudge; but the typing was readable for all that. Despite the grime and the rough erasures of text and over-typing, the sergeant felt compelled to read. He held it under the table lamp and began.

"It was one of those miserable wintry nights when everything was the color of second hand pewter. I had gone again to the graveyard to think, to try to straighten things out, get a hold of myself and play it like I had always played it—winner take all and the Devil take the hindmost. But my thoughts wouldn't organize. I was conscious only of sitting on top of a slab of polished granite that held down the frozen soul of some long departed village elder. It was not the first time I had sat on a cold tombstone but this time I sensed the numbness of my hips and thighs and wondered how I had ever withstood the cold before. But who feels the cold of a tombstone when the blood is boiling in your veins. I stood up to relieve the biting cramp. Opposite me was a heap of soil that had settled into a weathered mound. A few weeds had favored it during the past summer. Now their shriveled rosettes were hunkered down close to the sore earth to wait out the winter.

There was still no headstone, just a small numbered square of metal beside the graveled path. How long I stood there just seeing, not really conscious, I don't know. I hadn't heard him come up even though the gravel crunches underfoot. But there he was, the black raincoat and somber hat of his trade between me and the sorry grave. I was conscious then of the whiteness of the dog collar around his neck and the porridge color of his face.

There were bluish crescents below the pale gray eyes that held onto mine.

We looked at each other for some time. His lips began to move silently like the two halves of a worm that had been sliced through by a spade. "Confucius say," the ugly mouth of him spat, "he who screw in graveyard is fucking near dead!"

There is no way to answer that one especially when it comes at you like ghost-whispered words out of the past; especially when, in that moment it made everything click together; especially when I looked into the cold gray eyes of the Reverend Gabriel M'Goophen, I had that sudden flash of realization that all my troubles were just about to end."

Sergeant Kilroy laid aside the manuscript and asked, "How's it going there, Doc?"

The Doctor paused a few seconds while he completed another check of the body's pulse. "He's alive. Let's move him."

The Sergeant nodded. "All set?"

"Just give us another couple of minutes and we're off."

Sergeant Kilroy looked at the still figure on the stretcher. Who would have thought, he asked himself. Poor bastard. The room was a shambles; empty likker bottles scattered around the floor, scraps of half-eaten portions of food, unwashed clothing strewn over furniture. The man had lived like a pig. Now it had come to this. Suicide!

"That's it," said Doctor Jones checking the adhesives on the wrists. "We'll take him over to my surgery."

"Right. Grab hold!"

They took the patient to Doctor Jones surgery and laid him out on a cot. His face was pale and he stank of whisky.

"He's lucky this time," commented Doctor Jones. "Aye. He'll live to try it a second try, so he will."

"Why?"

"Agh, he's an unfortunate fellow, just a drunk, Sergeant, an alcoholic. They do these things you know, nothing to live for. Despair, it's called."

"You're probably right." Sergeant Kilroy thought of the manuscript he had left behind on the table at the scene. What if someone else found it? "I think I'm going back there. Investigate a bit more. I'll go over everything again. He may have left some notion of why he'd want to do such a thing."

"Yeah!" the Doctor said tiredly. "Let me know. I'll clean him up in the meantime."

"Maybe, Doctor, we could keep this quiet for an hour or so. Alright?"
"Sure. Just another sick patient."
The Sergeant withdrew into the cold of the night and walked the short distance to Tom Burke's home. He picked up the manuscript. It certainly was interesting reading!

"How can one come to know a man of the cloth who can make a bald-headed remark like that? Confucius! It took me back through the years. We had grown up together in this same village. Moreover we went to University together. That again was a kind of destiny. We were the first ever from our village to go on to college, Gabriel and I. Well, not exactly. There was Phoebe. Yes, there was Phoebe. It's funny how I always forget about Phoebe. Maybe that's because I grew up in this male society and females were often forgotten.

All through school we three had been the so-called special students, which was not difficult. Imagine a small village associated with farming; Gabriel, the son of the schoolteacher, Phoebe, the daughter of the old parson, the one before Gabriel received the call, and my father the doctor. Our houses were the only ones with books. Our fathers were on all the committees, always consulted, always in the know.

In school Gabriel was brilliant at history but had a special passion for religious studies. He was often about the parsonage borrowing books on the Bible and discussing impossible theological topics with old Reverend Botham, Phoebe's father. He never seemed to notice Phoebe nor could anyone blame him. Poor girl, she was a drab, heavy thing and colorless. She was also very good at math and when she wasn't solving some indescribable problem she was reading some indescribable detective novel. The lending library from the next town sent a van once a week and Phoebe was possibly the only customer.

I know I ought to remember more about them from our teenage days but I can't think of anything important. I didn't have much in common with either. Certainly I was a good student, but my fun was sports or running with the village lads to dances and feeling in the petticoats of every girl for miles around.

At university we tended to avoid each other, which in itself was not difficult as we were in different faculties distributed in different parts of Belfast. Gabriel was in the School of Divinity and Phoebe in the Faculty of Arts. I was studying medicine, hoping to fill my father's shoes as a doctor.

My time at University was not, for me, the best years of my life but certainly the years in which I made two great discoveries that afterwards were to determine the direction of my life. The first of these was that I was a man of strong passions with deep uncontrollable desires. It may seem strange that this should be a discovery but it was. I had been reared in the strict Puritan principles of the Dissenter Church and had behaved until then with proper decorum, never probing beyond a few skirmishes among the petticoats of village girls and the nurses at the hospital. But I discovered the villain within me in my third year of studies the night I met Lila.

The second discovery occurred later in the External Department of the Hospital one day as I was examining a bad case of piles. Peeping up an anus with a flashlight I suddenly saw my whole future staring at me. I just calmly switched off the light and left. I was probably halfway to South America before it was noticed that I was not on duty.

I don't think the world has missed me as a doctor yet, this decision was the pivot about which all else balanced and was eventually to settle on the head of my lovely Lila."

"How's it going, Sergeant? You're wife said I'd find you here." Constable McDoltt called from the open doorway. "Do you need a hand? It's damned cold out, so it is!"

"Aye, Constable. I can leave now." The Sergeant slipped the manuscript back into the large envelope and, turning his back on the constable, slipped it into the folds of his tunic. He drew on his greatcoat against the coming blast of cold air outside. "Right!" He glanced once more around the disheveled room then switched out the light, locked the door and put the key in his pocket. "Back to the barracks, Constable. Lets go!" The police car moved quietly along the village street.

"Do you think he'll make it?" asked Constable McDoltt.

"How do you mean?"

"Didn't he try to do himself in?"

"Nah! Just dead drunk." An inner warning told the Sergeant to go easy on what was said. So far only he and the doctor had observed the scene.

"Is that all?"

"Aye! But it hardly matters none. Burke threw his life away a good wheen of years ago anyway."

"Aye, you could be right."

"Damned fool."

At the police barracks in the village Sergeant Kilroy went to his office. "Put on the kettle there, Matt. We need warming up." He threw off his greatcoat and tunic, poked the fire into life and threw on a scuttle of coals. Goddamit! he thought. What now? It was a good job old Doctor Burke was dead, not to have to see the sight of his son lying on a stretcher, a derelict, a drunk, an attempted suicide. He stared for a while into the coals.

"Your tea, Sergeant."

Sergeant Kilroy took the steaming mug and settled himself at his desk. "Can you close that door Matt? I've got some work here and I don't want to be disturbed. See to it, won't you?" He extracted the manuscript from the envelope, took a mouthful of hot tea and began to read.

"Lila was beautiful. She had red hair. She was the only red-haired woman that ever attracted me. Long golden red hair. She had it all rolled up under her hat so you wouldn't have known the night I saw her for the first time. I saw her standing in Shaftesbury Square playing in a Jesus-Loves-You band. She was playing the cornet, a beautiful ludicrous sight in that ridiculous black Victorian outfit with its maroon ribbon and the golden hair of her hidden under a bonnet.

She played with her eyes closed. That's what I noticed about her first; playing with her eyes closed like she was enjoying it. And when she opened them we were staring right at each other. Even by the streetlight I could see that the color of her eyes was pure aquamarine. I couldn't take my eyes from her's except to notice the slow movement of the tip of her tongue over the depression left by the cornet's mouthpiece on the red of her upper lip.

It is said that those who play the cornet have special kinds of lips. Certainly Lila had special lips, lips to kiss with, lips to smile with. She smiled and I knew, I knew as sure as God's in His Heaven that we were meant for each other. God, how I loved that woman!

There are things that hardly seem real now—the wild passions. Gabriel M'Goophen was with me that night. He'd caught up with me as I was walking back to the student's hostel. It was his idea to listen to the Jesus-Loves-You band, only natural he being a divinity student. I can still see him, the bastard, his eyes closed tight and muttering to himself during the praying while she and I stared at each other as if the world did not exist. I remember how, after the prayer, Gabriel had to go over and congratulate the General in charge. Lila and I just walked off together like it was the most natural thing in the world. Away out past the University, I holding her hand and the cornet in its wee black case in the other like I was carrying her books home from school."

"Constable!"

"Aye!"

"Bring us another cup, like a good fellow. Make it hot. And I'll have two of sugar this time. No milk."

He laid the manuscript aside while he took up the poker. He tapped the coals. Some hissing yellow gas caught fire.

"Your tea, sir," said the Constable. "And it's nearing ten o'clock already and I'm off duty. McKilt will be here any minute, so he will. There he is now and I'm off. Is that alright?"

Sergeant Kilroy gave his consent. "Tell McKilt to come in here for a minute."

"Right!"

Constable McKilt entered, his red face a sign of the cold winds that blew outside.

"Sit down, McKilt, and let me bring you up to the minute for I have to go home soon and get some sleep. We had a bad case of a drunk this night. Do you know the late Doctor Burke's son, thon fellow that came back from overseas about a year ago?"

"I do. Aye."

"Well, he took the notion sometime the night to get himself dead drunk and maybe a bit violent."

"Agh, naw!"

"Aye! I got a phone call at home telling me to get over there quick like. I called Doctor Jones."

"And?"

"We got him probably just in time. Took him over to Doctor Jones' surgery. That's where he is now. The doc's probably pumping him out."

"Dear blessus!"

"Well, I'm here for another few minutes. Thought you needed to know because there may be some busy bodies calling in and you'll know why. Keep notes."

"I will, Sergeant. Sure I will that." He went to his desk and laid out a pencil and pad. Not much ever happened in Pigsbrae, an occasional drunk and disorderly, a family disagreement now and then. Last year's suicide! That was something and a half. Though once there was the Spitfire crashed in forty-two when he was a wee lad at school. That was really an event, but not likely to happen again. "Boys-a-dear!" He could see the Sergeant through the glass panel reading something. He was a smart fellow the Sergeant.

"The excitement of that woman passed from her hand to mine. It was an electric charge. I couldn't wait to get her into some dark doorway to lay my hands about her. I don't recall that we spoke. She talked to me with her fingers, weaving them through mine. We walked and she led me into the old churchyard by the museum. I had never been in a graveyard at that hour of the night before. And yet I wasn't afraid or hesitant. It seemed the most natural thing to do. Even when we made love on top of the tomb of one Samuel John Biggins, born 1852, died 1907, and his beloved wife Sarah, born 1860 died 1920.

When we emerged from there life for me had changed. Gabriel was standing opposite the iron-gate his mouth working to find the words that would express the outrage staring out of his pale gray eyes. It took him near fifteen years to find the right words but he found them a few nights ago. He found them by lifting a quotation from the immortal sayings of the venerable Confucius.

Yes, near fifteen years have passed since that night. Much has happened, not just to me but to Lila and the Reverend Gabriel. The worst that can happen has happened to my dear Lila. She is dead. The mound of rude earth out there is still waiting for a headstone. But one has been ordered from up in Belfast, in polished black granite with lettering in gold.

Lila, beloved wife of Rev. Gabriel M'Goophen.
Born July 1935, died November 1971.

That was just a year ago. I've had plenty of time to think about it, calmly, after the first terrible distress had worn off. And I am more certain now than I ever was that Lila, my Lila, was murdered. I can't prove it. That is the tragic thing because I, myself, destroyed the evidence."

Police Sergeant Kilroy felt the cold chill of fear pass over him. Though there were still many pages yet to read, he laid the manuscript down. Murder in a small village such as Pigsbrae? He dared not think about it. The inhabitants, all God-fearing people, were still not adjusted to the shock of Mrs. Lila M'Goophen's death, now almost a year ago. The county coroner had ruled it a suicide. Suicide? It had to be a suicide. The coroner said so. But murder? Murder! Murder which had escaped notice and which would have gone on escaping notice had not this drunkard, this degenerate, typed up these ridiculous pages before trying to commit suicide. He put the pages back into the envelope, addressed it to himself and locked it in his desk drawer. He dared not let anyone read it. A murder! Not just a murder but a murder announced in the most peculiar way—a lurid biography, as if for a novel. But a novel it could not be. No one writes a novel using the actual names of people and describing actual incidents. No! Tom Burke meant to have the pages found. He meant to draw attention by his suicide. Sergeant Kilroy was disturbed. To let this manuscript out of his hands would not only have the detective squad down from Belfast but every newspaper reporter from all the national papers asking questions, disturbing the village. Moreover there was his own job to think about; and Sergeant Kilroy was not one to run risks with his job. He had worked hard to become a sergeant even as it was, for the present, in a small country village. There were all those days and nights on the beat in Belfast, the study, the examinations. He saw his future drown as a murder, unobserved and revealed only at last, by a drunken scut of a suicide, headlined in every newspaper. There would be no living it down. There would be a whole-scale investigation, the whys and the wherefores that the beautiful wife of the local reverend should commit suicide or, as he now saw the headlines, get murdered. The more he thought about it the more he felt certain that the thing to do was to keep the whole matter hushed up. Sergeant Kilroy rose, put on his cap. "I'm heading over to Doctor Jones' surgery," he said to the Constable on duty. "Then I'll probably go home to get some sleep. It's been a long night."

"Right!"

"Hold the fort."

Perhaps with some luck the would-be suicide was already dead. If so, there the matter would end.

"He's alive and well!" said Doctor Jones. "It's a lucky thing he was drunk. If he'd been sober he wouldn't have botched the job like he did."

"How?" Sergeant Kilroy scarcely concealed his disappointment.

"Cut too far round on his wrists. Missed the main blood vessels, and not deep enough. It hardly seems like he was in earnest. It's really only a superficial wound. He'll survive it."

"Good!" said Kilroy. "I'm glad to hear that." He hoped his voice carried a ring of truth. "If it's such a minor thing maybe it could be called an accident. You know what I mean. A second suicide inside a year is not a good thing for the village. It would lead to all kinds of gossip."

"True."

"I would be prepared to delay my report or even omit it to avoid upsetting the village, so to speak, but more especially to give him a chance to pull himself together without everybody looking at him sideways as if he were some kind of freak. You know, he's not altogether the most welcome man in the village, as it is."

"You could be right. It pains me to see a fellow like him waste away his life. I understand he studied medicine once."

"So I've heard."

"Well, I'll get him on his feet and maybe we can encourage him to pick up a normal life."

Sergeant Kilroy thanked the Doctor for all his skill and understanding and went home. He felt nervously drained, exhausted from anxiety. He needed a strong cup of tea and he knew that by now Phoebe would be getting ready for bed and would have the kettle on to boil for the last cup of tea of the day, and a slice of toast.

Since the day he had married Phoebe, Sergeant Kilroy had had ample time to realize the degree of emotional control that his wife possessed. He had never seen her exhibit strong emotion, never seen her laugh beyond a controlled smile, never seen her cry or, for that matter, show anger. He had accepted this not only as part of her training as a schoolteacher but as a temperament which, in the beginning, he much admired. Sergeant Kilroy had married her in the strong belief that he was marrying up out of his social and educational level. It was something he had done deliberately, fully conscious that she was not a beautiful woman. But she was an M.A. He had rolled the sound of that around in his imagination the first time he had met her. Phoebe Botham, Master of Arts. He weighed the fact that her late father had been a Doctor of Divinity, albeit, lost away in a small village. It was a world foreign to his but a world to which Sergeant Kilroy desired to belong, as far away as possible from the teeming back streets of Belfast. He had already been able to profit from his one great asset, his huge physique. This had helped him survive not only the streets but got him into the police. He was also not without intelligence as he had adequately proved in the police examinations; but the success had whetted his appetite for more. After several postings as a constable to various parts of the province he had arrived at the village of Pigsbrae as the Sargent of Police. Better than nothing, a mere stepping-stone. He was soon to meet Phoebe, the schoolmistress. She was a big woman whose size, as well as her education, had scared off many a more qualified country suitor. But the Sergeant was a big man and she, a spinster on the shelf, had accepted him when he proposed. Sergeant Kilroy felt he had advanced in life. He had married an asset.

His career to date in the village had been exemplary. Nothing happened. No crime other than the occasional drunk and family squabble, and those were few. His domain also took in the surrounding townlands where farming families led a quiet life. Thus, the death a year ago of Mrs. Lila M'Goophen had been a shock to everyone. Fortunately it made only the county newspapers. Her death *while the balance of the mind was disturbed* seemed to satisfy everyone's conscience. It was not his responsibility, a doctor's problem perhaps, but certainly not his, was how he saw it. Everything was going well. All he had to do was wait for the next promotion, until now. This thing had happened. The village's only drunk. A bum! Goddamn the man for trying to start a scandal. And thinking of this misfortune he wondered again at his wife's control. It had long ago begun to gnaw at him for sergeant Kilroy was a man who, on occasions, was known to roar with laughter or, when provoked, to bellow with rage. He had passions. What he could not understand now about his wife was how she had walked calmly through two streets of the village to the Police Barracks to say, "Robert! I think Tom Burke has done himself in!"

"Are you sure, woman?"

"I'm sure." Never once had she raised her voice above normal nor her face expressed an emotion.

Sergeant Kilroy stirred his tea and said to her unspoken question, "He'll live."

She did not answer nor had he expected her to. He remembered how the manuscript had described her. 'She was a drab, heavy girl and colorless.' And emotionless, he added to himself, for he was a lusty man and often felt the need for a lusty woman. But Phoebe, so correct for his career ambitions, did not stimulate him to the passions that his soul desired.

His wife was already in bed when he went upstairs. He slipped off his boots and trousers and went to the bathroom in his shirttail. The window looked out over the graveyard. He stood looking at the somber darkness for some time, his thoughts engrossed by the typed pages he read. 'God how I loved that woman!' The phrase was a cry in the darkness of his thoughts. 'The most natural thing to do!' Scenes from the graveyard flickered in his mind as if some slowly turning silent picture show. 'She is dead!' He knew the village graveyard well even to the mound of earth where she lay. 'My dear Lila!' "Goddamn it!" he muttered to himself. "Why hadn't the bastard died?"

Sergeant Kilroy returned to the bedroom and put out the lights before pulling back the curtains. He could see the lights in several houses across the village. He wondered what was going on out there in the night. He thought of the violent passions that stirred a man to love, to love as if nothing else mattered, to be absorbed within the emotions for a woman. Sergeant Kilroy felt his life strangely empty. He felt a great hunger for someone, some woman who could give him pains in the groin in his desire for her. Goddamn Tom Burke! Goddamn the reverend's wife! The savagery of her emotions held him. What a woman! The thought began to make him feel sexually aroused. He turned towards the bed taking off his shirt, socks and vest. His wife was lying with her eyes closed, the face a calm passionless thing. He stopped. Would red hair have made any difference? He raised the cold sheets and got into bed. "Good night!" he said simply.

The Reverend Gabriel M'Goophen was surprised the next morning to find that he had a visitor in the person of Sergeant Kilroy. Gabriel, a softly built man of medium stature, felt uncomfortable in the presence of big men like Kilroy. That he was visiting him in the deep bottle-green uniform and black waterproof coat of a policeman on duty disquietened him even more. He sought some kind of mastery of himself and of the big visitor by giving his voice the pompous tones he so much admired in his bishop. "Sergeant, my good man. What can I do for you? Won't you come in?" He deliberately ushered the Sergeant into the library where the rows of books in their mahogany and glass cabinets were calculated to impress, even intimidate. "I do seldom see you in uniform. Am I honored with some official police business?"

It had always surprised Sergeant Kilroy, when he first came to the village of Pigsbrae, that the Reverend M'Goophin had such a strikingly good-looking wife. It was not so much that Lila was beautiful but that she radiated a sexuality that few men of experience could fail to notice. When the Reverend M'Goophin had arrived back in his hometown to take over the duties of the parish there had been comments on his choice of wife. But these had died as Lila demonstrated her skills to the women's community and led them into social affairs that the late Reverend Botham, a widower, had been unable to do. Yet to Sergeant Kilroy it seemed strange that she had married this soft ineffectual man. 'A woman like Lila!' To the Reverend's question he said, "No Reverend, not really. I was just on my way to the barracks. That's why I'm in uniform. No, I'm here just as one of your parishioners you might say. Though it does touch on police work."

"Oh! How so?"

"We had a spot of bother in the village last night."

The Reverend nodded kindly indicating that he was willing to hear and help.

"Tom Burke....he...well...he tried to do himself in. I'm sorry to have to break the news to you so soon after your own tragic....but.."

"Yes, Sergeant, I know. He tried, you said?"

"Aye, but he's alive. Doctor Jones saved his life."

The Reverend nodded.

"The thing is Reverend, since he's alive and, knowing how the gossip flows in this village, I thought maybe it would be best if Doctor Jones and I ...well, if it didn't become general knowledge."

"Tom Burke himself will think that very generous of you, I'm sure, but why do you come to me. I know he ought to be one of my parishioners but the man's a degenerate, a reprobate and, its no secret, an atheist."

"Reverend, only Doctor Jones and I know that this has happened and I felt you ought to know too."

"I see. Why, pray?"

"To avoid another.... emotional upset in the village."

"Each one must suffer the consequences of his own actions," the Reverend said. "He made his bed. Now let him lie in it. Even if he suffers." He frowned. "Even as I have suffered."

"Reverend, lets not be uncharitable. There's more to it than that."

The Reverend had the sinking feeling he had taken too pompous a stance and he was just about to lose out to this bumpkin fellow with the big hands. "Yes?"

"He was slashed on the wrists in just the same way as your...late wife."

"I see!"

"Only this time we found the instrument, a surgical scalpel"

"He was free to leave this world by any method he should choose." But the Reverend was upset. "Couldn't he have used a rope?"

"And, Reverend, he left a typed many-paged manuscript, a life-story you could say, saying that your wife had been murdered."

"My God!" The Reverend Gabriel M'Goophen started out of his chair but, half way, composed himself. "Would you care for a cup of tea?"

The Reverend M'Goophen did not have a live-in housekeeper, which would have been improper. Instead, a woman from the congregation came twice a week to clean up. He cooked for himself and, as now, made tea and carried the tray and pot to his visitor. "I find this deeply disturbing. I refuse to believe it!"

"Believe me, I do too. I have, of course, put the document under lock and key and have shown it to no-one."

"Very good thinking."

"We all know Tom Burke is the man he is."

"Quite!"

"And I feel that, instead of stirring up trouble in this township, he would be better under treatment in some hospital or institute well away from here."

"Quite!"

"That would be for his own good."

"Of course."

"We would need good grounds though."

"Decidedly."

"You knew him at school and up at the University? Could you give me something we could work on?"

"I doubt it very much. He was a moral degenerate even then. I was a divinity student. Even though we were childhood colleagues here at the school I could hardly associate with him, now could I?"

"He studied medicine, I'm told."

"Yes. He was a scholarship student too."

"What was his problem?"

"Women. It was rumored. Some scandal. He was rusticated I believe and disappeared overseas. Then, like the bad penny he is, he showed up here last year. One would think that he would have the goodness to stay away."

"He had known your wife before?"

"Good gracious! Certainly not! She was not the kind of woman men of Tom Burk's low moral character are ever likely to meet. Lila was the most Godly woman I've ever known. Of sound Christian upbringing."

As Sergeant Kilroy listened to Reverend M'Goophin's pompous tone he could not help seeing the shadowed graveyard and hear the stifled cries of a woman in love. '..lips to kiss with, lips to smile with....God how I loved that woman!'

The Reverend had stopped talking and was sitting, his two hands touching along the fingertips like some medieval saint. The meaty lips were pursed and the sergeant toyed with the idea of them mouthing a Confucian obscenity. It hardly seemed possible.

"I do realize, Reverend, it has been hard for you. I hadn't the pleasure of meeting her family."

"Oh, she was an orphan. We never told that to anyone. She was an orphan. Had been cared for by The Mission, an excellent body of Christians. But she was attracted to the more formal ritual of my denomination. Lila was too sophisticated for fundamentalist religion."

"Yes, indeed," said the Sergeant, not knowing quite what to say next. "Yes...well..." He felt lost. "I think this business of Tom Burke is a terrible affair. The man should be put away."

"Of course. A psychiatrist is the answer. A man who wanders in the graveyard at night sitting on the headstones as he has done since he returned, drinking, is hardly sane."

"He wandered in the graveyard?"

"Oh, yes. It's right back fornenst the church and parsonage. You can even see into it from your own house. Yes, I've often seen him there, sitting drinking from a bottle and talking. Long conversations they were. A few days ago I tried to speak to him. It was getting on my nerves and I still have some pity for the fellow." The Sergeant nodded. He had not expected any of Gabriel's version of Burke's life to agree with the manuscript. Certainly not in matters relating to his wife's past. To hear the Reverend admit to speaking to Burke in the graveyard was one point of interesting co-incidence. "I thought if I spoke to him I might be able to influence him."

"Yes?"

"But he called me filthy, vile names. You can't imagine the foulness of his tongue."

"What did you say?"

"I quoted the scriptures. Jesus said, 'Come onto me all ye who labor and are heavy laden and I will give you rest'. But he blasphemed. I reminded him, 'The wages of sin is death but the gift of God is Eternal Life!'"

"Nothing more?"

"No. He was so iniquitous I couldn't bear to be in his presence anymore."

"Of course."

"You can imagine my distress at such language near where my poor departed wife was laid to rest. Not to mention his own father. When I came back home here I went upstairs and there he was still, talking away. I could see him from the window, having a long conversation."

"With whom?" the Sergeant asked anxiously.

"With the Devil, no doubt!"

Sergeant Kilroy sat once again at his desk. He unlocked the drawer and retrieved the envelope. There were still several pages to read. He took a gulp of his tea, swallowed, laid the mug aside and began to read.

"TRAVEL! I have traveled the world. I never had any desire to make a fortune, just the experience, see strange places, strange peoples and their customs and most of all, something of interest to my young and foolish heart, screw a woman of every race, color and creed I chanced upon.

Travel is said to broaden the mind. It does. After a few years I was growing tired of this pursuit and taking to sorting out the names and faces of those women who had meant something to me. I could think of none, none except Lila. Lila! But I couldn't return. While I had grown tired of seeking new experiences I had not yet matured to a decision on what it was I really wanted. But Lila was always with me in my more sobering thoughts. Then my old father died two years ago and a nostalgia with a power stronger than any I had ever known, took hold of me and I had to return home. It took a year before I could gather up the money to do this. I came back.

Coming back was not what I imagined. No one seemed especially pleased to see me. I was a prodigal no one wanted. While I had not expected a welcoming committee it was a surprise to find my lovely Lila married to Gabriel M'Goophen, old school pal, divinity student and shepherd to the village flock. She was still the same Lila, but in a more mature way; and there was a yearning in her heart for a love that once only I could give. I read it in her eyes and the self-conscious movement of her lips.

She was in the village grocery when I went to buy cigarettes a few days after I returned. The fat grocer—we had been to school together—in his

green apron said, 'Tom! You haven't met Mrs. Gabriel M'Goophen?'
I said, 'No. I don't think I've had the pleasure.'
She was very pale as she recognized my face. The grocer was beaming. He thought me some kind of Marco Polo and was wallowing in the pleasure it gave him to introduce me.
'How do you do?' she said.
'Tom Burke,' I replied, smiling as I saw her uneasiness.
The fat grocer, still beaming from the thrill of knowing Marco Polo personally, said, 'Tom Burke's the only man from these parts has ever seen the world. Isn't that so Tom?'
I nodded agreement, taking note of how ill at ease she was.
'How nice,' she said. 'Will you stay long?'
'Perhaps. It depends.' And from my voice and eyes it must have been obvious to her what I already had in mind. I left her. At McCuddy's Bar I bought a bottle of whisky and that night, as I thought of her and how life held these strange surprises, I got drunk. But life had not finished with me yet. Not by a long shot."

"Aren't you going to eat?" Constable Matt called in the door.
"Oh! Is it that time?"
"Sure it is."
"Well then, I might as well."
The Sergeant put the manuscript in the envelope, put the envelope inside his tunic, took his bicycle and rode the few yards to his house. There was no one at home. Phoebe was at the school and she had a sandwich with her for lunch. The Sergeant buttered some bread, added a slice of ham and sat to eat. A fear was rising in him. There were secrets in the village that could come to light and destroy its calm. Tom Burke's manuscript was only part of it. There were other hidden secrets that had best stay that way. He mulled over what he had read and what he knew himself from the village. He was indeed fearful.

He poured himself a glass of milk, drank it and decided to go once again to Tom Burke's house. He was impatient now to read the last few pages but he wanted to read them in the atmosphere of the location. Then he would act. He rode over and unlocked the door. The smell of the room was appalling. He opened a window despite the cold and sat at the desk.

"I was certain of what I had seen in Lila's face. I saw it again as I dreamt wild, wild desires about her. And I drank the harder as I remembered that she

was the wife of the Reverend Gabriel M'Goophen. I don't recall how many nights afterwards it was that, in a fit of remorse, I went to the graveyard. It was a very dark night. Though I was in a befuddled drunken state of mind I hesitated to go in through the main gate that was never locked. Instead, perhaps it was the nostalgia, I went by the river path that bordered the graveyard on its forth side, to the small wooden door set into the wall. Every inch of this path was stamped in my memory from the days when, as a boy, I had walked with village girls under the big trees that spread over the shallow river.

The door was ajar. But it mostly was. I went in. It was dark but I knew my way. Perhaps I had only taken two or three steps when I stopped to listen. I knew the sounds, those little cries that had echoed in my heart over the years. I stopped and the world stopped too. Lila was there, my Lila, the Lila who had kept my soul alive for years. But she was in the arms of another man.

Life had kicked me in the guts before and I have always kicked back, flailing out viciously at the injustice. Sometimes I deserved it because I have always played to win, winner takes all and the Devil takes the hindmost. But life still hadn't finished. I went again to the graveyard the following week on the same night. I wanted to know who the bastard was. It wasn't that I had planned to do anything to him. What right had I? She wasn't my wife. And I found her, my foot striking against her outstretched arm. She had already bled profusely from cuts on her wrists. I could see that in the glow from the match that I struck. And she was quite dead.

Had she been alive I would have tried to save her. Now my first thought was to save myself for beside where she lay—it was clearly visible in the match light—was the instrument with which she had cut her wrists—for I imagined it was suicide—a medical scalpel of an early design which I knew came from my late father's surgery. Her suicide would be linked to me. In an instant I had picked it up and hidden it under a loose slab of a tomb. It would be a rusted strip of metal by the time it would be found.

There was nothing I could do now but go home. I got drunk like I've never got drunk in my life. But John Barleycorn only helps a little. One must also have time. But even then I was not allowed to escape for I had been seen. Yes! I had been seen, dark night as it was.

When Phoebe came to my house I was far from sober. 'Tom Burke!' she called.

I remember I invited her to have a snortful of whisky and even poured my own glass full to the brim and offered it to her. She refused, still standing *there, her face expressionless. I asked her what I could offer her. Quite simply she said, 'I saw you in the graveyard that night.'*

I have been known to drink a lot of alcohol and still keep my faculties. Yet this had a decided sobering effect. It indeed had been a dark night. I had only struck one match. No, two, the second when I had placed the scalpel in the old tomb.

'I saw you hide something in a tomb.'

I had nothing to say. When these moments come one must listen.

'I have it here, the scalpel that killed Lila. It's yours.'

I asked her what she was going to do with it.

'Nothing!' Still the calm face, the calm voice. 'Here, I'll put it in this desk drawer.'

Eventually I said, 'That was kind of you. How can I ever repay you?'

Phoebe was perhaps the most clever woman I have ever known. She was never beautiful, plain rather, as a girl at school, big and given to puppy fat. But that night when she stood in my parlor she was a woman. 'Love me, Tom Burke!' She said it simply. There was nothing in her voice, just the same voice she always used. But it was in her eyes I saw the pain, the despair of the lonely woman. I knew the look. I have seen it in the eyes of countless women around the world. 'Love me!'

She opened her heavy coat and unbuttoned her dress. Underneath she had nothing. She had come to me naked. 'Love me, Tom Burke!'

There was nothing more to read. It was the last page.

Sergeant Kilroy had known anger, even fear, but this was the first time in his life he had ever felt anguish. He groaned as though he had been kicked in the groin. He sat rigid, gripping the arms of the chair while he trembled with an inner chill and the cold sweat beaded on his forehead. Gradually, as if heavy weights were being tied about his body, he became calm and gathered his wits. The thought ran through his head that there might be other pages somewhere in the desk. He began rapidly to look through the other drawers. One lower drawer was empty except for a singly page. On it was typed a single sentence.

"*I am certain now who murdered my Lila!*"

Sargent Kilroy looked at the man in the white surgery bed. Not only was the aseptic air of the room in marked contrast with the shambles of the room he had just left but Tom Burke seemed a new man. He was washed and shaved and dressed in a clean pajama. He was, Kilroy noted, sober. His arms rested on the white bedcover, a bandage visible on each wrist. He was not reading, just staring ahead of him, no marked expression on his face.

"Tom Burke!"

"Sergeant!"

They looked at each other in awkward silence for a while.

"How do you feel?" asked the Sergeant.

"Fine. Just fine. The doc tells me I have you and your wife to thank for saving my life."

"Sort of."

"Thanks. I've just been wondering if you did the right thing. Draw up a chair there."

The Sergeant sat down. "You're a hardy man Tom Burke."

Burke nodded. Silence again.

"Tom, you left some papers on the desk over at your house and, ah, I read them. Papers you typed yourself."

"Papers? I'm afraid I'm not remembering too well all that happened, Sergeant. That must have been one hell of a drunk I was on. I just don't remember typing any papers."

"Well, I have them all here. There were two different lots. This lot I found the night we brought you here, lying on top of your typewriter. Today I went past to make sure you hadn't left the gas on, you know, I was worried, and this page I found in the bottom drawer. Sorry I searched but, here, read them first."

Tom Burke settled back into the pile of cushions and read. Sergeant Kilroy waited.

"Remarkable!" said Tom at last, laying down the manuscript.

"What is?"

"Damned good reading. Whoever wrote that should go in for writing detective stories."

"Is that all you have to say?"

"What else can I say?"

"Is any of it true or did you invent it as some kind of malicious joke?"

"Oh, hold on. Of course whoever wrote it has exaggerated here and there but it's still damned good reading."

"Did you have an affair with Mrs. Gabriel M'Goophen?"

"I could tell you to go to hell, Sergeant, but," he shrugged, "what the hell.

That was years ago, old man. Nothing for the Reverend Gabriel to take an exception to."

"And Phoebe? Is it true about my wife?"

"You haven't come here to strike me, have you?"

"No, I haven't!"

"You'll behave like a civilized fellow?"

"I just want to know. Is it true?"

"I'm afraid so! Yes! Afraid so! Sorry about that."

The Sergeant, silent, kept himself in control, the only visible sign of his distress being the working of the muscles of his jaws.

"You bastard!"

"I wouldn't for anything have had you find out."

"Then Goddamn it, why write it down? Why? Why try to let the whole world know?"

"That's the main point of why it's so remarkable. I didn't. Not one word was written by me! I think! I never saw the damned thing in my life before."

Phoebe saw the black figure cycle in through the school gates. She knew the moment had to come sooner or later. She had been waiting for it for some time now. She left the blackboard where she had been writing and went to the window. He was cycling without undue hurry, almost as if deliberately taking his time, up the tar-macadam surface of the schoolyard. He dismounted. She was calm as she watched him. He was pushing his bicycle the last few yards, walking slowly and looking towards the windows. Their eyes met. He stopped. She could see the hard set of his mouth and the white color of anger settling into his cheeks. Some children left their desks to go to the window and stare. She knew she had to remain calm. There was silence. They looked at each other. Her heart began to beat furiously. Then into the silence he let the bicycle crash over onto the ground and lay there, its rear wheel spinning foolishly. He was already moving in a quick stride for the main entrance. Phoebe's calm failed her. She began to run. Out through the rear door and across the playground. There was a thorn hedge with gaps between the bushes. She rushed through an opening without caring for the scratching thorns and on, running through the rushes and damp grass of a pasture. Behind her she heard the joyous shouts of the children as they hurried out of doors to cheer and laugh and shout.

Sergeant Kilroy saw his wife run and the squad of children take to the schoolyard. Some, in their excitement, had run after their teacher as if it was all part of some new game. "Back into school!" the Sergeant roared. Their shouting and laughter died. They knew the authority of this man. Not just because he was the Police Sergeant or because he was so big but it was the uniform, the deep bottle green uniform with the glazed scoop to the peaked cap and the black great-coat. That was authority. They scampered back into the school and crowded to the window to watch.

Sergeant Kilroy saw his wife turn once to look at him, then stumble on across the field. With deliberate, long measured stride he followed. He knew she could not get away, that she would tire. He knew the children would not follow and that there was a dip in the ground out of sight in the next field. She was there when he arrived. She could run no more. She had collapsed on a stone wall that divided the fields and lay across it. The wild gulping for air was the sobbing of an animal.

"Phoebe!"

She raised her head to look at him. He saw in her face an emotion. It was not fear. It was the emotion that he himself had recently felt and knew and hated to see in her, in that face which had never shown emotion before. Anguish!

"Goddamn you!" he yelled and felled her across the face with his huge right hand.

"You're in civvies tonight, Sergeant, I see," said Tom Burke.

"Aye. Though you'd better call me Robert. I'm not the Sergeant anymore."

"Is that so now?"

"Aye! I resigned."

Burke tossed a couple of lumps of coal onto the fire and wiped the black dust off on his trousers. "How about a glass? Here!" and he poured a couple of fingers of whisky into a tumbler. "What'll you do now?" Tom asked.

"I'm heading out to some foreign place. Maybe you could head me in the right direction. With your experience and all."

Tom thought for a moment. "You add up what you have in your pocket and you buy a ticket to the farthest place the money will take you. It doesn't matter where. Every place is the same."

"I hardly think it. There's Australia. Or South Africa and I hear tell that a man can do great for himself in Alaska."

"Aye, well, Robert. I can't tell you and you'll not know yourself till you've done it. Just get on the boat and don't look back. Keep going. Do you hear now?"

Robert Kilroy nodded.

"Robert, what made you give Phoebe such a beating? That was hardly the act of a civilized man." Robert Kilroy did not answer. "And Robert, what made you think Phoebe wrote that nice biography of me? It was good you know. There were times reading it I felt touched. She has a rare talent. She should have been writing books instead of teaching school. Sure, like the poet said, 'Full many a flower is born to bloom unseen and waste its sweetness in the desert air.' Eh? Isn't that the way of it? Phoebe should have been writing books. How's your glass there?" Robert let his hand shift slightly to indicate the glass was in good shape. "And poor Mrs. M'Goophen, Lila, murdered?" Tom shook his head drunkenly. "I went into the graveyard that night in a fit of remorse over my father's death. I would sit and talk to his ghost, as it were. I had nothing to do with Lila when I came back here. Do you believe that?"

"I do."

"But when I saw the old scalpel lying there I...I couldn't leave it lying. Maybe I panicked. Anyway I hid it. Are you sure your glass is full?"

"Fine now. Fine."

"Maybe I shouldn't have done what I did but when Phoebe came over and told me she had seen it all and brought me the scalpel..." Tom Burke drank hard from his glass. "Robert! I'd been without a woman for so long. And...and it...she wasn't a stranger...God, Robert, there's a lot of woman there, in Phoebe. And I was weak." He drank. "You're not that angry, I see. In fact, Robert, looking at you as I am now, you're not any wee bit angry."

"Tom," said Robert, ignoring this. "You should know that Phoebe murdered Lila!"

"Oh!" Tom looked drunkenly at Robert. "That puts a different face on it!"

"She also typed up that story about you."

"I know. You've already told me that."

"And when she had you in the right drunken state she slashed your wrists with the scalpel that she slashed Lila with."

"This is all on the level, Robert?"

"It is, damn it to hell. When you told me you hadn't written the damned thing it could only have been one or two people. The Reverend or Phoebe."

"Why?"

"Because of the intimate knowledge about yourself and them. Only they could have known so much about you or about each other. Those bits that happened in Belfast. But it couldn't have been the Reverend. He wouldn't disclose the shady past of his wife. I know. He told me she was an angel, practically. It had to have been Phoebe, since it wasn't you."

"Hhhmmm!"

"It had to be. She was deliberately telling the world through the typescript that she was... a desirable woman, like the books say. I'm afraid I'd ignored her something terribly. I couldn't help it. She was such...you know...no life in her at all." Robert Kilroy drank from his glass to hide his emotion. "She went to you." He looked at Tom. "After a while you ignored her too."

"I did."

"Tell me, Tom, how could she have known you and Lila made it out in the graveyard when you were a student?"

"You have me there," said Tom and watched Robert closely for signs of doubt.

Robert was taking another sip and beginning to show the heavy lids of a man getting warmed by too much whisky.

"But," said Tom, hastily seeking a new topic, "why would she want to murder poor innocent Lila? Explain me that!"

"Agh, she wasn't so innocent," said Robert, twisting up the side of his mouth in a corner-boy sneer.

"How so?"

"Because I was the one. I was the one," he repeated with drunken pride. "I was Lila's lover!" He threw back the whisky. "All the time! I was Lila's lover, so I was. It was me you saw in the graveyard with her that night." It sounded like a boast.

Tom poured him another glass. "You're a bastard, Robert Kilroy, so you are."

"You're a bastard yourself, Tom Burke."

"Aye, we're both bastards!"

They sat in silence after this deep comment. Tom turned to the fireplace and gave it a blatter with the poker. He threw material on and the flames shot up the chimney. "What'll happen to poor old Phoebe?" he asked.

"Nothing! I haven't told anyone. Have you?"

"No!"

"There are just those ten pages of typing. That's the only evidence."

"There were ten pages of typing, Robert."

"Oh?"

"I lit those nice flames with them a minute ago."

Robert stared somewhat unsteadily at the fire. "There's a great warmth from it. There's a great draw from that chimney, I'm thinking."

"There is."

They both sipped thoughtfully from their drinks.

"The law will not punish her, then?" Tom asked.

"No! What they don't know won't do them any harm." He sighed a great sigh. "You see, Tom Burke, I've just discovered that living with oneself is worse than hanging."

"True."

"And Phoebe has a lot of it ahead of her, living in this wee village, looking out over the wall at the graveyard. Seeing the reverend every day. And you. And she'll be alone. Now won't she?"

"That, Robert, isn't going to be a punishment. That's going to be Hell."

Robert Kilroy put down his glass. He rose slowly. He had drank a lot. "I must be going." He went to the door, opening it and going out into the cool night air. Tom followed to the step. Kilroy was a few yards down the pavement when he turned. "Tom Burke! You're right! It's going to be Hell!"

It was late into the night. Tom Burke was sitting at the typewriter when the tap came at the door. It was a tap he knew well. He called for his visitor to come in. He turned towards her as she came into the light and he could see that the bruises had still not left her face. There was a smile on her lips. He got up from his chair and kissed her, feeling tenderly with his finger tips the blue flesh on her cheek. "I'm sorry about that," he said. "I didn't think he was such a violent man."

Phoebe kissed him. "It was worth it, considering." She moved to the typewriter. "Another story?"

"Yes. Got an idea at last."

"Can you tell me?"

"Of course." He went to the sideboard and got two glasses. "It's about a fellow who returns from overseas after a long absence to find that a childhood sweetheart had married, in the interim, a policeman. She is very unhappy because the policeman in question is having an affair with the Reverend's wife. Not knowing which way to turn, she enlists the help of this same old sweetheart who has just returned from overseas. Together they take advantage of the sudden suicide of the reverend's wife who is one and the same person as the policeman's clandestine mistress. You follow me?"

"But Tom, I think I've heard this story before, except that the Reverend's wife, alias the policeman's mistress, was murdered."

"Yes, my love. That is the story they concoct, to wit, a murder. But you know and I know that the reverend's wife is mentally unstable and really did commit suicide. The murder bit is just a ruse."

"But, Tom, in the original the prodigal attempted suicide also. Will that be in your new story?"

"Of course! Clever! What! He has been a medical student and knows just what to cut and what not to cut."

"Do you think the policeman would fall for it?"

"Any policeman would who was afraid of, shall we say, scandalous revelations about the goings on in a certain graveyard."

"That's a strange story, Tom. No one will believe it. I mean, why would a wife, even an unhappy one, run the risk of being accused of murder?"

"For the same reason that the prodigal runs the risk of suicide." He looked into her clear blue eyes, covering the bruise with one hand. "For love!"

The Land of Eternal Youth

Yesterday was the twenty-eighth of August. It is a day I will always remember for it is my birthday. It is a day with its own enchantment and the day on which I had my strangest adventure.

I remember how, on the sunny afternoon of my ninth birthday I ran out of school and along the country road to the path where my dog would meet me. I remember how disappointed he was that I did not stop to pat his head; but I was in a hurry. I had presents and it had been a long day; too long I thought since the hour before dawn when I had set off for school, when only my mother was up to light the fire and get me ready and the rooster was still roosting in the barn. All day I sat wondering what presents I'd get. Now my boots scudding off the loose stones of the lane silenced the birds and the grasshoppers ahead of me and I was almost home.

The table was laid out for me just as it always was. My soup and the potatoes were ladled out and I had to eat before touching the presents piled beyond my plate. And then, the plate cleaned to its willow pattern, I untied my few parcels. There was a book from my father – The Piper of Hamlin, a box of sweets, such a rare thing then during the war, socks from my aunt and a new schoolbag from my mother who always saw the practical side of things. And there was a note from Gran'pa.

Gran'pa was an old man nearing ninety-seven. He was not well and lately had been confined to bed in his room just off the farmhouse kitchen. From there he could hear everything that went on and he would call specially for me when I came home from school. Gran'pa was my best friend. I would sit by him and talk and do my homework. But those last few days his voice had grown weak and he did not call me. I went less often to see him then so as not to tax his strength. Now his note asked me to come.

I gathered up my presents and thumbed down the latch of the door. Gran'pa was waiting, his one eye – for he had lost the other in the Boer War

MUSIC ON THE WIND

– twinkled at me from amid the range of pink folds pressed there by the pillow and the turn of his head. There was a mask over his nose and a tube that led to a long vertical cylinder set on wheels. It had been explained to me that it contained oxygen that Gran'pa needed to breathe. He had been that way for some time. It was the face to which I had become accustomed.

He nodded to me in a way that caused his wispy hair to rise and fall. It was whiter than the pillow and made strange contrast to the black band that crossed his forehead and held a black shade for the missing eye.

"Look, Gran'pa, my presents," I said.

Gran'pa was very weak and I had to unfold each and turn it around so that he could see it clearly. Each time he nodded and smiled. Then he motioned me close. He whispered to me as I bent my ear down beside the mask and the concave of his lips. "Something in the top drawer," he whispered.

I opened the top drawer and there, lying on the silk of his Orange Order sash, was a flute. I lifted it out and felt that strange moment of not knowing whether to be glad or disappointed. A flute! Just like any other flute played on the Twelfth of July though this was apparently Gran'pa's flute. And yet I had never seen him play it. I did not even know it was hidden away in that drawer.

Gran'pa smiled happily when he saw that I had it and I tried hard to smile back. "'Tis the best...legacy I can...give you Kevin...'tis the best flute....this side of the Boyne."

"I never knew you could play one of these," I said.

He shook his head as if that was unimportant and motioned that I should go out and sport myself and I left him. My dog followed me to the yard where I stood a moment, one hand clutching the perforated chestnut piece of wood, the other my book. I wanted to go somewhere quiet, some place where I could read undisturbed. My dog waited patiently. Then, in an impulsive moment, I strode to the orchard.

Our orchard was not really an orchard at all. It was a great mound that had once been used by an ancient Celtic people as a burying place. The archeologists said it was honeycombed with rooms and passages but no one ever knew for sure since the only opening led into a room and then a passage that, after a little distance, became impassable. This opening had long since been grown over with grass and nettles; and it would have been quite concealed had not the rain washed the lentil stone bare of its shallow coating of sod.

It was the shallowness of the sod that prevented the apple trees from lasting. Great Gran'pa had planted them but they had not rooted properly and the wind blew them over in their gnarled old age. Now their twisted trunks harbored the long grass among the branches and snail tracks were on the bark. Their roots stuck out unevenly like snatching fingers on the end of a wizened arm. They were dead like the heroes of old and even the birds avoided them. Around this mound with its dead apple trees there flourished a necklace of beech, sycamore, chestnut and the silver barked rowan. Birds sang here from morning to night. Nests abounded in spring and in the harvest sparrows gathered there before swooping down to land like shower-hail among the stubble of the corn.

I loved the orchard for all its contrasts. I loved especially the farthest side from the farmhouse where the sun warmed all the day, where there was a kind of hollow and the grass was soft and the tall weeds on the rim hid me from around. It was the perfect place to hide and read a book.

I settled down in the warm stillness with only the occasional tweet of a bird or the rustle of a hopper in the grass. My dog lay down beyond me and let the drowsiness of the sun lull him into sleep. I opened my book to read The Piper of Hamlin.

I read easily for it is a story often told and as I read the words were somehow hardly new. So, soon I laid the book aside and rested back to watch the sky awhile. New sounds appeared, of insects and a blackbird 'way beyond. Then a rustling in the thorn by the beech trees and a bird sat there. He whistled out his tune and I listened wondering at the notes he sang. I tried to whistle back but he flew away. I was sad. Had my whistle been an unfamiliar language? Or had the notes been harsh and angry? I could not understand and yet....the flute lay there before me.

I picked it up and wondered new again. Then I placed my fingers and pursed my lips to blow over the little hole. The note was like a seagull's, harsh and shrill. I tried again, and again and gradually the notes came cool and lilting like a songbird in the trees above. I closed my eyes and rested back. And I blew. And the sun shone warmly and the air about was filled with music that cascaded and tumbled here and there among the gently moving branches. I was happy and felt the glow that birds must feel when they are singing. I was entranced with the beauty of the flute. I was unconscious of the change around me, the slow creeping quiet of the orchard. I did not know until a voice rang harsh yet clear to shatter the beauty of my tune. I opened my eyes and there before me was the biggest rat I had ever seen. He was standing on his two back legs. I wanted to cry out but he spoke to me in a gentle way. "Kevin!

Kevin McMuire! Do not be afraid. You will find I shall be an old friend." The voice was comforting and yet somehow familiar. I was no longer afraid and let my eyes leave him to wander to those things around me that I had so far missed.

The rat was not alone. There were dozens of other animals besides – rabbits, hedgehogs, mice and birds. All were standing mute and still as if caught by a witch's spell. Then the rat began to speak again. "Kevin McMuire, you have played the flute, the flute that I have lived a thousand years to hear; what music that can control the minds of those who listen. Look at my friends around me, caught in a witch's spell, drawn by their youth closer and closer to its trap. But I, I am old. I am tone deaf and so immune. So it was I who yelled to break the spell but a moment ago, I who have waited a thousand years."

I watched the rat and, as I watched, something stranger still was happening. I was slowly growing smaller all the time until now, jumping to my feet, I was but little taller than the grass. I yelled to my dog. He came running to my feet no larger than a mouse. I gathered him up in my arms. The rat laughed. "Look at you. You're now my size."

I looked at him face to face and saw for the first time that he wore a patch over one eye. It was black like Gran'pa's. "You have an eye-patch just like Gran'pa," I exclaimed.

"True, Kevin, true."

"And your voice is just like his."

"I have the voice of many people." He smiled again in his gentle way and added, "Please come with me."

There was little I could do for the animals fell in behind me and I was carried forward before them. The rat walked in front, limping slightly as Gran'pa did and leaning on a black thorn stick. It was uncanny how I could see in him shades of Gran'pa. And how odd it felt to walk among the blades of grass and step aside for daisies; to stand beside a weed taller then than me; and the trees – they were beanstalks to the sky.

"Here we are now," he said, stepping aside to show me a door set in the side of a tree stump that had a crooked branch on top. I hesitated but he motioned me on with a slight nodding of his head.

It was a large room, low of ceiling and with a tiny knothole window in the wall opposite the door. And there was a huge hearth with a chimney that seemed to lead to the odd shaped branch I had seen outside. It was like a dream yet it smelled of sawn wood and leaves.

"Like it?" he asked. I moved my head in answer as I set my dog on the earthen floor. "Yeah," he said, looking around with a kind or pride. "I carved it out myself a couple of centuries or so ago."

"Are you that old?"

He drew up a rocking chair from the shadowed corner and sat down to look at me with some sadness in his eyes. "Kevin, I am as old as mankind itself."

The rat puzzled me. I could not understand what those words meant. But he seemed to sense my puzzlement for he spoke to me again. "Do not wonder why I am. Just listen and I will tell you who I have been, then I must ask you for your help. So take that stool by over there and I will tell you my tale." His eyes seemed to reach beyond me into a time gone past and I might have been alone in the dim room but for his voice. "A long time ago in Hamlin there was a plague of rats. Rats somewhat like me. There were hundreds of us, hungry and ravenous for the Hamlin people were greedy people who left not a scrap at meals. So we ran the streets and roofs looking for food. Even the cats avoided us. We became a menace for there were more of us than them and the people were afraid. They cried to the Aldermen for help. And the Aldermen, being afraid also, offered ten thousand pounds to any man who could rid the town of rats. But no one came to take the offer until, one day in the bright sun of the early morning, a stranger came to town; a stranger like we had never seen before, a stranger dressed in scarlet and yellow hose, with a purple and orange coat. He carried a flute and they called him the Pied Piper.

"There was a smile upon his lips and laughter in his eyes and with him went the air of life and jest. The children loved him for he seemed as one of them. But the people laughed when he offered to rid the town of rats. And the Aldermen laughed, 'We will give you twice the sum if you do!' So the jester put to his lips the flute he carried and he played. Music, magic music that promised life and joy and jest; and all around me rats cried, 'Listen! Listen to the promise!' But I could not hear for I am tone deaf. So the piper played and played and out of every corner came my friends dancing and cajoling to follow the piper on his way.

"It was evening when he returned to say that all my friends were dead, drowned in the river that flows out of the Green Hills. And I was sad as I listened but somehow did not really care for I was hungry. But the people cried with joy and the Aldermen laughed with glee.

'Give me my money,' said the Piper, 'for I must go.'

'No!' said the Aldermen, 'No!'

MUSIC ON THE WIND

'Then I shall take your children away with me,' said the Piper.

'Try!' said the Aldermen. 'Try!'

"Then the Piper raised his flute to his lips again and blew. And the streets were filled with children hunting the promise of the music, of a better life far away, where none ever grew old, where life was fun and jest and joy. They danced and cajoled in the streets to follow the Piper on his way. Then the people cried in fear but it was too late. And I, I who am tone deaf did nothing but satisfy my hunger at their forgotten plates.

"In the morning when I awoke the town was filled with sorrow for there were no children there. 'He has taken them into the heart of the Green Hills,' they cried. And I was ashamed of myself then for I knew that I could have saved them as I could have saved my friends, as I did today to break the spell of your music. But I was greedy to eat. And greed is folly. Night came and I was alone. Morning came and I began to search for my friends, but no one wanted me. I was alone, an outcast. And I was ashamed. Everywhere I went rats stepped aside to let me pass and I became know as Death.

"Time passed endlessly until I found that I could not die. I found that I had lived a thousand endless years alone. No one wanted me. Everyone feared me. I was alone. And in my loneliness I wandered the earth searching to undo what I had done. I learned that I had to find the Green Hills for the children lived there still. But the way was through a cavern unknown to anyone until I found it a century or two ago."

"And have you been there?" I asked.

"No Kevin, I cannot, for the way is barred. I need music. I need your help."

"To play my flute?"

"Yes! To play your flute for your flute is like the Piper's, made of some mysterious wood that conjures magic."

"Then I will play."

"Then we will leave at once."

The rat led me out from the cool of the room into the warm caress of the sun. My dog followed behind my heels, a little awed by the great size of the rat. I patted his head and comforted him but of no use, his tail sagged greatly at the sight of the rat and his friends. They formed a group around the rat who talked to them in undertones. They seemed overjoyed with what he said and they danced around, happy at his words. Then the rat addressed me. "Kevin! We are all going. They have heard the promise of your music and want to follow." Then like a General marshalling his troops, he formed them into rows. "Play, Kevin, play!"

I put the flute to my lips to play and joined the rat with my dog on the other side. The rat limped forward, his thorn stick held aloft, and we headed towards his cave. The tall grass swept around my shoulders obscuring my direction until a bunch of nettles loomed ahead. The rat parted them with the point of his stick to show a cavern's mouth yawning like some great beast. Its lentil stone was washed bare of its covering sod. Now I knew, I stood on tiptoes and out of the corner of my eyes looked far past the line of trees and the drumlins to the Green Hills of Antrim. Now I knew. Why had I not guessed before?

The blackness swallowed us as we descended into the throat of the cave. Behind us the daylight grew smaller to a pinpoint in the furthering darkness. And my music, flowing out to hit the walls, rebounded in countless echoes until not just one flute but many it seemed were playing all at once. The animals danced with joy at this effect. Even my dog got the call and joined in their play. But the rat, peering into the darkness ahead, led me onward, down, ever down into the dungeons of the earth.

Soon the blackness changed to blue and I could see sufficiently around to notice how the cave was formed. Boulder sat upon boulder to form the walls and roof. But, as we went along, this changed to rock of sparkling bluish brilliance like endless walls of moonstone and bits of bottle glass. From the roof hung teeth of stone; even from the floor they grew in such numbers until it seemed that we walked through giant jaws. And all the while the light was blue and our skins of a haunted hue.

Then the floor ceased to slope and the narrow passage widened to enclose a lake. It was large and still. Little wisps of mist blew across it here and there. I wondered where the wind came from and then I saw a waterfall tumbling down into some unknown depths. Its noise and the rushing wind drowned the music and the animals fled in fear. The rat stopped and took my arm to point. Ahead and across the torrent ran a bridge scarcely wide enough to let one person pass. On it was a round-eyed creature with a long tubular body. It ran on wheels breathing noisy air from a tube. Our way was barred.

We stood on the balcony while the rat surveyed the creature on the bridge.

"It is just a machine," I said noting that it looked very like the cylinder attached by a tube to Gran'pa.

"It's the ogre that bars the way. We must destroy it. Play our music."

I put the flute to my lips and played but only the roar of the torrent could be heard. "Music is useless," I cried into this ear. "It can't be heard."

"Then our way is barred." He sat down helplessly on the damp rock. "To think an ogre stops us from the land beyond."

I laughed for I could not understand. "A machine can do no harm," I yelled. "Watch! I'll show you how. I'll go first. You must not be afraid."

He called to me but I was already on the bridge and crossing over, my arms in the air to hold my balance. I passed the creature and heard its pulse beats loud and clear. But it could not harm me for I was not afraid. At the other side I stopped and called to my dog. He came, bounding over in great leaps without a glance to right or left. I called then to the rat to tell the animals not to be afraid. But none came so the rat set out alone to cross as I had done. At last at my side he looked back as if to give the past a last farewell then, arm in arm we continued, my dog trotting on ahead.

The cavern's blueness changed to green and we knew we were in the Green Hills. Ahead, a grayness, like gauze filtered light, told of our journey's end. The rat began to run. I followed him out into a land of sunshine and gold and sparkling rivers, with skies like china blue and the smell of blossoms in the air. All around were children and as far as the eye could see was happiness.

"So it is true," said the rat. "We are really there."

"Where?" I asked.

"The Land of Eternal Youth," he said. "I've been wrong. It really does exist!"

"What?"

"Happiness," he said.

I did not understand and looking at his eyes I was even more puzzled. "Who are you?" I asked.

He smiled, his eyes seeing only the landscape of happiness. "It's not who I am but who I have been." He paused. "I was death!"

His white wispy hair made strange contrast to the black band that crossed his forehead and held a black shade for the missing eye. He turned. I stared into the face of Gran'pa. "Goodbye, Kevin, goodbye!"

As in a hurry he turned towards the sun. I wanted to call to him, to say "wait!", but the dazzle from the sun slowly hid him from my view. I cried out in silence as the sun passed into gray and the scene was slipping from my view. I was falling, falling, down, down. A voice called "Kevin!" in the distance of my mind.

The warm afternoon had passed to the cold of the evening. White heavy-laden clouds drifted over the treetops and the dew was settling on the grass. The ground was damp so I arose taking up my book and flute.

Again a voice called "Kevin!" I whistled for my dog and walked across the uneven ground of the orchard to the farmyard. My boots sounded hollow on the cobblestones. The house was silent and the blinds were drawn. My mother stood in the door. Her face was strained with weeping and her voice was full of tears. "Gran'pa! He has passed…"

"To the Land of Eternal Youth?" I asked. Looking up I thought I saw a ray of light in the darkness of her sorrow.

Say It with Flowers

Hearing her husband's car pull into the driveway made her heart leap. He had been gone four days, since Monday. The nightly phone calls from the conference center had not filled the emptiness, nor had the companionship of her dog that had been invited to sleep on the carpet by her bedroom door. The absence, a rare event at this stage in their lives, had again reinforced the role he played in her life—someone to love, someone to be loved by, someone to be there, knowing he was there always. After thirty-six years of marriage they lived for each other. The children, now adults with their own independent lives, came next.

On opening the door the dog bounded out to greet him but Frank brushed the animal off. That was not his usual way. She could tell by the set of his face that something was wrong. The dog bounced around but Frank was still unresponsive and the dog, called to nature by a nearby bush, forsook him. Frank came up the path.

"Frank, what's wrong?"

She laid a hand on her husband's arm as he entered their home noting that he had not given her the hug that was their ritual after any time away from each other. She began to feel that something was terribly wrong. It was written on his face. In all their married life he had never been able to leave his work behind at the office. And, although he sometimes talked about those problems, silent brooding on business matters meant an evening in which she felt cut off. He would sit in his study and work on the contents of his brief case. Often he would sit watching some banal program on TV.

"Why?" she once asked.

"It helps me relax," he explained. "I don't have to think."

She had learned to wait and let him work his way to sharing his problems with her. Now, even though he had been away for almost a week and she had a need to communicate with him, to hold hands and share feelings, she waited. He hung his coat in the closet and turned to look at her. "Kate! Kate!" He reached for her and enveloped her in his arms. She could tell by the force that he had more than missed her. Something indeed was wrong.

"What is it, darling? What is it?" she asked. She led him to the family room and made him lay back on the sofa. "Tell me. What happened? How was the seminar?"

He shook his head in despair. The dog barked, asking for the door to be opened. She rose. "Can I get you a drink?" He shook his head again. The phone rang. "That must be Janet, George's wife. I was to meet with her tonight to discuss our flower business deal, but I'll cancel. Hello!" She spoke into the phone. "Janet?" She listened for a few moments. "Oh! Well, don't worry. It'll all work out. Talk to you later. Bye!" She poured some whiskey over ice and added a splash of soda water. "Here. Sip some of that. You'll feel better."

"Thanks. What did Janet want?" His voice was weary.

"Just to cancel our get-together tonight, something about George and his manias. Good job too, you in the state you are in. I'd have called her to cancel anyway. Good thing she called me first." She realized she was talking just to fill up the space between them and fell silent. He sipped his drink. An involuntary heavy sigh escaped him. That was good. The tension was beginning to wind down. "I'll get the dinner ready," she said, knowing that with a little time he would begin to share. She opened the front door and the dog bounded in to lay his paws on Frank's lap.

As she watched her husband fondle the dog's neck with both hands she knew that recovery was on its way. Just give it time. The dog poured out its affection. Frank bent to hug the animal. Kate followed the rich smell of casserole back into the kitchen. Yes, just give it time and a good dinner.

"Kate?" There was a cracked note in his voice.

"Yes?" she called.

"Today at the conference we had some candid comments."

"And?"

"I was told I was not a team player."

"Yes, Frank? So? What does that signify?"

There was silence from the other room, a long silence. She remembered the often-used expression of waiting for the other shoe to drop. It had seemed humorous. Once. Now this was it. She waited. The silence was too long. She moved to the door of the family room. Frank still sat motionless, staring at the floor.

"Yes Frank?"

"All the contributions I have made to the company's bottom line." He spoke the sentence as a declaration; something to stand alone, to be considered for it's worth. "To be told! By some of my colleagues!" Kate watched him. She had never seen such stress on his face before. "That last product introduction I did. Sixty million dollars! The largest first year's sales for a new product in the company's history."

"So why are you so upset. You have a great track record."

"But you know what they told me?"

She went to kneel before him, the better to look up into his eyes and see the anguish.

"It didn't really count! They told me I'm not a team player. Just not a team player. Being a team player is what counts."

"What's that mean?"

"That's the question I asked."

"So?"

"It's the new corporate game."

"And so? Team players? What's that got to do with it?"

"Everything apparently. The world has changed since I was a young fellow. Teams! No one talks of leaders anymore."

"All of this came out in the seminar? It took four days?"

"Yeah!" He sighed. "They have something planned. That's what George says. There's something in the wind."

"What went on? Can't you tell me?"

He reflected for a moment, a quick glance backward at the events of the week. "Later. Not just now. I feel very tired. Let me be for a moment."

"Lie back then." She fixed a cushion behind his head. "I'll call you when dinner is ready."

The seminar had been held several hours' drive from the company offices at a conference center selected for its rural setting. There was a golf course, a physical fitness center and, for the less athletic, a billiards room. There was no television in the bedrooms since that would encourage individuals to retreat from the collective experience in favor of some entertainment of lesser value. Emphasis was on atmosphere that offered people the maximum opportunity to get to know one another, and, while that was happening, no interruption from phones and daily business demands. Those of management and their support staff, who had been nominated for the experience, arrived on the Monday morning ready to begin the team-building seminar at one in the afternoon. There was a measure of suspense. "What do you think this is about?" was a question often asked. No one had attended anything like this before and there was great speculation. But the brochure each participant received had given the assurance that it was a leap forward in people relations, an exercise that would lead to greater productivity through better understanding of each other. The team! There were skeptics. George, Frank's colleague in marketing was one. "Right! Lets go!" George said with mock impatience five minutes before the start. "If we're late they'll think we're not committed, not totally involved, not part of the team." George mimicked a facial expression of great concern that he held for a few minutes, then dispelled with a smile and several wiggles of his eyebrows. "The team is waiting!" George strode off purposefully. "Coming?"

Frank noted that the seminar room was set up with chairs around the walls and, somewhat docile with expectation of the unknown, soon found himself sitting in one. A large, overweight woman in a loose fitting dress that tried valiantly to hide her bulk, introduced herself and encouraged everyone to turn to their neighbor and shake hands. "Now think," she said, "how well do you know the person sitting beside you? Think about it. You've worked with that person for several years. Do you really know that person? Do you really know what makes them tick? How much do you care for that person? Is that person on your team? Are you on theirs?" She smiled confidently, turning her face slowly around the room so that everyone could benefit. "Well, in the next few days we're going to find out." She stepped back and cleared her throat. "Now, let's begin with a very simple exercise. Like this! Everyone belongs to something, a religious belief, for example. Everyone who is Roman Catholic come up here beside me." A number of people strode forward aimlessly. What was it all about? "Now those of you who are Presbyterians." A similar migration took place from the chairs to the center of the floor. "Baptists!" There were a few. "Jews!" A lone figure crossed the floor. "Muslim?" None. "Anyone else?" Several self-conscious persons reluctantly went forward. "And what are your beliefs?"

"Mormon!" two replied simultaneously.

"Pentecostal!" said another.

"I'm a biologist," a middle-aged man replied.

"Ahh!" She was at a loss. "Well then, you see, everyone belongs to something. Everyone shares beliefs with others."

George looked surreptitiously at Frank and, finding eye contact, did his eyebrow dance. Frank suppressed a smile.

"Now, take your seats and let me introduce Doctor Max, my colleague and business partner. Max!"

Doctor Max was tall and gaunt. He wore jeans that had been washed of their original color, a faded plaid shirt and tasseled loafers that were scuffed by constant wear and lack of polish. There were salt stains on the sides. He gave the impression of a careless dresser, one for whom clothes meant nothing, yet, every item was deliberately chosen to make a personal statement—that he was really a humble person and not there to scare or intimidate. He was, in his own estimation, a fellow student around campus. His hair was cut to give a wind-blown effect that was at odds with his age. "Look how youthful I am!" it seemed to cry out.

"So!" he smiled. "I'm the other facilitator for this seminar. Let me begin by saying something about myself and then each of you can describe yourselves however you wish and prefer, to the group."

He gave a summary of his suburban life and the struggle to find himself in a material world. He described his discovery of everyman's need for self-realization and his own pursuit of those skills that would fit him to reach out and help. He pronounced selected words with great emphasis, a foundation, as it were, that afforded an opportunity to detail his academic career in a most apologetic manner as if someone else was to blame for his intellect. Then, having established the persona of Max, a really friendly fellow, Doctor of Philosophy, formerly assistant professor in humble-ology, now a missionary in the field where executives too need to find themselves, the floor was open.

There was a hesitant beginning, a degree of reticence to talk about oneself but soon volunteers were vying with each other to be next in-line. There was a motley of life stories and personal revelations as each one struggled to offer some meaningful description of themselves as per the model of Doctor Max. Several found the effort too emotional and broke down into tears as they described personal and emotional hardship. Doctor Max listened intently, nodding his head in a caring manner. Frank heard himself say, "I'm Frank Lewis, marketing manager, married, three children, all grown up, thirty years with the company, and I enjoy my work. And oh, yes, I studied economics at a mid-west college and took a Masters in business administration rather late in life, studied part-time. My hobby is gardening and wood-work and eating my wife's cooking." There was a ripple of laughter from the men. The women seemed not to find this amusing. "And yes, we're a one income family. My wife is a graduate in fine arts but she wanted to be a home-maker." He felt that needed more explanation so added, "She has done a wonderful job in rearing our children. I feel blessed that they reached adulthood without becoming involved in drugs or promiscuity. She has been a wonderful wife and mother and I'm a very happy person."

"But is she?" a female voice called, emphasizing the word *she*.

"Now, now!" scolded Doctor Max. "Let each person say what they want to say. We'll have time later to exchange viewpoints. Continue!" he added, turning to Frank.

"That's all!" Frank quite regretted the glimpse of his personal life. "Really, that's all I want to say."

"How interesting!" Doctor Max looked around him. "Well now. Let's talk about the concept of the team. Shall we? Anthropologists believe that a major advancement in social evolution occurred when early caveman formed teams to hunt more successfully. Together, you see! In a team!"

"Ahem!" George was on the edge of his seat, nodding his head vigorously. "Shouldn't that be cave-person? I mean there were at least two genders present even then. Correct?"

At some time in Doctor Max's evolution he had exchanged thick glasses for contact lens but the habit of peering had not gone away. He peered around the group with an intensely serious face looking for the source of this attack. "I wish," he said, "you would refrain from facetious comments. Of course the word caveman is generic. Quite generic. But, if you will, I'll say early humans who lived in caves."

"Quite all right." George waved a hand as if granting a pardon. "I like the word caveman myself."

Doctor Max had lost the thread of his discourse. He stared around him. His audience stared back. In a moment he had repeated his opening lines and continued. "But teamwork really exploded with the advent of the Industrial Revolution and mass production." He paused again, searching the ceiling for the next sentence that he had memorized verbatim, something he had gleaned from a book now featured prominently on his bookshelf. "No change has had more impact than the growth of work teams. And team members say they are happier than ever in their jobs. They feel good about themselves—valuable contributors in the workplace."

The voice of Dr. Max faded off into the distance as Frank thought of his vegetable patch and tomatoes that needed to be harvested before the frosts began. He decided he would buy a load of new soil for his raised beds. Next weekend he would need to check out the wood chipper in readiness for the fall. The garage needed clearing also. He felt a hand shaking his shoulder. "Oh, Kate! It's you. I must have dozed off. What time is it?"

"Just after seven. Time for dinner."

"Already?" There was a provoking aroma of casserole. They sat down at the dining table and held hands across the space between them.

"While you were sleeping I phoned Janet again for a longer chat. She feels she cannot go ahead with the flowers idea. Her husband George is against it. He has other plans."

"Oh?"

"Says he needs her taking care of the house and being there when he comes home. God! Some men! Can't he see she's bored to death? The son married and the daughter in the army. A maid comes in twice a week to clean up. She plays golf most mornings just to get out of the house. She's fed up!"

Frank rested his fork, drank from his glass of water and asked calmly, "Kate, are you fed up?"

"Not fed up, Frank. Just that I'd like to do something now that our own kids are through college. Face a challenge where I'm making decisions. Yes! Maybe I am a little fed up, but not as you might think. I want to get out and do something while there's still time."

"Well, then, go ahead. I thought the flowers gig was a good idea."

"I know you did. But that pompous ass, George, Janet's husband, do you know what he did? He bribed her with a new car. My God! A bribe! And she can't see it. 'It's because he loves me!' she said. Can you believe that? Oh! I could have shaken her."

"Ah well. Let it go for a few days. Something will work out." Then a thought struck him. "Kate, I love you but I don't buy you a new car," he said teasingly. "Are you disappointed?"

"Terribly!"

"I've calculated it's cheaper to let you do the flowers thing. Besides, you just might make enough money to buy me a new car. I could do with a new one, you know. What were you going to call the business, anyway?"

"Say It With Flowers!"

"That nice. With Flowers! Quite a message hidden there."

"That's the point."

She had a feeling Frank was deliberately staying away from his problems. "Frank, aren't you going to tell me something about your week? I've never seen you this way before. What happened really?"

"According to George the whole thing was a god-damn corporate commune; the hippie generation in a corporate setting. Sitting around trying to emote and solve the world's problems whether it needs it or not. He says someone in the boardroom downtown is smoking pot if they think this will improve productivity."

"What do you think, Frank?"

"I think I'm just too old for all these new-fangled ways of doing things. I've just been too happy at work to ask myself if I'm unhappy. It seems that people today have got to be unhappy otherwise they're not getting enough out of life."

"Frank, that's silly."

"It is! I know that. But don't tell anyone. There's an industry out there living off unhappiness."

"Frank? Is the water boiling?"

"Coming!" Frank brought the two teacups filled with hot water, the tea bags and the sugar bowl on a tray. He laid them on the low table before his seated wife.

"So tell me," she said. "What happened?"

"There was an outside speaker, a consultant of sorts, a Doctor Max, who spoke the first day on being team members. Quite good actually. But George was a hot item. Sniping here and there with odd questions."

"Like what?"

"Oh, twenty people stuffed into a room trying to reach agreement, he said, was summed up generations ago as 'too many cooks spoil the broth'! 'What has changed?' he asked. 'The recipe? The cooks?' It was quite interesting."

"Poor George. He needs to argue."

"He wanted to know in a team who took responsibility if the taste was off? No one! he said. Doctor Max was not amused."

"Is that all?"

"Day two was even stranger. We practiced being open and honest with each other. Differences of opinion and perspective were supposed to be valued. And we were to try managing conflict."

"Good grief. And George?"

"It wasn't George this time. His secretary Marcia said that she couldn't find the strength to come to work on a Monday because George made her sick to her stomach. That was why she had been absent so many Mondays. Sick!"

"And George?"

"George kept quiet. It was old Harold spoke up. 'Isn't it true Marcia that you have been working in Hepburn and Partridge's at the Mall, every weekend, Saturday, Sunday and Monday. That's an eight-day week,' he says. 'Five theoretically for the company and three part-time at the Mall.'"

"Oh goodness. Poor girl. She must have died."

"Very nearly. And a big woman too. She broke down in tears and rushed out of the meeting, all two hundred and thirty pounds of her. The woman facilitator rushed after her. Neither of them came back for the rest of the day. Marcia was very, very quiet the rest of the week."

"Who thinks these sessions up, Frank? Seems very unsettling to me. What good comes of it?"

"Ah, who knows? The social engineers of academia are what George calls them. The Doctor Max's of this world. They certainly charge plenty. Do you know what that little episode cost the company?"

"Don't tell me. Your last raise was a mere pittance."

"Day three was interesting too."

"Frank, enough. You're dwelling on the whole thing too much. It'll all blow over and everything will be back to order. This is just a storm in a tea cup."

"I wish. I really wish."

"Well, it's time for bed. The morning comes early. Tomorrow's Friday and then you have all day Saturday and Sunday to relax. Come on."

Frank could not sleep. He heard the pendulum clock in the family room strike midnight. The third day had been a doozey. Diversity! He had never imagined there was so much hatred amongst people.

"Frank! You're awake aren't you?"

"Yes."

"Can't you sleep?"

"No!"

"What's the matter?"

"The whole thing. Life has become very different."

"Shall I make some hot milk?"

"Why not."

"Well, lets go down. You can tell me all about it. Come on."

The dog came to lay its nose against his knee and ask to be fondled. He cupped its ears in his hands and bent to rub his nose on the dog's head.

"That's not sanitary, Frank. I suppose you'll want to rub noses with me now."

"He's my old friend. Aren't you puppy?" The dog wagged his tail; the tone of voice of his master was assurance enough. "People should be more like dogs. Trusting! There's too much bitterness and unhappiness. Have you ever seen an unhappy dog?"

"There are lots. Go down to the dog pound."

"You've got a point." He reflected for a moment. "I think the company has become a dog pound."

"What's eating you Frank?"

He took hold of her hand. "Have I always treated you well, Kate?"

"How do you mean?"

"Have I been caring? Or have I been uncaring, treating you like a chattel?"

She caressed him. "No Frank. You have always led and I have always followed because that is what I wanted, a strong man to take care of me. And the children."

"But weren't you conditioned to that as a child? To take second place, as it were, to men? To play with dolls instead of toy soldiers? To learn to cook instead of fix the car?"

"Never! I liked dolls. I like to cook."

"Didn't you want to use your degree to have a profession?"

"Frank, rearing three children was my profession. You finding the money to take care of us all was your profession. We were a team, Frank. A team of two."

"Do you believe that? A team? Of two?"

"Judge for yourself. Bill's an attorney. Helen's a psychiatrist, and Jill is following your steps in business. They all three were top students; high grade-point-averages and will lead productive lives. No drugs. No teen-age pregnancies. Imagine! We reared three children to be good citizens despite the times."

"You did, Kate. You did. I'm very grateful."

"I know you are, Frank. But you provided."

"You know Kate, I look forward every day to coming home, to you, this house, your cooking. It's part of my life."

"You're a success, Frank. We both are."

"But, Kate, don't you still want something more?"

"Why not? It's to keep busy, to continue being a success. Look at it that way."

"Success? I've always wondered how one should define that word. How would you?"

Kate pursed her lips in thought. "I'd say, being at peace with one's-self in a mad, mad world. Yes! That's how I'd define success."

"You know Kate. I'm not at peace with myself. I thought I was, until this team-building seminar. It's made me think of all kinds of things. Things I had never questioned before."

"Frank, I love you. Don't question that. Come! You need a good night's sleep. Look, it's already one something. You've only got about five hours left. You'll be miserable tomorrow. Remember it's Friday and then you have all the week end."

On the staircase he stopped. "Say it with flowers? Hmmm! Catchy!"

He closed his eyes and waited for sleep to descend. Janet's head was nestled on his arm and from her breathing he knew she was already asleep. In the distance of the night a police car siren whined. With his free arm he switched on the bedside light and reached for a book. But it was no use. The events of the past week were in re-run, the faces, the voices and the body language of every participant re-enacted in total recall.

"Nah! Damnit!" said George, his mood one of surpressed anger. "All this goddamn crap! What's it all about any way? Team building! The only team any of these folks are going to be on is some softball team and even that's in doubt. Softball requires talent and coordination. God, these people. And the company's paying for this. That silly ass Doctor Max! Doesn't he know that people who share common goals can work together whether they're called teams or not. It sorts itself out, like basketball. The guy who can't share the ball is a goner. You know why? The money! It's the money. The reward! What's so goddamn new about that? A million-dollar contract for some seven-foot talent or a woolly mammoth for the caveman! Reward! Ah, I see it all now. It's getting through to me. This is bright stuff, man. We've been living in the dark ages. All this time we've been producing millions for the old company but never knew we had a team. God! Now I know. It has a vocabulary! Eureka!" He shook his head in mock amazement.

"You sound like you're not committed to progress?" Harold said.

"I'm committed to making money. That's what I'm committed to. That's what business is about. Creating wealth! Wealth, the only reward for effort. All else is subsidized. And by what? Money! And what is money? Only the sweat of effort. I work, therefore I am."

"Well, times have changed," said Mike.

"They sure have. Hey! Fellows. The agony will soon be over. Let's have a bit of a giggle. Did you hear the one about the case of this young thaing?" He pronounced the last word in the manner of the South.

"Can't say I have." Mike was always eager for raunchy stories. "How's it go?"

George launched into a bawdy tale of a young woman with a speech impediment that, as was his custom, he found hard to tell without laughing. "B..b..before she c..c..could s..s..say she w..w..wasn't t..t..that k..k..kind of a g..g..girl, she was!" George laughed so hard he choked and began to cough.

"Christ, George. Watch out." Harold looked around nervously. "One of the dragons will hear you and hand you your ass in a sling. You're not being very politically correct."

"Eaaah! Politically correct my ancient grandmother's keister. It's all a farce! Crap! What we need is to kick ass and take names and then we'd get some results. People don't do what is expected. They do what is inspected!"

"Let's wait and see what the meeting is all about. Keep an open mind."

"I'm here because, like you," George waved an arm energetically, "I was told to attend and I'm also, like you, over fifty and an old fart in the eyes of this new politically correct generation. The hippie generation in a business suit. Holding hands in the corporate commune! It's crazy! I just don't believe in a corporate Camelot. Ah, what the hell! I'll behave. I got payments on that new Cherokee, don't I? And the alimony for my first wife, God bless her! That's the bottom line. Keeping the old head above water."

"Well, let's not push it. Let's keep our mouths shut and feel our way. Who knows what notes are being taken. Say the wrong thing and it's goodbye birdie."

"Like hell. I'll get me an attorney. Let them try. Age discrimination it's called. I know an attorney who would be frothing at the bit. How many of these young scamps have a track record like mine? Or yours? Hmm? Ass holes! Like that Dr. Max! Good God! Where did the company find him?"

"Keep it down, George. Anyone can hear."

"Brrrrp!" He made a rude noise with wet lips.

The Friday morning traffic to work ambled along at its usual thirty-five miles per hour, stopping at frequent traffic lights. Frank listened to the local news on the radio—a shooting downtown, the search for a serial rapist, a break-in and robbery of a jewelery store, an abandoned house set on fire, a case of spousal assault and battery. The national news came on with horror stories of the ethnic cleansing in Bosnia, a massacre of rebels in Chechnya and Irish terrorists had detonated a bomb in Belfast with several dead. He pressed the search-knob on the radio dial and found an early morning talk show. Someone was calling in to plead the case of protection from child molesters. It was enough. He stabbed the off-button. He felt depressed and realized that going to work had become a trial of will power. Maybe the secretary who had accused George of making her sick to her stomach had been right. How much better for Marcia to work in the friendly atmosphere of a shop at the Mall surrounded by relaxed people. Yet there had been a time when each day at work had brought excitement. There were challenging things to do, decisions to make, goals to reach, interesting people to discuss things with, a feeling of accomplishment at the end of every day.

The traffic came to a stop at a traffic light. There were cars before, behind and to each side, queued up waiting. A woman across the way adjusted her rear-view mirror and put on makeup, dickering herself to enhance the plainness of an intelligent face. What were her hopes? What were her hidden demons? A man sipped coffee from a large plastic cup, symbol of McDonalds clearly visible—a late riser? Or a bachelor making do? Or just a wife still in bed too unconcerned to prepare breakfast? A young couple stared straight ahead, strangers to each other the morning after. Frank began to smile, enjoying his little foray into analysis. The lights changed to green and the race was on again.

"Hi there Frank. How goes it? What's your feeling on the down-sizing?" Walt, from plastics, greeted him in the corridor.

"What down-sizing?"

"It was just announced. Where you been?"

"At a conference all week. When was it announced?"

"It's on the screen this morning. They must have entered it last night."

"Oh God! How many?"

"Several hundreds. It'll be on your computer screen. Pull it up."

"I will. Anyone I know got caught in the net?"

"It's voluntary. At least to start with. I'm taking it. Had enough. Retiring to a place I bought years ago for just this occasion, down in South Carolina. The wife and I are looking forward to it. Going to sign up today for the deal."

"Good luck, Walt. That's a brave step. I congratulate you. I wish I could see clearly on a matter like that."

In the corridor the large figure of Marcia, George's secretary, came towards him. "Mr. Lewis, can I have a minute." He invited her in and bade her sit down opposite him. "Mr. Lewis!" She held a half filled packet of chocolate cookies in one hand and in the other a cookie from which a bite had been taken. "I'm having a problem in my life and I don't know what I should do. My husband has gone to live with a girl I went to school with and was one of my bridesmaids and he's never coming back." Tears began to well in her eyes. Instead of reaching for a handkerchief she pushed the remains of the cookie into her mouth and stolidly chewed on it. Frank handed her a tissue from a box he kept to clean the screen of his monitor. She dabbed futilely at what had now become a stream. She rocked gently on the seat in her anguish, the rolls of fat settling down on each other. A hand kept rustling cookies from the packet.

"Frank!" George stepped into the office. "Sorry!" and as quickly spun on his heels. An expression of pending calamity distorted his face.

"Every God-damned morning," George had said during a break at the seminar, "that bitch comes into my office to spill her forlorn love life and marital problems all over my carpet and wastes two hours of my time. I can't get anything done, damnit. I'm not a marriage counselor! I'm not a priest! I'm a businessman. Trying to make a buck for the company. And I'm expected to listen to that drivel! So I'm uncaring because I tell her I've got work to do. I disgust her, she says! She disgusts herself! Probably disgusted her husband too. I should have told her to stop eating. If she wasn't so fat and ugly her husband would still be in her bed."

Frank watched the bedraggled figure before him. "Marcia," he said gently. "Have you talked to your priest or pastor?" She shook her head. "Marcia, I'm not qualified to give advice, you know. But those people are. What's your pastor's name and I'll be happy to arrange for you to talk to him. Or would you prefer I call someone else?"

She blew her nose. "Would you, please?"

Frank got up and closed the door for more privacy. He called personnel. A woman colleague answered. He talked quietly and asked for her to come to his office. During the few minutes wait he removed the packet of cookies and held the woman's hands, gently and firmly. She sat with closed eyes letting the tears stream down her face. "I needed the money," she said.

"I hope you're going to relax this coming weekend," Kate said. He held her to him and laid his face on the warmth of her neck. He could feel the softness of her skin and gentle tumble of her hair. Thirty-six years of marriage had not diminished the pleasure and comfort he got from her presence.

"I'll work on the garden. Maybe clean out the garage."

"Don't forget the basement. How was your day?"

"George's secretary is on the verge of a nervous breakdown."

"Poor girl. What happened?"

"She came to my office and told me the whole story of her husband running off with another woman and why she had to work at the Mall. Ah ho!" He ended with a sigh.

"Shall I get you something to help relax you?"

"No. That's the last thing I want to do when things turn bad, is to turn to alcohol. How about a glass of iced tea and you come and sit here beside me." He went to the sofa in the family room.

Frank sipped his tea. He put his feet up on a stool and lay back. "Several of us went out for lunch together, today. George, a couple of guys you've never met, Harold, Mike and myself."

"Where'd you go?"

"Kate, that's not important. We just went out to lunch. Now listen."

"It is important. Were you overheard talking because I'm certain you all talked at the top of your voices. Especially George."

"O.K. We went to that new place out route seven, The Tortilla or something. Serves Mexican. There were very few people there. O.K?"

"Don't be sharp. I'm just concerned."

"Sorry. I'm a bit on edge. George thinks he has an outside offer and the others are near panic. They want to leave but after thirty years of security within the company they are afraid of the outside world."

"And you, Frank?"

"Me too. The last time I made a job application was a long time ago. Thirty years to be exact."

"But you're not going to take the early retirement offer. You're going to stay until you're sixty-five. Aren't you Frank?"

"Sure. If they let me."

She could see the stress in his face. "They're not going to fire you, are they?"

"No, not fire me. It's a voluntary early retirement. They say!"

"Good then. So there's no worry? Tell me about the lunch."

"Mike got near drunk, for one. George held forth on the hypocrisy and deceit of upper management. Harold said that it was all an excuse to fill management with women and minorities and all white men who were considered uncaring and unsympathetic to the cause were being pressured to go."

"Is that true?"

"Not really, yet somewhat."

"And where do you stand?"

"I just want to keep working until I'm sixty five."

"But don't you agree with more women and minorities in management?"

"Sure, why not. There are enough incompetent white men already. We could do with a little diversity."

"Frank, you're getting bitter. There's the oven ringing. Let's eat."

The lamb chops were laid on a serving plate on the table. There was a delicious smell.

"Let me serve you, Frank. Are you very hungry?"

She was a wonderful cook. Every meal was a delight. She was wonderful to come home to.

"So what are you going to do with the flower idea now that Janet has dropped out?"

"I want to have another talk with her. Do you think you could take a look at the financial side of it tonight and give me your unbiased opinion of our chances of success? I've all the background research ready. All you have to do is check it out and make certain that I haven't forgotten anything."

He cut a piece of lamb-chop, then stopped to look at her. "It's so nice to come home. So many of the people in the company don't have this, you know. I made the point during the open discussion."

"Frank, you didn't?"

"I did. I'm proud of my home life. Why shouldn't I say what is open and honest about how we live?"

"What did you say?"

"When they were discussing how some people had no time for building relationships I said that some folks seemed to come to work only to meet their friends and exchange gossip. I said that was evident by the amount of time people spent in the smoking areas or drinking coffee."

"And what then?"

"Well, most of the smokers seem to be women so that was taken as an attack on them."

"What did you say?"

"Well I said no, that was not it, but it did seem that many people had no friends outside the company, lived lonely lives, single or divorced or alienated by whatever and hence came to work looking for something their lives otherwise didn't have."

"Frank, you shouldn't have. That's probably true, but cruel to say it. Weren't they upset?"

"It kinda hit home. But I then said that I myself did not come into work in the morning looking for love and affection because I had a happy and loving relationship with my wife and family. I came to work in the morning to work. Just that! To work! And at the end of the day I had a loving home and wife to go home to."

"Frank!" She reached for his hand. "That was a lot to say. How was it taken?"

"Silence. About a good half minute of silence. The women facilitator was a bit put-about, I guess by the honesty of it, but more I guess by the fact that it is true. And she divorced her husband. At one point in the meeting she told us how she planned the divorce so as to take the maximum cash from her husband as punishment for his ignoring her on weekends. He preferred to play golf, you see." He looked deep into Kate's eyes. "What I have with you is very rare."

"What did she say?"

"Strange, she quoted the Bible. Of all things!"

"She did?"

"Yes. She said, 'They that are whole need not a physician!'"

"Frank, that was a put down. Sarcasm. She was trying to say that you were too good to be true."

"Maybe. I think she was envious. She's divorced, single and probably unloved. So many people are, it seems. Unloved!"

"Frank, that's the nicest thing you've said to me in a long while."

He leaned over and kissed her on the cheek. She smelled so feminine, so soft the touch of her skin. She really was nice to come home to. His voice was troubled as he said, "George decided this afternoon to take the early retirement offer."

"He did? After all his bravado?"

"Yeah! Said he had enough of social engineering."

"Whoa! Will he get a payout?"

"Yep!"

"So what's the problem? He's better off, isn't he?"

"I guess so."

"So why the long face?"

"It's not the same. The whole company is changing. New upper management. New philosophy."

"So? You can change with the times, can't you."

"It's not the change exactly. It's what doesn't change."

"And? What's that?"

"The same old kiss-ass syndrome."

"So tell me once again, you don't kiss ass?"

"Nope! Never have."

"That's politics, you know."

"And I'm not very good at it."

"Tell me what's happened."

"Oh, the new management has surrounded itself with the usual party liners. Not an iota in their heads but yes, sir! No, sir! Three bags full, sir! Let me kiss your ass, sir, or madam as the case may be. Pumping sunshine!"

"Are they asking you to take retirement?"

"They've kinda hinted at it."

"You can't you know. Not yet."

"I know."

"You're only fifty nine, Frank. You won't be sixty until November. And there's still the mortgage on this house. Frank, they're not going to give you the push, are they?"

"I don't know. They seem to want younger people. George's replacement appears to be a person in their thirties."

"How do you mean a person? Their thirties? Their? You mean a woman, don't you?"

"Yes. That's right. A woman. But it's not that. She's very competent. Good track record. She earns about half of what George earned. It's a question of age and economics. They're trying to save money. Us older folks earn too much after thirty years."

"Humph! How many others?"

"Several. But the company may have leaned on George."

"Didn't he have a good track record too?"

"The best. He's a top man. Gets powerful results."

"What then? Was he messing with the secretaries?"

"Nah! George just wasn't very reverent with his comments. A bit too outspoken."

"Isn't that what they want? Isn't that what they call exchange of ideas?"

"Not if it makes certain upper managers feel like fools."
"Oh well. That's the world all over."
"So I've learned."
"If the company was considering downsizing why on earth did they hold the seminar? Couldn't they have saved the expense?"
"Already paid for in advance, probably. Corporate confusion!" He thought for a moment. "Or it gives them the basis now to tell people they are not team players."

Friday night dinner was over and the dish washing machine was on. The flowers had been set back in the middle of the dining table. The dog fed. Kate slipped on her tweed coat. "Don't forget to review those financial figures. It's important."

"I will." He looked up. "I say, where are you going? It's late. Almost seven thirty."

"Out. Just for a while. I need to see Janet. Maybe she'll change her mind."

"About backing out of the flowers gig? All George's fault?"

"Certainly. Wait up! You can fill me in on more details when I get back, around ten probably. Her phone number's on the fridge door if you need me for anything. Bye."

He kissed her cheek. The door closed and he watched her through the panes. She waved back at him as she drove off. He felt deprived of her company. He went back to the sofa and reached for the hot cup of herbal tea he liked so much that she had left for him on the side-table. He sat down before the television and surfed the channels. Violence! Men and women yelling and screaming! Beatings! Car chases! Harsh background music! He could feel his nerves begin to stand on end. He found a public channel with an English comedy but the shrill voices and strange accents only added to his distress. He switched off. The dog came to sit by his feet and rest its muzzle on his knee. But all Frank could think about was the week that passed, and George, George the dragon killer.

"Ahh, now wait a minute, Doctor Max," said George, rocking back and forward in his chair with discomfort at what he heard. "Are you saying, number one, that we must go back to being cavemen, or, number two, teamwork was not involved in assembling the Ford Model T?"

"I'm saying that team work has been re-discovered and is contributing to strides in quality, productivity and customer service."

"Ah, I see. We can kill more woolly mammoths and bring more meat back to the cave for the little women if we work together. I get you. Proceed."

The term little women caused a rustle of body language amongst several women. Dr. Max showed his discomfort. "I would like to ask you to please wait until the end of my presentation to ask questions and make comments. That way you will be able to evaluate the whole in its entirety rather than piecemeal, for the better understanding of each and all. Now, the essential about teams is that everyone is involved. And hence, everyone feels better about themselves."

An audible sigh escaped from George.

Frank sat up, acutely aware that time had passed and his wife was still not home. He remembered his promise to her and reached for the pages she had given him. The folder had a white label on the cover on which was printed in a neat hand, *Say It With Flowers*. Frank felt a warm feeling and ran his fingers over the letters. He was so proud that his wife had decided to use her artistic talents. He opened the folder to the financial data and tried to study the numbers. But George had already got a job. Frank had looked at him in great surprise. "How?"

"Networking! Called everybody I knew."

"And what about the attorney you had on a string?"

"Nah! No point. I've got full pension and a job waiting for me. Delta Marketing! Across town! Don't even have to move. I'm off, man! Dah-da-da-dah!" George was a picture of happiness.

"I'm going to stay," said Harold. "I'm certain I have security here. Give them a few more days. They need a man like me with direct marketing experience. No problem!"

"They?" said George scathingly.

Frank went over the numbers again for the umpteenth time. The pension payments, having to wait two more years for social security, the probability of finding another professional job at sixty that would pay what he now earned, the mortgage payments and the amount in his Savings and Investment Plan. And Kate's plan to be in floral arrangement. He had promised her to analyze the matter. With no great enthusiasm he opened the folder once more and began to study. After a few minutes concentration he went to the desk and found a sheaf of paper and pen. He took the raw data and prepared a cash flow extended out for one year and then beyond that according to three different scenarios. It certainly was a project that had a better than even chance of success, with some luck. He double-checked his analysis. The front door opened and she was with him again. "Here, feel my hands. There may be a frost tonight. Ah, you've been working. Good! Well?"

"How was Janet?"

"She's not sure. I'll tell you later." She settled beside him on the sofa. "What's your verdict on the numbers?"

"Kate, the critical success factor in all of this is your ability to build a reputation as a wedding florist and of course for other events, too. Will you always have a supply of flowers?

"Yes indeed. The supplier list is in the green folder. And in the red folder is how I'll build the business. You'll see the list of churches etcetera where I'll build my contacts. You'd be surprised at how many weddings there are each week. And do you see the number of golf clubs around this part of the state? They have banquet rooms and have a high rate of bookings. Wedding receptions mostly, but other things as well. It would be up to me to win their custom."

"And how would you do that?"

"Better service than they can get else where."

"Service? Is that all?"

"Well, there's my talent for arranging flowers and there's my skill with people, or so I'm told."

"Hmmm. Well, it's a pity Janet's not interested. At least you would have somebody to hold your hand as the business goes belly up."

"Belly up? Heavens Frank! Is it that bad a proposition?"

"Not at all. It's a very good proposition. It's just that Janet is not the person to be in partnership with."

"Why?"

"Can't you see? She gave in to old George's manias. So how would she behave if the going got rough in business? And George is certain to interfere. Why not look for another partner. Someone with guts who can share your own enthusiasm and not keel over when there's a disappointment?"

"Yes. That's right. But who?"

"Well, a catchy name like *Say It With Flowers* should get someone interested."

"Frank, you're poking fun."

All that Saturday morning Frank worked his vegetables, mowed the lawn and cleaned up around his yard. It was relaxing. The physical exercise left his mind free to drift over things. He thought about his son developing his career in law, already an assistant attorney and had appeared in one case reported in the national press. Frank had enjoyed the reference to how his son had turned the defense witness into a witness for the prosecution and virtually sealed the case. He hoped his son's marriage was happy and that his wife, also an attorney, would someday enjoy the fulfillment of having children. They were still young, still eager to develop careers. They were almost competitive with each other, she somewhat ahead and earning more in private legal practice. His son was proud of that. "So what?" said his son. "She's a terrific lawyer."

He thought of his daughter Helen still in residency at the psychiatric hospital. She still had a year to go. She was unmarried. And had no plans that he knew of. Was she happy? But she was a mature woman of thirty-two. Only she could decide. Frank had long ago realized that where Helen was concerned she had a mind of her own.

"Let her follow her own decision, Frank!" His wife had often said. "She's her own person."

And there was Jill. Already she was the product manager of a well-known brand of detergent; her husband in the stock market and their apartment decorated by a professional. What could it have cost? He was proud of his three children. They had returned the love and affection Kate and he had given them by trying hard and making their lives productive. They were a success. There was that word again. What did it mean? Being at peace with oneself? as Katy had defined. Peace? What was peace? Did George have peace? Or Harold? And Doctor Max? Especially Doctor Max! And the woman who led the seminar! Wasn't peace having enough money in the bank so as not to worry? Wasn't peace being able to overcome change without changing oneself? To be at peace despite whatever? And to be loved!

A rabbit ambled across the back yard in a leisurely fashion and sat down immobile when it realized Frank had seen it. Frank watched, amused by the nonchalance of the animal. Such confidence! It could handle come what may. Frank straightened up. The rabbit took notice but stayed immobile, watching. Frank took a few strides towards it out of curiosity of what it would do. The rabbit kept an eye cocked. As Frank got closer the animal ambled off and squeezed through the fence. Once on the other side it sat there, confident it had the power to keep ahead of the game.

"Kate!" A thought had come to Frank. "Kate!" Frank made for the patio door. "Kate!" He was filled with excitement as the realization came to him.

"Frank, what is it?"

MUSIC ON THE WIND

"Kate, why do you need a partner?"
She looked at his eager face.
"Are you alright Frank? What's the matter?"
"Why do you need Janet as a partner?"
"To share the responsibility, that's why."
"But you can handle the responsibility by yourself, can't you? Haven't you ever thought of that? You have the ability!"
"Frank what is it? I haven't seen you like this in a long time. Not since Helen got into medical school. What's up?"
"Kate, I've just had a realization. I'm not at peace with myself. The changes that are happening are too much for me to handle within the company. And I can't handle being pushed aside for a younger person. I need responsibility and decision. Abdicating that is too much of a change for me. I want out. I need to get up in the morning knowing that I'm essential as an individual, not just a cog in a wheel."
"But, Frank, what's that got to do with Janet and me. What?"
"Don't you see? You start your business. I'll be your partner. We already are. We can both continue to be a success. Together."
"Do you mean that? It would be my business? What would you do?"
"I could keep the books. Drive the van. Make bookings if you like. Do whatever you want me to do. It would be your business. Your business!"
"But I'd give the orders." She kept her face serious, but there was a smile beginning on her lips.
"Yes!"
"And if you get uppity?"
"You can fire me!"
"Fire my husband?"
"No! Fire me as your employee. But never as your husband."
"You mean that, don't you?"
"I do."
"Do you love me?"
"I do."
"Do you promise to love, honor and obey as an employee?"
"I do!"
"What will you tell George?"
"To hell with George!"
"And Harold?"
"Harold can make his own team!"

"And the mortgage?"

"I checked the numbers, remember. It will work out."

"Frank, you'd be working for a woman! You realize that?"

"I do. But haven't I been working for a woman for these last thirty six years?"

"True!"

"And haven't I enjoyed every minute of it."

"Kiss me!"

"You know something?"

"What?"

"There's something wrong with this world."

"So what's new?"

He kissed her again. The phone rang. As Kate went towards it Frank rushed forward and picked it up. There was a boyish look on his face. "Say It With Flowers!" he said, a certain music in his voice. "How may I help you?"

Kate smiled and felt happier than she had all week.

THE QUARK SYNDROME

They had been in orbit for over three months. In the first week they had launched a probe to search for signs of life in the universe. After only one day's scanning they had discovered a repetitive beep from somewhere within the galaxy. The instruments were locked onto the sound and it was channeled along to the experts on earth, but it was unidentifiable.

In the days that followed they performed several other scientific experiments that were successful and duly recorded. They had also done research on each other, testing responses to different exercises and stresses both physical and psychological and to selected drugs being developed for long term space travel. The data was significant and critical to future voyages within and beyond the solar system. Eventually all the scheduled tasks were behind them and they began to relax and let the last twenty-four hours tick by. The voice from Command on earth advised, "The relief craft is on its way and should dock with you in exactly twenty three hours and thirty five minutes. So relax folks! You've done a great job! Watch one of the videos! Get some sleep! Get ready for the trip back to earth."

They all looked forward to the return; to be with family and friends, see the reportage on TV and have a beer with old buddies, shake hands and exchange stories, show candid photos of high-jinks in the weightlessness of the space cabin, be interviewed and finally, simply call it a day and go back to teaching, flying or engineering. They were all tiredly excited. All, that is, except one! He had no one to return to, no family, no friends. He knew that the time had come to put the rest of the plan in place. A plan they knew nothing about; a plan that only he, and the people from whom he took orders, knew. He looked around at his colleagues. He had spent two years with them in training and simulation. It was the closest he had ever come to having a family. The knowledge he had acquired was invaluable. Now he had to do it. He had been ordered. They would not know what happened. And he would have no regrets. It had to be.

The five astronauts were so deeply involved in the tasks that had been set by the Space Agency that there was little time for small talk. Now, the work behind them, they were beginning to open up.

"What about a movie like Command says?" Holly, the physicist, floated over towards the library and withdrew a slim black cassette. "How about The Quark Syndrome. That should be good for a laugh."

There was general agreement except from Dr. Joyce. "It's just a lot of Hollywood nonsense. Sheer rubbish!" he said sharply and immediately regretted having spoken.

"Aw, come on! Who cares? It's fun," she said.

"Forget your science for once, Dr. Joyce," said Kebbins. "Relax!"

Though all the astronauts had doctorates in their respective sciences, Dr. Joyce was the only person on board who was addressed by his title. It was not that he insisted, simply that he somehow appeared so distant that they felt more comfortable calling him Doctor.

"Live a little," continued Kebbins, the navigator. "You're far too serious! Enjoy life a bit more!"

Dr. Joyce nodded. Enjoying life was what he had been doing for several years, had they only known. But they were not to know. Now it was getting near the time to go. He dare not reveal the slightest hint. They must not know. "Why not!" he said letting a smile convince his colleagues he was just another one of the gang. "Sure! Let's go! Roll it!" He was proud of his skill with the language.

The video began with a flash of several spacecraft hurtling through the heavens, guns firing, and fierce explosions taking place. Strange humanoid creatures shouted orders.

"Look how that one vaporizes and re-appears on another planet," hooted Cranson. "Boy! I'd like to be able to do that!"

"Why not?" said Dr. Joyce, "It should be possible some day for humans. If they're still around, that is."

"What?" Cranson screwed up his face in disbelief that a fellow scientist could even think such a thing. "Never!"

"He's theorizing about quarks," said Holly. "Those sub-atomic particles that're making the scientific news. It's the explanation for everything these days."

Dr. Joyce shrugged his shoulders as if it mattered little whether they thought it possible or not, a kind of if-you-say-so shrug.

MUSIC ON THE WIND

"I like those bumps on that one's forehead," Sharon Miller, the craft's pilot, commented with a laugh. "Brainy looking sort. And look at that one. Yeeach! He looks like a shag carpet made into a moppet doll." She giggled. "And there's the lizard man. Wow!"

"Rubbish!" muttered Dr. Joyce. "All Hollywood rubbish!" The movie was annoying to a person of his intellect. There was a detectable sneer on his face. Everyone but Dr Joyce was in high spirits as the video progressed. "It's earthly arrogance," he sneered, "to believe that aliens must have some variant of human form."

"Why not?" countered Cranson, the space walking specialist.

"It's nonsense to think that humans are the optimum expression of evolution." But no one was listening. They were engrossed in the escapade of aliens shooting ray guns and hurtling their spacecraft through galaxies at the speed of light. There were hoots of laughter as each imaginative creature played out their villainous or heroic role.

"Well, at least the good guys won," Cranson said.

"Yet, once again," said Kebbins, "I'd like to see a movie where the bad ones get away with it. What do you think, Dr. Joyce?"

The biologist kept his thoughts to himself responding with a non-committal smile. He still had plenty of time, a few hours.

"Well?" asked Sharon. "Give us your critique." She looked at the others. "Lets have Dr. Joyce analyze the movie for us. From a biologist's scientific point of view."

He knew she was teasing him. It was not the first time. He was the only man in the extended team of astronauts and ground staff that did not respond to her attractiveness. He had deliberately not permitted himself to be drawn into any emotion that would interfere with his mission. What she took to be a rebuff had led her to tease him. She did so frequently, a sort of female revenge. Now she wanted to have a little more fun at his expense. He wondered did the others notice. Perhaps they didn't. Later he would have something special for her. Later! But now he decided to respond in a manner fitting to her question. "The film doesn't make sense!" He reached to take the cassette out of the player and watched it slowly glide upwards. He put his hand up, caught it and placed it in the proper receptacle. "It really makes no sense."

"Do you mean earthly sense or intergalactic sense?" Cranson was doing a slow revolution that resembled a performer in water ballet.

"Why, earthly of course," said Dr. Joyce cautiously.

"So its irrelevant." Cranson caught the edge of his bunk and held on.

"Not really," Kebbins interjected into this exchange. "Dr. Joyce is right. We can use our earthly sense to try to interpret what might happen in space. The laws of physics are the same throughout the universe. Aren't they Holly? You're our physicist. Give us your views."

"Physics, yes," said Holly. "They're the same everywhere. But I think Dr. Joyce is talking about life in outer space. Aren't you?"

"Thank you," he acknowledged. "Earthly scientific sense indicates that life in outer space may bear no relationship to what we know on earth."

"How come? The same atoms exist throughout the universe." Kebbins was a great aeronautical engineer but limited in his general scientific knowledge. Like most engineers he was a specialist. "Can't one expect the same evolutionary trends? After all, the best molecular basis for life is still carbon, oxygen and hydrogen. That's what I'm told."

The feeling of hilarity induced by the movie was fading away and faces began to reflect the serious direction of the conversation. A question was on the table and they looked to Dr. Joyce, the instigator of the discussion, to lead the conversation into greater depths. Serious thinking, as would be expected from such highly educated and intelligent people, was their profession and they were enjoying this interplay of thoughts. It was the first and only time they had the opportunity to talk on matters other than the tasks and research they had been carrying out. In its way it was relaxing, even more so than the video.

"Yes! It is," Dr. Joyce confirmed. "The same atoms and molecules. But it's the form that it takes. You earthlings are prisoners of yourselves. You tend to believe that all life-forms in space should look like you."

"You earthlings?" Kebbins said. "Let's say us! Look like us! You too!"

"Quite so!" Dr. Joyce had a moment's panic. He must remember where he was. "Certainly. Like... us. Like we see on television. Or in the video."

"Exactly!" Sharon laughed. "I agree. Hollywood portrays all space travelers with a head, a body, arms, legs and at least one eye. That's humanoid. They can't very well do much else. After all, actors have to fit into those costumes. Somebody has to play the roles."

Through a porthole the earth could be seen suspended like a Christmas tree ornament—blue with wisps of white cloud. "Isn't it beautiful," Sharon said. "That will probably be my strongest memory of this trip. Looking down on earth."

All of them except Dr. Joyce looked down. There was silence for some time as each let their thoughts run. They thought of their families first and then of their duties that would bring them safely back home. They would get some sleep in preparation for the ordeal of descent. Get properly suited up, strapped in and review procedures yet once again. Everything had gone perfectly since blast off. It should go equally perfectly on the shuttle descent. Sharon would pilot the craft into its landing.

Suddenly Holly said, "This must be how aliens see earth. I wonder what they think?" She gave a short, happy giggle. "But, Dr. Joyce, why shouldn't aliens look like us?"

The others were brought back to the question. They looked quizzically at Dr. Joyce.

"Because," he made the conscious effort to use the correct word, "we.. we humans... are the result of an accident that happened sixty some million years ago. At the last extinction."

"Oh?"

"When the dinosaurs were extinguished, as you will recall from reading the latest scientific opinion, it left the opportunity for other creatures to fill the ecological niches that were vacated. Early mammals and so on."

"So? We all know that. Then what?"

"Explicitly, if we examine it closely," again he concentrated on using the word, "we... humans... have a head, a body, legs, arms, two eyes, fingers and an internal set of organs, all based on the same pattern as the dinosaurs. More or less that is! Even the embryos of humans and lizards look alike during the early period of development."

"As long as I'm not born all covered in scales, I'm happy!" Cranson said flippantly. There were smiles of agreement.

Dr. Joyce let the remark pass. Despite his colleagues' technical education and specialty they had no depth of philosophical thought. But what could one expect? He tried again. "First, if the dinosaurs had not been extinguished there would probably not have been a process of evolution that led to primates and humans. At least probably not to a higher intelligence that looks just like... humans..." Again the feeling of caution.

"You mean we could very well have ended up looking like lizards?" Cranson, the body-beautiful athlete and space walker, considered the matter a joke. He was a religious man and had definite views on how humans came to be on earth.

"That's one possibility," said Dr. Joyce.

"I disagree! Whether by creation or by evolution the perfection of mankind was, and still is, the goal of God's work. In His image."

"But of course." Dr. Joyce was careful to avoid controversy. He was at the end of his journey. Almost there. Just a few hours more. "I respect that. But there are those would say that believing humans are the ultimate goal of evolution is nothing more than earthly arrogance. Man in love with himself!"

"They can kiss my ass!" said Cranson with an aggressive expression on his face.

"And we'll help them," Sharon assured him. "Damn right, we will!"

Dr. Joyce waited until the laughter had receded. "But how can one say that on other planets of the cosmos, life followed the same paths it did on earth? One can't." He had the smug feeling of satisfaction that he very well knew the answer to that. "And it didn't!" he said with finality. Life elsewhere was indeed very different to that on earth. He knew!

"Are you saying that there are other forms of intelligent life?" Cranson was still spoiling for an argument.

Dr. Joyce explored the possibilities of his response for a second. "I know!" He began, then realized he was becoming careless. "I mean...the question is, what form does it take?"

"No head like we have?' joked Holly, shaking her head in a girlish way.

"No!"

"No body, arms or legs?"

"I'd say not."

"Two eyes?"

"It may not have eyes at all. Or twenty, like a spider, for all you know."

"Preposterous!" Cranson shook his head. "How could life function? We need all of our senses just to survive on this planet."

"But why not?" Dr Joyce gave a broad smile of satisfaction. He knew.

"You're right, Cranson," offered Kebbins. "You have a very important point. Lookit! As I see it, a brain is necessary to think intelligently. I think, therefore I am! Descartes, I believe. No brain, no creative thought, no inventions. Hands and fingers are needed to translate the creative thoughts of the brain into material form. Eyes are needed to see and appraise it and a mouth to communicate to others that it exists. Like art! Otherwise why do it? And those other creatures need eyes to verify it's there. And hands to cart it away and brains to appreciate it. Simple really." He began to laugh at his own ingeniousness.

"Perfect!" Cranson was grinning and gave thumbs up salute to Kebbins. "That's one up!" he said to Dr. Joyce. "Your turn!"

Dr. Joyce shifted over onto his side. He resembled a slim shark hanging in the mid-depths of the ocean. "Because you think like earthlings. Consider! Snakes get by just with taste on the tip of their tongue. Bats need only a piercing voice and good hearing. Eagles depend on sight and dogs do pretty well with smell. And they've all been around longer than humans. Humans are the Johnnys-come-lately in this earthly gig, probably just a temporary blip in the species spectrum of this planet. Cockroaches were here before humans and will no doubt out-survive them. Us, I mean!"

"So what's the point?" Cranson's tone of voice indicated his impatience with Dr. Joyce. The man was too clever by far. No spiritual anchor. No beliefs.

"Ask yourself," said Dr. Joyce quietly, realizing this was dangerous ground, "what are the options to the human form."

"I can't rightly see any," said Cranson belligerently. "God made man in his own image. So you tell me what goes on in other planets!"

"Well, I agree with the brain part, as Kebbins outlined. Some structure is required to project higher intelligence, thought, inventiveness, memory and so on."

"Yes, and like Kebbins says," Holly held up her well kept hands, the nails perfectly manicured, "once you have invention you are going to need some physical means of constructing the invention."

"Maybe. But remember our hands are based on the structures of our animal-like forebears and that goes all the way back to the first lungfish and their fins. We ended up with five fingers. It might have been three or seven? But why have fingers at all? Why not a suction cup? Like an octopus? And they're very brainy creatures."

"Eyes? What do you substitute for eyes?" asked Sharon. "Imagine, nowhere to use mascara. No false eyelashes. Boy!" She laughed. "That would make the mornings a lot easier."

"How about radar!" Cranson said jokingly, catching her mood.

"But," said Holly defending her turf as a physicist, "that would mean some means of emitting and receiving, built into the brain of this extra-terrestrial creature."

"Why not?" said Dr. Joyce.

"Little antenna sticking out of their heads." Cranson held a finger up at each side of his head and made a face. "Now we're back to Hollywood. You've been reading too many comics!"

The seriousness of the topic had noticeably slipped and a fun aspect was taking over.

"You mean they would sense each other, know each other's where-abouts and even communicate by radio waves," laughed Kebbins.

"Oh!" Sharon said with a shudder. "That's invasion of privacy! There should be a law!"

There was more laughter.

"Sure. Why not?" said Dr. Joyce, his face still serious. But they were not listening to him any more.

"Sounds to me like telepathy," said Kebbins. "Even some humans can do that."

"I still think the human form is the best form of all," said Sharon. "Especially when you consider how we're packaged in two different versions."

"What? Tall and short? Fat and thin?" Holly was beginning to giggle again.

"That's silly. I mean male and female."

"Ah!" Holly pretended serious thought about that, and getting the point, nodded sagely. "So how do aliens reproduce? Tell us Dr. Joyce?" The question was meant to poke fun.

Dr Joyce stayed quiet until he was certain they were ready for it. "Who said they need to?"

"If they don't, poor things they," laughed Kebbins.

"You're thinking earthly again," giggled Holly. "Or is it earthy!"

"One of the things I've always wondered about," said Sharon, "is the life and death of us humans. It's such a waste. Why can't we be recycled? Rebuilt to be even better than we were before. Oh the possibilities!" She made a pantomime of looking at her butt.

"You sound like a Hindu," Cranson was serious again. The thought offended his beliefs. "Re-incarnation up the ladder of perfection. Good grief!"

Dr. Joyce listened with tolerance. Poor people! So limited! He was glad in a way that his journey through their existence was at an end. Soon he would be far beyond in the heavens where he belonged. He had a feeling of superiority as he continued. "What if aliens had solved all that? What if they had achieved some level of evolution that did not require reproduction?"

"Yeeacch! Sounds amoeboid and slimey!" Sharon shuddered.

"What if they could be and yet at times not be?" he continued.

"Ah, that is the question," said Kebbins. "'To be or not to be? Whether 'tis more noble...."

"You mean, move around like spirits?" Sharon interposed.

"Something,' continued Dr. Joyce, "something beyond the current comprehension of the earthly human mind."

"Rubbish!" said Cranson and moved to a panel of dials where he turned several knobs. A look of surprise showed on his face. "Hey! Listen folks! Do you hear that? Those signals we've been hearing seem to be getting clearer. Closer!" He turned the sound up. They all listened intently nodding heads in agreement. Ping! Ping! "It sounds like what you'd hear in a submarine." Cranson peered out a porthole as if expecting an enemy ship to drop a depth charge.

"Well, let Mission Control worry about it. Our task is over. I think we should all get some rest," said Sharon. "We can leave the question of life in outer space to another day. I'm turning in. I've got to land the shuttlecraft tomorrow. I need sleep!"

"How about warm milk everyone?" suggested Dr. Joyce amiably. "I'll get it. Help you all sleep peacefully."

Milk was one of the few foods transported in its original form, frozen of course, but not dehydrated or condensed. It had been found to have a soothing effect on mind and stomach, especially towards the last days of a flight. There was general agreement and Dr. Joyce floated towards the galley. He placed four frozen containers in the microwave. His colleagues strapped themselves into their resting couches. In a few moments Dr. Joyce returned with the specially designed containers, each with a straw-like tube protruding. "Catch!" He floated a container across the cabin to each person. "I'm scheduled for this watch," he said. He went to the console of instruments and waited. It would only take a few minutes for the drug to work. "Idiots!" he thought. The radar-like pinging noise was certainly getting closer. He could hear it quite clearly even without the array of instruments and speakers on the console. He placed the earphones over his head in the appearance that was expected of him. The sound was deafening. He turned the instrument off. He could hear perfectly well without them.

Kebbins closed his eyes. He felt extraordinarily drowsy. It was probably the after-effect of all the excitement from realizing that tomorrow he would be home. In a day or two he would be tossing a ball to his son's bat. The barbecue pit would be hot with smoke curling up and a smell of steaks cooking. His wife would be giving him hugs and kisses and generally fussing around him. Three months was a long time. He forced his eyes open for a second and could see that Sharon seemed to be asleep. Holly too. Cranson was snoring lightly. Yes, they were all exhausted. It had been a tiring trip. He was glad it was over. He saw Dr. Joyce over by the console. He looked busy. What was he doing? Listening? Talking? Maybe a message had come in from Mission Command. Ah well, Joyce could take care of it. He dozed back into a never-never land suspended between sleep and wakefulness. The discussion with Dr. Joyce floated through his mind; phrases repeated, responses given, laughter heard. There was a pinging sound somewhere in the background, as if a radar instrument was beneath his headrest. But the very repetitiousness of the sound lulled him into an even deeper rest where images began to flicker behind his eyes. He began to dream of an alien space craft of a kind never imagined by Hollywood becoming visible in the porthole nearest his head. It seemed to glow with a silver iridescence. He wanted to ask Dr. Joyce if he too had seen the apparition but no sound came from his throat.

In a way Kebbins knew he was dreaming but it was not unpleasant. Not yet a nightmare. He always seemed to know when he was having a nightmare and could force himself awake. This was a pleasant dream. Enjoy, he felt. He could see, in his inner dream state, Dr. Joyce rise from the console and calmly drift to the battened door leading to the airlock chamber that was used in preparation for space walks. Joyce seemed enveloped in the same strange iridescent glow as the space ship hovering outside. He was not wearing a space walker's suit and helmet. Kebbins tried again to speak, to warn him of the danger but again no sound came from his throat. He shouted. No sound. Joyce twirled the radial handle. The door was opened a fraction. An indefinable and formless cloud entered into the cabin and hovered, turning this way and that. Dr Joyce pointed to the sleeping bodies strapped into their couches and the iridescent cloud moved over as if to inspect them. It enveloped the body of Cranson. Cranson suddenly sat up into a sitting position jerking his arms and legs in a spasmodic fashion. Just as suddenly he relaxed back again. The iridescent cloud rose slowly from his body and moved to the person of Holly. It seemed to fade into her body from head to toe. She too sat up suddenly and jerked her arms and legs about. Dr. Joyce looked on, a rare smile on his face, and, as if in some kind of joke, he too jerked his arms and kicked his legs as he floated. "Didn't I tell you?" He gave a short cackly laugh.

The iridescent cloud floated to the still open door and hung there. Dr. Joyce waved a hand as if to say, "Wait!" and made his way to the couch of

MUSIC ON THE WIND

Sharon. He looked at her in a tender way for a moment and then, leaning forward laid a soft kiss on her lips. He stood back, continued to look at her as if regretfully and floated over to his couch. Dr. Joyce strapped himself in and closed his eyes. He gave one deep sigh and lay backwards.

Kebbins struggled within the depths of his dream to break into consciousness. He could feel his thighs straining against the straps that held him; the subconscious struggling to surface into the reality of wakefulness but it was no use. It was a drowning sensation. He cried for help, "Dr. Joyce!" But still no sound came. "Dr. Joyce!" He could see the iridescent glow that surrounded Dr Joyce's body begin to rise and float towards the door. The other iridescence glow quickly slipped through, the second iridescence followed. The door closed and the radial handle spun. "Help!" shouted Kebbins. Nothing! "Help!" He struggled and slowly, like a drowning man coming up for air, he gasped a cry. This time he heard his own voice. He blinked awake. Perspiration glistened on his forehead. He looked around. Everyone was asleep. Even Dr. Joyce was snug on his couch, strapped in and at peace. He shook his head to clear his thoughts. He looked through the porthole. A faint light seemed to speed away into the distance and was gone. He laid his head back on the rest. Oh God! Another nightmare! Gradually sleep once again took over and he slid into unconsciousness.

The irritant voice of Mission Control woke Stebbens.

"Wakey wakey!" it said. "Time to get ready folks!"

"Damn!"

"Is that you, Kebbins? Are you awake? Can you come to the mike?"

"Hold on! Hold on!" Kebbins floated to the console noting as he did so that Cranson, Holly and Sharon were stretching their arms and yawning.

"I'm here!"

"Are you O.K? You sound groggy!"

"I am groggy. Just awakened from a nightmare. I'm still a bit spaced out."

"And well you should be." He could hear laughter from the ground crew.

"Sorry! Didn't mean to make a pun."

"Looks like everything is on schedule," continued ground control. "You folks get ready and we'll have you back in no time at all."

"O.K! It's a deal!"

Kebbins still felt groggy from the disturbed sleep. What a night! Sharon floated over beside him. "That's the worst sleep I've had this whole trip. What a nightmare I had."

"Don't talk about nightmares!" said Holly. "I had the worst!"

"Me too." Kebbins did not want to say more. "Must be the excitement of our last night."

"Did you folks say nightmares?" Cranson was sitting up shaking his head as if to clear cobwebs. "I had a doozey. Man! Am I glad to see Dr. Joyce safe in bed. You won't believe the nightmare I had. And him in it! Jeeze!"

"That milk must have been full of bugs," suggested Holly. "I dreamt Dr. Joyce simply floated out through that door and disappeared."

Kebbins listened. He was afraid to speak. The similarity was too much.

"Did you see the glow that appeared at that porthole?" said Cranson. "If I hadn't known it was a nightmare I'd have sworn it was real. An iridescence! Shaped something like a ghost ship. Like you'd see in a horror movie."

"Just look at Dr. Joyce. Sleeping like a baby," said Holly. "What right does he have to be so cool. Upsetting everyone's sleep like he did."

"All of you had nightmares that involved Dr. Joyce?" asked Kebbins.

"I'll not tell you what I dreamt," said Sharon.

"Oh, come on. It was only a nightmare, pleaded Holly. "We all had them. What was yours?"

"I dreamt that..." she leaned forward to whisper, "...that creep Dr. Joyce came to me and kissed me. Right on the lips. Yeeach!"

"But he did!" said Kebbins. "I saw him." There was silence. "I mean, in my dream I saw him. It was a nightmare really."

"Heavens!" said Cranson. "How come we've all had the same nightmare? This is something weird!"

"Wake him up!" Holly said with a giggle. "Let him explain himself. What's he been doing wandering around in our nightmares. The nerve! I'm pissed off. Go on! Wake him up." No one moved. "Then I will." She laughed as she floated across the cabin. "This guy's got a lot of explaining to do."

They watched silently. Holly shook Dr. Joyce by the shoulder. He did not respond. "Say, this guy's a deep sleeper." She shook again. "He's kinda stiff." She touched his cheek. "He's cold!" She felt the artery of his neck. They could see the look of disbelief creep over her face. She turned. "He's dead!" She pulled her hand away quickly. "He's really dead. I'm not joking! Dr. Joyce is dead!"

As of one thought the four of them pressed towards the porthole. None spoke as they peered out into the vast distance of space.